THE ULTIMATE ESOTERIC WISDOM COLLECTION

History's Most Influential Texts on Hermeticism , Alchemy, Mysticism & Occult Philosophy

A Modern Translation

Adapted for the Contemporary Reader

Hermes Trismegistus | The Three Initiates Julian the Theurgist | Paracelsus

Translated by Tim Zengerink

Table of Contents

Preface - Message to the Reader

Rebuilding the Greatest Library in Human History

Thousands of years ago, the Library of Alexandria was the heart of global knowledge — until it was lost.

Now, we're rebuilding it — and you're invited to join.

At the Modern Library of Alexandria, our mission is simple: make *every book* available to *every person*, in every language, format, and edition.

Here's how we do it:

- **Deluxe Print Editions at True Printing Cost** - Order paperbacks, hardcovers, or boxsets at the exact printing cost — no markup.

- **Unlimited Access to the Greatest Works** - Explore thousands of timeless classics in modern eBook and audiobook editions. Free for every reader, everywhere.

- **Modern Translations for Every Language & Dialect** -Clear, accessible versions of the world's greatest works, translated into every language and dialect.

When you visit **LibraryofAlexandria.com**, you're not just accessing books — you're joining a global movement to restore, preserve, and share the wisdom of civilization.

Join us today at LibraryofAlexandria.com

Together, we'll ensure the light of human wisdom never fades again.

With gratitude,

The Modern Library of Alexandria Team

Visit:

www.libraryofalexandria.com

Or scan the code below:

The Kybalion

The Three Initiates

Introduction

We are pleased to present this little book to students and seekers of the Secret Doctrines, based on the ancient Hermetic teachings. Even though many writings on occultism refer to these teachings, surprisingly little has been written about them directly. For this reason, we believe that those who are eager to uncover hidden truths will welcome the release of this volume.

The goal of this book is not to promote a specific philosophy or doctrine. Instead, it aims to provide students with a clear understanding of the Truth, helping them connect and make sense of the different pieces of occult knowledge they may have encountered. These bits of knowledge can often seem to contradict each other, discouraging beginners. We are not trying to build a new "Temple of Knowledge" with this book. Rather, we offer it as a "Master-Key" that will help students unlock the many doors within the Temple of Mystery they have already entered.

Throughout history, no part of the world's occult knowledge has been as closely guarded as the Hermetic teachings. These teachings have been carefully passed down for thousands of years from their founder, Hermes Trismegistus, known as the "scribe of the gods." He lived in ancient Egypt at a time when humanity was still in its early stages. Legend has it that Hermes not only lived during the time of Abraham but also taught the wise sage himself. Hermes has always been seen as a guiding light in occultism, illuminating many teachings that have spread through the centuries. Many of the core ideas found in the mystical teachings of various cultures can be traced back to Hermes. Even the oldest teachings from India seem to have their roots in Hermetic thought.

It is said that many advanced spiritual seekers from India traveled to Egypt to learn from Hermes himself. These travelers gained the "Master-Key" from him, which helped them understand and connect their different beliefs. In this way, the Secret Doctrine became well established. People from many lands considered Hermes the "Master of Masters," and his influence was so powerful that even after centuries of changes, similarities remain in the spiritual ideas taught by different cultures today. Students of religion can see traces of Hermetic teachings in every significant religion, whether ancient or modern. Despite the differences between various beliefs, the Hermetic teachings act as a bridge, uniting them.

Hermes' mission was not to create a school of thought that would dominate the world's ideas. Instead, he planted the seeds of truth, allowing them to grow in many forms. Throughout history, a few dedicated individuals have preserved the original purity of his teachings. These individuals refused to share the teachings widely, reserving them for the few who were ready to understand them. These truths were passed down quietly, from teacher to student, by word of mouth. In every generation, in different parts of the world, there have been a few Initiates who kept the sacred flame of Hermetic wisdom alive. These guardians of the truth have always been willing to share their light to rekindle the lamps of those whose understanding had grown dim. They faithfully tended the "Perpetual Lamp of Wisdom," ensuring that it never went out, just as a poet once wrote: "O, let not the flame die out! Cherished age after age in its dark cavern—in its holy temples cherished. Fed by pure ministers of love—let not the flame die out!"

These dedicated teachers were never interested in gaining approval from the public or gathering large followings. They understood that only a few people in each generation would be ready to receive the truth or recognize it when presented. They kept the deeper teachings—what they called the "strong meat"—for the few who could handle it, while others received simpler lessons—"milk for babes." They saved their most valuable teachings for those who truly appreciated them, rather than sharing them with those who would not understand and instead treat them with contempt. However, these teachers always followed the teachings of Hermes, who said, "Where fall the footsteps of the Master, the ears of those ready for his Teaching open wide." They also lived by the saying, "When the ears of the student are ready to hear, then cometh the lips to fill them with wisdom." Still, their wisdom was kept hidden, as expressed in another Hermetic teaching: "The lips of Wisdom are closed, except to the ears of Understanding."

Some have criticized the Hermetic approach, saying that their secrecy was unhelpful. But history shows the wisdom of the Masters, who knew it was pointless to teach what the world was not prepared to accept. The Hermetists did not try to become martyrs. Instead, they chose to stay silent, watching patiently as others were persecuted and misunderstood for trying to share advanced truths with those who were not ready. Even now, persecution continues, and there are still parts of the Hermetic teachings that, if shared openly, would provoke hostility and scorn from the masses, just as in the past when people cried, "Crucify! Crucify!"

In this book, we aim to introduce the key ideas of The Kybalion, focusing on practical principles that you can apply yourself. Rather than offering all the details, we leave it to the true student to explore and use these teachings. If you are genuinely ready to learn, you will discover how to apply these principles. If not, you will need to grow into the kind of person who can understand them. Otherwise, the Hermetic teachings will be nothing more than "words, words, words" to you.

Chapter I

Hermetic Philosophy. "The lips of wisdom are closed, except to the ears of Understanding."—The Kybalion.

The foundational esoteric and mystical teachings that have influenced the philosophies of nations and cultures for thousands of years originated in ancient Egypt. Egypt, known for the Pyramids and the Sphinx, was the birthplace of hidden wisdom and spiritual teachings. Many nations borrowed from its Secret Doctrine. Countries such as India, Persia, Chaldea, Medea, China, Japan, Assyria, Greece, Rome, and others benefited greatly from the knowledge offered by the wise teachers and masters of Egypt to those prepared to receive it.

In ancient Egypt lived great masters and adepts who have rarely been equaled, much less surpassed, throughout history. The greatest of all mystical schools was located in Egypt, and the students who entered its temples later became masters and teachers themselves, spreading this sacred knowledge to different parts of the world. All serious students of the occult acknowledge the wisdom they owe to these ancient masters of Egypt.

Among these remarkable masters was one called "The Master of Masters." This figure, Hermes Trismegistus, lived in Egypt in ancient times. He is recognized as the founder of occult wisdom, the creator of astrology, and the discoverer of alchemy. His life story has been lost over the centuries, though various countries have argued over which one could claim to be his birthplace, thousands of years ago. No one knows the exact time of his final presence in Egypt, but scholars place it during the earliest dynasties—long before the time of Moses. Some believe he lived during the time of Abraham, and certain traditions suggest that Abraham learned some of his mystical knowledge from Hermes himself.

According to tradition, Hermes lived for 300 years. After his death, the Egyptians honored him as a god, calling him Thoth. Many years later, the Greeks also worshipped him as a god, referring to him as Hermes, the god of wisdom. The Egyptians revered him for countless centuries, calling him "the scribe of the gods" and giving him the title "Trismegistus," meaning "the thrice-great," a name that reflected his unmatched greatness. Throughout the ancient world, the name Hermes Trismegistus became synonymous with the source of wisdom.

Even today, the word "hermetic" refers to something secret or tightly sealed, a nod to the fact that Hermes' followers kept their teachings hidden. They followed the principle that wisdom should not be shared with those unprepared to understand it, summarizing this idea with the phrase "milk for babes, meat for strong men." This principle, though familiar in Christian texts, was used by the Egyptians long before Christianity.

This careful sharing of knowledge has always defined the Hermetic tradition, and it continues to do so today. Hermetic teachings exist in many religions and countries but have never been tied to any specific place or religious group. The ancient teachers warned against turning these teachings into rigid beliefs. History shows the wisdom of this caution. The mystical knowledge of ancient India and Persia faded because religious leaders blended it with theology, burying it under superstition and dogma. The same happened in ancient Greece and Rome. Similarly, the Hermetic teachings of the Gnostics and early Christians were lost during the time of Constantine, when philosophy was replaced with theology. The Christian Church lost much of its original spirit and had to search for centuries to reconnect with its ancient beliefs. Now, in the twentieth century, it seems the Church is once again striving to rediscover these ancient mystical truths.

However, some faithful individuals have always kept the flame of truth alive. These devoted souls carefully guarded this knowledge, ensuring it was never lost. Thanks to their dedication, we still have access to these teachings today. But they are not widely available in books. Instead, this wisdom has been passed down directly from master to student. Even when it was written, the meaning was hidden in the language of alchemy and astrology, so only those with the right understanding could grasp it. This secrecy was necessary to protect the teachings from religious persecution during the Middle Ages when the truth was often met with fire, torture, and execution. Even now, few reliable books on Hermetic philosophy exist, though references to it can be found in many writings on occult subjects. However, Hermetic philosophy remains the "Master-Key" that can unlock all occult teachings.

In the early days, a collection of essential Hermetic teachings was compiled and passed from teacher to student. This collection was called "The Kybalion," though the meaning of the title has been lost over time. These teachings have been transmitted orally through the generations. They consist of maxims, axioms, and principles that are not clear to outsiders but become understandable to students once explained by Hermetic initiates. These teachings form the foundation of "The Art of Hermetic Alchemy," which focuses on mastering mental forces rather than manipulating physical materials. The legend of the "Philosopher's Stone," said to turn base metals into gold, is actually an allegory about transforming mental energy, understood by true students of Hermeticism.

In this book, which serves as the first lesson, we invite students to explore the teachings of The Kybalion. These teachings are explained here by us, humble students of the tradition, who still learn from the wisdom of Hermes, the Master. We present many of the maxims, axioms, and principles from The Kybalion, accompanied by explanations and examples to make the ideas easier to understand for modern readers, as the original text is intentionally written in complex terms.

The original sayings from The Kybalion appear in quotation marks, with proper credit given. Our explanations are integrated into the main text. We hope that this book will be as valuable to today's students as it has been to those who have walked this path before, following the teachings of Hermes Trismegistus—the greatest of all masters. As The

Kybalion says: "Where fall the footsteps of the Master, the ears of those ready for his Teaching open wide." And, "When the ears of the student are ready to hear, then cometh the lips to fill them with Wisdom."

According to these teachings, this book will reach those who are ready to receive its lessons. Likewise, when a student is ready for the truth, the necessary book or teacher will appear. This reflects the Hermetic Principle of Cause and Effect, also known as The Law of Attraction, which brings together students and teachers at the right time. So it is, and so it shall be!

Chapter II

The Seven Hermetic Principles. "There are seven Principles of Truth. Anyone who truly understands them holds the Magic Key that opens all the Doors of the Temple." — The Kybalion. The Seven Hermetic Principles, which form the foundation of the entire Hermetic Philosophy, are: I. The Principle of Mentalism. II. The Principle of Correspondence. III. The Principle of Vibration. IV. The Principle of Polarity. V. The Principle of Rhythm. VI. The Principle of Cause and Effect. VII. The Principle of Gender. These Seven Principles will be discussed and explained throughout these lessons. But first, here's a brief explanation of each one.

The Principle of Mentalism. "THE ALL is MIND; The Universe is Mental." — The Kybalion. This Principle teaches that "All is Mind." It explains that THE ALL (the true reality behind everything we see and experience as "The Material Universe," "Life," "Matter," "Energy," and all that we perceive with our physical senses) is actually SPIRIT. This spirit, while beyond our full understanding or ability to define, can be thought of as an Infinite, Universal, Living Mind. It also teaches that the whole universe, as well as everything within it, exists in the Mind of THE ALL and follows the Laws of Created Things. We "live and move and have our being" within this Mind. By understanding this, we can explain all the mental and psychic phenomena that grab so much public attention, which otherwise seem impossible to understand through science. Knowing this great Hermetic Principle of Mentalism helps people to easily understand the rules of the Mental Universe and use them to improve their lives. The Hermetic Student can then wisely apply the great Mental Laws, instead of just using them randomly. With this Master-Key in hand, the student can unlock many doors in the mental and psychic temple of knowledge, and walk through them with understanding. This Principle also explains the true nature of "Energy," "Power," and "Matter," and shows why and how they are all controlled by the Mastery of Mind. One of the ancient Hermetic Masters wrote long ago, "He who understands the truth about the Mental Nature of the Universe is well on his way to Mastery." These words are just as true today as they were back then. Without this Master-Key, Mastery is impossible, and the student will knock in vain on the many doors of The Temple.

The Principle of Correspondence. "As above, so below; as below, so above." — The Kybalion. This Principle teaches that there is always a relationship between the laws and events on different planes of Being and Life. The old Hermetic saying goes, "As above, so below; as below, so above." Understanding this Principle gives people the ability to solve many puzzles and unlock hidden secrets of Nature. There are planes beyond our understanding, but by using the Principle of Correspondence, we can comprehend much more than we otherwise could. This Principle applies universally to all levels of the material, mental, and spiritual universe—it is a Universal Law. The ancient Hermeticists considered this Principle one of the most important mental tools for clearing away the barriers hiding the Unknown. Using this Principle could even lift the Veil of Isis, allowing a glimpse of the goddess's face. Just as knowledge of Geometry allows people to measure distant stars while sitting in their observatories, knowledge of the Principle of Correspondence lets them reason from the Known to the Unknown. By studying the smallest things, they can understand the greatest.

The Principle of Vibration. "Nothing rests; everything moves; everything vibrates." — The Kybalion. This Principle teaches that "everything is in motion"; "everything vibrates"; "nothing stays still." These facts are supported by modern science, and every new discovery further confirms them. But this Hermetic Principle was known thousands of years ago by the Ancient Egyptian Masters. It explains that the differences between various manifestations of Matter, Energy, Mind, and even Spirit are mainly caused by different rates of vibration. From THE ALL, which is Pure Spirit, down to the grossest form of Matter, everything vibrates—

the higher the vibration, the higher the position on the scale. The vibration of Spirit is so incredibly fast that it seems motionless—just like how a rapidly spinning wheel can appear to stand still. At the other end of the scale, there are forms of matter whose vibrations are so slow that they appear to be at rest. Between these extremes are countless degrees of vibration. From tiny particles like electrons and atoms to planets and galaxies, everything is moving and vibrating. This is true not just in the material world, but also on the levels of energy, force, and the mind, where different states depend on vibration, and even on spiritual levels. Understanding this Principle, along with the right methods, allows Hermetic students to control their own mental vibrations and even influence those of others. The Masters use this Principle to control Nature's phenomena in various ways. "He who understands the Principle of Vibration holds the sceptre of power," one ancient writer said.

The Principle of Polarity. "Everything is dual; everything has poles; everything has its pair of opposites. Things that seem alike can be different, and things that seem opposite are really connected in nature, just differing in degree. Extremes meet. All truths are only half-truths, and every paradox can be solved." — The Kybalion. This principle teaches that everything has two sides or two poles. Every aspect of life has a pair of opposites, a concept rooted in ancient Hermetic teachings. It also clarifies many puzzling contradictions like "Thesis and antithesis are identical but differ in degree," "Opposites are the same, just varying in degree," and "All opposites can be harmonized." It reveals how two sides that seem far apart are, in fact, just the outermost ends of the same thing, with many degrees between them. For example, heat and cold are considered opposites, but they are simply different degrees of the same thing. If you look at a thermometer, there's no clear point where heat ends and cold begins. There's no such thing as absolute heat or cold—just varying levels of temperature, which are expressions of vibration. In this way, heat and cold are just two extremes of what we call "temperature."

This principle also applies to light and darkness, which are different degrees of the same thing. Where does darkness end and light begin? What's the difference between big and small, hard and soft, or loud and quiet? These are just shifts in degree between two poles. Even love and hate—two emotions that seem completely opposite—are connected by a spectrum, with feelings like "liking" or "disliking" in the middle. You might find yourself not knowing whether you like or dislike something because both are just different points on the same emotional scale. This idea also explains how feelings can shift quickly. Many people have experienced a sudden change from love to hate or hate to love. These changes happen naturally, but Hermetic teachings show that you can intentionally change these feelings by using your willpower and specific methods. Good and evil are also two ends of the same thing. Hermetic practitioners know how to turn negative emotions into positive ones by using the Principle of Polarity. This practice, called "Mental Alchemy," is a key part of the ancient and modern Hermetic tradition. Anyone who masters this principle can change their emotional state and even influence others if they put in the necessary time and effort.

The Principle of Rhythm. "Everything flows in and out, like tides. Everything rises and falls. The swing of a pendulum happens in all things. The distance it swings to one side will be matched by the distance it swings to the other. Rhythm balances everything." — The Kybalion. This principle teaches that everything in life moves like a pendulum, with a back-and-forth motion, like the ebb and flow of tides. This rhythmic motion happens between the two poles of everything, as described by the Principle of Polarity. There is always a flow forward and a pullback, an advance and a retreat, and a rise followed by a fall. This rhythm can be seen in all areas of life: the creation and destruction of worlds, the rise and fall of nations, and the lives of people, animals, and even thoughts. Hermetic students find this principle especially important in understanding how their minds work. They've discovered ways to lessen the effects of rhythm on their thoughts by applying specific methods and mental exercises. Although it's impossible to stop rhythm from happening, they've learned how to avoid being controlled by it. Instead, they consciously use it to their advantage.

The Hermetic masters can position themselves at the emotional or mental state they prefer and neutralize the natural swing of the pendulum that would pull them to the opposite side. Many people unknowingly resist these shifts to some degree, but masters do it deliberately and with focused willpower. This gives them a sense of stability and peace that may seem unbelievable to others, who are often tossed around by their emotions like a swinging pendulum. Hermeticists have studied the principles of polarity and rhythm closely and have developed ways to counteract their effects. Learning to control these natural forces is a core part of what Hermetics call "Mental Alchemy."

The Principle of Cause and Effect. "Every cause has its effect, and every effect has its cause. Everything happens according to laws. What people call 'chance' is just a law that hasn't been recognized yet. There are many levels of causation, but nothing escapes the law." — The Kybalion. This principle states that everything that happens has a cause, and every cause produces an effect. Nothing happens randomly; everything follows a set of laws. Even events that seem like chance are simply the result of laws that people don't understand. While there are many levels of cause and effect, with higher causes influencing lower ones, nothing escapes this universal law.

Hermetic practitioners have learned how to rise above the normal cycle of cause and effect by moving their minds to a higher plane. By doing this, they become the ones causing events, rather than being affected by them. Most people are controlled by external causes—like their environment, other people's wills, or their own habits and emotions—without realizing it. They are like pieces on a chessboard, moved by outside forces. However, those who understand this principle become players in the game of life. They take control of their thoughts, emotions, and actions, and they shape their environment instead of being shaped by it. While even the masters must follow the laws of higher planes, they learn to take charge of their lives on their own level.

The Principle of Gender. "Gender is in everything. Everything has both masculine and feminine principles, which are present on every level of existence." — The Kybalion. This principle teaches that gender exists in everything. Masculine and feminine energies are always at work, not only in the physical world but also on mental and spiritual levels. In the physical world, this principle appears as biological sex, but on higher levels, it takes different forms. No creation—whether physical, mental, or spiritual—can happen without both masculine and feminine principles working together. Understanding how these principles work sheds light on many of life's mysteries.

Every person and every thing contains both masculine and feminine qualities. For example, even men have feminine traits, and women have masculine traits. To fully understand mental and spiritual creation, you must study and understand this principle. It holds the answers to many puzzles about life. However, Hermetic teachings warn against mistaking this principle for the immoral ideas promoted by some groups. These distorted beliefs, which focus on indulgence and misuse of natural principles, have no place in Hermetic philosophy. The Hermetic tradition strongly condemns such practices, which only harm the mind, body, and soul. Hermetic teachings are pure, and those who seek base or corrupt ideas must look elsewhere. As the saying goes, "To the pure, all things are pure; to the corrupt, all things are corrupt.

Chapter III

Mental Transmutation "Mind, just like metals and elements, can be changed from one state to another, from one degree to the next, from one condition to another, from one extreme to the opposite, and from one kind of vibration to another. True Hermetic Transmutation is a Mental Art."—The Kybalion.

As mentioned before, the Hermetists were the first alchemists, astrologers, and psychologists, with Hermes being the founder of these fields of thought. Modern astronomy evolved from astrology, modern chemistry grew from alchemy, and modern psychology developed from the mystical psychology of the ancients. However, it would be wrong to assume that the ancient people were unaware of the knowledge that modern schools believe to be their unique discovery. Ancient Egyptian records carved in stone clearly show that they had a deep understanding of astronomy, with the design of the Pyramids reflecting their knowledge of the science. They were also familiar with chemistry since fragments of their writings reveal they understood the chemical properties of materials. In fact, many ancient ideas about physics are now being confirmed by new scientific discoveries, particularly in areas related to the structure of matter. Furthermore, the ancient Egyptians were highly skilled in psychology, especially in aspects that are often overlooked by modern science. Today, these overlooked areas are being rediscovered under the term "psychic science," which has puzzled modern psychologists and made them reluctantly admit that there might be some truth to it.

The truth is that beyond material chemistry, astronomy, and psychology—meaning psychology in terms of how the brain works—the ancients possessed knowledge of a higher form of each subject. They studied astrology, which is a deeper form of astronomy; alchemy, which is a deeper form of chemistry; and mystic psychology, which goes beyond the surface level of modern psychology. They had both inner knowledge, which modern scientists lack, and outer knowledge, which is the only kind of understanding most modern scientists possess. Among the many secret skills of the Hermetists was something called Mental Transmutation, which is the focus of this lesson.

"Transmutation" generally refers to the ancient practice of changing metals—especially turning base metals into gold. According to Webster's dictionary, "to transmute" means "to change the nature, form, or substance of something into another." In the same way, "Mental Transmutation" is about transforming mental states, forms, and conditions into different ones. You could call it "Mental Chemistry" if that helps—a kind of practical mystic psychology.

But there is more to Mental Transmutation than it might seem at first. Transmutation, whether we talk about alchemy, chemistry, or mental work, is powerful enough by itself. Even if it stopped at just changing thoughts, it would still be one of the most important areas of study. But this is just the beginning—let's explore why.

The first of the Seven Hermetic Principles is the Principle of Mentalism, which states: "THE ALL is Mind; the Universe is Mental." This means that the true nature of everything in the Universe is the Mind, and that the entire Universe exists within the Mind of THE ALL. We will explore this principle in more detail later, but for now, let's think about what happens if this principle is true.

If the entire Universe is made of Mind, then Mental Transmutation is the art of changing the Universe itself through mental effort. This means transforming things related to matter, energy, and thought. Mental Transmutation is what the ancient mystics referred to as "Magic," although they provided few practical instructions on how to do it. If everything is fundamentally mental, then mastering the ability to change mental conditions gives a person control over both mental and material conditions.

Only the most advanced Mental Alchemists have reached the level of mastery needed to control physical forces, such as influencing the elements of nature, stopping storms, or even causing or preventing earthquakes and other powerful events. While these abilities may sound unbelievable, many experienced occultists believe that people with these abilities—called Masters—have existed and still exist today. Reliable teachers assure their students of this, based on personal experiences that support these claims. These Masters do not show off their powers in public but prefer to live in seclusion, focusing on their personal growth along the Path of Attainment. We mention them here to highlight that their powers are purely mental, working according to the Hermetic Principle of Mentalism. "The Universe is Mental"—The Kybalion.

Even though not everyone reaches the level of a Master, many Initiates and Teachers can work effectively on the Mental Plane, practicing Mental Transmutation. In fact, all forms of "psychic phenomena," "mental influence," "mental science," and "new-thought" practices operate on the same principle, regardless of what they are called.

Students and practitioners of Mental Transmutation work within the Mental Plane, transforming mental states and conditions according to specific methods. These methods include various "treatments," "affirmations," and "denials" used by schools of mental science. However, most of these methods are imperfect and lack the deep understanding possessed by the ancient masters. Modern practitioners often work without knowing the true principles that underlie their efforts.

Using Hermetic methods, a person can not only change their own mental states but also influence the mental states of others, sometimes without even realizing it. In many cases, this influence happens consciously, especially when the person affected does not know how to protect themselves mentally. Furthermore, as many practitioners of modern mental science know, people's thoughts and desires can even change the external conditions of their lives, as long as those conditions are connected to the minds of other people.

Since the public is already familiar with these ideas, we won't go into them in detail. Instead, we want to show how the Hermetic Principle of Polarity is at work in all these practices, whether they are used for good or bad purposes. The same mental force can be directed in opposite ways, depending on how it is applied.

This little book will outline the key principles of Mental Transmutation so that anyone who reads it can understand the core ideas and use them as a master key to unlock many aspects of the Principle of Polarity.

We will now move on to the first of the Hermetic Seven Principles: the Principle of Mentalism, which teaches that "THE ALL is Mind; the Universe is Mental," as written in The Kybalion. We ask readers to pay close attention and study this principle carefully because it is the foundation of the entire Hermetic philosophy and the Mental Art of Transmutation.

Chapter IV

The All "Behind the Universe of Time, Space, and Change, there is always the Substantial Reality—the Fundamental Truth."—The Kybalion.

"Substance" refers to what lies beneath all outward appearances—it is the essence, the core reality, the thing itself. "Substantial" means something that truly exists, that is essential and real. "Reality" refers to the state of being real—something that lasts, remains true, and holds firm.

Behind everything we see and experience, there must be a Substantial Reality. This is the law. When a person reflects on the Universe, of which they are a part, they see nothing but constant change—matter changes, forces change, and even mental states change. Nothing simply stays as it is; everything is always in the process of becoming something else. Nothing remains still—everything is born, grows, and eventually dies. The moment something reaches its peak, it begins to decline. This constant rise and fall follow the law of rhythm. Nothing remains the same; everything shifts and transforms. Creation and destruction, birth, growth, and death are always happening in cycles.

A thoughtful person will eventually realize that all these changing things must be mere appearances or expressions of a deeper force—some kind of Substantial Reality that lies beneath them all. Throughout history, across different cultures and eras, thinkers have acknowledged the need to recognize this Substantial Reality. Every philosophy that has earned respect has been based on this idea. People have called this Reality by many names. Some have referred to it as God, using various titles. Others have called it the Infinite and Eternal Energy, while some have tried to name it Matter. Regardless of the name, all these thinkers have agreed that this Reality exists. Its existence is obvious and requires no proof.

In these lessons, we follow the example of great thinkers, both ancient and modern—especially the Hermetic Masters—by calling this Substantial Reality "THE ALL." We believe this term is the best way to refer to what is beyond names and descriptions. We accept the teachings of these wise thinkers and those enlightened beings who have reached higher levels of understanding. They have all said that the true nature of THE ALL is unknowable. Only THE ALL can fully understand itself.

The Hermetists teach that THE ALL, in its essence, must always remain unknowable. They see all the attempts by theologians and philosophers to define or describe the nature of THE ALL as the limited efforts of human minds trying to grasp the infinite. These efforts always fail and will continue to fail, given the nature of the task. People who pursue such inquiries get lost in endless thoughts, leading them nowhere and leaving them unprepared for the practical challenges of life. They are like a squirrel running in circles on a wheel, going nowhere and ending up where they started—still trapped.

Even worse are those who try to assign human traits, emotions, or qualities to THE ALL. They imagine it has the same emotions as people, including jealousy or the desire for praise and offerings. Such ideas reflect the childish thinking of early humanity and are now being abandoned by mature minds.

It's important to clarify the difference between Religion and Theology, as well as Philosophy and Metaphysics. Religion, to us, is the personal realization of THE ALL's existence and a person's relationship with it. Theology, on the other hand, involves people assigning personal qualities and desires to THE ALL and acting as intermediaries between it and others. Philosophy is the pursuit of knowledge within the realm of the knowable, while Metaphysics tries to explore what is beyond understanding—much like theology. In our view, Religion and Philosophy are grounded in reality, while Theology and Metaphysics are shaky, offering no real support for the human mind or soul. We don't demand that our students agree with these definitions but offer them to clarify our position. You won't hear much about Theology or Metaphysics in these lessons.

While the true nature of THE ALL is beyond our understanding, there are certain truths about its existence that our minds must accept. These truths align with the insights of enlightened beings from higher levels of awareness, and they are worth exploring. We now invite you to join us in this exploration.

"The Fundamental Truth—the Substantial Reality—cannot be named, but wise people call it THE ALL."—The Kybalion.

"In its essence, THE ALL is unknowable."—The Kybalion.

"Still, reason's insights must be accepted and respected."—The Kybalion.

Human reason gives us certain truths about THE ALL that we must accept if we are to think clearly, even though these truths do not remove the mystery surrounding THE ALL.

THE ALL must be everything that truly exists. Nothing can exist outside of it, or else THE ALL would not be complete. THE ALL must be infinite because nothing exists to limit, define, or restrict it. It must be infinite in time, meaning eternal, since there is nothing else that could have created it. Something cannot come from nothing, and if THE ALL had ever not existed, it would not exist now. It must continue to exist forever, as nothing can destroy it. THE ALL must also be infinite in space, meaning it must be everywhere, without interruption or separation. There is nothing outside of it to break its continuity. It must also be infinite in power, or absolute, as nothing exists to limit or challenge it. THE ALL is subject to no other power because no other power exists.

THE ALL must be unchangeable because there is nothing to cause it to change. There is nothing into which it could transform and nothing from which it could have transformed. It cannot gain or lose anything and cannot become more or less than it already is. THE ALL has always been and will always remain exactly as it is. Nothing else exists for it to become.

Because THE ALL is infinite, eternal, and unchangeable, anything that is temporary or limited cannot truly be THE ALL. Since nothing exists outside of THE ALL, all finite things must ultimately amount to nothing. Don't be alarmed by this idea. We are not leading you toward the teachings of Christian Science under the cover of Hermetic Philosophy. There is a way to resolve these seemingly conflicting ideas, and we will get to it soon.

We observe what we call "matter," which serves as the foundation for all physical forms. But is THE ALL simply matter? No, because matter cannot give rise to life or mind. Since life and mind are present in the Universe, THE ALL cannot be merely matter. Nothing can rise higher than its source. An effect cannot contain more than what is present in its cause. Also, modern science tells us that matter is not truly solid but is energy or force vibrating at a low frequency. As one modern thinker said, "Matter has melted into mystery." Science now rests on the idea of energy, not matter.

But is THE ALL just energy or force? No, because energy and force, as defined by materialists, are mechanical and lifeless. Life and mind cannot come from something without life or intelligence. As we said earlier, nothing can rise higher than its source. Since life and mind exist, THE ALL cannot be only energy or force. We know this to be true because we are alive and capable of thinking about this question, as are those who argue that energy is everything.

What, then, is greater than matter or energy? Life and mind, in all their many forms, stand above them. But is THE ALL simply life and mind as we know them? Yes and no. THE ALL is not life or mind in the way we experience them. Instead, it is something far greater—something the enlightened call "Spirit." THE ALL is Infinite Living Mind, as far beyond our understanding of life and mind as life and mind are beyond mechanical forces or matter. It is what the illumined refer to when they say the word "SPIRIT."

THE ALL is Infinite Living Mind—what the enlightened call SPIRIT.

Chapter V

The Mental Universe "The Universe is Mental—held in the Mind of THE ALL."—The Kybalion.

THE ALL is SPIRIT. But what exactly is Spirit? It's hard to define Spirit because it is essentially the same as THE ALL, which cannot be explained or fully understood. Spirit is just a name people use to describe the highest idea of Infinite Living Mind. It refers to the Real Essence—Living Mind that is far beyond the life and mind we know, just as life and mind are superior to mechanical energy and matter. Spirit is something beyond what we can fully grasp, and we use the word only to help us think and talk about THE ALL. For the sake of understanding, we can think of Spirit as Infinite Living Mind, even though we admit that we can't truly understand it. We must either approach it in this way or stop thinking about it altogether.

Now let's consider the nature of the Universe, both as a whole and in its individual parts. What is the Universe? We know that nothing can exist outside of THE ALL. But does that mean the Universe is the same as THE ALL? No, because the Universe is made up of many things, is constantly changing, and doesn't fit the characteristics we know to be true about THE ALL. If the Universe is not THE ALL, does that mean it is nothing? That idea doesn't feel right either, because we know the Universe exists in some way. If the Universe is neither THE ALL nor nothing, what can it be? Let's explore this more carefully.

If the Universe exists, it must have come from THE ALL, since something cannot come from nothing. But how could THE ALL create the Universe? Some philosophers say that THE ALL made the Universe out of itself, from its own being. But this idea doesn't work, because THE ALL cannot be divided or reduced. Also, if every part of the Universe were a piece of THE ALL, each part would have to know it was THE ALL, and THE ALL could not forget its own nature and become a simple object or creature. Some people, realizing that THE ALL is everything, have claimed that they are identical to THE ALL, declaring, "I AM GOD," much to the amusement of ordinary people and the concern of wise thinkers. This claim would be as strange as a tiny cell in your body shouting, "I am the entire human being!"

So, if the Universe is not THE ALL and wasn't made by dividing THE ALL, what else could it be? The answer lies in the "Principle of Correspondence." This principle says that what happens on one level of existence mirrors what happens on other levels. The Hermetic saying, "As above, so below," applies here. Let's try to understand how THE ALL might create by looking at how we create things in our own experience.

On our level, humans can create things in two main ways. First, we can make something by using materials from the outside world. But this cannot apply to THE ALL, because there is nothing outside of it to use. Second, we reproduce by creating new life, passing part of ourselves to our offspring. But this also cannot apply to THE ALL, since it cannot give away or divide any part of itself, nor can it multiply or increase. This leaves only one other way to create: through thought. Humans create mental images and ideas without using physical materials or reproducing themselves, yet these mental creations are still real within their own minds.

Following the Principle of Correspondence, we can say that THE ALL creates the Universe in a similar way—mentally. Just as humans create thoughts and images in their minds, THE ALL creates the Universe within its Infinite Mind. This idea agrees with the teachings of the wise and enlightened throughout history. THE ALL creates everything mentally, without using materials or dividing itself. There is no other way it could create.

Just as you, as a person, can create a world of thoughts within your mind, THE ALL creates many Universes within its own Mind. However, your mind is limited, while THE ALL's Mind is infinite. The two are alike in nature but different in scale. As we continue, we will explore the process of creation in more detail. But for now, keep this in mind: the Universe and everything in it is a Mental Creation of THE ALL. In truth, everything is Mind!

"THE ALL creates countless Universes in its Infinite Mind. To THE ALL, the birth, growth, and end of millions of Universes is as brief as the blink of an eye."—The Kybalion. "The Infinite Mind of THE ALL is the womb of Universes."—The Kybalion.

The Principle of Gender applies to everything, whether physical, mental, or spiritual. But gender, in this sense, is not the same as biological sex. Instead, gender refers to the concept of creation and generation. Wherever anything is created, the Principle of Gender is at work, including in the creation of Universes.

It's important not to misunderstand this teaching. We are not saying that there is a male and female God or Creator. That idea is just a distorted version of older teachings. The truth is that THE ALL is beyond gender, just as it is beyond all other laws, including time and space. THE ALL is the source of all laws but is not bound by them. However, when THE ALL creates on a lower level of existence, it follows the laws and principles of that level, including the Principle of Gender. On the mental plane, this principle appears as two aspects: the Masculine and the Feminine.

This may sound surprising at first, but you already accept this idea without realizing it. People talk about God as the Father and Nature as the Mother. They refer to the Divine Father and the Universal Mother, instinctively recognizing the Principle of Gender in the Universe.

However, the Hermetic teaching does not imply that there are two separate beings. THE ALL is One. The two aspects—Masculine and Feminine—are just different ways that THE ALL expresses itself. The Masculine aspect represents the Will of THE ALL, which directs and sets things in motion. The Feminine aspect, which we might call Nature, carries out the work of creation and evolution, developing everything from simple forms to human beings and beyond, all according to natural laws. You can think of the Masculine aspect as the Divine Father and the Feminine aspect as the Universal Mother, from whom all things are born. But remember, these are only metaphors to help us understand the process. The truth is that the entire Universe is created and exists within the Infinite Mind of THE ALL.

You can better understand this idea by applying the Law of Correspondence to yourself. In your mind, there is a part of you that observes your thoughts and mental images—the part you call "I." There is also the part that generates those thoughts, which you might call "Me." Just as you witness your own mental creations, THE ALL creates and observes the Universe within its Mind.

It's no wonder that people feel a natural sense of reverence toward THE ALL. This feeling is what we call "religion"—a deep respect for the Father Mind. And when we look at the wonders of Nature, we are filled with awe, sensing a connection to the Mother Mind, just as a child feels safe and comforted in a parent's embrace.

Don't make the mistake of thinking that the world you see around you—the Earth, which is just a tiny speck in the vast Universe—is the whole of existence. There are countless other worlds, some far greater than ours, and many Universes exist within the Infinite Mind of THE ALL. Even within our solar system, there are levels of life far higher than our own. Compared to the beings that exist on these higher levels, we are like the simple creatures that live at the bottom of the ocean compared to humans. Yet these higher beings were once like us, and we too will evolve and rise to even greater heights, for that is the destiny of humanity, as the wise have taught.

Death is not an end but a transition into a new life. You will continue to grow, rising to higher and higher levels of existence over endless ages. The Universe is your home, and you will explore its farthest reaches long before the end of time. You are a part of the Infinite Mind of THE ALL, and your possibilities are limitless in both time and space.

When the grand cycle of existence eventually draws to a close, and THE ALL reabsorbs all its creations, you will return willingly, for you will finally understand the full truth of being one with THE ALL. This is what the enlightened have seen and shared with us.

Until then, rest assured that you are safe, protected by the infinite power of the Father-Mother Mind.

"Within the Father-Mother Mind, mortal children are at home."—The Kybalion. "There is no one in the Universe without a Father or a Mother."—The Kybalion.

Chapter VI

The Divine Paradox. The half-wise, noticing that the Universe isn't completely real, think they can ignore its laws. These people are arrogant and foolish, and they end up suffering because of it, like someone being thrown against rocks and torn apart by the forces of nature. The truly wise, however, understand how the Universe works and know how to use higher laws to overcome lower ones. They master the art of Alchemy, transforming bad things into good ones, and through this skill, they succeed. True mastery isn't about strange dreams, wild visions, or unrealistic ideas. It's about using higher forces to rise above the lower ones, freeing yourself from the hardships of the lower planes by living at a higher level. The real tool of the Master is transformation, not denial or arrogance.

This is the Paradox of the Universe, which appears because of the Principle of Polarity. This principle is at work when THE ALL begins to create. It teaches us the difference between half-wisdom and real wisdom. While the Infinite ALL sees the Universe and everything in it as something like a dream or a meditation, to all things that are finite, the Universe must be treated as real. Life, actions, and thoughts should follow the rules of the Universe, even as we remember the higher truth behind it. Everything must work according to its own plane and laws. If THE ALL were to believe the Universe was fully real, there would be no way for anything to rise to a higher level. The Universe would stop growing, and progress would end. Similarly, if a person, through half-wisdom, acts as though the Universe is only a dream, like one of their own dreams, they will get stuck. They'll wander aimlessly, making no real progress, until the natural laws they ignored force them awake, leaving them hurt and confused. Keep your mind focused on your goals, but also watch where you step, or you'll trip while looking upward. Remember the Divine Paradox: while the Universe isn't truly real, it still exists. Always keep in mind the two sides of truth—the Absolute and the Relative—and be careful of accepting only half-truths.

The Hermetic teaching called the Law of Paradox is tied to the Principle of Polarity. Hermetic writings often refer to this paradox when discussing life and existence. Teachers frequently warn students not to overlook the "other side" of any topic. This warning is especially import-ant when thinking about the Absolute and the Relative, which can con-fuse many students and lead them away from common sense. Students are reminded to understand the Divine Paradox between the Absolute and the Relative, or they may get lost in half-truths. This lesson is meant to make this concept clear. Read it carefully.

The first thought that comes to someone who learns that the Universe is a mental creation of THE ALL is that everything in the Universe is just an illusion, a dream. This idea can be hard to accept. However, like all great truths, it needs to be understood from both the Absolute and the Relative perspectives. From the Absolute point of view, the Universe is like a dream, something fleeting and unreal compared to THE ALL. We see hints of this idea in everyday life when we talk about the world as temporary, always changing, with things coming and going. All philos-ophers, scientists, and religious thinkers agree that anything created must be temporary and imperfect compared to the infinite nature of THE ALL. This idea isn't unique to Hermetic teachings—it can be found in many different schools of thought.

The Hermetic teachings don't claim the Universe is unreal any more than other philosophies do, though their way of presenting the idea may sound more surprising. Anything with a beginning and an end is, in some sense, unreal, and all philosophies agree on this point. From the Absolute view, only THE ALL is truly real. Whether the Universe is made of matter or is a mental creation in THE ALL's mind, it is temporary and ever-changing. It's important to understand this before judging the Hermetic idea that the Universe is a mental creation. Think about other ideas and see if they don't also align with this truth.

But focusing only on the Absolute view shows only one side of things. The Relative view also matters. Absolute Truth means seeing things as THE ALL sees them, while Relative Truth means seeing things as hu-mans understand them. While THE ALL may view the Universe as just a dream, for the finite beings within it, the Universe feels real and must be treated as such. Although we know the Universe isn't the ultimate reality, we still have to live and act as though it is. We aren't THE ALL, after all.

For example, we know that matter seems real to our senses, even though science tells us it's made up of atoms and particles of energy in constant motion. If we kick a stone, it feels solid, even though we understand it's just a collection of vibrating particles. But remember, our foot and brain are also made of these particles, and without our mind, we wouldn't even be aware of the stone or the foot at all.

Similarly, an artist's idea or a writer's characters feel real to them, even though they only exist in their minds. If this is true for humans, how much more real must the mental images in THE ALL's mind feel? To us, this mental Universe is the only reality we can know, no matter how high we rise in understanding. As we move closer to understanding THE ALL, we begin to see how temporary things are. But only when THE ALL brings us fully into itself will the illusion completely disappear.

So, instead of worrying about whether the Universe is an illusion, we should focus on understanding and using its mental laws. These laws are just as real and unchangeable as any physical laws, and we are all bound by them. Everything except THE ALL must follow these laws, because THE ALL is the source of all laws. No being, no matter how powerful, can escape the laws. Even the most advanced Masters, who seem like gods to us, must obey the laws of the Universe. If these high beings must follow the laws, it's foolish for ordinary people to think they can ignore them just because they understand the Universe is mental in nature.

The Hermetic Principle of Mentalism explains that everything in the Universe is mental in nature, but it doesn't change scientific ideas about the Universe, life, or evolution. In fact, science supports the Hermetic teachings. The only difference is that science calls the foundation of the Universe "energy," while Hermeticism calls it "mind." The philosopher Herbert Spencer's idea of "infinite and eternal energy" aligns closely with Hermetic thought, though Hermetic teachings add that this energy is part of THE ALL's mind.

Students of Hermeticism don't have to abandon their scientific beliefs. They only need to understand that "THE ALL is Mind, and the Universe is mental." The other six Hermetic principles will fit naturally with scientific knowledge, helping to clarify complex ideas. This alignment shouldn't be surprising since Hermetic thought influenced the early Greek philosophers, whose ideas form the foundation of modern science. The main difference between science and Hermeticism lies in the acceptance of the Principle of Mentalism, but science is slowly moving toward this understanding.

This lesson aims to show that the Universe, its laws, and its phenomena are just as real to us as they would be under other philosophical systems, even though everything is always changing and temporary. Regardless of what we believe, we must live as though these things are real. The difference with Mentalism is that it recognizes mental power as the greatest force, which can transform life for those who understand and use it.

Students must learn the advantages of Mentalism and apply its laws. But they should avoid the mistake of thinking the world isn't real and ignoring their responsibilities, as the half-wise do. Those who make this mistake end up suffering because of their foolishness. Instead, students should follow the example of the wise, using higher laws to overcome lower ones and transforming negative things into positive ones. As the Kybalion teaches, mastery lies not in strange dreams or fantasies, but in using higher forces to overcome lower ones, escaping pain by rising to a higher level. Always remember: transformation, not denial, is the key tool of the Master.

We don't live in a dream world, but in a Universe that feels real and demands our effort. Our goal isn't to deny the Universe, but to live fully, using its laws to rise higher and higher. Life's meaning may be beyond our understanding, but the wisest advice is to live according to the best in us and follow the Universe's upward path, no matter how things appear. We are all on a journey, with resting places along the way. Read the Kybalion carefully, and follow the example of the wise, avoiding the mistakes of the half-wise, who suffer because of their ignorance.

Chapter VII

"The All" in All. "While All is in THE ALL, it is equally true that THE ALL is in All. To the one who truly understands this truth, great knowledge has come."—The Kybalion. Many people have often heard the idea that their God (called by many names) is "All in All," but very few have realized the deeper, hidden truth behind these words, which are usually spoken without much thought. This common phrase is actually a remnant of the ancient Hermetic teaching quoted above. As the Kybalion says: "To the one who truly understands this truth, great knowledge has come." Since this is the case, let us search for this truth, because understanding it holds great importance. This Hermetic principle hides one of the most powerful truths in philosophy, science, and religion.

We have already explained the Hermetic teaching that the nature of the Universe is mental—that "the Universe is Mental, existing within the Mind of THE ALL." As the Kybalion says in the passage we just quoted: "All is in THE ALL." But there is also a related truth that must not be overlooked: "It is equally true that THE ALL is in All." Though these two ideas might seem to contradict each other, they actually make sense when viewed through the Law of Paradox. This law helps us understand the relationship between THE ALL and the mental universe it creates. We've talked about how "All is in THE ALL." Now, let's explore what it means that "THE ALL is in All."

Hermetic teachings tell us that THE ALL is present within its creation—it exists in every part, particle, and combination in the Universe. This idea is often explained using the Principle of Correspondence. Teachers encourage students to imagine something in their minds, such as a person, an idea, or a character. A writer or playwright, for example, might picture their characters, just as a painter or sculptor imagines what they want to create. In each case, the mental image exists only within the creator's mind. At the same time, the creator is also present within the image they form. In other words, the life, spirit, and meaning of the mental image come from the mind of the person who created it. Think about this idea carefully until you fully understand it.

To make this clearer, let's use Shakespeare's characters as an example. At the time Shakespeare imagined Othello, Iago, Hamlet, or King Lear, these characters only existed in his mind. Yet, Shakespeare was also "inside" each of these characters, giving them their personality, life, and purpose. Similarly, when we think about characters like Micawber, Oliver Twist, or Uriah Heep, we might ask: Are these characters separate, independent beings, or are they extensions of Dickens, their creator? Do famous sculptures or paintings, like the Venus of Medici or the Sistine Madonna, have spirits of their own, or do they reflect the creative power of their artists? According to the Law of Paradox, both ideas are true depending on how we look at them. Micawber is both Micawber and, at the same time, part of Dickens. But although we can say Micawber reflects Dickens, they are not exactly the same.

In the same way, a person might say: "The spirit of my creator is within me, but I am not my creator." This view is very different from the mistaken belief that some people loudly claim when they say, "I am God!" Imagine how strange it would sound if Micawber or the sneaky Uriah Heep declared, "I am Dickens!" Or if some of Shakespeare's lowly characters proudly announced, "I am Shakespeare!" THE ALL exists in the earthworm, but the earthworm is not THE ALL. Yet the mystery remains: Even though the earthworm is just a small part of the creation, living entirely within the Mind of THE ALL, THE ALL is still present within the earthworm and within every particle that makes it. Is there any greater mystery than this idea: "All in THE ALL, and THE ALL in All"?

Of course, these examples are limited and cannot fully capture this idea, since they describe the creation of mental images by finite human minds, while the Universe is the creation of an Infinite Mind. The difference between these two types of creation is vast. Yet, the same principle applies to both. The Principle of Correspondence shows that what is true on one level is also true on another—"As above, so below; as below, so above."

The more a person becomes aware of the spirit that exists within them, the higher they will rise in their spiritual development. This awareness, recognition, and expression of the spirit within us is the true meaning of spiritual growth. Remember this: Spiritual development is the recognition, realization, and manifestation of the spirit within us. This is the essence of true religion.

There are many levels of existence in the Universe, ranging from the lowest forms of matter to the highest forms of spirit, which are very close to the essence of THE ALL. Everything in the Universe is constantly moving upward on this scale of life. Even though things might seem to move in different directions at times, everything is ultimately progressing toward THE ALL. This upward movement is a journey of returning home, and no matter how things may appear, all progress leads back to THE ALL. This is the message of enlightened teachings.

The Hermetic teachings explain that the Universe was created mentally by THE ALL. At the start of creation, THE ALL, in its state of "Being," directed its Will toward "Becoming," and this is how the creative process began. This process involves lowering the level of vibration until it reaches a point where the densest form of matter appears. This phase is known as Involution, during which THE ALL becomes deeply connected with its creation. Hermetic teachings compare this to the way an artist or writer becomes so absorbed in their work that they almost forget themselves, living entirely within their creation. If we replace the word "wrapped" with "rapt," it may help us better understand this concept.

This first stage of creation is sometimes called the "Outpouring" of divine energy, while the next stage, Evolution, is called the "Indrawing." At the furthest point of the Outpouring, the vibrations are at their lowest, and this is the point furthest from THE ALL. When the Evolution stage begins, the pendulum of Rhythm starts swinging back toward home. Hermetic teachings describe this as a return journey.

During the Outpouring, creation is unified and whole. But as Evolution begins, the Law of Individualization takes over. This means that creation begins to separate into individual units of force. What started as unformed energy returns to THE ALL as countless developed life forms that have grown through physical, mental, and spiritual evolution. These beings rise higher and higher along the scale of life, becoming more advanced as they move closer to their source.

The ancient Hermetists often use the word "Meditation" to describe how the Universe was created mentally in the Mind of THE ALL. They also sometimes use the word "Contemplation." But what they really seem to mean is the use of Divine Attention. The word "Attention" comes from a Latin root meaning "to reach out" or "to stretch out," so paying attention is like mentally stretching out or extending your mind's energy. Once you understand the real meaning of "Attention," this idea becomes much clearer.

The Hermetic Teachings about Evolution say that THE ALL began the process of Creation by meditating on the Universe. In doing so, it set the foundations of the material world and brought it into existence through thought. After this, THE ALL gradually awakens from its Meditation, and this awakening sparks the beginning of Evolution. This process unfolds step by step on the material, mental, and spiritual levels. Everything begins to move toward the spiritual. Matter becomes less heavy, new forms of life start appearing, and combinations of elements form. Life grows and shows itself in higher forms, and Mind becomes more visible as the vibrations rise higher and higher. The entire Evolution process moves forward following the laws of the "Indrawing" phase. This whole process takes countless ages, each lasting millions of years, but the Illumined tell us that the entire creation—both Involution and Evolution—is only like the blink of an eye to THE ALL.

When these endless cycles of time finally come to an end, THE ALL pulls back its Attention, Contemplation, and Meditation from the Universe because the Great Work is complete. At that point, everything returns to THE ALL, where it first came from. Yet, the mystery remains: even though all things return to THE ALL, the spirit of each soul is not destroyed—it expands infinitely. The Creator and the Created become one. This is what the Illumined tell us.

This example of THE ALL meditating and then awakening is only an attempt by teachers to explain something infinite using a simple idea. Even so, "As Below, so Above" applies. The difference is only in degree. Just as THE ALL wakes up from its meditation on the Universe, people also stop focusing on the material world over time and instead turn more toward the Spirit within, which is "The Divine Ego."

There is another point we want to mention, even though it touches on metaphysical ideas, which we usually avoid because such thoughts often lead nowhere. But it's important to address a question that everyone who seeks truth eventually asks: "Why does THE ALL create Universes?" This question takes different forms, but it all comes down to this same curiosity.

Many people have tried to answer this, but no answer fully explains it. Some suggest that THE ALL creates to gain something, but that makes no sense since THE ALL already has everything. Others think THE ALL created the Universe to have something to love or for amusement, or maybe because it felt lonely or wanted to show its power. These are all childish ideas from an immature way of thinking.

Some thinkers suggest that THE ALL creates because it feels an inner need or instinct to create. While this idea is more advanced than others, it still has a flaw. If THE ALL were forced to act by its own nature or creative instinct, then that instinct would be more powerful than THE ALL, and that makes no sense. However, THE ALL does create, and it seems to experience some kind of satisfaction in doing so. It's hard to avoid the conclusion that THE ALL might have something similar to an inner nature, a creative instinct like humans, but on an infinite scale, with infinite desire and will. It wouldn't act unless it wanted to, and it wouldn't want to unless it found satisfaction in acting. This inner nature can be understood through the Law of Correspondence.

Even with that said, it is better to think of THE ALL as acting completely freely, without any internal or external force influencing it. This is the heart of the problem—and the challenge of understanding it.

In truth, there is no "reason" why THE ALL acts, because having a reason would suggest a cause. And THE ALL is beyond the law of cause and effect, except when it decides to set that law into motion. In the end, the nature of THE ALL is impossible to fully understand—just as THE ALL itself is unknowable. We can only say that "THE ALL acts because it acts." THE ALL is its own reason, law, and action, all at once. THE ALL, its reason, its law, and its action are all the same thing—just different ways of naming the same truth.

The teachers sharing these ideas believe that the answer to this mystery is hidden deep within THE ALL, along with the secret of its existence. The Law of Correspondence helps us understand only part of THE ALL, the part connected to "Becoming." Beyond that lies the aspect of "Being," where all laws dissolve into one Law, and all principles merge into one Principle. In that state, THE ALL, Principle, and Being are one and the same. This is why trying to explain these things through metaphysics is pointless. We mention this only to acknowledge the question and show that the usual answers from metaphysics and theology are inadequate.

Some ancient and modern Hermetic teachers have leaned toward the idea that THE ALL has an inner nature, following the Law of Correspondence. However, the legends say that when advanced students asked Hermes, the Great, about this mystery, he pressed his lips together and stayed silent, showing that there is no answer. Perhaps he was applying the saying, "The lips of Wisdom are closed, except to the ears of Understanding," meaning even his advanced students didn't yet have the understanding needed for the answer. If Hermes knew the secret, he didn't share it. And if Hermes remained silent, what ordinary person would dare to teach it?

Whatever the answer may be—if there even is one—the truth remains: "While All is in THE ALL, it is equally true that THE ALL is in All." This teaching is essential. And we can add one final reminder: "To the one who truly understands this truth, great knowledge has come.

Chapter VIII

The Planes of Correspondence. "As above, so below; as below, so above."—The Kybalion. The second great Hermetic principle explains that there is harmony, agreement, and connection between all the different levels of life, existence, and reality. This truth is fundamental because everything in the Universe comes from the same source, and the same laws, principles, and qualities apply to every unit and every combination of forces as they operate on their respective levels of existence.

For easier understanding, Hermetic philosophy divides the Universe into three main types of phenomena, known as the Three Great Planes: The Great Physical Plane, the Great Mental Plane, and the Great Spiritual Plane. These divisions are not absolute but are more like steps along the continuous scale of life, starting from the lowest form of undifferentiated matter and rising to the highest point, which is pure spirit. The boundaries between these planes blend into one another, so it is difficult to clearly separate the higher forms of the physical from the lower forms of the mental, or the higher mental from the lower spiritual.

In short, the Three Great Planes are like broad categories representing different levels of how life manifests. Although we won't go into deep detail about these planes here, it is useful to give a general description to help with understanding.

One question that beginners often ask is: "What exactly is a plane?" This word has been used a lot in occult writings, but it is not always clearly explained. People often wonder if a plane is a physical place with size and dimensions or if it's just a state of mind or condition. The answer is that it is neither a place nor simply a condition. It is more like a degree or level in a scale that can be measured, but not in the usual sense of dimensions like length, width, and height. This concept may seem strange at first, but let's explore it further.

In everyday life, a "dimension" refers to measurements such as length, width, and height—or sometimes thickness or circumference. However, occultists and some scientists recognize another dimension beyond these physical ones. This extra dimension is often referred to as the "Fourth Dimension," which is used to measure the different degrees or levels of existence, called "planes."

This Fourth Dimension could be described as the Dimension of Vibration. Both modern science and Hermetic teachings recognize that everything in the Universe is constantly moving and vibrating—nothing ever stays still. Every object and form, from the lowest to the highest, vibrates at a specific rate. These vibrations differ not only in speed but also in the way they move and behave. The degree of vibration determines the level, or plane, on which something exists. The higher the vibration, the higher the plane and the more advanced the form of life on that plane. So, even though a plane is not a physical location or a simple state of being, it shares qualities with both.

It's important to keep in mind that the Three Great Planes are not actual separations within the Universe but are used by Hermetic thinkers to help us study and understand the different levels and forms of life. Whether it's an atom, a force, the mind of a human, or the being of an angel, all are different levels within the same system. The only difference between them is the degree of their vibration, and everything in the Universe is a creation of THE ALL, existing within the Infinite Mind of THE ALL.

Each of the Three Great Planes is further divided into Seven Minor Planes, and each Minor Plane is again divided into seven sub-planes. These divisions are not strict and rigid; instead, they smoothly transition into one another. They are mainly used to help us study and understand the complex activities and forces at work in the Universe.

The Great Physical Plane and its Seven Minor Planes cover all things related to physical matter and energy. This includes everything we recognize as material objects, forces, and physical energy. However, the Hermetic teachings emphasize that matter is not a separate thing by itself. Matter is just one form of energy, vibrating at a very low frequency. Hermetic teachings classify matter under the category of energy, assigning three of the Seven Minor Planes of the Physical Plane to it.

The Seven Minor Physical Planes are: The Plane of Matter (A), the Plane of Matter (B), the Plane of Matter (C), the Plane of Ethereal Substance, the Plane of Energy (A), the Plane of Energy (B), and the Plane of Energy (C).

The Plane of Matter (A) includes the forms of matter we are familiar with—solids, liquids, and gases—as described in physics textbooks. The Plane of Matter (B) contains higher, more refined forms of matter, which science is only beginning to understand, such as the energy associated with radioactive elements like radium. The Plane of Matter (C) holds the most subtle and delicate forms of matter, which modern science has not yet discovered.

The Plane of Ethereal Substance includes what scientists call "the Ether," a highly flexible and nearly weightless substance that fills all space. This ether acts as a medium for transmitting energy waves like light, heat, and electricity. It serves as a link between matter and energy because it shares qualities with both. According to Hermetic teachings, this plane is further divided into seven sub-levels. In fact, there are seven types of ether, not just one.

Above the Plane of Ethereal Substance is the Plane of Energy (A). This plane consists of the ordinary forms of energy that science recognizes, with seven sub-planes: Heat, Light, Magnetism, Electricity, and Attraction (including forces like Gravity, Cohesion, and Chemical Affinity). There are also other kinds of energy that scientific experiments have detected, though they have not yet been named or classified. The Plane of Energy (B) consists of seven sub-planes of more advanced energy forms, which science has yet to discover. These forces are sometimes called "Nature's Finer Forces," and they are involved in mental phenomena, making such events possible. The Plane of Energy (C) contains seven sub-planes of energy that are so advanced they resemble life itself. However, this energy is beyond what ordinary human minds can understand. It is only accessible to beings from the Spiritual Plane, and it can be thought of as a kind of divine power. These beings, compared to the most advanced humans, seem like gods.

The Great Mental Plane includes all living beings we know, along with other types that are less familiar to most people but are known to occultists. The seven minor planes of the Mental Plane can be described as follows, though this classification is somewhat simplified and not meant to be fully detailed here.

The Plane of Mineral Mind involves the states and conditions of the entities that give life to minerals and chemicals. These entities are not the same as the molecules, atoms, or particles that make up minerals. Instead, they are like the souls that animate these physical forms, just as a human body is not the same as the soul that inhabits it. These entities have low levels of life, mind, and development—just slightly more advanced than the energy units found on the higher physical planes. Most people don't think that minerals have mind, soul, or life, but occultists know they do, and modern science is starting to agree. Molecules, atoms, and particles show behaviors that could be described as attraction, repulsion, love, and dislike. Some modern scientists even believe that the emotions and desires of atoms are just a simpler version of those found in humans.

The Plane of Elemental Mind (A) includes the mental and vital development of beings that are unknown to most people but are recognized by occultists. These entities are invisible to ordinary human senses, but they play important roles in the Universe. Their intelligence is between that of minerals and plants.

The Plane of Plant Mind consists of the mental and life states of the beings that make up the plant world. The idea that plants have life, mind, and even souls is becoming more accepted, with recent scientific studies showing new insights into how plants live and think.

The Plane of Elemental Mind (B) involves more advanced elemental beings that are part of the natural order. They exist between the mental levels of plants and animals and share characteristics of both.

The Plane of Animal Mind includes the mental states of beings that animate animals, which are familiar to us all. There's no need to describe this level further, as the world of animals is well-known.

The Plane of Elemental Mind (C) consists of beings that are still invisible but have qualities that blend both animal and human traits. The most advanced of these beings have intelligence that is nearly human.

The Plane of Human Mind contains all the mental and life experiences of human beings, divided into seven levels. Most people today exist on the fourth level, and only the most intelligent have reached the fifth. It has taken humanity millions of years to reach this point, and it will take many more years to reach the sixth and seventh levels. However, earlier civilizations have already moved through these levels and advanced to higher planes. Some people today have already reached the sixth and seventh levels and gone beyond. Those who reach the sixth level will be like "Super-Men," while those on the seventh will be "Over-Men."

While we've mentioned the Elementary Planes briefly, we won't go into too much detail here, as it's beyond the scope of this discussion. These planes serve a similar role to the black keys on a piano, which complement the white keys. While the white keys alone can create music, the black keys are essential for certain scales and harmonies. In the same way, the Elementary Planes connect the other planes and allow for transitions between them. Some forms of evolution happen on these planes, and those who understand these ideas can gain new insights into how life moves from one kingdom to another. The great elemental beings are well-known to all occultists, and their presence is mentioned throughout esoteric writings. Readers of stories like Bulwer's Zanoni will recognize the kinds of beings that inhabit these planes of life.

Moving from the Great Mental Plane to the Great Spiritual Plane, how can we describe these higher states of Being, Life, and Mind? It is hard to explain them to minds that are not yet ready to understand even the deeper levels of the Human Mind. It is like trying to describe light to someone born blind, sweetness to someone who has never tasted anything sweet, or harmony to someone born deaf. We can only speak about them in very general terms.

The seven minor planes of the Great Spiritual Plane, each with its seven sub-divisions, are home to beings whose Life, Mind, and Forms are far beyond anything we can imagine. These beings are as advanced beyond today's humans as humans are beyond earthworms, minerals, or even certain forms of energy or matter. Their lives are so far above ours that we cannot fully grasp the details. Their minds are so far ahead of ours that, to them, our thinking seems more like a mechanical process. The matter that makes up their forms belongs to the highest planes, and some are even said to be made of pure energy. What can we say about such beings?

On these seven minor planes exist beings that we might call Angels, Archangels, and Demi-Gods. On the lower levels are great souls known as Masters and Adepts. Above them are the vast Angelic Hosts, beings so advanced that they are beyond human imagination. Higher still are beings so great that they can be called "gods" without disrespect, for their intelligence, power, and existence resemble what humans imagine when thinking of Deity. These divine beings, as well as the Angelic Hosts, take a deep interest in the Universe and play a major role in guiding evolution and cosmic progress. Their influence can be seen throughout human history, inspiring many legends, religions, and traditions. Over time, they have shared their knowledge and power with the world, always following the laws of THE ALL.

Even though these advanced beings are extraordinary, they are still creations within the Mind of THE ALL. They follow the same cosmic laws and processes as everything else in the Universe. They are mortal beings. We may call them "gods," but they are really like older siblings to humanity—souls who have grown far beyond the rest of us and have chosen to delay their union with THE ALL so they can help others on their journey along the Path. However, these beings still belong to the Universe and are subject to its rules. They are not Absolute Spirit.

Only the most advanced Hermetists can understand the deeper teachings about the powers and experiences of the Spiritual Planes. These ideas are so advanced that they can easily confuse anyone without years of study in Hermetic philosophy. Those who understand these teachings are often souls who have carried knowledge from previous lifetimes. Much of this wisdom is considered too sacred and powerful to share openly, as it can be dangerous if misunderstood. Those who study Hermeticism will recognize that the word "Spirit," in this context, means something much deeper than religious or holy ideas. For Hermetists, "Spirit" refers to the Animating Principle, the force that gives life and energy, similar to living power or inner essence.

This power can be used for both good and evil purposes, following the Principle of Polarity. Many religions recognize this dual nature in their ideas of the Devil, Satan, or fallen angels. Because of this danger, knowledge of the Spiritual Planes is kept secret within the inner circles of esoteric and occult orders. Those who misuse spiritual power face a terrible fate. The law of Rhythm will pull them back to the lowest levels of material existence, where they must slowly make their way back toward Spirit. These fallen souls are burdened by the memory of the heights they once reached and lost. The legends of fallen angels are based on real events, as advanced occultists know. Any attempt to gain power selfishly on the Spiritual Planes will cause a soul to lose balance and fall, no matter how far they had risen. However, even these fallen souls are given the chance to return, though they must face the consequences of their actions and work their way back according to the universal laws.

We must always remember that the Principle of Correspondence applies to every plane of existence. "As Above, so Below; as Below, so Above." All seven Hermetic principles are active on every level—physical, mental, and spiritual. The Principle of Mental Substance applies to all planes, as everything exists within the Mind of THE ALL. The Principle of Correspondence reveals the harmony between different planes. The Principle of Vibration explains the differences between planes, since everything vibrates at a unique rate. The Principle of Polarity shows that all things exist in pairs of opposites. The Principle of Rhythm is seen in the rise and fall of events on every plane. The Principle of Cause and Effect teaches that every cause creates an effect, and every effect has a cause. The Principle of Gender is always present, with creative energy expressing both masculine and feminine qualities.

"As Above, so Below; as Below, so Above." This ancient Hermetic truth explains how the same principles apply at every level of existence. As we explore the remaining principles, we will see even more clearly how this great principle of Correspondence connects everything in the Universe.

Chapter IX

Vibration. "Nothing rests; everything moves; everything vibrates."—The Kybalion. The third great Hermetic principle, the Principle of Vibration, teaches that everything in the Universe is in motion. Nothing stays still—everything moves, vibrates, and revolves. Some early Greek philosophers understood this truth and included it in their teachings, but it was later forgotten by most thinkers outside of Hermetic circles. In the 19th century, physical science rediscovered this principle, and discoveries in the 20th century provided even more proof that this ancient teaching was correct.

The Hermetic teachings say that not only does everything move and vibrate constantly, but the differences between all forms of energy and matter exist because of their varying rates and types of vibration. Even THE ALL vibrates, though it does so at such a high intensity and speed that it appears to be perfectly still—just like a spinning wheel can seem motionless when it spins fast enough. According to these teachings, Spirit exists at one extreme of the vibration scale, and at the other extreme are the densest forms of matter. Between these two ends, there are countless levels of vibration, each creating a different form of existence.

Modern science now agrees that everything we think of as matter and energy is just different forms of vibratory motion. Some scientists are even beginning to explore the idea that mental processes might also be forms of vibration. Let's look at what science says about vibration in matter and energy.

Science shows that all matter vibrates to some degree, with these vibrations tied to heat. Whether an object is cold or hot, it vibrates at a certain rate, meaning it is always in motion. Every part of the Universe is in motion, from the smallest particles to the largest celestial bodies. Planets orbit around stars, many spinning on their axes, while stars revolve around larger centers. These centers, in turn, may revolve around even greater ones, continuing infinitely. On a smaller scale, molecules within matter are constantly moving, vibrating around and against each other. Molecules are made up of atoms, which also move and vibrate. Atoms contain even smaller parts—called electrons, ions, or corpuscles—which orbit each other and vibrate rapidly. All forms of matter, from the smallest to the largest, follow the Principle of Vibration.

The same principle applies to all forms of energy. Light, heat, magnetism, and electricity are all forms of vibratory motion, likely originating from the ether. While science does not fully understand forces like cohesion (which holds molecules together), chemical attraction (which binds atoms), or gravity (which draws all matter together), Hermetic teachings suggest that these forces are also forms of vibratory energy. Hermetists have taught this idea for ages, even though science is only beginning to explore it.

The ether, which science describes but does not yet fully understand, is considered by Hermetists to be a higher form of matter. They call it the "Ethereal Substance," believing it is made of matter vibrating at a higher rate. This substance is incredibly fine and elastic, filling all of space and serving as a medium for transmitting energy, such as light, heat, and electricity. It acts as a bridge between matter and energy, possessing its own unique vibrations.

Scientists often use the example of a spinning wheel, top, or cylinder to illustrate how increased vibration affects an object. Imagine a wheel spinning slowly. At first, it is easy to see, and you hear no sound from it. As the speed increases, you start to hear a low hum or growl. As it spins even faster, the sound becomes a musical note that rises higher on the scale with each increase in speed. Eventually, it reaches a point where the sound becomes too high for human ears to hear, and silence returns.

If the wheel's speed keeps increasing, it will start to glow red. As the vibration rises, the red turns to orange, then yellow, and continues through green, blue, indigo, and violet. Beyond violet, the colors disappear, as the human eye can no longer register them. Yet, even though we can't see them, the object continues to emit rays—like those used in photography—and eventually gives off X-rays and other powerful forms of energy. When it reaches the correct vibration, it also begins to release electricity and magnetism.

If the wheel continues to accelerate, its molecules will break apart, turning into their original atoms. These atoms will then separate into their smaller components, such as electrons or corpuscles, following the Principle of Vibration. Eventually, even these particles will dissolve, and the wheel will no longer be made of matter—it will have become Ethereal Substance. At this point, science can no longer follow the process, but Hermetic teachings say that if vibration keeps increasing, the object will go through higher stages of existence. It will rise beyond material form, moving through mental and spiritual levels, until it finally returns to THE ALL, the source of all things.

Though the wheel will have stopped being an "object" long before reaching the level of Ethereal Substance, the example still helps us understand the effect of increasing vibration. It's also important to remember that when the object emits light, heat, or other energies, it is not actually turning into those forms of energy. Instead, it reaches a vibration that allows these energies, which were trapped within it, to be released. These forms of energy are usually confined within material objects because energy interacts with and becomes entangled in material forms. This process of creation—where the force that creates something becomes wrapped up within the creation—is something that happens on all levels of existence.

The Hermetic teachings go far beyond what modern science teaches. They explain that every thought, emotion, reason, will, or desire—any mental state—creates vibrations. Some of these vibrations are released and can affect the minds of other people through a process called "induction." This is the principle behind phenomena like telepathy, mental influence, and other ways one mind can affect another. Today, these ideas are becoming more familiar to the public, thanks to the spread of occult knowledge by various schools, teachers, and movements.

Every thought, emotion, or mental state has a specific rate and pattern of vibration. With enough focus and effort, a person can reproduce these mental states, just as a musical note can be recreated by making an instrument vibrate at the right frequency or as a specific color can appear when vibrations match. By understanding how the Principle of Vibration applies to mental processes, a person can adjust their mind to any state they desire, gaining control over their thoughts, moods, and emotions. This same understanding also allows them to influence the minds of others, creating specific mental states in those around them. In a way, this is like producing mental vibrations at will, just as science produces physical vibrations. However, mastering this power requires proper instruction, practice, and effort. This ability is part of what Hermetists call Mental Transmutation, which is a branch of the Hermetic Arts.

Thinking carefully about these ideas reveals that the Principle of Vibration is at the heart of the abilities shown by Masters and Adepts. These advanced individuals appear to bypass the laws of nature, but in reality, they are simply using one natural law to counteract another. They achieve their extraordinary results by changing the vibrations of physical objects or forms of energy, which leads to what many people call "miracles."

As one of the old Hermetic writers wisely said, "He who understands the Principle of Vibration has grasped the scepter of Power."

Chapter X

Polarity. "Everything is dual; everything has poles; everything has its pair of opposites; like and unlike are the same; opposites are identical in nature, but different in degree; extremes meet; all truths are but half-truths; all paradoxes may be reconciled."—The Kybalion. The fourth Hermetic principle, the Principle of Polarity, explains that everything in existence has two sides, two aspects, or two poles. Each thing has a pair of opposites, with many degrees in between the two extremes. The old paradoxes that have confused people for ages can be explained by understanding this principle. People have always noticed something similar to this idea and have expressed it through sayings such as, "Everything is and isn't at the same time," "All truths are only half-truths," "Every truth contains some falsehood," and "There are two sides to everything."

The Hermetic teachings explain that the differences between things that seem completely opposite are only differences in degree. They show that opposites can be reconciled and that "thesis" and "antithesis" are the same in nature, only varying in degree. Understanding this principle makes it possible to see how opposites can come together as part of the same truth. For example, Spirit and Matter are just two poles of the same thing, with many stages of vibration in between. The ALL and the Many are also the same, with the difference being a matter of mental manifestation. Likewise, Law and laws, Principle and principles, and Infinite Mind and finite minds are opposite poles of the same concept.

On the physical level, we can see this principle in action with temperature. Heat and cold are not completely different things but are two ends of the same scale. A thermometer shows different degrees of temperature, with one end labeled as "cold" and the other as "hot." Between these two extremes are many degrees of warmth, and the same measurement can be called either "hotter" or "colder" depending on your perspective. There is no absolute point where heat ends, and cold begins—it is all just a matter of higher or lower vibration. The terms "high" and "low" are also relative and are just two sides of the same thing.

This principle applies to many other areas as well. If you travel east far enough, you will eventually find yourself going west, and the same is true if you travel north or south. Light and darkness are two ends of the same spectrum, with many levels between them. In music, the scale is made up of notes that rise until they repeat in a higher octave, showing how one thing flows into another. The same is true with colors, which are just different vibrations—red being a lower vibration and violet a higher one. Size is also relative, with large and small being two ends of the same concept. Noise and quiet, hard and soft, sharp and dull—each of these are poles of the same thing with many degrees in between.

Good and bad are not absolute but depend on where they fall on the same scale. Something may be "less good" than another thing above it, but it is still "more good" than something lower on the scale. This "more or less" way of thinking applies to everything, and the differences are always about degree rather than kind.

On the mental level, love and hate seem like complete opposites that cannot be reconciled. However, the Principle of Polarity shows that love and hate are just two ends of the same scale. There is no such thing as pure love or pure hate—they are simply terms for different levels of the same thing. As you move up the scale, you find more love and less hate, and as you move down, the reverse is true. Somewhere in the middle, love and hate are so balanced that they become hard to tell apart, turning into a neutral state of like or dislike. The same principle applies to courage and fear. Every mental state has its opposite, and wherever you find one, you will find the other.

This understanding allows Hermetists to transform one mental state into another by shifting along the scale of polarity. Things from different categories cannot be changed into one another—love can't turn into east, and red can't become courage—but things within the same class can shift from one pole to the other. For example, love can turn into hate, and hate can turn back into love by adjusting their polarity. The same is true for courage and fear, as well as many other states. A fearful person can raise their mental vibration along the fear-courage scale until they feel fearless. Similarly, a lazy person can shift their vibration and become active and energetic.

Anyone familiar with how mental practices work may already understand how these ideas are applied to change mental states. However, the Principle of Polarity makes it clear that these changes happen by shifting degrees along the same scale, not by turning one thing into something entirely different. This is a crucial difference. On the physical level, heat cannot turn into sharpness or loudness, but it can be lowered until it becomes cold. In the same way, love can turn into hate, and fear can turn into courage, but love cannot become courage, nor can fear turn into hate. Each mental state belongs to a specific class, with two poles along which transformation is possible.

The positive and negative poles exist in every mental state and physical phenomenon. Love is positive compared to hate, courage is positive compared to fear, and activity is positive compared to inactivity. Even without knowing the Principle of Vibration, most people recognize that the positive pole feels higher and tends to dominate the negative pole. Nature always seems to favor the positive side.

This principle also explains how one person's mental state can influence another's. When someone changes their mental polarity, they can affect the minds of others through induction, causing similar changes in them. For example, a person feeling sad and fearful can be helped by someone who has trained their mind to be positive and courageous. The

51

helper raises their own mental vibration and then, through induction, influences the other person, shifting their mind toward the positive end of the scale. As a result, the fearful person begins to feel courageous and hopeful. Most mental changes follow this principle of shifting along a scale rather than becoming something entirely different.

Knowing about this important Hermetic Principle will help students better understand their own mental states and those of others. They will realize that all mental states are just a matter of degree. With this understanding, they will learn to raise or lower their mental vibrations whenever they choose, shifting their mental polarity. In doing so, they will gain control over their thoughts and emotions, becoming masters of their mental states instead of being controlled by them. This knowledge will also allow them to help others wisely, using the right methods to shift another person's polarity when needed. We encourage all students to study and become familiar with this Principle of Polarity, as understanding it will bring clarity to many challenging topics.

Chapter XI

Rhythm. "Everything flows out and in; everything has its tides; all things rise and fall; the pendulum-swing manifests in everything; the measure of the swing to the right is the measure of the swing to the left; rhythm compensates."—The Kybalion. The fifth Hermetic principle, the Principle of Rhythm, teaches that everything in the Universe follows a pattern of movement. There is always a flow in and out, a swing forward and backward, like the swing of a pendulum or the rise and fall of tides. This movement occurs between the two poles of existence found on the physical, mental, and spiritual levels. Rhythm works together with the Principle of Polarity, which explains that everything has two sides. Rhythm moves back and forth between these opposites, though it rarely reaches the extremes at either end. Instead, it constantly moves toward one pole and then the other in a never-ending cycle.

This pattern of movement is found everywhere in the Universe. Everything moves from action to reaction, from growth to decline. Suns and planets form, grow in power, and eventually fade into lifeless matter, waiting to begin a new cycle of life. In the same way, worlds are born, live, and die, only to be reborn once more. This process applies to all living things, which are born, grow, die, and then are reborn again. It also applies to philosophies, religions, governments, fashions, and societies, which all go through stages of birth, growth, maturity, decline, and rebirth. The pendulum of life is always in motion.

We see this swing of rhythm everywhere. Day turns into night, and night becomes day again. The seasons change from summer to winter and back to summer. Even the smallest particles of matter follow rhythmic cycles, just as larger objects like planets do. Nothing ever rests completely, and all movement follows the principle of rhythm. This principle applies to every area of life and can explain many aspects of human behavior as well. The rhythm of life always swings between the two poles, and the pendulum is always moving. Life's tides rise and fall according to law.

Science understands the Principle of Rhythm as a natural law that applies to physical things. But Hermetists take this idea further, understanding that rhythm also affects human thoughts and emotions. It explains why people experience sudden shifts in moods and feelings, which can seem confusing or frustrating. However, Hermetists have studied this principle closely and have discovered how to escape some of its effects through Transmutation.

The Hermetic masters learned that although rhythm is always present in the mind, it works on two levels. There is a higher plane of consciousness and a lower plane. By understanding this, they learned how to rise to the higher plane, where they could avoid being affected by the back-and-forth swing of rhythm on the lower level. In other words, the swing of the pendulum still happens, but it only affects the unconscious mind, leaving the conscious mind unaffected. This technique is called the Law of Neutralization. It works by raising the self, or Ego, above the level of unconscious thoughts, so the backward swing of the mental pendulum doesn't disturb the conscious mind. This is similar to rising above a storm and watching it pass beneath you without being touched by it.

A Hermetic master or advanced student can place themselves at the desired pole of their mental state and, by refusing to engage with the backward swing of rhythm, they stay firm in their chosen mindset. They let the pendulum swing back on the unconscious level, without letting it affect their conscious thoughts. Many people who have gained self-control do this naturally, even if they don't fully understand how it works. They avoid being overwhelmed by moods or negative thoughts by instinctively applying the Law of Neutralization. However, a master achieves a much higher level of control, using their will to maintain a state of poise and mental strength that may seem impossible to others who allow their emotions to control them.

Anyone who reflects on their life will realize how much these rhythmic swings of mood and emotion have affected them. Moments of excitement are often followed by feelings of sadness. Times of courage are replaced by fear. Most people are constantly carried back and forth by these emotional tides without ever knowing why it happens. By understanding the Principle of Rhythm, a person can gain mastery over these emotional swings and come to know themselves better. With this knowledge, they can avoid being swept away by the constant flow of changing moods.

The will of a person is stronger than the conscious effects of rhythm, though the principle itself cannot be stopped. While it is impossible to eliminate rhythm entirely, it is possible to escape its influence by learning how to avoid being caught up in the swing. The pendulum will continue to swing, but those who understand this principle can rise above it and no longer be controlled by its movement.

There are other aspects of the Principle of Rhythm that we need to discuss here. One of these is the Law of Compensation. The word "compensate" means "to balance or counterbalance," which is how the Hermetists use the term. This is the idea behind the Kybalion's statement: "The measure of the swing to the right is the measure of the swing to the left; rhythm compensates."

The Law of Compensation explains that every movement in one direction determines an equal movement in the opposite direction. Every swing toward one pole is balanced by a swing toward the other pole. On the physical level, there are many examples of this law. The pendulum of a clock swings a certain distance to the right and then swings back the same distance to the left. The seasons balance each other in the same way, as do the tides. Wherever rhythm is present, the Law of Compensation is at work. A short swing in one direction will only allow for a short

54

swing in the other direction, while a long swing to one side will result in an equally long swing back. An object thrown high into the air must travel the same distance when it falls back to the ground. The force used to throw it upward matches the force it generates when it returns to the earth. This law is constant on the physical level and can be observed in many areas of life.

However, Hermetists take this law further and apply it to mental and emotional states. According to their teachings, a person who experiences great joy will also be capable of deep suffering. On the other hand, someone who feels little pain will experience little joy. For example, a pig does not suffer much mentally, but it also does not experience much joy—it is balanced. In contrast, some animals feel great joy but also suffer greatly because of their sensitive nature. The same is true for humans. Some people are only capable of mild pleasure and mild pain, while others can experience intense joy but also suffer deeply. This balance between joy and pain is an example of the Law of Compensation at work.

Hermetists go even further, teaching that to experience a certain amount of joy, a person must first go through an equal amount of pain. However, this does not mean that after experiencing pleasure, the person will have to "pay" for it with future suffering. Instead, the pleasure is seen as the balancing result of pain experienced earlier—either in this life or in a past one. This understanding provides new insight into the purpose of suffering.

Hermetists view life as a continuous chain, with each life forming part of a greater whole. The swing between pain and pleasure only makes sense when reincarnation is considered. Without the idea of previous lives, the Law of Compensation would seem confusing.

They also teach that advanced students and masters can avoid much of the suffering caused by this rhythmic swing by using the Law of Neutralization. By raising their awareness to the higher plane of the Ego, they can escape many of the experiences that affect those who remain on the lower plane of consciousness.

The Law of Compensation plays a major role in people's lives. It is easy to see that everything we gain in life requires us to give up something else in return. For example, no one can "keep their penny and eat the cake" at the same time. Every positive thing has its downside, and every gain involves some loss. The rich have wealth that the poor do not, but the poor often have things the rich cannot enjoy. A wealthy person may have access to fine foods and luxuries, but they may lack the appetite to enjoy them. Meanwhile, a poor laborer may take great pleasure in simple meals, enjoying them more than the rich person ever could. Their different habits, desires, and conditions make this balance possible.

This balancing act continues throughout life. The Law of Compensation ensures that everything is balanced in the end, even if it takes several lifetimes for the pendulum of rhythm to swing back to its opposite pole.

Chapter XII

Causation. "Every Cause has its Effect; every Effect has its Cause; everything happens according to Law; Chance is but a name for Law not recognized; there are many planes of causation, but nothing escapes the Law."—The Kybalion. The Sixth Hermetic Principle, the Principle of Cause and Effect, teaches that everything in the universe follows a law. Nothing happens by chance. What people call "chance" is just a name for causes that we don't understand or haven't noticed yet. All events follow one another without breaks, and nothing happens outside of this law.

The Principle of Cause and Effect is a foundation for all scientific thinking, both ancient and modern, and it was first taught by the earliest Hermetic teachers. Although different schools of thought have debated the details over time, most thinkers agree with this principle. To reject it would mean denying that the universe operates under law and order, which would leave everything to randomness—something people have called "chance."

If we look closer, we'll see that there is no such thing as pure chance. The dictionary defines chance as something that happens without law or purpose. But if we think deeply, we'll realize that nothing in the universe works outside of law and cause. Everything follows rules and patterns. To believe in something outside of these laws would mean believing in something greater than the natural order of the universe, which is impossible. Nothing exists outside of THE ALL, which itself is the source of all laws. If such a thing as pure chance existed, it would break all the natural laws and cause the universe to fall into complete disorder.

When we talk about chance, we are really talking about causes that are hidden from us. The word "chance" comes from a word that means "to fall," like the falling of dice. People often think that when a die lands on a certain number, it's just random. But if we look closer, we'll see that even the roll of a die follows specific causes, just like the planets follow their orbits. The outcome depends on the angle of the die in the box, the force used to throw it, and the surface it lands on. These are all visible causes. Behind these, however, are many unseen causes, which also affect the result.

If you throw a die many times, the numbers will eventually even out, with each number appearing roughly the same amount of times. The same thing happens when you flip a coin—over many flips, the heads and tails will balance out. This is called the law of averages, but both the average and the individual tosses are part of the same Law of Cause and Effect. If we could trace every single cause leading up to a die roll or coin toss, we'd see that the outcome couldn't have been any different under the same circumstances. Every event has a cause, or more precisely, a chain of causes.

Some people get confused by this principle because they struggle to understand how one thing causes another. But in truth, no single thing ever causes or creates another thing. Cause and Effect refer to events, not objects. An event is simply something that happens as a result of a previous event. Events don't create each other; they are just links in a continuous chain of actions that flow from the energy of THE ALL. Every event is connected to what came before it and to what will follow it.

Take, for example, a stone falling from a mountain and crashing into the roof of a house. At first, this may seem like a random accident. But when we look deeper, we see a chain of causes behind it. Rain may have softened the soil, causing the stone to loosen. The stone itself was part of a larger rock that broke apart over time due to weathering. That larger rock was formed by natural forces, such as earthquakes and volcanic activity. If we keep tracing back, we can find more and more causes, each connected to the next.

This chain of cause and effect is endless. It's like tracing your family tree. You have two parents, four grandparents, eight great-grandparents, and so on. If you go back forty generations, you'll have millions of ancestors. In the same way, every event has countless causes behind it, even something as small as a speck of soot floating by. That speck of soot may have once been part of a tree, which became coal, and later turned into soot as it burned. And that speck's journey isn't over—it will continue moving through time, causing new events in the future.

Even this text is part of the chain. The act of writing these words and your act of reading them will have effects on both of us, as well as on many others now and in the future. Each thought we think and every action we take sets new events into motion, adding more links to the endless chain of Cause and Effect.

This principle also shows us how deeply connected everything is. If two people had not met in ancient times, neither you nor I would be here today. If they had not crossed paths, this conversation wouldn't exist, and many other events would be different. Everything we do, no matter how small, creates ripples that affect the lives of others, both now and in the future.

We won't dive into debates about free will versus fate here. The truth, according to Hermetic teachings, is that both sides are partly right. The Principle of Polarity teaches us that these two ideas are just opposite ends of the same truth. A person can be both free and bound by necessity, depending on how we define those terms and from which level of understanding we view them. As the ancient teachings say, "The further from the center something is, the more it is bound; the closer it moves toward the center, the freer it becomes."

Most people are controlled by their environment, upbringing, and emotions, showing little real freedom. They are influenced by the opinions and expectations of others, as well as by their own moods and feelings. They may believe they are acting freely, but they fail to see where their desires and preferences come from. What makes them want one thing instead of another? What makes them feel pleased by one choice and not by another? There are causes behind these feelings too, even if they are not always visible.

A master, however, learns to change their desires and preferences by shifting their mental state. Instead of acting on impulse or external influences, the master chooses to act with intention. They "will to will," meaning they act based on conscious choice rather than being driven by emotions, moods, or circumstances.

Most people are carried through life like a falling stone, easily influenced by their surroundings, emotions, desires, and the will of others stronger than themselves. They are shaped by heredity, environment, and suggestions without resisting or using their own will. Like pawns on a chessboard, they play their roles until the game ends, at which point they are set aside. However, Masters, who understand the rules of the game, rise above the material world. By connecting with the higher aspects of their nature, they take control of their moods, character, qualities, and polarity, as well as the environment around them. In doing so, they become the ones who move the game, not just pieces to be moved—they become Causes, not Effects. Masters do not avoid the higher laws, but they align themselves with them, mastering circumstances on the lower plane. This allows them to consciously participate in the law instead of being blindly controlled by it. While they serve on the higher levels of existence, they rule over the material world.

Whether on higher or lower levels, the Law always operates. There is no such thing as chance. The idea of a blind goddess controlling fate has been replaced by reason and understanding. With the clarity that knowledge brings, we now know that everything is governed by universal laws. All the countless smaller laws are expressions of one Great Law—the LAW, which is THE ALL. As the scriptures say, not even a sparrow falls unnoticed by the Mind of THE ALL, and even the hairs on our head are numbered. Nothing exists outside the Law, and nothing happens that goes against it.

But do not think that this means humans are helpless machines with no freedom. The Hermetic teachings say that we can use one law to rise above others. The higher laws always have power over the lower ones until, eventually, we reach the point where we find refuge in the LAW itself and no longer feel limited by the smaller, temporary laws of the material world. Can you grasp the deeper meaning of this?

Chapter XIII

Gender. "Gender is in everything; everything has its Masculine and Feminine Principles; Gender manifests on all planes."—The Kybalion. The Seventh Hermetic Principle, the Principle of Gender, teaches that Gender is present in everything. Both Masculine and Feminine principles are always active and influence every part of life, on all levels of existence. However, it's important to understand that Gender, in the Hermetic sense, is not the same as what people usually mean by "sex."

The word "Gender" comes from a Latin word meaning "to create, generate, or produce." This meaning goes beyond just the biological differences between male and female. Sex is only one way that Gender shows itself, and it only appears on the physical level where organic life exists. We need to be clear about this difference because some people have misunderstood the Hermetic teachings, confusing the Principle of Gender with strange ideas and theories about sex that have little to do with the true meaning of this principle.

Gender's purpose is to create, generate, and produce, and we can see its effects at every level of existence. Although science hasn't fully recognized the universality of this principle, some scientific discoveries hint at it. For example, the principle of Gender can be seen in how atoms are formed. Scientists have discovered that atoms are made up of smaller parts called corpuscles, electrons, or ions, which are constantly moving and vibrating. An atom forms when many negatively charged corpuscles gather around a positively charged one. The positive particle influences the negative ones, causing them to arrange themselves in a specific way, and this process creates the atom. This aligns with ancient Hermetic teachings, which associate the Masculine principle with the positive pole and the Feminine principle with the negative pole of energy.

It's worth noting that the term "Negative" is often misunderstood. People tend to think of "positive" as strong and real, while "negative" suggests weakness or lack. However, in electrical phenomena, this isn't accurate. The so-called "Negative" pole is actually the point where creation and production take place. Some scientists now use the word "Cathode" instead of "Negative." The word "Cathode" comes from a Greek word meaning "descent" or "path of creation." It is from the Cathode, or the

Negative pole, that electrons and powerful energy rays are released. These rays have revolutionized scientific thinking in recent years, challenging many old ideas. The Cathode, or Feminine pole, is the source of new forms of matter and energy. For this reason, we replace the word "Negative" with "Feminine" when referring to this pole, since it aligns with both scientific discoveries and Hermetic teachings.

Modern science also shows that the creative particles, or electrons, carry what they call "negative" electricity, which we describe as Feminine energy. A Feminine particle separates from a Masculine particle and begins a new journey, naturally seeking union with another Masculine particle. This union is driven by the desire to create new forms of matter or energy. Some scientists even say that the particle actively seeks this union. This constant separation and joining of particles is the basis for most chemical reactions. When a Feminine particle unites with a Masculine one, the Masculine energy activates the Feminine, causing it to move quickly and create new forms. The result of this union is the birth of a new atom. Once the atom forms, it becomes a distinct entity with its own properties and no longer acts as free electricity. The process of separating the Feminine particles is called ionization. These particles are among the most active forces in nature, and their interactions create phenomena such as light, heat, electricity, magnetism, attraction, and repulsion.

The Masculine principle directs energy toward the Feminine principle, which responds by creating new forms. However, neither principle can function without the other. Both are needed for creation, and this balance is present at every level of life. In some forms of life, both principles are combined within a single organism. In fact, everything in the organic world contains both Masculine and Feminine qualities. Even in things that appear purely Feminine or purely Masculine, both principles are always present.

Hermetic teachings contain much more about how these two principles work together to create energy and matter, but we won't go into those details here since science hasn't yet caught up with these ideas. Still, the example of how atoms form shows that science is moving in the right direction and helps us understand the deeper meaning of this principle.

Some leading scientists have suggested that crystal formation may involve something similar to "sexual activity." This idea is another small hint about the direction scientific thinking is moving. As time passes, more evidence will emerge to confirm the Hermetic Principle of Gender. It will become clear that Gender is always present and active, not only in living things but also in the realm of energy, force, and even in non-living matter. Today, many scientists believe that all forms of energy can eventually be traced back to electricity. The latest scientific theory, known as the "Electrical Theory of the Universe," is gaining widespread acceptance. If we can find clear evidence of Gender in the workings of electricity—right at its source—then we have good reason to believe that science is finally offering proof that the Principle of Gender operates throughout all universal phenomena.

There's no need to go into detail about the well-known processes of attraction and repulsion between atoms, chemical bonds, or how molecules stick together. These concepts are already familiar. But have you ever thought about the fact that all these processes are expressions of the Principle of Gender? Can you see how these phenomena align perfectly with what we know about electrons and corpuscles? And beyond that, doesn't it make sense that the Hermetic teachings might be correct when they suggest that even gravity—the mysterious force pulling all matter together—might be another expression of the Principle of Gender? This principle reflects the natural attraction between Masculine and Feminine energies. While we don't yet have scientific proof of this idea, try looking at these phenomena through the lens of Hermetic teachings. You may find that it offers a clearer explanation than many current scientific theories.

We encourage you to apply this principle to all forms of physical phenomena. If you do, you'll see that the Principle of Gender is always present. Now, let's explore how this principle operates on the Mental Plane, where even more fascinating insights await.

Chapter XIV

Mental Gender. Psychology students studying mental phenomena have noticed that over the past ten to fifteen years, many theories about a "dual mind" have emerged. These ideas have inspired several different explanations about how these two minds might work. Back in 1893, Thomson J. Hudson became well-known for his theory of the "objective and subjective minds," which he believed were present in every person. Other thinkers have explored similar ideas, like the "conscious and subconscious minds," the "voluntary and involuntary minds," or the "active and passive minds." Even though these theories differ, they all revolve around the same basic idea: the mind has two parts.

A student of Hermetic Philosophy might smile at how these modern theories claim to have "discovered" the truth about the dual mind, even though the Hermetic teachings have discussed Mental Gender for centuries. If you look at the early teachings of Hermeticism, you will find that they have always recognized the existence of Mental Gender. In fact, they explained the dual mind long ago using this concept. The Masculine aspect of the mind aligns with what modern thinkers call the Objective Mind, the Conscious Mind, or the Active Mind. Meanwhile, the Feminine aspect matches what some call the Subjective Mind, the Subconscious Mind, or the Passive Mind. However, Hermetic teachings do not completely agree with many of these newer theories or their conclusions. Some of these ideas are not well-supported by evidence, and the Hermetic view offers a different perspective. We only mention these similarities to help students connect what they already know with Hermetic teachings.

In the second chapter of The Law of Psychic Phenomena, Hudson admits that the Hermetic ideas align with the concept of the dual mind. He suggests that the Hermetic teachings contain the same core idea, though he refers to them as "mystic jargon." If Hudson had spent more time studying these ancient ideas, he might have gained deeper insights into the dual mind. However, without that, his own work may not have gained the same attention. Now, let's explore the Hermetic view of Mental Gender.

Hermetic teachers instruct their students to focus inward, examining their own consciousness to understand Mental Gender. They encourage students to reflect on their sense of self, starting with the awareness of their existence, often expressed as "I Am." At first, this statement seems to be the final understanding of the Self, but with more reflection, it becomes clear that this "I Am" has two distinct aspects. These two parts work together, but they are still separate.

While it first feels like there is only one "I," closer examination shows that there are actually two parts: an "I" and a "Me." These two parts of the mind have different qualities, and understanding how they interact can provide insight into mental influence.

Let's start by examining the "Me," which is often confused with the "I." When people think about themselves as the "Me," they tend to identify with their emotions, likes, dislikes, habits, and personality traits. These qualities form their sense of self, both in their own minds and in the way others see them. However, these emotions and traits are not fixed—they change over time, following the natural rhythms of life, and shifting between different extremes. People also associate the "Me" with the knowledge and experiences they have collected, seeing these things as part of who they are.

For some people, the "Me" is closely tied to their body and physical desires. Their sense of self is so connected to their body that they feel like they "live" in it. Some even see their clothes as part of who they are, believing that their identity depends on their appearance. As one writer joked, people are made up of "soul, body, and clothes." For someone like this, losing their clothes would feel like losing a piece of themselves. Even those who do not focus so much on clothes often still see their body as a key part of their identity, unable to imagine a Self separate from the body.

As people grow in awareness, they begin to see the body as something they "have," rather than something they "are." They start to understand that their body is just one part of their experience, and their mind is more than just a tool belonging to the body. However, even at this stage, people often continue to identify with their mental states, emotions, and habits, believing these things are who they are. They might not realize that these feelings and thoughts are only temporary states that exist within them, but are not their true Self.

With effort, people can learn to separate these mental states from their deeper sense of self. They come to see these feelings, habits, and thoughts as things they "own," not things they "are." This process takes mental focus and self-awareness, but it is possible, even for those just starting on this path. By imagining this separation, a person can begin to understand the difference between their true Self and the thoughts and emotions that pass through their mind.

Once a person learns to set aside these mental states, they begin to recognize the two aspects of their mind: the "I" and the "Me." The "Me" can be seen as a kind of mental space where thoughts, ideas, emotions, and other mental states are generated. It acts like a "mental womb," as ancient teachings describe it, capable of producing many types of thoughts and creations. The "Me" holds enormous creative potential, but it requires some form of energy from the "I" or another source before it can create anything. This realization gives a person a deep sense of their creative abilities and mental power.

However, the student soon discovers that the "I" has its own unique qualities. The "I" is the part of the mind that can choose to direct the "Me" to create along certain lines. It can observe the creative process of the "Me" and even step back to watch it unfold. The "I" holds the power to project energy toward the "Me," initiating the process of mental creation. While the "Me" is responsible for the active creation, the "I" is the guiding force, able to will these creations into existence.

This dual nature exists within every person. The "I" represents the Masculine Principle of Mental Gender, while the "Me" represents the Feminine Principle. The "I" reflects the state of being, while the "Me" represents the process of becoming. This principle operates not only within the mind but also in the larger universe. Just as the two aspects of Mental Gender work together within a person, they reflect the greater workings of the cosmos. As the Hermetic principle says, "As above, so below; as below, so above."

These two parts of the mind—the Masculine and Feminine principles, or the "I" and the "Me"—help explain many of the mental and psychic phenomena we observe. The principle of Mental Gender offers the key to understanding how mental influence works.

The Feminine principle tends to receive impressions, while the Masculine principle focuses on expressing and giving out energy. The Feminine aspect plays a more active role in generating new thoughts, ideas, and imaginative concepts. The Masculine aspect, on the other hand, drives the process through the power of Will. However, without the Will of the Masculine principle, the Feminine mind tends to simply process external impressions rather than create original ideas.

People who are capable of deep focus use both mental principles. The Feminine side actively generates ideas, while the Masculine Will energizes the mind, pushing it toward action. Most people, however, use very little of the Masculine principle. They passively absorb thoughts and ideas from the minds of others rather than creating their own. They rely on others to think and will for them. We won't focus on this part too much here since it's covered in many psychology books, but the key to understanding it lies in recognizing Mental Gender.

Anyone familiar with psychic phenomena knows about things like telepathy, mental influence, suggestion, and hypnotism. Many have tried to explain these events by referring to theories about the dual mind. While these theories are partially correct, a clearer explanation emerges when you view these phenomena through the lens of Mental Gender and Vibration.

In telepathy, the Masculine principle sends out a wave of energy toward the Feminine principle of another person, where the idea takes root and grows. Suggestion and hypnotism work similarly. The Will of the person giving the suggestion sends a stream of energy toward the other person's Feminine mind, which accepts the idea and acts on it. Once implanted, this idea grows and feels like the person's own, much like how a cuckoo egg placed in a sparrow's nest becomes accepted as the sparrow's offspring.

Ideally, the Masculine and Feminine principles within a person should work together in harmony. Unfortunately, many people rely heavily on their Feminine mind while allowing their Masculine principle, which contains the Will, to remain inactive. As a result, they are easily influenced by the thoughts and wills of others. This is why so few people have original ideas or act independently. Most live their lives as reflections or echoes of those with stronger minds and wills.

The most successful and influential people in the world demonstrate strong Masculine Will. They shape their own thoughts and dominate their minds instead of passively accepting ideas from others. These individuals also influence the minds of others, planting their thoughts like seeds that take root and grow within the masses. This is why so many people seem to follow the ideas of others without question, acting more like sheep than independent thinkers.

We see examples of Mental Gender at work all around us. People with magnetic personalities use the Masculine principle to impress their ideas onto others. Actors who make their audience cry or laugh are using this principle. So are effective speakers, politicians, preachers, and writers. The personal influence that some people seem to naturally possess is rooted in the principle of Mental Gender, which operates through the vibrations of thought and energy. This principle is also the foundation of hypnotism, personal magnetism, and fascination.

Anyone familiar with psychic phenomena knows how important suggestion is. Suggestion is the process of planting an idea in someone's mind in such a way that the person accepts it and acts on it. Understanding how suggestion works is essential for studying psychic phenomena, but knowing about Mental Gender and Vibration is just as important. The entire process of suggestion depends on these principles.

Many teachers explain suggestion by saying that the conscious mind makes an impression on the subconscious mind. However, they often fail to provide a clear explanation of how this works or how it mirrors natural processes. If you look at it through the Hermetic teachings, you'll see that it aligns with the natural laws of energy. The Masculine principle energizes the Feminine principle, leading to the creation of new mental states. This dynamic reflects the way the universe operates on every level, from the spiritual and mental to the physical.

The Hermetic axiom "As above, so below; as below, so above" reminds us that the same principles apply on all levels of existence. Once you understand the principle of Mental Gender, you'll find it much easier to organize and study psychological phenomena. This principle works in practice because it is based on the unchanging, universal laws of life.

We will not go into a long discussion or detailed description of the many types of mental influence or psychic activity. There are plenty of books on these topics, many of which are quite good. While the main ideas in these books are accurate, each author tends to explain the phenomena according to their personal theories. Students who study these subjects and apply the principle of Mental Gender will be able to organize these ideas and make sense of the conflicting theories. If they wish, they can even master these subjects by using this principle.

The purpose of this work is not to provide a detailed exploration of psychic phenomena. Instead, it offers a master key that can unlock the doors to many areas of knowledge for those who want to explore them. We believe that the teachings in The Kybalion can offer explanations that will clear up many confusing ideas and serve as a key to understanding a wide range of topics. There is no need to cover every aspect of mental and psychic phenomena if we can provide students with the tools they need to understand any topic that interests them.

With the insights from The Kybalion, a student can revisit any occult library with fresh understanding, using ancient wisdom from Egypt to shed light on difficult or obscure ideas. This is the purpose of this book—not to introduce a new philosophy, but to provide the framework of an ancient teaching that will clarify the ideas of others. It serves as a tool to bring together different theories and opposing beliefs, acting as a guide to help reconcile them.

Chapter XV

Hermetic Axioms. "Having knowledge without showing it through actions is like hoarding gold and silver—it's pointless and foolish. Knowledge, like wealth, is meant to be used. The Law of Use applies everywhere, and anyone who ignores it will struggle because they are working against nature."—The Kybalion. The Hermetic Teachings have always been carefully guarded in the minds of those who hold them, as we have explained before. However, they were never meant to be hidden away or kept secret forever. The Law of Use is emphasized throughout these teachings, as the quote from The Kybalion explains. Knowledge without action is useless, helping neither the person who has it nor anyone else. Be careful not to become stingy with your thoughts—take what you've learned and put it into action. Study these Axioms and Aphorisms, but be sure to also apply them in your life. Here are some important Hermetic Axioms from The Kybalion, with comments added for deeper understanding. Make these ideas your own by practicing them, because they won't truly belong to you until you put them into use. "To change your mood or mental state—change your vibration."—The Kybalion. You can shift your mental state by using your willpower to focus on a more positive mindset. Your will guides your attention, and your attention changes your inner vibration. If you learn how to focus through your will, you unlock the ability to control your thoughts and emotions. "To get rid of an unwanted mental state, use the Principle of Polarity and focus on the opposite of what you want to overcome. Destroy the negative by changing its polarity."—The Kybalion. This is one of the most important Hermetic techniques, grounded in scientific understanding. A mental state and its opposite are just two sides of the same thing. Through Mental Transmutation, you can reverse their polarity. Modern psychology uses a similar approach when helping people overcome bad habits—rather than fighting the habit, they focus on building its opposite. If you're struggling with fear, for example, don't waste energy fighting it directly. Instead, focus on building courage, and fear will fade away. Think of it like a dark room—you don't need to sweep out the darkness. You just open the windows, and the light drives the darkness away. To get rid of a negative feeling, focus on its positive counterpart. Slowly, the negative will fade, and you will be left aligned with the positive. But the opposite is also true—if you let yourself stay in negative states too often, they will take hold. Mastering your moods by shifting your polarity will allow you to change your mental states, reshape your personality, and build a stronger character. Much of the mastery achieved by advanced Hermetics comes from applying this principle of Polarity, which is an essential part of Mental Transmutation. Remember this Hermetic Axiom: "Mind (like metals and elements) can be changed from one state to another, from one level to another, from one condition to another, from one pole to the opposite, and from one vibration to another."—The Kybalion. Mastering Polarity is the key to Mental Transmutation, also known as Mental Alchemy. Without learning to change your own polarity, you won't be able to affect the world around you. Understanding this principle gives you the ability to change both your own state and the states of others. But it takes time, care, study, and constant practice to master it. The principle is true, but how well it works depends entirely on how patient and persistent you are in practicing it. "Rhythm can be balanced out through the Art of Polarization."—The Kybalion. As we mentioned earlier, the Hermetic teachings say that Rhythm affects both the mental and physical levels. This constant back-and-forth motion explains the changing moods, emotions, and thoughts we experience. The Law of Neutralization helps us overcome the effects of Rhythm. There is both a Higher Plane and a Lower Plane of consciousness. By mentally rising to the Higher Plane, you can allow the swing of the pendulum to happen only on the Lower Plane. When you stay on the Higher Plane, you won't feel the back-and-forth motion as strongly. This shift happens by focusing on your Higher Self and raising your mental vibrations above the usual level of thought. It's like rising above a wave and watching it pass underneath you. The advanced Hermetic practitioner keeps their focus on the Positive Pole—the "I Am" within—rather than getting caught up in the shifting personality and emotions. By refusing to let Rhythm pull them back and forth, they stay grounded in their true self. Those who have achieved even some level of self-mastery do this, even if they don't fully understand the principle. They simply refuse to get pulled around by moods and emotions and remain steady by holding on to their inner strength. The Master takes this a step further, using their Will to achieve a calmness and mental stability that others find hard to believe.

It's important to note that you don't actually destroy the Principle of Rhythm—it can't be destroyed. Instead, you counterbalance it with another law to maintain stability. Just as balance and counterbalance exist in the physical world, they also apply to the mind. When you understand how to use these principles, it might seem like you are breaking the laws of nature, but you are simply using one law to offset another. "Nothing escapes the Principle of Cause and Effect, but there are many levels of causes. You can use the laws of a higher level to overcome those of a lower level."—The Kybalion. By mastering Polarity, the Hermetic student rises to a higher level of Cause and Effect. At this higher level, they become the cause of things rather than being controlled by causes outside of themselves. They are no longer at the mercy of their environment, other people's desires, or inherited tendencies. Instead of being moved around like chess pieces, they become players in the game of life. Through control of their emotions, impulses, and thoughts, they build new qualities and abilities, shaping their character and breaking free from the limitations of their surroundings. They no longer react blindly to life but make deliberate choices. While they remain under the laws of Cause and Effect on higher levels, on lower levels, they become masters of these laws. As The Kybalion says:

The wise serve on the higher levels, but they rule on the lower ones. They follow the laws that come from those above them, but within their own world and in the realms below them, they take charge and give orders. Yet, in doing so, they work as part of the universal Principle, not against it. A wise person moves with the flow of the Law, and by understanding how it works, they control it instead of being controlled by it. Just like a skilled swimmer moves through water by choosing when to turn and where to go, rather than drifting like a piece of wood carried by the current—so the wise person lives compared to the ordinary person. However, both the swimmer and the log, the wise person and the fool, are still governed by the same Law. Understanding this truth brings a person closer to achieving mastery.

To wrap up, let's reflect again on the Hermetic Axiom: "True Hermetic Transmutation is a Mental Art."—The Kybalion.

This axiom teaches that the power to influence and change your surroundings is achieved through the mind. Since the entire Universe is fundamentally mental, it can only be governed by the power of thought. This understanding explains many of the mental phenomena and abilities that have drawn so much interest and study in the early years of the twentieth century. Beneath the teachings of different groups and schools of thought lies the unchanging idea that the Universe is made of mental substance. If the essence of the Universe is mental, then it makes sense that changing your mind can change the world around you. And if everything is based on the mind, then mental power must be the greatest force shaping reality. When this is understood, what people call "miracles" and "wonders" become clear—they are simply the results of mastering this truth.

"THE ALL is MIND; The Universe is Mental."—The Kybalion.

Corpus Hermeticum

Hermes Trismegistus

Corpus Hermeticum

An Introduction to the Corpus Hermeticum

The fifteen writings of the Corpus Hermeticum, along with the Perfect Sermon or Asclepius, are key texts in Hermetic philosophy. These writings were created by unknown authors in Egypt sometime before the third century C.E. They were part of a larger collection that was linked to Hermes Trismegistus, a mythical figure combining the Greek god Hermes and the Egyptian god Thoth. These texts emerged during a period of religious and philosophical growth, the same era that saw the rise of Neoplatonism, Christianity, and a variety of teachings grouped under the term "Gnosticism." This movement grew from the influence of Platonic thought on the older traditions of the Hellenistic world. While each of these traditions had its own unique approach to life's big questions, they shared certain themes and ideas.

The Corpus Hermeticum was eventually gathered into a single volume during the Byzantine period. One copy of this collection was discovered by agents working for Lorenzo de Medici in the fifteenth century. Marsilio Ficino, the head of the Florentine Academy, was tasked with translating these texts into Latin. He was instructed to prioritize translating the Corpus Hermeticum over the works of Plato. Ficino's Latin version was published in 1463 and was reprinted at least twenty-two times over the following 150 years.

The treatises within the Corpus Hermeticum can be grouped based on their content. The first writing, called "Poemandres," describes a revelation given to Hermes Trismegistus by a being named Poemandres, also known as the "Man-Shepherd," who represents the universal Mind. The next eight writings are known as the "General Sermons" and contain short conversations and teachings about the core ideas of Hermetic philosophy. Following these is the "Key," which summarizes the previous sermons. There is also a group of four texts—"Mind unto Hermes," "About the Common Mind," "The Secret Sermon on the Mountain," and the "Letter of Hermes to Asclepius"—which explore the more mystical parts of Hermetic thought. The collection concludes with the "Definitions of Asclepius unto King Ammon," which seems to be made up of three fragments from larger works.

The Perfect Sermon, or Asclepius, came to the Renaissance through a different path. It had been translated into Latin in ancient times, supposedly by Lucius Apuleius of Madaura, the author of The Golden Ass. This work provides valuable insights into the worship of the goddess Isis in the Roman Empire. Saint Augustine refers to the old Latin translation of the Perfect Sermon in his City of God, and this translation remained in circulation throughout medieval Europe, all the way to the Renaissance. The original Greek version was lost, though some parts of it have been preserved through quotations in other ancient texts. The Perfect Sermon is longer than any other surviving Hermetic text. While it covers many topics found in the Corpus Hermeticum, it also addresses other subjects, including instructions on creating divine statues and a bleak prophecy about the loss of Hermetic wisdom and the end of the world.

The arrival of the Corpus Hermeticum had a powerful impact on late medieval European philosophy. Some early Christian writers, like the Church Fathers, referenced Hermetic literature to support their points, and they believed that Hermes Trismegistus lived around the same time as Moses. Because the Hermetic writings included ideas from Jewish scriptures and Platonic philosophy, Renaissance thinkers believed these texts had influenced both traditions. Hermetic philosophy was regarded as an ancient form of wisdom, linked to the "Wisdom of the Egyptians" mentioned in the Bible's book of Exodus and praised in Plato's Timaeus. Many intellectuals used this view to challenge the dominance of Aristotelian philosophy, which controlled universities at the time.

The Hermetic texts also became a key part of another rebellion during the Renaissance—the effort to restore magic as a respectable spiritual practice in Christian Europe. There was another body of work linked to Hermes Trismegistus, which included writings about astrology, alchemy, and magic. If Hermes were considered a real historical figure, as Renaissance scholars believed, and if early Christian leaders had quoted his works with approval, and if these writings aligned with certain Christian beliefs, then the Hermetic approach to magic could be seen as compatible with Christianity. However, this effort ultimately failed. The dramatic changes in Western Christianity during the Reformation and Counter-Reformation solidified strict religious rules, and by the sixteenth century, practices that had once been accepted were now considered heretical. Some people were even executed for actions that had previously been viewed as signs of devotion.

Despite this failure, the ideas and language of the Hermetic writings remained influential in post-medieval Western magic.

I. Poemandres, the Shepherd of Men

This is the most well-known Hermetic text, telling a story about a vision of how the universe was created and the nature and destiny of humanity. Writers from the Renaissance onward have noted that its creation story seems partly inspired by the Bible's Book of Genesis, but it also presents a different take. In this version, the Fall is about the descent of the Primal Man through the spheres of the planets into the natural world. This descent isn't caused by disobedience but by love, and it happens with God's blessing.

The seven rulers of fate mentioned in various sections are the archons, or rulers, of the seven planets. These archons also appear in Plato's Timaeus and in other ancient texts often grouped under the term "Gnostic." In this text, these rulers have a complicated role. They represent the forces of Harmony, yet they are also responsible for humanity's tendency toward evil.

One day, as I was deep in thought, reflecting on the nature of existence, my mind rose to a great height while my physical senses seemed to fall away—like when someone drifts into a deep sleep from exhaustion or after a heavy meal. Suddenly, I felt a presence, a vast being beyond all measure, calling my name. It asked, "What do you wish to see and hear? What do you want to understand and learn?"

I asked, "Who are you?" The presence replied, "I am the Man-Shepherd, Poemandres, the Mind of Mastery. I know what you want, and I am with you everywhere."

I said, "I want to learn about the things that exist, to understand their nature, and to know God. This is what I want to learn." The being answered, "Hold these thoughts close, and I will teach you."

As soon as he said this, his form began to change. In an instant, everything around me opened up, and I saw a limitless vision. All things were filled with light, a sweet and joyful light, and I felt overwhelmed with wonder as I gazed at it. But soon, part of the vision darkened. The darkness was heavy and eerie, coiling like a serpent. It then transformed into a moist, shifting substance that was beyond words to describe. It gave off smoke, as if from fire, and made a deep groaning sound that was impossible to explain. After that, a strange, unrecognizable voice emerged from the darkness, like the sound of fire speaking.

Then, from the light, a Holy Word—the Logos—descended upon that chaotic nature. Suddenly, pure fire shot up from the moist substance, moving swiftly and brightly. The air followed the fire, rising from the water and earth, as if suspended by the fire. However, the earth and water remained mixed together, making it impossible to tell them apart. Even so, they were moved by the presence of the Spirit-Word, which filled everything.

The Man-Shepherd asked me, "Do you understand what this vision means?" I answered, "Not yet." He said, "That light you saw is me, your God and the Mind, which came before the moist nature that arose from darkness. The Logos, which emerged from the Mind, is the Son of God." I asked, "What does this mean?" He explained, "Know that what sees and hears within you is the Logos, the Word of the Lord. And the Mind is the Father-God. They are not separate from each other; their unity is what gives life." I said, "Thank you." He told me, "Understand the light and become one with it."

He looked deeply into my eyes, and I trembled under his gaze. Then he lifted his head, and in my mind, I saw the light once again. But now, it was accompanied by countless powers, and the universe had grown beyond measure. The fire I had seen before was now encircled by a mighty power and had been brought to rest. I realized the meaning of these things through the words of the Man-Shepherd.

While I was still lost in amazement, he told me, "What you have seen in your mind is the Archetypal Form, which exists before time and has no end." I asked him, "Where do the elements of nature come from?" He replied, "They come from the Will of God. Nature received the Word, and by looking upon the beauty of the cosmos, it shaped itself into a new world through its own elements and by the creation of souls."

He continued, "God, who is both male and female, existing as both light and life, brought forth another Mind to shape the universe. This

Mind, being divine and filled with fire and spirit, created the seven rulers who govern the visible world. People call these rulers Fate."

He explained further, "From the lower elements, the Logos rose up to unite with the Formative Mind, since it was one with it in essence. The lower elements were left without reason, becoming mere matter."

Then the Formative Mind, which was now one with the Logos, began to shape the spheres and set them in motion. They began spinning in harmony, without a beginning or an end, because the movement was willed by the Mind. Nature, using the lower elements, created life without reason, since the Logos had not been extended to them. Air produced creatures that could fly, and water gave rise to those that swim. The earth and water then separated as the Mind willed, and from the earth came all kinds of living creatures—some with four legs, some that crawl, and others both wild and tame.

The All-Father Mind, being both Life and Light, brought forth Man as an equal to Himself. He loved him deeply, as Man was His child and a reflection of His own perfect image. In truth, God fell in love with His own form and gave Man all the powers of creation.

When Man saw the creations shaped by the Enformer within the Father, he also wished to create. The Father granted him permission. Changing his state to enter the realm of creation, where he would have full authority, Man observed the beings created by his Brother. These creatures were drawn to him and each offered him a share of their own nature. After learning their essence and becoming part of their being, Man desired to go beyond the boundaries of their realms. He wanted to overcome the forces restraining the Fire and transcend them.

With power over all living beings in the cosmos—both rational and irrational—Man turned downward through the Harmony, breaking through its strength. He revealed God's beautiful form to the lower world of Nature. When Nature saw this divine beauty, she was enchanted, for he carried within him the energies of all seven Rulers, as well as the form of God. It was as if Nature saw Man's perfect image reflected in her waters and his shadow upon her earth. Man, in turn, saw his likeness within her waters and loved it, desiring to live within it. And with this desire came action—he brought life to the form that had no reason.

Nature embraced the object of her love, entwining herself completely with Man. They became one, united as lovers.

This is why, above all creatures on earth, man is dual in nature. His body is mortal, but his true essence is immortal. Although he is eternal and holds power over all things, he still experiences suffering like a mortal and is bound by Fate. Though man exists above the Harmony, within it he becomes a servant to its laws. He is both male and female, like his Father, and though he comes from a sleepless source, he is overcome by sleep.

I asked, "Teach me more, O Mind, for I too love the Word, the Logos." The Shepherd replied, "This is a mystery that has been hidden until now. Man and Nature together gave birth to something wondrous. Since Man carried within him the essence of the seven Rulers—made from Fire and Spirit—Nature wasted no time. She created seven beings, reflecting the qualities of the seven Rulers, each one both male and female, moving through the air."

I said, "O Shepherd, tell me more! I am filled with desire to learn; do not leave me now." The Shepherd responded, "Be still, for I have not yet unfolded the first of these truths to you." "I am listening," I said.

And so, as I have explained, the seven beings came into existence. The earth acted as a woman, and her waters were filled with desire. She took ripeness from Fire and spirit from Aether. With these elements, Nature created forms to match the image of Man. Man himself transformed, shifting from Light and Life into soul and mind—moving from Life to soul, and from Light to mind. The physical world continued in this way, cycling through endings and new beginnings.

"Now," the Shepherd continued, "listen to the rest of the teaching you have been waiting to hear."

When the cycle reached its completion, the bond holding everything together was loosened by God's will. All living creatures, which had originally been male and female in one form, were separated. Some became male and others female. Then God spoke through His Holy Word, the Logos: "Grow and multiply in great numbers, all creatures and beings. And man, who holds the Mind within him, must learn to understand that he is immortal, though the cause of death is love, for Love is all."

After speaking these words, God's Forethought worked through Fate and Harmony to bring beings together and establish their generations. In this way, everything multiplied according to its kind.

Those who come to know themselves achieve a goodness that goes beyond all abundance. But those who are led astray by a misguided love, focusing only on the desires of the body, remain trapped in darkness. They suffer through their senses and experience death.

I asked, "What great mistake do the ignorant make that causes them to lose their immortality?" The Shepherd responded, "It seems you have not truly thought about what you've heard. Did I not ask you to reflect on it?" "Yes, I have thought about it and I remember," I answered. "I am grateful for what You've taught me." "If you have reflected on it," He said, "then tell me: Why do those who are already in Death deserve to die?"

I replied, "It is because the dark, shadowy nature lies at the root of the material body. The moist nature came from it, and from this, the physical body was made. And it is from this body that death drains the waters of life."

"Well done," the Shepherd said. "But tell me, how does one who knows himself return to God, as the Logos has declared?"

I replied, "The Father of all things consists of Light and Life, and from Him, Man was born." "You speak correctly," the Shepherd said. "Light and Life are the essence of the Father-God, and from Him, Man came forth. If you understand that you are made of Light and Life and realize that you have become separated from them, you will return to Life once again."

The Man-Shepherd continued, "But tell me more, O Mind, how can one return to Life? For God has said, 'The man who holds the Mind within him must know that he is deathless.'"

I asked, "Does every person have the Mind within them?" "You are right to ask," the Shepherd said. "I, the Mind, am present with those who are holy, good, pure, and compassionate—those who live righteously. My presence helps them, and they quickly gain knowledge of all things, earning the love of the Father through their pure lives. They offer thanks to Him, calling down blessings, singing hymns, and focusing their love entirely on Him.

Before they leave their bodies behind in death, they become indifferent to physical sensations and the knowledge tied to bodily functions. I, the Mind, do not allow the body's activities to take their natural course. As the gatekeeper, I close all the pathways through which base and evil influences might enter, and I cut off harmful thoughts and actions from reaching the mind."

To those who live without Mind—the wicked, selfish, jealous, and impious—I am distant, giving way to the Avenging Daimon. This force fuels their inner fire, tormenting them and driving their desires to even greater excess. It controls them through their senses, pushing them toward more wrongdoing, leading to deeper suffering. These people are trapped in endless cravings, consumed by their insatiable desires, lost in darkness.

Thank you for teaching me all that I wanted to know, O Mind. Now, please tell me more about the path to ascend above. The Man-Shepherd replied: When the material body dissolves, you first surrender it to the natural process of change, and the form you once had disappears. Your way of life, along with its energy, is then handed over to the Daimon. The senses return to their original sources, transforming into separate energies, and passion and desire return to their original state, which lacks reason.

This is how a person begins their ascent through the Harmony. At the first level, they release the energy of growth and decay. At the second level, they let go of the tendency toward evil, now made powerless. At the third, they leave behind the deceptive pull of desires. At the fourth, they release their arrogance and pride. At the fifth, they give up reckless daring and boldness. At the sixth, they let go of greed and the pursuit of wealth through corrupt means. At the seventh and final level, they shed all falsehood, leaving it powerless.

With the energies of the lower realms stripped away, the person becomes clothed in their true power and ascends to the realm of the Eighth. There, they join others in singing hymns to the Father. These beings welcome the new arrival with joy, and the person becomes like them, hearing the songs of praise from those even higher, beyond the

Eighth realm. Together, they proceed to the Father, willingly offering themselves to the higher Powers. In doing so, they also become Powers, united with God. This is the ultimate end for those who have achieved Gnosis: to become one with God.

Why delay any longer? You have received all that you need. Now you must guide others who are ready, so that through you, humanity may be saved by God. After these words, the Man-Shepherd merged with the Powers.

Filled with gratitude and blessings for the Father of all, I felt free, empowered by the knowledge the Man-Shepherd had poured into me. He revealed to me the nature of all things and granted me the highest Vision. I began preaching to others about the beauty of devotion and the power of Gnosis: "O people, born of the earth, you who have given yourselves over to drunkenness, sleep, and ignorance of God—wake up! Stop drowning in excess and break free from the spell of mindless sleep."

When the people heard my words, they came together as one. I said to them: "Why have you surrendered to death, even though you have the power to share in immortality? Turn back, you who walk with Error and dine with Ignorance. Leave the darkness behind and take your place in immortality. Forsake the path of destruction!"

Some laughed and mocked me, choosing to follow the way of death. But others begged to learn, throwing themselves at my feet. I helped them rise and became a guide for them on the path back home, teaching them the words of wisdom and how they might be saved. I planted in them the seeds of knowledge, and they drank from the waters of immortality.

When evening came and the sun's light began to fade, I asked them all to give thanks to God. When they finished giving thanks, each returned to their place of rest. I kept in my heart the kindness shown to me by the Man-Shepherd, feeling that all my hopes had been fulfilled. For the sleep of the body became the awakening of the soul, and the closing of my eyes led to true vision. My silence was filled with goodness, and the words I spoke gave birth to good things.

Everything I experienced came from the Mind, the Man-Shepherd, the

Logos of all mastery. Through Him, I became inspired by God and found my way to the Plain of Truth. Therefore, with all my soul and strength, I give thanks to the Father-God.

Holy are You, O God, Father of all things. Holy are You, O God, whose Will is fulfilled through Your own Powers. Holy are You, O God, who desire to be known and are known by Your own. Holy are You, who through the Word brought all things into being. Holy are You, whose creation reflects Your image. Holy are You, whose Form Nature could never contain. Holy are You, more powerful than all power. Holy are You, beyond all greatness. Holy are You, greater than all praise.

Accept my offering of reason, pure and from the soul, always reaching toward You. O God, You are beyond words, beyond speech—only silence can speak Your Name.

Hear my prayer that I may never be without Gnosis, for Gnosis is the true nature of our being. Fill me with Your Power and Grace so that I may share the Light with my brothers and sisters who still live in ignorance. They are Your children too.

For this reason, I believe and bear witness: I go toward Life and Light. Blessed are You, O Father. Your Man will become holy as You are holy, for You have given him the authority to be so.

II. To Asclepius

Hermes: Everything that moves, Asclepius, must move within something and be moved by something, right? Asclepius: Yes, that's true. H: And whatever space it moves within must be larger than the thing moving, right? A: It must be. H: And whatever causes it to move must have greater power than the thing being moved? A: Yes, it must. H: And the nature of the space in which it moves must be different from the nature of the thing that is moving? A: Absolutely.

H: Isn't the cosmos incredibly vast, with no body larger than it? A: Yes, it is. H: And it is filled with many great things, containing all other bodies within it? A: It is. H: And the cosmos itself is a body, right? A: Yes, it is a body. H: And this body moves?

A: It does. H: Then the space in which the cosmos moves must be even larger than the cosmos itself, don't you think? This space must be vast enough to allow the cosmos to move freely without being cramped or restricted. A: Yes, it must be something immensely vast, Thrice-greatest one.

H: And what kind of nature would this space have? Wouldn't it need to be the opposite of a body? And isn't the opposite of body something bodiless? A: Yes, I agree. H: So, space must be bodiless. But what is bodiless could be either something divine or God Himself. When I say "divine," I don't mean something created, but something that exists without being created.

If space is something divine, it has substance. But if it is God, it is beyond substance. Yet, we should think of it as something different from God. God can be thought about by us, but not in the same way by Himself, because whatever is thought about must be separate from the thinker. Since God is what He thinks, He cannot think of Himself as something different. However, to us, He is something distinct that we can think about.

So, when we think about space, it should be seen as space and not as God. And when we think about God, we should not confuse Him with space but understand Him as the force that contains all space. Everything that moves must move in something that is stable. And whatever causes something else to move must remain still, because it cannot move along with the thing it moves.

A: But, Thrice-greatest one, how is it that things here on earth move along with other moving things? Didn't you say that the wandering stars are moved by the fixed stars? H: It's not that they move together, Asclepius, but that they move in opposition to each other. They don't move in harmony but in contrast. Their opposing movements create resistance, and this resistance produces stability. In fact, resistance is the source of rest in motion.

The wandering stars move in opposition to the fixed stars, and through their opposing forces, they are moved by each other. This movement through opposition also comes from the stable stars. It couldn't happen any other way. Look at the constellations of the Bears—Ursa Major and Ursa Minor. They never set or rise. Do you think they are moving or staying still? A: They are moving, Thrice-greatest one. H: And what kind of movement is that? A: They move in a circular path, always returning to the same place. H: Exactly. But movement in a circle is a form of stability because the movement always stays within the same boundaries. Circular motion is fixed because it does not go beyond its set path. Stability is achieved through this continuous cycle of opposing movements.

Let me give you an example you can observe on earth. Look at someone swimming. Even though the water is moving, the swimmer's hands and feet push against the water, creating resistance. This resistance keeps the swimmer steady, preventing him from being carried away or sinking. A: That is a very clear example, Thrice-greatest one. H: All motion, then, is caused by something stationary. Stability is necessary for movement to occur. The motion of the cosmos, like all other material things, is not caused by external forces. Instead, it is driven by internal forces, like the soul or spirit, which are incorporeal.

A body on its own cannot create motion, not even the vast body of the universe. Even a lifeless body cannot move without something within it that causes movement.

A: What do you mean, Thrice-greatest one? Isn't it physical bodies that move things like stones and other lifeless objects? H: No, Asclepius. The force inside the body that moves things is not a physical body itself. It moves both the lifter and the object being lifted. A lifeless thing cannot move another lifeless thing. Only something alive has the power to create movement.

Do you see now how much work the soul carries? It moves both the body it inhabits and the objects it interacts with. This shows that everything that moves must not only move within something but also be moved by something.

A: Yes, Thrice-greatest one, it is clear that everything that moves must move within some kind of emptiness or space.

Hermes: You speak well, Asclepius! Nothing that truly exists can be empty. Only what does not exist can be void, for what exists cannot simply become nothing. Asclepius: But what about things like an empty jar, a cup, or a vat? Aren't these examples of empty things? H: Oh, Asclepius, you are far from the truth! Do you really think that things filled to the brim with something are empty?

A: What do you mean, Thrice-greatest one? H: Isn't air a type of body?

A: Yes, it is. H: And doesn't this body of air fill all things? And since air is a body made from the blending of the four elements, everything you call empty is actually full of air. If it contains air, it also contains the four elements.

On the other hand, what you call full isn't filled with air, because other substances occupy that space. This means that what you call empty should really be called hollow, not void. These things are not truly empty—they are filled with air and spirit.

A: Your explanation makes sense, Thrice-greatest one. Air is indeed a body, and it fills all things. But what, then, should we call the space in which everything moves? H: That space is bodiless, Asclepius. A: And what exactly is bodiless? H: It is Mind and Reason—complete in itself, containing everything, without body or flaw. It cannot be touched or perceived by physical senses. It holds everything within itself and preserves everything that exists. Think of it like rays of Goodness, Truth, and Light that are beyond any physical light. It is also the Archetype of the soul.

A: And what is God? H: God is none of these things. God is the cause of all things—He makes Mind, Spirit, and Light exist. God isn't Mind, Spirit, or Light Himself, but He is the source of them all. Because of this, God is best honored by the names "Good" and "Father." These names belong only to Him.

None of the other gods, nor any human or spirit, can truly be called Good. Only God is Good, and nothing else can share that nature. All other beings are made of soul and body, which cannot contain the nature of the Good.

The greatness of the Good is as vast as all existence, including both physical and non-physical things. The Good touches everything, from what is seen to what is only understood. Do not call anything else "Good," for that would be wrong. And do not call anything else "God" except the Good, for that too would be impious.

Although many people speak of the Good, not everyone understands what it truly is. The same is true for God. Some people mistakenly call gods or even humans "Good," though they can never actually be or become Good. The nature of these beings is entirely different from God, and the Good cannot be separated from God, because God and the Good are one and the same.

Other immortal beings may be called gods, but they are called gods out of tradition, not because they share the nature of the Good. God alone is Good by His very nature. His nature and the Good are the same. From this unity, all other things come into being.

The Good is the one who gives everything and takes nothing. God gives all things freely without needing anything in return. Therefore, God is Good, and Good is God.

The other name of God is Father, for He is the creator of everything. A father's role is to create life. That is why bringing children into the world is considered one of the greatest and most sacred acts. Those who think rightly understand that leaving the world without children is a great loss and an act of impiety. After death, those who have no children are punished by the daimones.

Their punishment is this: their souls are condemned to take on a body that is neither male nor female, a cursed state under the sun. Therefore, Asclepius, do not feel sorry for the childless man. Instead, recognize the misfortune that awaits him and pity his fate.

Let all I have told you serve as your introduction to the knowledge of the nature of all things.

III. The Sacred Sermon

The source of everything is God, who embodies both Mind and Nature, as well as Matter and Wisdom, which reveals all things. God is also the origin of Energy, Necessity, Renewal, and the natural order. In the beginning, there was boundless Darkness in the Abyss, along with Water and an intelligent Breath. These elements were stirred by the power of God within Chaos. Then, Holy Light appeared, and from the moist essence, the Elements began to form, settling beneath the dry expanse. The Gods divided these things from the fertile Nature.

At first, everything was unshaped and unfinished. The lighter things were sent upward, while the heavier ones settled beneath the moist expanse. The universal elements were held together by Fire and suspended in Breath to keep them balanced. Heaven took shape in seven circular layers, with its Gods appearing as stars, each marked by signs.

Nature's parts came together in harmony with the Gods, and Heaven's edge moved in a continuous cycle, driven by God's Breath.

Each God brought forth what was assigned to him. This is how animals, crawling creatures, fish, birds, plants, flowers, and grasses came into existence. Every living thing carried within itself the seeds of future renewal. The Gods gave humans the special gift of understanding the works of God and the power of Nature. Humanity was meant to rule over everything under Heaven and to gain knowledge of the world's blessings. Humans were to grow in numbers and multiply, with their souls cycling through different lives under the guidance of the Gods. They were also meant to observe the wonders of Heaven, learn about the works of God and Nature, and understand the consequences of good and bad actions, mastering useful skills along the way.

Thus, their lives begin, shaped by the fates determined by the cycles of the Gods, and they pass away when their time is done. Their efforts on Earth leave behind memories, though they will fade when the cycles begin anew. Every life, every creation, and every effort will eventually decay, but they will also be renewed through the workings of the Gods and the rhythmic turning of Nature's wheel.

The divine nature of God constantly renews the mixture of the cosmos, and Nature itself is intertwined with this divine renewal.

IV. The Cup or Monad

Hermes: The World-maker created the universe not with hands but through Reason, so you should think of Him as always present, the source of all things, and the One and Only who brought everything into existence through His Will. His Body cannot be touched, seen, or measured, and it is unlike anything else. It is neither fire, water, air, nor breath, though all these come from it. Because He is Good, He dedicated this Body to Himself and arranged and adorned the earth.

He sent the universe down to earth through man, a being with both mortal and immortal life. Man is superior to all other living things because of the Reason and Mind within him. He became an observer of God's works, marveling at them and striving to understand their Creator.

God gave Reason to all people, but He did not yet give everyone Mind.

This was not because He withheld it, for God holds no grudges. Instead, selfishness belongs to those souls without Mind.

Tat: Then why didn't God give everyone Mind, Father? Hermes: God placed Mind in the world like a prize for souls to seek.

Tat: Where did He place it? Hermes: He filled a great Cup with it and sent it down, along with a Herald, who was told to proclaim these words to the hearts of men: "Baptize yourself with the water of this Cup if you have the faith to ascend to the One who sent it. Understand why you were created and rise to Him." Those who understood the message and accepted the Mind became part of the Gnosis. When they received the Mind, they became complete beings. But those who didn't understand the message remained without Mind and were left unaware of the reason for their existence.

The senses of such people are like those of irrational animals. Their lives are guided by feelings and impulses, and they fail to recognize what is truly worth contemplating. They focus only on the pleasures and desires of the body, believing that these are the reason for human existence.

But those who have received God's gift show, through their actions, that they have broken free from death. They embrace all things in their Mind—things on earth, things in the heavens, and even things beyond the heavens, if such things exist. Once they reach this understanding, they see the Good and view their time on earth as an accident. They reject both physical and non-physical desires and rush toward the One and Only.

This, Tat, is the knowledge of the Mind—the vision of divine things. It is the knowledge of God, for the Cup belongs to Him.

Tat: Father, I want to be baptized as well. Hermes: You cannot love your true Self unless you first reject the body, my son. And if you love your true Self, you will gain Mind, and with Mind, you will share in the Gnosis.

Tat: What do you mean, Father? Hermes: It is not possible to devote yourself to both perishable things and divine things at the same time. All things belong to one of two realms—either the physical or the non-physical, the perishable or the divine. Each person must choose between them, for they can never exist together. When someone chooses one path, the other fades away.

Choosing the Better path not only brings great fortune to the person who makes the choice, but it also honors God. On the other hand, choosing the Worse path leads to destruction, though it only disturbs God's harmony to a small extent—like a procession passing along a road without stopping others from moving. People who follow the desires of their bodies move aimlessly through life, led by their pleasures.

So, Tat, what comes from God is already ours, and it always will be. But what depends on us should not be delayed. It is not God but ourselves who cause evil by choosing it over good.

Do you see, my son, how many obstacles we must pass through? There are many bodies to overcome, many spirits to encounter, and the vast movements of the stars lie along our path toward the One and Only God. There is no other destination beyond the Good. It has no limits or end and, for itself, no beginning—though for us, its beginning is found in Gnosis.

For the Good, Gnosis is not a beginning. But for us, it is the first step toward understanding the Good. Let us take hold of this beginning and move swiftly through the challenges before us.

It is hard to leave behind the things we are familiar with, the things that surround us and please our senses, and to return to the ancient path. Visible things attract us, while things we cannot see are harder to believe in. Evil is more obvious, while the Good remains hidden from our eyes. It has no shape or form that can be seen.

The Good is like nothing else and cannot be compared to anything. Since it has no body, it cannot appear to those who only see with their eyes.

The superiority of what is alike and the inferiority of what is unlike lie in this: the One, which is the source and root of all things, is present within everything as its source. Nothing can exist without this source, but the source itself comes from nothing else—it is its own beginning and origin.

Because the One is the source of all, it contains all numbers but is not contained by any. It creates every number, yet it is not created by any other.

All things created are imperfect. They can be divided, increased, and diminished. But the Perfect One is not subject to any of these. What is capable of increasing does so by drawing from the One, but it weakens when it can no longer hold onto the One.

Now, my son, I have shown you a glimpse of God's image as much as possible. If you focus on this image with the eyes of your heart, you will find the path leading upward. This image will guide you, for divine vision has a unique power—it draws in those who open their eyes to see it, just as a magnet pulls iron toward it.

V. Though Unmanifest God Is Most Manifest

I will share this teaching with you, Tat, so you may no longer be unaware of the mysteries of the God beyond all names. Pay close attention, and you will see that what seems hidden to most will become clear to you. If it were already clear, it would not truly be what it is, for everything that is revealed is part of the process of becoming. The Unseen remains eternal, not needing to be made visible, for it already exists and gives form to all things. Being itself unmanifest, God makes all other things visible without becoming visible Himself. God is not made; instead, by thinking things into existence, He brings them forth. This act of creation is what I call "thinking-manifest."

Only what is created can be thought into existence, and since God is uncreated, He is beyond this process and remains unmanifest. Even though He brings all things into being, God reveals Himself through all things, but especially in those things He chooses. So, Tat, pray to the One-and-Only Lord and Father, the source of all things, to grant you His mercy. Through this mercy, you may catch a glimpse of the greatness of God—a single ray of His light shining into your thoughts. Only thought can see the Unseen, for thought itself is unmanifest.

If you open your mind, God will reveal Himself to you. The Lord does not withhold Himself but reveals Himself through the entire universe. You have the power to think, see, and grasp this truth with your mind, as if you were holding it in your hands. You can gaze upon God's Image within yourself. But if what is within you remains unseen to you, how can you hope to see God within yourself using only your outer eyes?

If you want to see Him, reflect on the sun, the moon's path, and the order of the stars. Who watches over this order? Every part of creation has its boundaries set by place and number. The sun is the greatest god among the heavenly bodies, and the other celestial beings respect him as their king. The sun, larger than the earth and sea, allows smaller stars to circle above him. Out of respect for whom, or out of fear of whom, does he do this?

Each star follows a unique path in the sky. Who sets the course for their movements and defines their limits? The Bear constellations, which circle endlessly in the heavens and carry the cosmos with them—who controls these? Who established the boundaries of the sea and set the earth in its place? There must be a Maker and Master over all these things. Without someone to guide them, neither number, place, nor measure could exist. Order cannot come from something that lacks place and measure. Even things without order must be beneath a higher power that has not yet brought them into order.

If only you could grow wings, soar into the sky, and hover between earth and heaven. From there, you could see the earth's stability, the sea's flowing waters, the vastness of the air, the speed of fire, the movement of the stars, and the swift rotation of the heavens. What a blessed sight it would be to see all these things working together under one command—the stillness within motion, the invisible made visible, creating the order of the cosmos we see around us.

If you want to see God through mortal things, think about how a human body is formed in the womb. Examine the skill involved in shaping such a perfect and divine image. Who carves the circles of the eyes? Who opens the nostrils and ears? Who shapes the mouth? Who stretches and connects the nerves? Who channels the veins and strengthens the bones? Who wraps the flesh with skin? Who separates the fingers and joints? Who forms the feet and prepares them to walk? Who creates the organs, spreads the spleen, shapes the heart like a pyramid, arranges the ribs, expands the liver, makes the lungs spongy, and stretches the belly? Who makes the honorable parts visible while hiding the less honorable ones from sight?

See how many arts and labors are used on one single form, each part made perfectly and in harmony with the others. Who but God, unmanifest and almighty, could create such beauty by His Will?

No one believes that a statue or painting can exist without a sculptor or painter. How, then, can such a masterpiece as the human body exist without a Creator? What blindness, ignorance, and disrespect it is to deny the existence of the Worker behind all things. Never forget, Tat, that all works must have a Maker.

God is greater than all names, the Father of everything that exists. His work is to be a father, creating all things. Creation itself shows His nature. This is why bringing life into the world is so sacred, and why failing to do so is seen as a loss.

If I may speak boldly, God's very existence is an act of creating and sustaining all things. Just as nothing can exist without a maker, God would not be who He is unless He were continually creating all things—whether in the heavens, the air, the earth, the seas, or throughout the entire cosmos. Everything, seen and unseen, is part of Him, for there is nothing in the universe that is not connected to Him.

He is both what is and what is not. The things that exist are revealed by Him, while the things that do not exist remain within Him. He is the God beyond all names, both unmanifest and fully revealed. He is known by the mind, but also seen with the eyes. He has no body, yet He is within all bodies. In fact, He is within everything.

There is nothing that God is not. He is all things, and all things are within Him. This is why He has every name, for all names belong to the Father. And yet, He has no single name, for He is the Father of all.

Who could ever praise God fully? Where should I direct my gaze to sing His praises—above, below, inside, or outside? There is no place where He is not, and nothing exists apart from Him. All things come from Him, and He gives all without taking anything, for He already possesses everything.

When, O Father, shall I sing to You? No one can capture Your time or hour. What shall I sing about—the things You have created or the things You have kept hidden? How shall I praise You—as myself, as someone with my own identity, or as something different from You? For You are everything I could ever be, everything I could ever do, and everything I could ever say.

You are all things, and there is nothing You are not. You are everything that exists, and You are also what does not exist. When You think, You are Mind. When You create, You are Father. When You act, You are God. You are Goodness itself and the Creator of all things.

The finest part of matter is air. Beyond air is the soul, beyond the soul is the mind, and beyond the mind is God.

VI. In God Alone Is Good And Elsewhere Nowhere

Good, Asclepius, is found only in God and nowhere else. In fact, Good is God Himself, eternal and unchanging. Since this is true, Good must be a perfect essence, free from any kind of movement or change. It is always full, never lacking or excessive, and it is the source of all things. Whatever provides for everything is Good, and only God holds this quality. He needs nothing, so He cannot desire anything in a way that would make Him bad. Nothing can be taken from Him that would cause Him pain, for pain is part of what is bad.

There is nothing greater than Him to overpower Him, nothing equal to Him that could wrong Him, and nothing that ignores Him to make Him angry. There is no one wiser than Him, so He has no reason to envy anyone.

Because none of these negative qualities exist in God, only Good is left. Just as badness has no place in God, Good cannot be found in anything else. Everything else—whether small or great, whether an individual or the vast cosmos—contains all the other qualities that are not Good.

Things that are born are filled with passions, and birth itself is tied to suffering. Where there is passion, there is no Good, and where there is Good, there is no passion. Just like how day cannot exist where there is night, and night cannot exist where there is day, Good cannot exist where there is birth and change. Good belongs only to what is uncreated and eternal.

Since matter shares in everything, it also shares in some form of Good. This is why the cosmos is considered good, but only in the sense that it creates things. In all other ways, the cosmos is not Good. It is subject to suffering, change, and the creation of things that suffer.

In humans, good is determined by how much badness is present. What is considered "not too bad" is called good here, but the good we experience is just a small part of what is bad. Therefore, there can never be a pure good in this world. What is called good here is mixed with bad, and once it is mixed, it is no longer truly good.

Only in God is there true Good, or rather, Good is God Himself. So, Asclepius, the word "Good" exists among humans, but the reality of Good does not. It cannot exist here because no material body can contain it. Our bodies are surrounded by bad things—like suffering, desires, emotions, errors, and foolish thoughts.

The worst thing of all, Asclepius, is that people here believe these bad things are the greatest goods. An even worse thing is the lust for food and pleasure, which leads all other bad desires and pulls us away from Good.

I am grateful to God for making me understand that true Good can never exist in the world. The world is filled with bad things, but God is full of Good, and Good comes from God. The pure and perfect qualities that surround Good are so pure that they may even be part of Good's very essence.

Asclepius, one might dare to say that God's essence is Beauty itself, and Beauty is also Good. But there is no Good that can come from physical things in the world. Everything we see is just an image or shadow of reality, while the real essence of Beauty and Good lies beyond what we can see.

Just as the human eye cannot see God, it cannot see true Beauty and Good either. These qualities are part of God and are inseparable from Him. God loves them, and they love Him in return. They are united with Him in a way that cannot be separated.

If you can understand God, you will also understand Beauty and Good. They are brighter than light itself, made even lighter by God. That Beauty cannot be compared to anything else, and that Good cannot be imitated, just like God Himself.

So, as you think of God, think also of Beauty and Good. They cannot be connected to anything else in the world because they are always united with God. If you seek God, you are also seeking the Beautiful. The only path to reach this is through devotion and knowledge.

Those who do not know this and do not follow the path of devotion dare to call people beautiful and good, even though they have never seen true Good. Instead, they are surrounded by all kinds of bad things, believing them to be good. They hold onto these bad things, fearing to lose them, and they work hard not only to keep them but also to gain more.

These are the things people call good and beautiful, Asclepius—things we cannot escape or avoid. The hardest part is that we need these things to survive, even though they are not truly good.

VII. The Greatest Ill Among Men is Ignorance of God

Where are you stumbling, fools, drunk on the wine of ignorance, unable to hold it in, already vomiting it back out? Stop for a moment, clear your minds, and look upward with the true eyes of your heart! And if not all of you can, then at least those who are able!

Ignorance spreads like a sickness across the earth, weighing down the soul trapped inside the body, keeping it from reaching the safe harbor of Salvation. Do not let yourselves be swept away by the raging flood of ignorance. Instead, those of you who can, fight against the current and make your way to the harbor of Salvation. Once there, seek someone to guide you to the gates of Gnosis, where pure Light shines, free from all darkness. There, no soul is intoxicated, but all are clear-headed, looking upon the One who wishes to be known, using the eyes of their hearts.

No ear can hear Him, no eye can see Him, and no tongue can speak of Him. He can only be understood by the mind and the heart. But first, you must strip away the heavy cloak you wear—the web of ignorance that is the root of all corruption, the shackle of decay, the living death. It is the burden of sensation that you carry with you, a tomb that holds your soul prisoner. This thief lives in your own house, loving things that harm you and hating things that could set you free.

This cloak is a curse, keeping you tied down so you cannot look upward. It stops you from seeing the Beauty of Truth and the Goodness that dwells within it. If you could see these things, you would hate the evil within you. You would realize how this evil works against you, dulling your senses and making you believe that what you experience is real.

Matter blocks and clogs your senses with desires and distractions, so you are blind to the things you need to see and deaf to the truths you need to hear.

Let's talk about the soul and the body now, my son—how the soul is immortal and how it directs the forming and dissolving of the body. Nothing truly dies. The idea of death is either a misunderstanding or just a mistake in language, for when we say "death," what we really mean is something closer to "deathless." Death implies destruction, but nothing in the cosmos is ever destroyed. Since the cosmos is the second god—a living being that cannot die—none of its parts can truly die either. Everything in the cosmos, especially humans as rational beings, is part of this eternal life.

First and foremost is God, the eternal Creator of all things. Second is the cosmos, made in His image. God brought the cosmos into being, nourishes it, and sustains it with eternal life. It lives forever, not by itself, but because its source is the Father. The difference between the eternal and what simply lives forever lies in their origin. God is truly eternal because He was not created by anyone else. But the cosmos, though it lives forever, did not exist on its own from the beginning. Its immortality is a gift from the Father.

From the matter below the cosmos, God formed a universal body and shaped it into a perfect sphere, wrapping life within it. This sphere is immortal, making even the physical world eternal in its way. Filled with His divine ideas, the Father scattered living beings throughout this sphere, enclosing them within it like creatures placed inside a cave. He did this to ensure that life would continue in all its forms.

God surrounded this universal body with immortality so that the material world would not break apart and fall back into disorder. Before matter was shaped into bodies, it was chaotic and without structure. Even now, this chaotic nature lingers in the physical world, affecting the small, earthly creatures that experience growth and decay—what people call life and death.

This disorder is tied to the earthly world, but the heavenly beings follow the orderly path assigned to them by the Father. They maintain their harmony through cycles of restoration, ensuring that their order remains unbroken. When bodies on earth are reassembled, this is also a kind of restoration. When they dissolve, they return to a state connected to bodies that do not experience death, only transformation. So, what we call the loss of life is not really destruction—it is just a change, not the end of existence.

The third type of life is humanity. Man is made in the image of the cosmos, with a mind that aligns with the Father's will, giving him a place above all earthly creatures. Humans not only experience life in the cosmos, but they also have the ability to understand the first God. We feel the presence of the cosmos as something physical, but we perceive the Father as something beyond the physical—a pure and divine Mind.

Tat: So, does this mean human life doesn't end? Hermes: Be still, my son, and try to understand what God is, what the cosmos is, and the difference between life that is eternal and life that dissolves. The cosmos exists within God and is sustained by Him. Humanity exists within the cosmos and is shaped by it. God is the origin, the foundation, and the limit of all things.

IX. On Thought and Sense

I gave the Perfect Sermon yesterday, Asclepius, and today I feel it's important to follow it with a detailed explanation about Sense. At first glance, sense and thought seem different—sense relates to physical things, while thought concerns deeper realities. But to me, they don't seem so different, at least not in people. In other creatures, sense is tied closely to nature, but in humans, sense and thought are connected. Mind is as different from thought as God is from divinity. Just as divinity comes from God, thought flows from the mind. Thought and the word (logos) work together as tools for each other—neither thought can be expressed without words, nor can words exist without thought.

In humans, sense and thought blend together, working as one. You can't truly think without sensing, and you can't sense without also thinking. Some say it's possible to think without sensing, like in dreams, but I believe both happen even in dreams. Sensing shifts from the sleeping state to the waking state, just as thought does. Human beings are divided between body and soul, and true understanding happens when both parts of our sense come together, allowing the mind to express what it has conceived.

The mind is where all thoughts are formed. It creates good thoughts when it receives inspiration from God. But it can also produce the opposite when influenced by daimons. No part of the cosmos is free from these daimons, who sneak into the light-filled parts of the soul and plant the seeds of their negative energy. These seeds grow into harmful actions—adultery, murder, betrayal, sacrilege, and other evils that come from dark daimons.

The seeds that come from God are fewer, but they are vast, beautiful, and good. They include virtues like self-control and devotion. Devotion is the knowledge of God, and those who truly know God become filled with good things. They think divine thoughts instead of the ordinary thoughts that most people have. Because of this, those with Gnosis often don't fit in with the rest of society. They are misunderstood, mocked, hated, and sometimes even killed. Badness must exist here on earth—it belongs here, not in the cosmos. The earth is its natural place, though some speak wrongly, claiming that badness is part of the cosmos too.

Those devoted to God learn to endure everything, once they understand the truth of Gnosis. To them, even things that seem bad to others are transformed into good. They deliberately connect all things, good or bad, to the knowledge they have gained. Amazingly, only those who have found Gnosis have the power to turn bad things into good.

Now, let me return to the topic of Sense. Sense, when combined with thought, defines what it means to be human. But not all people benefit from thought, as some are focused only on material things, while others embrace the deeper, substantial aspects of life. Material-minded people are drawn toward badness and receive their thoughts from daimons. Those who align with the Good are connected to God and are saved by Him.

God creates all things, shaping them to become like Himself. Yet, while people develop their goodness through their actions, they remain incomplete. The workings of the cosmos affect how things turn out, filling some with badness and cleansing others with goodness. Even the cosmos itself has its own kind of sense and thought, though it is simpler and purer than what humans possess.

The cosmos follows a single purpose: to create all things and then gather them back into itself. It serves as an instrument of God's will. It holds all the seeds of life from God, bringing them into existence, dissolving them when their time ends, and renewing them again—like a gardener who nurtures life, allowing it to flourish and then planting it anew. There is nothing the cosmos does not give life to. It takes in everything and makes it live, becoming both the home of life and its creator.

All material bodies are made from different elements—some from earth, some from water, some from air, and some from fire. Some bodies are more complex than others, with the heavier ones being more composed, and the lighter ones being simpler. The speed of the cosmos drives the diversity of life's forms, giving each body its unique qualities, along with the fullness of life.

God is the Father of the cosmos, and the cosmos gives life to everything within it. The cosmos is God's child, and all things within the cosmos come from it. That is why the cosmos is called "Order," for it arranges everything in perfect harmony. It gives life to every creature, keeps them all active, and ensures that nothing is left out. Its unending activity, precise structure, and careful organization are what define it.

The sense and thought of all living beings come to them from outside—breathed into them by the force that contains them. But the cosmos received its sense and thought all at once, when it first came into being, and it holds onto them as a gift from God.

Some people mistakenly believe that God is beyond sense and thought. But this is not true. Everything that exists is within God, created and sustained by Him. Every action that takes place in the physical world, every movement of the soul, every breath of life, and every process of renewal—all these depend on Him. In truth, He is not just the source of these things—He is these things. He does not receive them from outside Himself but gives them freely from within His own being.

This is God's way of thinking and sensing—constantly moving everything forward. There will never come a time when anything that exists will stop existing. When I say "anything that exists," I also mean anything that belongs to God. All things that exist are within God, and nothing exists outside of Him, just as He is never without anything.

Asclepius, if you truly understand these ideas, they will make sense to you and feel true. But if you do not understand, they will seem impossible to believe. Understanding leads to belief, and not believing shows a lack of understanding. My words guide you toward the truth, but the mind is powerful. When it is guided by words to a certain point, it can find the truth on its own.

When the mind reflects on these things and sees that they align with what reason has already confirmed, it finds peace in a deep trust. For those who, with God's help, can grasp the meaning of these teachings, they are easy to believe. But for those who cannot understand, they remain unbelievable. This is all that needs to be said about thought and sense.

X. The Key

Yesterday, I gave the Perfect Sermon to you, Asclepius. Today, I will dedicate my teaching to Tat, as this will serve as a summary of the General Sermons that were addressed to him. God, the Father, and the Good share the same essence, or more precisely, the same energy.

The term "nature" refers to things that grow or change, whether they move or stay still, whether they are human or divine. God wills all these things into being. However, energy refers to something deeper, as I explained in earlier teachings on both divine and human things. This is important to remember when we talk about the Good.

God's energy is expressed through His will. His very essence is the will for all things to exist. God, the Father, and the Good are one and the same—they are the source of everything that has not yet come into being. God is the foundation of everything that exists, and nothing can be added to Him. Although the cosmos, represented by the sun, brings life to all things that participate in it, the sun is not the true cause of life or goodness. Even if the sun is seen as a parent of life, it serves this role only through the goodwill of the Good, without which nothing could exist or come into being.

A parent, whether a father or a mother, creates only by participating in the creative will of the Good, which flows through the sun. It is the Good that holds the power to create. This power belongs to God alone, who takes nothing for Himself but brings everything into existence. I choose not to say that He "makes" things because making suggests imperfection—something that is done at one moment and not at another.

Makers are limited by time, sometimes producing things of one quality and sometimes of another. But God, the Father and the Good, is the reason everything exists. This truth becomes clear to those who are able to see it.

The Good exists by its own nature and is the reason everything else exists. It is the essence of all being. Other things exist only because of the Good. The defining feature of the Good is that it desires to be known. This, Tat, is the true nature of the Good.

Tat: Father, this vision of the Good is so beautiful that it feels like something I could worship. It fills my mind with such clarity that I feel it must be divine. Unlike the sun's light, which blinds the eyes, the radiance of the Good enhances our vision. It shines in a way that the mind can receive fully, and instead of causing harm, it fills us with life.

Those who experience this vision more deeply than others sometimes fall into a sleep-like state, lost in its beauty—just as it happened with Uranus and Cronus, our ancestors. I hope we, too, may share this experience one day, Father.

Hermes: Yes, may it happen for us, my son. But for now, we are not yet ready. We have not yet opened our mind's eye enough to behold the true Beauty of the Good—a beauty that can never be corrupted or fully understood. You will only see it when you can stop trying to describe it. Knowing the Good requires a holy silence and a rest from all sensory activity.

When someone perceives the Good, they can focus on nothing else. They stop seeing, hearing, or moving their body. Their senses and movements come to a complete halt. The light of the Good fills their mind and radiates through their soul, drawing them away from the physical world and transforming them into pure essence. Even while still in the body, a soul can become like God if it contemplates the Beauty of the Good.

Tat: How can a soul become like God, Father?

Hermes: Each soul experiences transformations, my son.

Tat: What do you mean by transformations?

Hermes: In the General Sermons, I explained that all individual souls come from one universal Soul, which spreads throughout the cosmos.

These souls undergo many changes—some move toward a better state, while others fall into worse conditions.

Some souls that once lived as crawling creatures transform into creatures of the sea. Others move from sea creatures to land animals, and some from land animals to birds. Eventually, souls that exist in the air can transform into human beings. Human souls, in turn, reach the first step toward immortality by becoming daimons.

Souls that become part of the choir of perfect gods join the ranks of the Inerrant Gods. There are two groups of gods: those who are without error and those who err. Reaching the company of the Inerrant Gods is the greatest achievement for a soul.

However, if a soul enters a human body and continues in ignorance, it will not experience immortality or partake in the Good. Instead, it will follow the path of degeneration, returning to a lower state, such as that of a creeping creature. This is the consequence of a soul's failure to grow. The root of the soul's failure is ignorance. A soul without knowledge of existence, its nature, or the Good becomes blinded by bodily desires and is tossed around by passions.

Such a soul, unaware of its true nature, becomes enslaved to the body. Rather than ruling over the body, the soul becomes its servant, burdened by physical form. This ignorance is the soul's downfall.

On the other hand, knowledge—Gnosis—is the soul's virtue. A person who has this knowledge is good, pious, and even divine, even while still on Earth.

Tat: Who, Father, is this kind of person?

Hermes: The one who neither talks too much nor listens to too much. Those who argue and debate endlessly only waste time on meaningless fights. God, the Father, and the Good cannot be found through endless speech or listening. Even so, senses exist in all beings because life cannot be experienced without them. But Gnosis is different from sense. While sense responds to things that control us, Gnosis is the goal of true knowledge, and it is a gift from God.

All knowledge is non-physical. It uses the mind as a tool, just as the mind uses the body. Both material things and mental things come into the body because everything must involve opposites and contrasts to exist.

Tat: Who is this material god you speak of?

Hermes: The cosmos is beautiful, but it is not truly good, because it is made of material things and can be affected by external forces. Though it is the highest of all material things, it is still second in rank and lacks self-sufficiency. The cosmos has no beginning in time—it has always existed. But it is in a state of constant change, always generating new qualities and forms. It is always moving, creating the source of all physical motion.

The underlying stillness of the mind gives rise to this motion. The cosmos is like a sphere, or a head. Everything at the top—the head—is non-material, while everything at the bottom—the feet—is purely physical. The mind, like the head, moves in a way that reflects the mind's nature. Those beings closest to the mind, or the "head," are more filled with soul and less with body. Because of this, they are free from death. However, those beings further from the mind, who have more body than soul, are subject to death.

The entire cosmos is alive, containing both material and spiritual elements. It is the first of all living things, and humans come next, though humans are the first among mortal beings. Humans share the same life force as other creatures but are not naturally good and are even capable of great evil, since they are subject to both change and death. Although the cosmos is also not entirely good, it is not evil because it does not experience death. Humans, however, are vulnerable to both motion and death, which makes them prone to evil.

The structure of humans works like this: the mind resides in reason, reason resides in the soul, the soul resides in the spirit, and the spirit resides in the body. The spirit flows through the body using veins, arteries, and blood, giving the body movement and carrying life. This is why some people mistakenly believe that the soul is in the blood, not understanding that at the moment of death, the spirit withdraws into the soul, causing the blood to stop flowing and the body to die.

All things originate from one Source, and that Source depends on the One, who is unmoving and eternal. There are three: God, the Father and the Good, the cosmos, and man. God contains the cosmos, and the cosmos contains man. The cosmos is God's child, and man is like a child of the cosmos.

God does not ignore humans; He knows them well and desires to be known by them. The only way for humans to be saved is through the knowledge of God. This knowledge leads the soul upward to a higher existence. Through this path, the soul becomes good—not occasionally good, but good by necessity.

Tat: What do you mean by this, Father?

Hermes: Think of an infant's soul, my son. The soul of a newborn has not yet been pulled down by the body, because the body is still small and not fully developed.

Tat: How is that possible?

Hermes: The soul of a child is a beautiful thing to witness, untainted by the body's desires and still connected to the Cosmic Soul. But as the body grows and weighs the soul down, the soul becomes disconnected and forgets its higher nature. This forgetfulness leads to vice.

The same thing happens when people leave their bodies at death. As the soul withdraws, the spirit contracts within the blood, and the soul retreats into the spirit. Once the mind sheds these layers, it becomes purely divine, taking on a body of fire and moving freely through the universe. The soul, however, remains behind to face whatever judgment or consequences it has earned.

Tat: What do you mean, Father? Are you saying that the mind, soul, and spirit separate from each other? I thought the soul was the mind's covering, and the spirit was the soul's covering.

Hermes: A listener must engage deeply with the speaker, breathing in sync with his words and understanding beyond what is said aloud. In an earthly body, the soul, mind, and spirit take on these layers. The mind cannot exist in its pure form within a physical body. The body cannot contain such immortality, nor can divine virtues remain in a physical form without being weighed down by suffering. So the mind takes the soul as a covering, and the soul uses the spirit as its covering, while the spirit spreads throughout the living being.

When the mind is freed from the body, it immediately takes on its true form—a robe of fire. It cannot remain in an earthly body, as the earth cannot contain fire without being consumed. That is why water surrounds the earth, acting as a barrier to keep fire at bay. The mind, being the fastest and most divine force, has fire as its natural body.

The mind uses fire as a tool to create all things. The divine Mind shapes everything, while the human mind can only create things on earth. Without the fire of divinity, the human mind cannot create anything divine—it remains tied to earthly things. However, not all souls are the same. A pious soul is both divine and connected to higher forces. When such a soul leaves the body and has lived righteously—by knowing God and doing no harm to others—it becomes entirely mind. But a soul without piety is trapped in ignorance, punishing itself and searching for a new human body to inhabit. No human soul can enter the body of a creature without reason, for God's law prevents such a violation.

Tat: How does a soul get punished, Father?

Hermes: The greatest punishment a soul can experience is the lack of piety. Nothing burns as fiercely as this absence, and no wild beast can wound the soul as deeply. The impious soul carries countless burdens. It cries out, "I am burning! I am in torment! I don't know what to say or do! I am surrounded by suffering and cannot see or hear!" These are the cries of a soul in anguish, not the result of being transformed into a beast, as some believe. That idea is a mistake.

The true punishment of the soul is that when the mind becomes a higher, divine force, it takes on a fiery form to serve God. It enters the impious soul, punishing it with the weight of its own sins. The soul then becomes trapped in acts of violence, blasphemy, and wrongdoing, harming both itself and others. In contrast, the mind lifts a righteous soul toward the light of Gnosis. Such a soul pours out blessings and kindness in both word and deed, imitating the goodness of its Creator.

This is why you must praise God and ask for the Good Mind to guide you. A soul on the right path cannot fall into a worse state. Souls interact with each other—those of gods with humans, and human souls with those of creatures without reason. The higher beings guide the lower ones: gods care for humans, and humans watch over animals. Above them all is God, who watches over everything and holds everything together. The cosmos obeys God, humans follow the cosmos, and animals are subject to humans. But God reigns over all of them and contains everything within Himself. God's energy radiates like beams of light. The cosmos expresses its nature through the elements, and humans act through arts and sciences. The flow of divine energy moves from God through the cosmos and down to humanity.

This structure reflects the order of the universe, which is rooted in the nature of the One and sustained by the divine Mind. Nothing is greater than the Mind, which connects gods and humans. The Good Mind is the highest blessing a soul can receive, while a soul without it is truly unfortunate.

Tat: Father, what do you mean by this?

Hermes: Not every soul contains the Good Mind, my son. I am speaking about the divine Mind, not the mind that punishes souls. A soul without the Good Mind cannot think or act properly. Sometimes, the mind leaves the soul, and when that happens, the soul becomes as if it had no reason. It cannot understand or perceive anything. The mind does not remain with a soul that is sluggish or tied too closely to the body. Such a soul is bound by the body and does not truly possess the Mind. A person with such a soul cannot be called a true human, for a human is a divine being. Humans are not measured alongside other earthly creatures but are compared to the gods in heaven. In fact, humans and gods are equal in power.

No god from heaven descends to earth, for they remain within their divine realm. Yet humans can ascend to the heavens and understand its workings. They know what is high and what is low, and they can learn all things. Even without leaving the earth, a person can reach heavenly knowledge through ecstasy. In this way, humans on earth can be seen as mortal gods, just as gods in heaven are immortal humans.

Thus, the entire order of creation is maintained through the connection between the cosmos and humanity, all guided by the One.

XI. Mind Unto Hermes

The divine Mind spoke to Hermes, saying, "Pay attention to this teaching and remember my words. I will explain things clearly without delay."

Hermes responded, "Many people say different things about the nature of God and the universe, and I still don't know the truth. Only you can give me the real answer, Master."

The Mind replied, "Listen closely, my son. I will explain the connection between God, eternity, the cosmos, time, and the process of creation. God creates eternity. Eternity brings the cosmos into existence. The cosmos gives rise to time, and time makes all things come into being. The essence of God is goodness, beauty, wisdom, and blessedness. For eternity, the essence is sameness. For the cosmos, it is order. For time, it is change. And for creation, it is life and death.

God's energies are mind and soul. Eternity holds immortality. The cosmos has restoration and decay. Time involves growth and decline. Creation brings about qualities. Eternity exists within God, the cosmos within eternity, time within the cosmos, and the process of creation takes place within time. Eternity surrounds God. The cosmos moves within eternity. Time fulfills its purpose within the cosmos, and creation unfolds within time.

Everything begins with God, whose essence is eternity. The material world is the cosmos. God's power flows through eternity, and eternity's work shapes the cosmos, which constantly changes and yet remains eternal through the power of eternity. Because eternity cannot be destroyed, the cosmos is also indestructible. Nothing in the cosmos truly perishes, for the whole of the cosmos is held together by eternity.

Hermes asked, "What is God's wisdom?"

The Mind answered, "God's wisdom is the Good, the Beautiful, and the source of virtue and blessedness. Eternity governs the cosmos, giving it the qualities of immortality and continuity. Everything begins with eternity, just as eternity comes from God. Time and the process of creation exist differently in heaven and on earth. In heaven, they are unchanging and eternal, but on earth, they are subject to change and destruction.

The soul of eternity is God. The soul of the cosmos is eternity. The soul of the earth comes from heaven. God is found in the mind, the mind in the soul, and the soul in matter. All of these exist through eternity. The cosmos, containing all things, is filled with soul. Soul is filled with mind, and mind is filled with God. The soul fills the cosmos from within and surrounds it from without, bringing life to everything. This perfect life encircles the entire cosmos and gives life to all within it. In heaven, things remain unchanging. On earth, they change and come into being.

Eternity preserves the cosmos, either by necessity, divine will, or natural law. However you understand it, everything is energized by God. God's energy is unmatched and cannot be compared to anything human or divine. Never imagine that anything above or below is like God, for God has no equal. Nothing else possesses the same power as God, for only God gives life, immortality, and transformation. God is not inactive; if He were, nothing could exist or act. Everything is full of God, and there is no such thing as inaction, for both what creates and what is created are always active.

All things must be created and continue to be made in harmony with their place in the universe. God works within everything He creates, not limited to one part of creation but present in all. He is the power within all things and works through them, though they remain subject to Him.

Look at the cosmos, Hermes, and admire its beauty. It is a perfect body, always young and full of life. It remains in a constant state of renewal, never growing old. Notice how the seven spheres are arranged, each fulfilling its purpose according to the order of eternity. Everything is filled with light, not fire, because light is born from the blending of opposites through God's energy. God, the source of all goodness and order, governs the movements of the seven spheres.

See how the moon leads the way for the other spheres, influencing nature and transforming the lower elements. The earth, at the center of everything, supports and nourishes life. Look at the many forms of life—some immortal, some mortal—and notice how the moon connects the two, standing between them.

All things are filled with soul and move according to their nature. Some revolve around heaven, while others orbit the earth. None move out of place—those above do not move below, and those below do not rise above. Everything follows the path of creation, as you have already learned. All bodies possess souls, and all souls are in motion.

It is impossible for all things to come together without someone to unite them. That someone must be entirely One. Since everything in the universe moves differently and has different forms, yet follows one unified order, there can only be one creator. If there were more than one, they would compete with each other, causing disorder. If one creator made mortal beings and another made immortal beings, each would desire to create the other's work. But if both matter and soul are one, who would decide how creation is divided? If both creators shared the task, who would take the greater part?

Every living being consists of both soul and matter, whether it is immortal, mortal, or irrational. All living things have souls, while things without life are only matter. Soul, when acting in accordance with its creator, gives life. The ultimate source of all life is the One who creates the deathless.

Hermes asked, "How are mortal beings different from immortal ones? Why does the creator of immortality also create beings that are not immortal?"

The divine Mind answered, "It is clear that there is one who creates these things, and that He is the One God. Soul, life, and matter are all part of this oneness. Who else but God could place souls in living beings? Just as you believe the cosmos, the sun, the moon, and the divine nature are each singular, you must also understand that God is One."

God creates everything in many ways. If you, a human, can do many things—seeing, hearing, speaking, walking, thinking, and breathing—all at once, how much greater is God, who gives life, soul, deathlessness, and change? Just as all these abilities in you belong to one person, everything in the universe belongs to the one God. Without Him, nothing could exist, just as you would no longer live if you stopped breathing and thinking. If God ever stopped creating (though it is impossible to imagine), He would no longer be God.

Nothing in existence can be inactive, least of all God. If there were anything He did not create, He would be incomplete. But God is perfect and creates everything. Stay with Me a moment longer, Hermes, and you will understand that all things exist because of God's continuous creation—whether they are being made now, were made in the past, or will be made in the future. This is life itself. This is beauty, goodness, and God.

If you wish to understand this more deeply, think about how you desire to create life yourself. But unlike you, God does not create out of enjoyment. He works alone, and everything He creates remains connected to Him. If He ever withdrew from His work, everything would collapse, and life would end. Since all things are alive, and life is one, God must also be one. All life, whether in heaven or on Earth, comes from one source—God. Life is the unity of mind and soul. Death is not the end, but the separation of soul and mind from their union.

Aeon is the image of God, the cosmos is the image of Aeon, the sun reflects the cosmos, and humans mirror the sun. People call change "death" because the body dissolves, and life retreats into the unseen realm. But just as the cosmos experiences daily changes without being destroyed, life itself does not end—it only transforms. The changes of the cosmos are part of its rhythm, with its rotations and hidden cycles renewing it constantly.

The cosmos contains all forms within itself. It does not need external forms because it transforms itself from within. If the cosmos has all forms, what must its creator be like? He cannot lack form, but if He had every form, He would resemble the cosmos. If He had only one form, He would be less than the cosmos. So, what can we say about Him without falling into confusion? God has one unique essence, which is beyond physical form. Though it is invisible, this essence makes all things visible through the bodies He creates. Do not be surprised that such an invisible essence exists—it is like the way mountaintops in a painting appear to rise from the canvas, though they are actually flat.

Consider this bold but true statement: just as humans cannot live without life, God cannot exist without doing good. His essence and movement are tied to the creation and sustaining of life. Some of these ideas may seem difficult, so listen closely.

All things exist within God, but not in the way objects exist within a physical space. A place is something physical and unmoving, while the things that exist within God are always in motion.

Things exist differently in the realm of the unseen than in the physical world. Think of the One who holds everything together. There is nothing faster, stronger, or greater than what is bodiless. It surpasses all in power, speed, and completeness.

Now, imagine telling your soul to travel anywhere—it will be there even before your thought is complete. Send it across the ocean, and instantly it arrives, not by moving step-by-step, but as if it is already present. Tell it to rise to the heavens, and it will go without wings or obstacles. Neither the sun's fire, nor the sky's winds, nor the stars will block its path. It will pass through them all and reach the farthest edge of the universe. And if you desire to go beyond the cosmos to see what lies beyond—if anything does—you are free to do so.

Recognize the incredible power and speed within you. If your soul can do all these things, how much more can God do? Know God by understanding that He holds all things within Himself, like thoughts, including the entire cosmos. But to know God, you must become like Him. Only by becoming like the divine can you truly know the divine.

Grow beyond all limitations. Rise above the body, surpass time, and become one with eternity. Imagine yourself as immortal, knowing all things—every art, science, and way of life. Be higher than the highest and lower than the lowest. Contain within yourself the senses of every creature—fire and water, dry and wet. Imagine yourself everywhere at once—on land, in the sea, in the sky. See yourself as unborn, in the womb, young, old, dead, and beyond death, all at the same time. If you can know all these things at once—every time, place, event, quality, and quantity—you will know God.

But if you trap your soul within your body and limit yourself by saying, "I don't know anything, I can't do anything, I'm afraid of the sea, I cannot reach the heavens, I don't know who I was or who I will be," you will remain disconnected from God. You cannot understand true beauty and goodness as long as you are attached to the body and filled with negativity.

The worst thing is not knowing the Good that comes from God. But the ability to know, to desire, and to hope for the Good is the path that leads directly to it. This path is easy to follow. The moment you take a step on it, the Good will reveal itself everywhere—when you expect it and when you don't. It will appear while you are awake or asleep, traveling or resting, in the day or night, whether you speak or stay silent.

Everything around you is a reflection of the Good.

Hermes asked, "Is God invisible?" The Mind answered, "Be silent! Who could be more visible than God? The whole reason He created everything is so that you could see Him through all things. This is the Goodness of God—His power to make Himself known through everything.

Even things without bodies are not truly invisible. The mind sees itself when it thinks, and God reveals Himself through His creation. Now, you have been shown these things, Thrice-greatest Hermes. Reflect on what you have learned, and apply the same understanding to everything else. If you do, you will not be misled.

XII. About The Common Mind

The Mind, Tat, is part of God's very essence—if it's even possible to define God's essence. Only the Mind truly understands what this essence is. The Mind is not separate from God but is united with Him, like light is connected to the sun. In humans, the Mind is God, which is why some people are like gods, their humanity closely linked with divinity. As the Good Daimon said, "Gods are immortal humans, and humans are mortal gods."

In animals without reason, the mind acts as their natural instinct. Wherever there is life, there is soul; wherever there is soul, there is mind. But in these creatures, the mind serves only as a function of nature. In humans, however, the Mind works for their betterment, guiding them toward what is good. For animals, the mind cooperates with their natural instincts, but in humans, it often opposes them. This is because every soul, once it enters a body, is immediately pulled toward pleasure and pain. Just as liquids mix and bubble inside a container, so do pleasure and pain swirl within the body, and the soul is thrown into this mixture when it enters.

When the Mind governs a soul, it brings light to it by opposing the desires that cloud it, much like a good doctor treats a sick body by using painful methods to heal it. In the same way, the Mind brings discomfort to the soul, pulling it away from harmful pleasures, which are the source of every evil. The worst evil for the soul is being disconnected from God. This disconnect leads to the desire for everything harmful and nothing good. The Mind acts to rescue the soul from this state, just as a physician restores health to a sick body.

However, when a human soul is not guided by the Mind, it becomes like the soul of an irrational animal. The Mind allows such souls to chase after whatever they desire, indulging in endless cravings, just as animals are driven by instinct. These souls are never satisfied and are constantly consumed by harmful desires and passions. God has placed the Mind as a judge over these destructive urges, to bring them under control.

Tat said, "But Father, doesn't this teaching about the Mind conflict with what you taught me about Fate? If it is destined for a person to commit a sin, such as theft or sacrilege, why should they be punished if they only acted according to Fate?"

Hermes replied, "Every action is connected to Fate. Nothing, whether good or bad, can happen without Fate. However, it is also part of Fate that those who do evil will suffer. They commit wrongs so that they can experience the consequences of those actions."

"But for now, let us leave the discussion of vice and Fate. We have covered that in other teachings. Our focus here is on the Mind—what it does and how it differs in humans and animals. In animals, the mind aligns with their nature, but in humans, it restrains destructive desires like anger and lust. Some people follow reason, while others live without it."

All humans are subject to Fate, which brings both birth and change. But those who are guided by reason—those led by the Mind—experience life differently. They are not trapped by vice and do not suffer from it, even though they still endure the challenges of life.

Tat asked, "But isn't a person who commits murder or theft considered bad? Aren't they punished for it?"

Hermes answered, "I don't mean that those who follow the Mind are free from life's trials. Even though they may not commit sins like murder or theft, they still experience suffering, as if they had. No one can escape the experiences of change and birth. However, those guided by the Mind can free themselves from vice, even if they still endure life's difficulties."

I have heard the Good Daimon say that if He had written His teachings down, humanity would have greatly benefited. As the firstborn of God,

He sees all things clearly and speaks divine truths. He once said, "Everything is one, especially the things the mind alone can perceive. Our life depends on God's energy, power, and eternal essence. God's Mind and Soul are both good. Since this is true, the things of the mind are never separated from one another. The Mind, which rules over all things and serves as the Soul of God, can do whatever it desires."

Tat, understand this and apply it to your question about the Mind and Fate. If you eliminate confusing arguments, you will see that the Mind, which is the Soul of God, governs everything—Fate, Law, and all else. Nothing is beyond its control. It can place a soul above Fate, or allow a soul to fall below it if the soul neglects what happens to it. Let this teaching from the Good Daimon be enough for now.

Tat responded, "These words are truly divine and helpful, Father. But I still have one more question. You said that the Mind works with the natural impulses of animals, but those impulses seem to be driven by passions. If the Mind works with these impulses, does that mean the Mind also takes on the nature of passion?"

Hermes replied, "That is a thoughtful question, my son. You are right to ask, and it deserves a careful answer."

All things that lack physical form are subject to emotion when they enter a body. In fact, they themselves are forms of emotion. Anything that moves on its own is formless, while anything that is moved by something else has a body. The formless is moved by the Mind, and motion itself is a kind of emotion. Both the one that moves and the one being moved are subject to emotion—the first governs, and the second is governed. But when someone frees themselves from the body, they also free themselves from emotion. However, strictly speaking, nothing is entirely without emotion. Everything is affected in some way. There is a difference between feeling emotion and being subject to it—one is active, and the other is passive.

Formless things act on themselves; they are either still or in motion, and both are forms of emotion. Bodies, on the other hand, are always acted upon, which makes them subject to emotion. Do not let these words confuse you—action and emotion are two sides of the same thing. It does no harm to use the word "action" because it sounds better.

Consider this, my son. God has given humanity two gifts that other living beings do not have—mind and speech. These gifts are equal to immortality. The mind allows us to know God, and speech gives us the ability to praise Him. If a person uses these gifts correctly, they will become like the immortals. When they leave the body, the mind and speech will guide them to join the company of the gods and the blessed.

Tat asked, "But don't other creatures also use speech?" Hermes replied, "No, my son. They use only sounds. Speech is very different from mere voice. All humans share the ability to speak, but each type of animal has its own unique sounds."

Tat continued, "But even among humans, speech differs by language." Hermes agreed, "Yes, son, but humanity is still one. Speech can be translated and understood, whether it's spoken in Egypt, Persia, or Greece. You seem to underestimate the power and importance of reason. The Good Daimon, the Blessed God, once said, 'The soul exists within the body, the mind within the soul, reason within the mind, and the mind within God. God is the Father of them all.'

Reason is the image of the Mind, just as the Mind is the image of God. The body reflects the form, and the form reflects the soul. The finest part of matter is air, from which comes soul; from soul comes mind, and from mind comes God. God surrounds everything and fills everything. The mind embraces the soul, the soul fills the air, and the air permeates matter.

Necessity, Providence, and Nature are the tools through which the cosmos and matter are arranged. In the realm of ideas, everything shares the same essence, and sameness is their defining quality. In the material world, every physical form is made of many parts. Although they transform from one state to another, they maintain their underlying essence.

Every composite thing has a set number of parts. Without numbers, there could be no structure, creation, or breakdown. Units give rise to numbers and can be divided and reabsorbed into themselves. Matter is one, and the entire cosmos is both a powerful god and the image of a greater God. It is unified with God and preserves the will and order of the Father. The cosmos is filled with life, and nothing within it—whether part or whole—has ever been, is now, or will ever be lifeless. The

Father intended it to be filled with life for as long as it exists. For this reason, the cosmos itself must be a god.

How could there be anything dead in the cosmos, which is the image of the living Father? Death is a form of decay, and decay is destruction. Nothing in the cosmos, which is free from decay, can be destroyed.

Tat asked, "Do the creatures within the cosmos not die, then?" Hermes replied, "Be silent, son! You are being misled by the common use of words. Creatures do not die; their bodies are simply broken down. The breakdown of a body is not death—it is the separation of its parts so they can be renewed. Life's activity is motion. Is there anything in the cosmos that does not move? No, my son, everything moves."

Tat asked, "But doesn't the Earth seem motionless?" Hermes answered, "No, my son. The Earth moves rapidly, even though it seems stable. How could the one that nurtures all things remain still? Creation requires movement. The idea that the Earth is motionless is laughable. Anything without motion is lifeless."

Understand, my son, that everything in the cosmos moves either to grow or to diminish. Movement is a sign of life. However, not everything that moves remains the same. The cosmos as a whole does not change, but its parts are constantly changing. Yet nothing within it is corrupted or destroyed. Confusion arises because people misuse words. Life is not defined by birth but by awareness. Death is not simply change but the loss of awareness.

Since this is true, everything—matter, life, spirit, mind, and soul—is immortal. Anything that lives owes its immortality to the Mind. This is especially true for humans, who are closely connected to God and share in His essence. God reveals the future to humanity through dreams, signs, and nature—through birds, winds, and trees. That is why humans claim to understand the past, present, and future.

Each type of creature lives in a specific part of the cosmos—fish in water, animals on land, and birds in the air. But humans interact with all the elements: Earth, water, air, and fire. They also see the heavens and connect with them through their senses. God, however, surrounds and fills everything. He is energy and power, and it is not difficult to understand God.

If you want to contemplate God, observe the order of the cosmos and how everything follows its proper arrangement. Notice how necessity governs what has been made, and how providence guides things as they change and develop. See how matter is filled with life, and how God moves everything, accompanied by gods, spirits, and humans.

Tat said, "But, Father, these things are just energies." Hermes responded, "And if they are energies, who do you think directs them except God? Just as heaven, Earth, water, and air are parts of the cosmos, so too are life, immortality, energy, spirit, necessity, providence, nature, soul, and mind parts of God. These things, along with eternity, are what we call the Good. There is nothing that has been made or is being made without God's presence.

Tat asked, "Then is God present even in matter?" Hermes replied, "Matter is separate from God so that it can serve as the space in which things exist. Without God's energy, matter would be nothing more than mass. But because it is energized, it must be directed by God. Every living thing is brought to life by God. Immortality comes from Him, and change is directed by Him. Whether you speak of matter, body, or essence, know that they are all forms of God's energy. Matter expresses energy through form; bodies express it through movement, and essence expresses it through being. This is God—the All.

Everything in existence is part of God. He is not bound by size, space, quality, form, or time. God is All, and He surrounds and fills everything.

Honor and worship this divine Reason, my son. There is only one way to worship God, and that is to live without doing harm."

XIII. The Secret Sermon on the Mountain

In your earlier teachings, Father, you spoke in ways I didn't fully understand, especially about divinity. You said no one could be saved without Rebirth, but you didn't explain what that meant. When I asked you for more guidance after our journey to the mountaintop, you told me I would learn about Rebirth when I became a stranger to the world. So I worked to detach my thoughts from worldly illusions. Now, please complete my understanding by sharing what you promised, whether through words or a hidden teaching. I still don't know where humanity comes from, or what seed and womb bring us into being.

Wisdom, which is found in silence, is both the matter and the womb from which humans are born, and the seed is the True Good.

Who plants this seed, Father? I am confused.

It is God's Will, my son.

What kind of being is born from this seed? I do not feel that I share in the essence that goes beyond the senses. Is the one born from this seed a child of God?

The one born is a being composed of all divine powers, fully united in one.

You speak in riddles, Father. Please explain it to me clearly.

This knowledge cannot be taught in the usual way, my son. When God wills it, the memory of the truth awakens within.

What you're saying seems impossible, Father. I need clear answers. Am I not your son, part of your lineage? Don't withhold this from me—I am ready to understand Rebirth.

What can I say, my son? I can only tell you this: when I receive the clear vision born from God's grace, I pass through my ordinary self into a new form that can never die. I become something entirely new, born in the Mind. This transformation is not something that can be taught, and it cannot be understood through the senses you use to see me now. My former self, the one made of many parts, is no longer who I am. I am no longer touched by things, yet I still have the ability to touch. I have form and dimension, yet I am no longer bound by them.

You see me with your eyes, but you cannot truly understand what I am, no matter how hard you try to grasp it with your body or your sight.

You've thrown me into confusion, Father. I can't even see myself clearly anymore.

I wish you could pass through yourself as well, just as those who dream but remain awake do.

Who creates Rebirth, Father?

The Son of God, the One Man, through God's Will.

Your words leave me stunned, Father. My senses are completely overwhelmed. I see that your true self is far greater than your outward appearance.

You misunderstand, my son. This mortal form changes every day. It grows and declines with time, showing that it is not truly real.

Then what is real, Father?

That which is unchanging, beyond all definition. It has no color, no shape, no change. It does not wear any garment or take any form. It gives light but is only known to itself. No body can contain it.

I feel like I'm losing my mind, Father. I thought I was gaining wisdom, but now my thoughts feel blocked.

This is the nature of the truth, my son. It rises like fire but settles like earth. It flows like water but moves like air. How can you understand what is beyond both solid and fluid, what cannot be grasped or bound? Only those who perceive the way of Rebirth through God can begin to understand it.

Does this mean I am not capable of understanding, Father?

No, my son. God forbid such a thought. Turn inward, and it will come to you. When you truly will it, it will happen. Silence the senses of your body, and your divine nature will be born. Free yourself from the tormenting attachments of the material world.

Are there tormentors within me, Father?

Yes, many, my son—fierce and numerous.

I don't know them, Father.

The first tormentor is ignorance, followed by grief. Then come indulgence, desire, injustice, greed, error, envy, deceit, anger, recklessness, and malice. These twelve are the main tormentors, but there are many others. They hide within the body, causing the soul to suffer through the senses. However, these tormentors begin to leave one by one when God shows mercy. This is the process of Rebirth.

Now, my son, remain still and keep silent. In this way, we allow the flow of God's mercy to continue uninterrupted.

Rejoice now, my son, for through God's powers you are being cleansed and prepared to receive the true Reason. When the knowledge of God enters us, ignorance is cast away. With the arrival of divine joy, sorrow leaves us, retreating to those who still make space for it. Now, I call upon self-control, the power that follows joy. O sweetest of powers, let us welcome it gladly, for it drives away all indulgence.

Next, I invoke the power of continence, which stands firm against desire. This power rests on the foundation of righteousness. Without effort, righteousness dispels injustice. We become righteous when injustice leaves us. Now, I summon the power that stands against greed—sharing with all. With greed gone, I call upon truth, and as truth enters, error departs. See how the fullness of the Good arrives, my son, with the coming of truth. Envy vanishes, and truth unites with the Good, bringing both life and light. No more do the torments of darkness dare approach us; defeated, they take flight.

Now, my son, you understand the process of rebirth. When the ten divine powers drive out the twelve tormentors, the birth of the true self—an intellectual birth—reaches completion. In this rebirth, we are made into gods. Through God's mercy, those who experience this rebirth leave behind the senses of the body. They come to know themselves as beings of light and life, filled with joy.

Tat exclaimed, "By God's power, Father, I no longer see the world through the eyes of my body, but through the energy of the Mind. I feel myself everywhere—in the heavens, on earth, in water, and air. I am in animals and plants. I exist in the womb, before birth, and after death—I am everywhere! But tell me, how do the twelve dark torments lose their power when faced with the ten divine powers? How does it work, O Thrice-Great One?"

This body we pass through, my son, is made from the circle of the twelve kinds of life, each representing an element. Though these twelve seem separate in our experience, they act together as one unified whole. Rashness cannot be separated from anger, nor can they even be distinguished. According to reason, these twelve tormentors withdraw naturally once the ten powers arrive, for the ten are the source of all souls. Where life and light unite, the One exists through the Spirit. Reason teaches us that the One contains the Ten, and the Ten hold the One.

Tat said, "Father, I see everything—I see the whole universe and myself within the Mind!"

Hermes replied, "This is the experience of rebirth, my son: no longer viewing the world from the body's limited perspective, but through the Mind. This teaching about rebirth is not shared with everyone, for God has willed that the mysteries of the All remain hidden from the masses."

Tat asked, "Father, is the body, which is made of the ten divine powers, ever dissolved?"

"Hush, my son. Do not speak of such impossibilities, for to think this way is to sin and darken the eye of your Mind. The physical body that we sense must dissolve, but the spiritual birth is beyond decay. The first body must perish, but the spiritual self is beyond the reach of death. You must know, my son, that you have been born a god, a child of the One, just as I am."

Tat then asked, "Father, I wish to hear the hymn of praise that you said you heard when you reached the eighth level of the Powers."

Hermes answered, "Just as the Shepherd foretold, I reached the eighth. You are eager to cast off your earthly body, and you are now purified. The Shepherd, who is the Mind that governs all, did not need to pass on more than what has been recorded, for He knew I would be able to learn all things on my own, hear what I needed, and see what I desired. He left the creation of beautiful things to me, and so the powers within me—and within all beings—sing in unison."

Tat said, "Father, I long to hear these things. Please tell me!"

Hermes replied, "Be silent, my son, and listen to the hymn of praise that keeps the soul in harmony. This hymn of rebirth is not usually shared, for it is meant to remain hidden in silence. Now stand in an open place, where the sky is clear. At sunset, face the southern wind and offer your worship. At sunrise, do the same, facing the east. Now, my son, be still."

Let every part of the world hear my hymn! Open, O Earth! Let the gates of the Abyss be unlocked. Be still, O trees! I am about to praise the Lord of all creation, the One who is both all things and beyond them. O heavens, open! Winds, be still! Let God's eternal sphere receive my words.

I sing to Him who created all things, who established the earth, hung the heavens in place, and commanded the oceans to provide fresh water to both inhabited and uninhabited lands for the benefit of all. He made the fire shine for the use of gods and humans. Let us all give praise to

Him, the Lord above the heavens and master of all things! He is the Mind's great vision—may He receive the praises of these powers within me!

O powers within me, sing with my will! Sing with me, O blessed Gnosis, for through you I see the light that only the Mind can perceive. I rejoice in the joy of the Mind. Sing with me, O powers! Sing with me, O self-control! Sing, O righteousness, the praises of the righteous! Sing, O sharing-with-all, the praises of the All! Through me, O truth, sing the praises of truth. Sing, O Goodness, the praises of the Good! O Life and Light, from us to you flow our endless praises!

Father, I thank You. You are the energy behind all my powers. I thank You, O God, the source of all my strength.

Your Word sings praises through me. Through my offering, return everything to Your divine Reason. The powers within me cry out, praising You. They follow Your will. From You comes Your will, and to You all things return. Receive from all of us our offering of Reason. Preserve the life within us, O Life. Illuminate us, O Light. Fill us with Your Spirit, O God.

It is Your Mind that guides Your Word, O Creator, the One who gives the Spirit to all beings.

Through fire, air, earth, water, and spirit, through all Your creations, I offer my praise to You, God. I have found joy in praising You, and in doing Your will, I have found rest.

I have seen how this hymn of praise is sung, Father, and I have brought it into my inner world as well.

Say it within the cosmos that only your mind can see, my son.

Yes, Father, I say it in the cosmos within my mind. Through Your hymn and praise, my mind has been filled with light. Now, I too want to offer my praise to God from the depths of my mind.

Do it mindfully, my son.

Yes, Father. I speak what I see in my mind. To You, the One who gave me life, I send my offering as I would to God. O God and Father, You are Lord and Mind. Accept my offering, as You will, for by Your will all things are made complete.

Offer your praise, my son, to God, the Father of all. But remember to add, "through the Word."

Thank you, Father, for teaching me how to sing such hymns.

I am happy, my son, that you have brought forth the good fruits of truth—fruits that will never die. Now that you have learned this lesson, promise to keep silent about your virtue. Do not reveal the knowledge of Rebirth to anyone, so that we will not be accused of misleading others.

We have both given enough attention to this teaching—you as the listener, and I as the teacher. In your mind, you have come to know yourself and our shared Father.

The Emerald Tablet

(Thoth the Atlantean)

Hermes Trismegistus

The Emerald Tablets of Thoth the Atlantean

The story behind these tablets is unusual and may seem unbelievable to modern scientists. They are said to be incredibly ancient, going back around 36,000 years before the common era. The author is Thoth, an Atlantean priest-king, who established a colony in Egypt after the destruction of Atlantis.

Thoth is credited with building the Great Pyramid of Giza, though it has been wrongly attributed to Cheops. In the pyramid, he stored his knowledge and preserved the records and tools from ancient Atlantis. Thoth ruled over Egypt for about 16,000 years, from around 52,000 to 36,000 BCE. Under his leadership, the once primitive people of Egypt rose to a high level of civilization.

Thoth had overcome death and could pass from life only when he chose, without actually dying. His great wisdom made him ruler over many Atlantean colonies, including those in South and Central America. When it was time for him to leave Egypt, he built the Great Pyramid over the entrance to the Halls of Amenti, where he placed his records and selected the most worthy people to guard his secrets.

In later times, these guardians became the priests of the pyramids, and Thoth was worshiped as a god of wisdom and the Recorder. In the age that followed his departure, the Halls of Amenti became known in legend as the underworld, where souls went after death for judgment.

Thoth's spirit continued to incarnate in human form, as described in the tablets. He returned three times, with his last appearance as Hermes, known as the "thrice-born." During this incarnation, he left behind writings known as the Emerald Tablets, a later and more simplified version of the ancient mysteries.

The tablets translated in this work are ten in total, originally placed in the Great Pyramid under the care of the pyramid priests. For convenience, the content has been divided into thirteen sections. The final two tablets contain such powerful knowledge that it is currently forbidden to release them to the public. However, the ones included here hold valuable secrets for those who are serious about seeking wisdom. They should not be read just once but studied many times, as only through careful reading can their deeper meanings be understood. A casual reading will provide glimpses of beauty, but true insight comes only through deep study.

Now, let me explain how these ancient secrets were brought back to light after being hidden for so long. Around 1,300 BCE, Egypt was in turmoil, and many priests were sent to other parts of the world. Among them were some of the pyramid priests carrying the Emerald Tablets. They used the tablets as a symbol of authority, allowing them to influence less advanced priesthoods in other regions descended from Atlantean colonies.

These priests eventually settled in South America, where they found the Mayan civilization, which had preserved much of the ancient wisdom. The priests stayed with the Mayans, and by the 10th century, the Mayan people had established themselves in the Yucatan. The Emerald Tablets were placed under the altar of a great Sun Temple.

After the Spanish conquest, the Mayan cities were abandoned, and the treasures within their temples were forgotten. It's important to understand that the Great Pyramid has always been a temple for initiation into the mysteries. Even figures like Jesus, Solomon, and Apollonius were initiated there.

The author of this translation, who is connected to the Great White Lodge that works through the pyramid priesthood, was instructed to retrieve the tablets and return them to the Great Pyramid. After many adventures, the tablets were recovered. Before returning them, permission was granted to translate and keep a copy of the wisdom they contain. This translation was completed in 1925, and only now has permission been given to release part of it to the public. Some people will doubt its authenticity, but true seekers will find wisdom within these words. If the light is already within you, the light in these tablets will resonate with your soul.

Now, let me describe the physical nature of the tablets. They are made of a bright emerald-green material, created through a process of alchemical transformation. These tablets are imperishable and immune to all natural elements, with their atomic structure remaining stable forever. In this way, they defy the natural laws of matter and ionization.

The ancient Atlantean language is engraved on their surfaces, and these inscriptions respond to focused thoughts, releasing mental vibrations that awaken understanding in the reader. The tablets are held together by hoops of a golden-colored alloy, suspended from a rod made of the same material.

The knowledge within these tablets forms the foundation of the ancient mysteries. Anyone who reads them with an open mind will greatly expand their wisdom. Read them, believe or not, but read them—and the vibrations within will awaken a response in your soul.

In the following pages, I will reveal some of the deeper mysteries hinted at in previous writings. Humanity's search for the laws that govern life has been constant, but the truth has always been hidden just beyond the veil that separates the higher realms from the material world. Those who seek knowledge must learn to look inward, for the answers lie in silence, beyond the distractions of the physical senses. Those who talk do not know, and those who know do not speak.

The highest truths cannot be spoken, for they exist beyond words and symbols. Symbols serve as keys to understanding deeper truths, but often people cannot see what lies beyond the symbols because they seem too overwhelming. If we realize that all material symbols are just representations of higher truths, we begin to develop the vision to see beyond the veil.

Everything in the universe moves according to law. The laws that govern the planets are no different from the laws that shape human life. One of the most important Cosmic Laws is the one that connects the material aspect of humanity with the spiritual. The key to this connection lies in the intellectual part of human nature, which bridges the material and spiritual worlds.

Those who seek higher knowledge must strengthen their minds and concentrate all their energy on their chosen path. The search for light, life, and love begins on the material plane, but it reaches its ultimate goal in complete unity with the universal consciousness. The material world is only the starting point; the true goal is spiritual enlightenment.

In the following pages, I will interpret the Emerald Tablets and reveal some of their hidden meanings. The words of Thoth contain many layers of truth, and these hidden meanings will become clear with thoughtful reflection. If your own inner light is awakened, the knowledge within these tablets will resonate with your soul.

TABLET 1 I, Thoth, the Atlantean, master of ancient mysteries, keeper of sacred knowledge, and mighty ruler, have lived through countless generations. As I prepare to enter the Halls of Amenti, I write down this wisdom for those who come after me. In the great city of Keor, on the island of Undal, I began this life long ago. The people of Atlantis were not like the men of today—they did not live short lives, but instead, they renewed their existence over and over through the Halls of Amenti, where the river of life flows eternally.

I have traveled down the dark path that leads to light a hundred times over, and just as many times I have returned from darkness, renewed in strength and power. Now, I leave once more, and the people of Khem (ancient Egypt) will no longer see me. But one day, I will rise again, mighty and powerful, to demand an account from those I left behind. Beware, people of Khem, if you have betrayed my teachings, for I will cast you down into the darkness from which you came.

Do not reveal my secrets to those from the North or the South, or my curse will fall upon you. Remember my words, for I will return and demand from you all that you have been entrusted with. Even from beyond time and death, I will return to reward or punish you according to how you have followed my truths.

My people were great in ancient times, far greater than the people who live now. We held knowledge that reached into the depths of the universe, uncovering wisdom from Earth's earliest days. We were wise with the knowledge of the Children of Light, who lived among us, and we drew power from the eternal fire. Among us, the greatest of all men was my father, Thotme, the keeper of the great temple and the link between the Children of Light and the people who lived across the ten islands of Atlantis. He was the voice of the Dweller of Unal, whose words the kings obeyed.

I grew up under my father's guidance, learning the ancient mysteries, and the fire of wisdom grew within me until it consumed my soul. On a great day, the Dweller of the Temple summoned me before him. Few men had looked upon his face and lived, for the Children of Light, when not in physical form, are not like the sons of men. I was chosen from among humanity to be taught by the Dweller, so that I might carry out his purposes, which were not yet born in the world.

For long ages, I lived in the temple, learning ever more wisdom until I reached the light of the great fire. The Dweller taught me the path to Amenti, the underworld where the great king sits on his throne of power. I bowed before the Lords of Life and Death, and they gave me the Key of Life. I was freed from the cycle of death and rebirth. I traveled to the stars, where space and time meant nothing, and after drinking deeply from the cup of wisdom, I looked into the hearts of men. There, I discovered even greater mysteries, and my soul was at peace.

Throughout the ages, I have watched people die and be reborn in the light of life. But as Atlantis declined, the consciousness that had once been one with me faded, replaced by lesser beings from distant stars. Following the laws of the universe, the word of the Master began to take form. The thoughts of the Atlanteans turned downward into darkness, and the Dweller awoke from his detachment, calling forth his power. Deep in the heart of the Earth, the Sons of Amenti heard his call. Using the power of the Logos, they directed the eternal fire, shifting its course.

A great flood swept over the world, shifting the balance of the Earth, and only the Temple of Light remained standing on the mountain of Undal, still rising above the water. Some among us survived the flood. The Master commanded me to gather my people and take them across the waters to the land of the barbarians who lived in caves. There, we would carry out the plan we knew so well.

I gathered my people, and we boarded the Master's great ship. As we rose into the morning sky, the Temple of Light disappeared beneath the rising waters. It vanished from the Earth until the appointed time when it would return. We fled toward the rising sun, and beneath us lay the land of the children of Khem. When we arrived, the barbarians came at us with spears and clubs, filled with rage and intent on destroying the Sons of Atlantis.

I raised my staff and directed a ray of vibration at them, freezing them in place like stones from the mountain. Then I spoke to them calmly, telling them of the greatness of Atlantis and explaining that we were messengers of the Sun. I used my knowledge of magic and science to subdue them until they bowed before me. When I released them, they groveled at my feet in fear.

We lived in the land of Khem for many long years. Following the Master's command, I eventually sent the Sons of Atlantis to distant lands, so that the wisdom of Atlantis could rise again in the future. Through the womb of time, knowledge would once more be reborn in those who seek it.

For a long time, I lived in the land of Khem, using my knowledge to perform great works. The people of Khem grew in understanding, nourished by the wisdom I shared. To retain my power, I opened a path to Amenti, allowing me to live through the ages as a Sun of Atlantis, preserving knowledge and records. The people of Khem became strong, conquering those around them and slowly rising in spiritual strength.

Now I must leave them and descend into the dark halls of Amenti, deep within the Earth, where I will stand once more before the Dweller. Above the entrance to Amenti, I raised a gateway—only a few have the courage to cross it. Over the portal, I built a mighty pyramid, harnessing the power that defies Earth's gravity. Inside, I placed a force-chamber, creating a circular passage that reaches near the top. At the summit, I set a crystal to send a ray through time and space, drawing energy from the ether and focusing it toward the gateway of Amenti.

I built other chambers that seem empty but hide the keys to Amenti within them. Only those who dare to explore the dark realms may enter, but first, they must purify themselves through fasting. Those who seek the mysteries must lie in the stone sarcophagus within my chamber, and then the hidden truths will be revealed. Even in the depths of the Earth, I will meet them. I, Thoth, the Lord of Wisdom, will dwell with them always.

I built the Great Pyramid, designing it to align with the forces of the Earth, so it would burn with energy for eternity and stand through the ages. Inside, I placed my knowledge of magic and science, ensuring I could return from Amenti. While my body sleeps in the halls, my soul will roam freely, incarnating among humans in different forms, including as Hermes, thrice-born.

I serve as the Dweller's messenger on Earth, following his commands to guide many toward enlightenment. Now I return to the halls of Amenti, leaving behind fragments of my wisdom. Keep the Dweller's command: Always lift your gaze toward the light. In time, you will become one with the Master, united with the All. I leave now, but remember my teachings. Live by them, and I will be with you, guiding you into the light. As the portal opens before me, I descend into the night's darkness.

Deep in the heart of the Earth lie the Halls of Amenti, beneath the sunken islands of Atlantis. These halls are places for both the living and the dead, illuminated by the fire of the infinite All. In a distant past, the Children of Light observed humanity's struggle, seeing that people were bound by forces beyond them. They knew that only by breaking free could humans rise from Earth toward the Sun. The Children of Light took human form and came down to Earth, saying, "We are beings formed from the dust of space, part of the infinite All. Though we live as humans, we are not entirely like them."

They created vast spaces beneath the Earth's surface, far from where humans lived, surrounding these halls with powerful forces to protect them from harm. They built other spaces nearby, filling them with life and light from above. In these hidden places, they built the Halls of Amenti to dwell there eternally, living with endless life.

Thirty-two of the Children of Light came among humans, seeking to free them from the darkness and the forces that bound them. In the Halls of Life, a bright, flaming flower grew, expanding and driving away the darkness. At its center, they placed a powerful ray, filling all who came near with life and light. Around the flower, they arranged thirty-two thrones, where the Children of Light sat, bathed in its radiance and filled with the eternal light.

Over the ages, they placed their original bodies in these halls, reawakening them every thousand years with the life-giving light, which quickened their spirits. Though they appeared to sleep, their souls moved freely through the bodies of men, guiding and teaching them. As their bodies rested, they incarnated among humans, leading them from darkness into the light. In the Halls of Life, they kept knowledge unknown to humanity, living forever beneath the cool fire of life.

At times, they awakened from their rest, coming forth as lights among people, infinite beings among finite men. Those who rise from darkness into light are freed from the Halls of Amenti and the Flower of Life. With wisdom as their guide, they pass from among men to join the Masters of Life, free from the bonds of darkness. In the center of the radiant flower sit seven Lords from realms beyond time, guiding humanity with infinite wisdom along the path through time. Though they are silent and hidden, their power is immense, and their knowledge is endless.

Drawing from the Life force, different yet connected to the children of men. Though different, they are also One with the Children of Light. They guard and watch over the forces that bind humanity, ready to release them when the time for enlightenment arrives.

At the forefront sits the Veiled Presence, the Lord of Lords, the infinite Nine, standing above the Lords of the Cycles—Three, Four, Five, Six, Seven, and Eight—each with a purpose and unique power, guiding and shaping human destiny. They sit in strength and wisdom, untouched by time or space. Though not of this world, they are connected to it, like Elder Brothers to humanity. With wisdom, they judge and observe, watching how the Light grows within mankind.

The Dweller led me before them, and I witnessed him blend with the ONE from above. A voice came forth, saying, "Thoth, you are great among the children of men. From this moment, you are free from the Halls of Amenti, a Master of Life among men. Death will come to you only if you desire it. Drink from the well of Life for all eternity, for Life is now yours to take. Death is yours to command at will. Stay here or leave when you wish; Amenti is open to you, a Sun among men. Take Life in any form you choose, Child of the Light who has grown among humanity.

Though free, you must always labor along the path of Light. You have taken one step on the endless journey upward, but the mountain of Light stretches infinitely before you. Every step you take raises the mountain higher; each bit of progress makes the goal seem farther away. You will forever move toward infinite Wisdom, but the goal will always stay just out of reach. You are now free from the Halls of Amenti."

The Divine Pymander

(Poimandres)

Hermes Trismegistus

Preface

This book claims to be the oldest of all books in the world, written hundreds of years before the time of Moses, and I will try to prove that. When we talk about the author of the book, there are four things to consider: his name, knowledge, country, and the time he lived in.

The name he is most known by is Hermes Trismegistus, which means "Mercury the Thrice Great" or "The greatest messenger three times over." He is called Hermes because he was the first person to share knowledge with mankind through writing or engraving. The title "Thrice Great" was given to him for reasons I'll explain later.

His wisdom can be seen through his writings, and it connects with the reason for his name. As for his country, he was a king of Egypt. The exact time he lived is debated. Some say he came after Moses because he was called "Thrice Great," meaning he rose through Egypt's ranks, becoming the top philosopher, the chief priest, and eventually the king. But I disagree with this reasoning, and here's why. According to the most learned followers of Hermes—such as Geber, Paracelsus, and Henricus Nollius—he was called "Thrice Great" because of his perfect understanding of everything in the world. He divided all things into three categories: minerals, plants, and animals, mastering knowledge of each. He also discovered the "Quintessence," the hidden essence of the entire universe, which he said was contained in these three parts. This knowledge, also known as the "Philosophers' Stone" or the "Great Elixir," holds both earthly and heavenly powers. Many have denied its existence, others have sought it at great cost, but only a few—some even in England, such as Ripley, Bacon, and Norton—have found it. It is said that this great treasure was inscribed on an Emerald Tablet discovered in the Valley of Hebron after the flood.

Thus, the idea that Hermes lived after Moses is not convincing. In fact, it seems unlikely he lived during Moses' time, even though some, like the scholar John Functius, believe Hermes lived twenty-one years before Moses received the law in the wilderness. Their arguments, however, are weaker than those that support the idea that Hermes lived before Moses.

One reason for this is that ancient traditions say Hermes was the first to invent writing and engraving to share knowledge with the world. If that's true, he must have come before Moses, who, as the Bible says, was skilled in Egyptian learning from his youth. Moses would have needed written texts to learn this knowledge, and those texts would not exist without Hermes.

Another reason is that Hermes is said to be either the son or the scribe of Saturn. According to historians, Saturn lived during the time of Sarug, Abraham's great-grandfather. Suidas, a respected historian, believes Hermes not only lived before Moses but long before. His words are: "I believe Hermes Trismegistus, the wise Egyptian, flourished before Pharaoh."

This ancient book holds more true knowledge about God and nature than any other book in the world, except for the sacred scriptures. Those who read it carefully and understand it well will have no need to read many other books that claim to explain the Creator and creation. If God ever revealed himself through a person, he did so through Hermes. It's remarkable that someone without the benefit of inherited knowledge—since he was the first to share knowledge with future generations through writing—could be such a profound philosopher and divine thinker. This suggests that his wisdom came more from God than from man, leading some to believe that Hermes came from heaven and was not born on earth.

This book contains the true philosophy, without which one cannot reach the highest level of piety and religion. A true philosopher, according to this philosophy, is someone who studies what things are, how they are ordered and governed, by whom, for what reason, and to what end. Anyone who does this will naturally give thanks to and admire the Creator who directs all things. A person with such gratitude can be called truly pious and religious, and the more religious they become, the more they will understand truth. As they learn more truth, they will become even more religious.

The aim of philosophy is to understand the greatest good, which is the source of all good things. How can we find the source without following the streams that flow from it? Nature's processes are like streams flowing from the fountain of goodness, which is God. I reject the foolish idea that the greatest philosophers are the greatest atheists. Knowing God's works and understanding how he operates through nature does not lead a person to deny God. The Bible calls this belief foolish, and experience shows it is untrue. Look at Hermes—he was the greatest philosopher, and therefore the greatest theologian.

Read this book carefully, and if you need help, use the detailed commentary written on it by Hanbal Offeli Alabar. The book will reveal more about its author than any person, including me, could explain.

Hermes Trismegistus, His First Book

My son, write this first book for the good of humanity and to show respect for God.

There is no truer or more just religion than knowing the truth about things and giving thanks to the one who created them. I will never stop doing this.

Father, how should a person live a good life, especially when there seems to be nothing true in this world?

Be devoted and faithful, my son. The one who lives this way is the greatest philosopher. Without philosophy, it's impossible to reach true faith and devotion.

Anyone who studies how things exist, how they are ordered, governed, and by whom, will give thanks to the Creator, just like a child thanks a good father, a kind caretaker, or a faithful steward. And those who give thanks will be devoted, and those who are devoted will understand where the truth is and what it means. By learning this, they will grow even more devoted.

A soul that seeks the good and true things while it is still in the body will never turn toward evil. It becomes deeply connected to what is good and forgets what is harmful. Once it knows its true Father and Creator, it cannot turn away from what is good.

This is the goal of faith and devotion, my son. Once you reach this point, you will live well and die in peace, knowing where your soul will return.

This, my son, is the path to truth. It is the way our ancestors followed, and by doing so, they found the good. It is a noble path, but even though it is clear, it is difficult for a soul still in a body to travel.

First, the soul must fight against itself. After much struggle, one part will win, because it's a battle of one against two. The soul tries to escape, while the other parts try to hold it back.

The two parts don't seek the same goal. One moves toward the good, while the other clings to evil. The part that loves the good desires freedom, but the part connected to evil prefers bondage.

If the two parts lose, they become quiet and accept the soul's leadership. But if they win, they pull the soul down, forcing it to stay and suffer in the body.

This, my son, is the guide to the way forward. You must detach yourself from the body before the end of life and win this inner struggle. Only then can you return to where you belong.

Now, my son, I will quickly explain the nature of all things. Pay attention and remember what you hear.

All things that move are different from what stays still.
Every physical body can change.
Not every body can be broken down.
Some bodies can be dissolved.
Not every living thing can die.
Some living things are immortal.
Things that can be broken down are also corruptible.
Things that remain unchanged are unbreakable.
What stays the same forever is eternal.
Things that are constantly made are also constantly destroyed.
What is made only once stays as it is and never becomes something else.
First is God. Second is the world. Third is humanity.
The world exists for humans, and humans exist for God.
A soul has two parts: the part connected to the senses is mortal, but the part that reasons is immortal.
Every true essence is immortal.

Every true essence is unchanging.

Everything that exists has a double nature.

Nothing stays still forever.

Not everything moves because of a soul, but everything that moves is moved by a soul.

Whatever feels pain can sense things, and whatever can sense things feels pain.

Everything that feels sorrow also experiences joy, and it is mortal.

Not everything that feels joy also experiences sorrow; such beings are eternal.

Not every body is sick, but every sick body can be dissolved.

The mind exists within God.

Reason exists within humans.

Reason is a part of the mind.

The mind does not experience pain.

No truth lies within physical bodies.

Whatever is without a body cannot lie.

Everything created can be corrupted.

There is nothing truly good on Earth, and nothing evil in Heaven.

God is good, and humans are evil.

Goodness acts freely and willingly.

Evil is forced and unwilling.

The gods choose good things because they are good.

Time is a divine creation.

Law is a human creation.

Malice feeds the world.

Time brings corruption to humans.

Nothing in Heaven can change.

Everything on Earth can change.

There are no servants in Heaven, and no one is free on Earth.

Nothing is hidden in Heaven, and nothing is fully known on Earth.

Earthly things do not connect with things in Heaven.

Everything in Heaven is beyond blame, but everything on Earth can be criticized.

What is immortal cannot be mortal, and what is mortal cannot be immortal.

Not everything that is planted is born, but everything that is born comes from something planted.

A body that can be broken down goes through two phases: first, being planted for life to begin, and second, moving from life toward death.

For a body that lasts forever, time starts only at its creation.

Bodies that can decay grow and shrink over time.

Matter that can decay shifts between opposites, like birth and death. But eternal matter stays the same, returning to its original state.

Human life begins with birth and ends in decay, but decay is also the start of new life.

Whatever gives birth to another thing was once born from something else.

Some things exist in physical form, while others only exist as ideas.

Whatever involves action or work takes place in a physical body.

What is immortal has no part in what is mortal.

Mortal things cannot enter an immortal body, but what is immortal can exist within something mortal.

Actions do not rise upwards; instead, they move downward.

What happens on Earth does not help what is in Heaven, but what is in Heaven benefits everything on Earth.

Heaven is the perfect place for eternal bodies, and Earth is where corruptible bodies belong.

The Earth is crude and unthinking, but Heaven is rational and wise.

Things in Heaven are arranged beneath it, while things on Earth are arranged upon it.

Heaven is the first of all elements.

Divine order is known as Providence.

Necessity serves as the tool or servant of Providence.

Chance is what happens without order—it's like a false idol of action, based only on opinion and illusion.

What is God? He is unchanging goodness.

What is man? He is a being marked by constant evil.

If you fully remember these points, you won't forget the longer explanations I gave before, as these are the key ideas in summary.

Avoid spending time with crowds or common people, because I don't want you to become envied or mocked by them.

Things that are similar attract each other, while things that are different do not get along. Teachings like these only appeal to a few listeners, and that's how it will likely remain, for they are meant for those few who understand them deeply.

These teachings can actually push wicked people toward more malice, so it is important to avoid the masses, as they do not grasp the power or value of these words.

What do you mean, Father?

This, my son: the entire nature of human beings leans toward wickedness. They grow familiar with it and even take pleasure in it. When someone like this learns that the world was created and everything happens according to Providence, Necessity, or Fate, they might become even worse. They may reject everything because it was created and use Fate as an excuse for evil deeds.

This is why we must be cautious with such people—if they stay in ignorance, their fear of the unknown might keep them from doing more harm.

The Second Book, Called, Poemander

One day, as I was deeply thinking about the nature of existence, my senses became dull, like how a person feels sleepy after eating too much or working hard. In this state, I felt as though a being of enormous size and power called me by name and asked, "What do you want to hear and see? What do you want to understand and know?"

I asked, "Who are you?" He replied, "I am Poemander, the mind of the great Lord, the most powerful ruler of all. I know what you want, and I am always with you."

I answered, "I want to understand the nature of things and learn about God." He said, "How do you want to learn?" I replied that I was eager to listen. Then he said, "Keep me in your mind, and I will teach you everything you wish to know."

After saying this, his form changed, and suddenly, in an instant, everything became clear to me. I saw an endless light that was sweet and beautiful, filling me with joy as I looked upon it.

But soon after, a darkness appeared, descending at an angle. It was terrifying and strange, becoming like a moist, chaotic substance that gave off smoke as if from a fire. From it came a sorrowful, wordless voice that seemed to come from the light itself.

Then a holy word came from the light and united with the moist substance. Out of the moistness rose a pure fire that was sharp and active. The air, which was also light, followed the spirit upward toward the fire, leaving the earth and water behind. The air seemed to depend on the fire and rise along with it.

The earth and water stayed together, so closely mixed that the water covered the earth entirely. They both moved under the influence of the spiritual word that hovered over them.

Poemander asked me, "Do you understand the meaning of this vision?" I replied, "I will understand." Then he said, "I am the light, the mind, your God. I existed before the moist substance that came from the darkness. The bright word that emerged from the mind is the Son of God."

I asked, "How can that be?" He replied, "What allows you to see and hear is the word of the Lord, which is the same as the mind of the Father, God. They are not separate from each other, and their union creates life." I thanked him, and he said, "First, understand the light in your mind and truly know it."

After saying this, we stared at each other for a long time. I trembled at his appearance.

Then he gave me a signal, and I saw in my mind the light that filled an endless and indescribable world. I saw that fire was contained within a great moist force, held in place by it.

I understood these things by looking at the word, Poemander. As I stood in awe, he asked me, "Have you seen the original form that existed before the infinite beginning?" I asked him, "Where do the elements of nature come from?" He answered, "They come from the will and wisdom of God. God saw the perfect world in his mind and created this world in its likeness, using principles and seeds of life from himself."

"God, who is both male and female, life and light, created another mind through his word. This second mind, being a god of fire and spirit, formed seven rulers. These rulers, through their movements, control the physical world, and their influence is called fate or destiny."

"The word of God rose from the lower elements into the pure workings of nature and joined with the mind that created everything, for they were of the same essence. The lower elements remained without reason, existing only as raw material."

"The creative mind, together with the word, spun the circles of the heavens like a wheel, guiding them endlessly. The cycles of creation have no beginning or end; they always start where they finish."

"As the mind directed, the movement of the elements gave rise to animals without reason—birds in the air and fish in the water."

"The earth and water were separated by the will of the mind, and the earth produced all kinds of creatures—both wild and tame, those that walk on four legs and those that crawl."

"The mind, which is both life and light, created humans in its own image and loved them as its own children, for they were beautiful and reflected the creator's form."

"God admired his own image so much that he gave humans all his creations. But when humans saw and understood the works of the creator, they wanted to create as well. This desire separated them from the Father, placing them within the realm of creation and action."

"Humans, having the power to understand the operations of the seven rulers, were embraced by them, and each ruler shared a part of their nature with them."

"Through careful learning and understanding, humans gained knowledge of the rulers' essence and their ways. They became determined to break through the boundaries of the circles and understand the power of the one who rules over fire."

"With the power to control mortal things and creatures, humans looked deeper into the harmony of creation. By breaking through the limits of the circles, they revealed the lower nature of things and reflected the beautiful image of God."

"When humans saw this image, filled with beauty and the operations of the seven rulers, they smiled with love, as if seeing their reflection in water or a shadow on the ground, capturing the most beautiful human form."

When he saw his reflection in the water, which looked just like him, he fell in love with it and wanted to be united with it. The moment he decided this, the action followed, creating an image without reason.

Nature, loving what she had embraced, wrapped herself around it, and they merged together because they both desired one another.

Because of this union, man is both mortal and immortal: mortal because of his body, but immortal because of his inner spirit. Even though he possesses immortality and power over all things, he still suffers from mortality and is subject to fate.

Although man is above the forces of harmony, he is also a servant to them. He is both male and female, guided by the will of the Father, who is also both male and female, and always watchful.

I then said, "You are my mind, and I love the wisdom you reveal."

Poemander replied, "This is a secret that has remained hidden until now. When nature joined with man, it created something marvelous.

Because man carries within him the harmony of the seven rulers—spirit and fire from the source I mentioned—nature quickly produced seven beings, each both male and female, in alignment with the qualities of the seven rulers."

I said, "Pimander, I have a great longing to hear more. Please continue and don't go off track."

He replied, "Stay silent, for I am not yet finished with the first part of my teaching."

I responded, "I am listening."

Poemander continued, "The creation of these seven beings happened in this way: Air, which is female, and Water, which desired union, absorbed the ripeness of Fire and the spirit from the ether. This mixture gave rise to physical bodies in the form of humans."

"Man was created from life and light. His soul came from life, and his mind from light."

"All the parts of the visible world continue to follow their course, generating life until the end of time."

"Now listen to the rest of what you wish to hear."

"When the time for completion came, the bond holding everything together was loosened by God's will. All living beings, who were originally both male and female, were separated into male and female forms."

"Then God said to the Holy Word, 'Multiply and increase all my creations. Let those with a mind know they are immortal, and let them understand that love for the body brings death. Let them seek to learn all things.'"

"With these words, Providence worked through the harmony of fate to establish the different kinds of creatures and their generations. Those who came to know themselves reached a higher state of existence and found lasting good."

"But those who, out of ignorance, loved the body wandered in darkness, experiencing suffering and death."

I asked, "Why do those who lack knowledge sin so much that they lose their chance at immortality?"

Poemander replied, "You do not seem to fully understand what you've

146

heard."

I answered, "Perhaps it seems that way to you, but I do understand and remember it well."

Poemander said, "If that is true, I am glad for your sake."

I asked, "Why do those who are already caught in death deserve death?"

He replied, "Because their bodies are accompanied by a heavy darkness. This darkness comes from the moist substance that makes up the physical body, and from it comes death. Do you understand this now?"

I asked, "But how does someone who understands himself find his way to God?"

Poemander answered, "The word of God says this: The Father of all things is life and light, and man was made from both."

I said, "You have spoken well."

He continued, "God, the Father, is life and light, and man was created from these. If you learn and believe that you are made of life and light, you will return to life."

I asked, "But tell me more, O my mind—how will I return to life?"

Poemander replied, "God says, 'Let man, who has a mind, carefully observe and understand himself.'"

I asked, "Do all men have a mind?"

He replied, "Be careful what you say. I, the mind, come only to those who are holy, good, pure, merciful, and who live faithfully. My presence helps them know all things. They pray to the Father with love and gratitude, giving thanks and singing hymns to Him. Before they surrender their bodies to death, they reject the desires of their senses, knowing the nature of their actions."

"As the mind, I do not allow the desires of the body to be fulfilled. I guard against evil and block the entrance to wickedness. I cut off impure thoughts and actions."

"But to those who are foolish, wicked, envious, greedy, violent, and impure, I remain far away. In my absence, the avenging spirit torments them with fire, driving them further into wickedness so they face greater punishment."

"These individuals are never satisfied. They have endless desires and continue to fight in darkness. The spirit torments them without rest, increasing the fire upon them more and more."

I said, "O mind, you have taught me well and answered my questions, but what happens after the body returns to its original state?"

Poemander replied, "When the physical body dissolves, it changes form and becomes invisible. Its habits are handed over to the avenging spirit, and the senses return to their sources, where they once belonged and now become active again."

"Anger and desire return to the lower, animal nature, while the rest of the soul strives upward through harmony."

"To the first level, it returns the power of growth and decay."

"To the second level, it returns the ability to plan evil and deceive others."

"To the third level, it returns the deceitful cravings of desire."

"To the fourth level, it returns ambition and an endless thirst for power."

In the fifth zone, it lets go of reckless boldness and the dangerous confidence that comes with it.

In the sixth zone, it releases the harmful pursuit of wealth through worthless means.

In the seventh zone, it surrenders sly falsehood, always waiting in secret to deceive.

Stripped of all the influences of the lower harmony, the soul rises to the eighth sphere, regaining its true power. There, it sings praises to the Father alongside everything that exists, and all those present welcome it with joy. Becoming like those it now dwells among, the soul also hears the higher powers beyond the eighth sphere singing their unique songs of praise to God.

In time, the soul returns to the Father, joining the higher powers and becoming one with God.

This is the ultimate good, the goal sought by all who understand.

So why do you ask what remains for you to do? Your task is to guide others and show the way to those who are ready, so that humanity can be saved through God.

When Poemander said this, he merged back with the powers above.

I gave thanks and blessed the Father of all things. Strengthened by what I had learned, I understood the nature of the entire universe and had seen the most wondrous vision.

I began to teach people about the beauty of a life rooted in piety and knowledge.

"O people of the earth," I said, "you who live in ignorance of God, indulging in drunkenness and sleep, wake up! Stop being drawn into mindless pleasure and the sleep of ignorance."

Those who listened came willingly, united in their desire to hear more. I continued,

"Why, O people born from the earth, have you chosen death when you have the power to gain immortality? Repent and change your ways. You who have wandered in error and darkness, turn back to the light.

Leave behind the darkness that deceives you. Become part of immortality and abandon what leads to decay."

Some who heard me mocked and scorned, choosing instead to follow the path toward death.

But others knelt before me, asking to be taught. I lifted them up and became their guide, showing them how to be saved. I planted the seeds of wisdom within them and nourished them with the water of immortality.

When evening came and the light began to fade, I told them to give thanks to God. After they finished their thanksgiving, each returned to their home.

In my heart, I carried the kindness and generosity of Poemander, and I was filled with joy, having received everything I desired.

The sleep of my body became the wakefulness of my mind, and when my eyes closed, I saw with true vision. My silence was filled with wisdom, and my words became the fruits of good things.

These experiences came to me through my mind, which is Poemander, the Lord of the Word. Through him, I was inspired by the truth of God.

For this, I give praise and blessing to God the Father with all my soul and strength.

Holy is God, the Father of all things.

Holy is God, whose will is accomplished through his own power.

Holy is God, who chooses to be known and is known by those who belong to him.

Holy are you, who created all things through your Word.

Holy are you, of whom all of nature is a reflection.

Holy are you, who were not made by nature.

Holy are you, who are stronger than all power.

Holy are you, who surpass all greatness.

Holy are you, who are greater than any praise.

Receive these thoughtful sacrifices from a pure soul and a heart reaching toward you.

O God, beyond words and beyond description, you are praised even in silence!

I ask that I may never stray from knowing you. Be merciful to me, strengthen me, and give your light to those who live in ignorance, my fellow humans who are also your children.

I believe in you and bear witness to you as I enter into life and light.

Blessed are you, O Father, for you have given humanity the power to be sanctified and made one with you."

The Third Book,
The Holy Sermon

THE glory of all things, God, and that which is Divine, and the Divine Nature, the beginning of things that are.

God, and the Mind, and Nature, and Matter, and Operation or Working, and Necessity, and Matter, and Operation or Working, and Necessity, and the End, and Renovation.

For there were in the Chaos an infinite darkness in the Abyss or bottomless Depth, and Water, and a subtle in Spirit intelligible in Power; and there went out the Holy Light, and the Elements were coagulated from the Sand out of the moist substance.

And all the Gods distinguished the Nature full of Seeds.

And when all things were interminated and unmade up, the light things were divided on high. And the heavy things were founded upon the moist Sand, all things being Terminated or Divided by Fire, and being sustained or hung up by the Spirit, they were so carried, and the Heaven was seen in Seven Circles.

And the Gods were seen in their Ideas of the Stars, with all their signs, and the Stars were numbered with the Gods in them. And the Sphere was all lined with Air, carried about in a circular motion by the Spirit of God.

And every God, by his internal power, did that which was commanded him; and there were made four-footed things, and creeping things, and such as live in the water, and such as fly, and every fruitful seed, and Grass, and the Flowers of all Greens, all which had sowed in themselves the Seeds of Regeneration.

As also the Generations of Men, to the Knowledge of the Divine Works, and a lively or working Testimony of Nature, and a multitude of men, and the dominion of all things under Heaven, and the Knowledge of good things, and to be increased in increasing, and multiplied in multitude.

And every Soul in Flesh, by the wonderful working of the Gods in the Circles, to the beholding of Heaven, the Gods Divine Works, and the operations of Nature; and for signs of good things, and the Knowledge of the Divine Power, and to find out every cunning Workmanship of good things.

So it beginneth to live in them, and to be wise according to the operation of the course of the circular Gods; and to be resolved into that which shall be great Monuments and Rememberances of the cunning Works done upon earth, leaving them to be read by the darkness of times.

And every Generation of living Flesh, of Fruit, Seed, and all Handicrafts, though they be lost, must of necessity be renewed by the renovation of the Gods, and of the Nature of a Circle, moving in number; for it is a Divine thing that every worldly temperature should be renewed by Nature; for in that which is Divine is Nature also established.

The Fourth Book, Called the Key

Yesterday's speech, Asclepius, I dedicated to you. Today, it is fitting to dedicate this one to Tat, as it summarizes the teachings given to him. God, the Father, and the Good share the same nature, or rather, they carry out the same action and purpose. There are two ways to describe existence—one applies to things that change, and the other to things that are unchanging and unmoving, like the divine and human realms. Every being follows the nature it chooses, but actions originate from somewhere else, whether divine or human, as we have taught before and must understand again here.

God's action is his will, and his very essence is to will all things into being. God, the Father, and the Good are the source of all things, both those that do not yet exist and those that already are. This is the essence of God, the Father, and the Good, and nothing else can compare or draw near to it. The world and the sun—though the sun may be called a father in some sense—are not the ultimate source of goodness or life for living beings. Even the sun acts according to the will of the Good, and without this will, neither being nor creation would be possible.

The Father is the source of his children, with a will that brings goodness into life through the sun. Goodness is always active, constantly creating, yet it comes from one who needs nothing but desires all things to exist. I avoid saying "creates" because creation implies limitations—like time, quantity, or quality—and there are moments when creation pauses or shifts. God, however, is the Father and the Good by being all things, both what he wills to be and what he already is. And all this exists entirely within himself for those who can truly see it.

All other things exist for this purpose: it is in the nature of goodness to be known. This, Tat, is what Good truly means. Tat responded, "You have opened my eyes, Father, and my mind feels purified by this vision." I replied, "I am not surprised, for seeing the Good is not like looking at the sun, which blinds the eye with its intense light. Instead, the vision of the Good sharpens and brightens the mind's eye, making it more capable of understanding."

This sight is swift and clear, gentle yet full of immortality. Those who can grasp it often find themselves drawn out of the body into this beautiful vision. Our ancestors, Celius and Saturn, achieved this state. Tat said, "I wish we could experience that too, Father." I replied, "I wish the same, my son, but for now, we are not focused enough to open the eyes of our minds and behold the pure beauty of the Good. We will see it only when we have no words left to describe it."

The knowledge of the Good is found in divine silence and in the stillness of all senses. When someone understands it, they cannot comprehend anything else, nor can they see, hear, or move their body in the same way. The Good surrounds the entire mind, illuminating the soul and freeing it from the body's senses and movements, drawing it closer to the essence of God.

It is possible, my son, for the soul to become divine even while it still resides in the body—if it contemplates the beauty of the Good. Tat asked, "What do you mean by becoming divine, Father?" I answered, "Every soul is different, my son." Tat continued, "How do these differences affect the soul's journey?" I replied, "Have you not heard from the earlier teachings that all souls come from the same universal soul, though they are scattered throughout the world? Some souls improve their condition, while others decline. For example, souls in lower forms like crawling creatures can rise to higher forms like aquatic beings, and those in water can rise to land creatures. Airy beings may become human, and human souls that seek immortality transform into divine spirits."

These spirits ascend to join the realm of the eternal gods. There are two groups of gods—those that move and those that remain fixed. Achieving union with these divine realms is the ultimate fulfillment for the soul. However, when a soul enters a human body and becomes corrupted by evil, it loses access to immortality and cannot partake in the Good. Such a soul regresses, returning to lower forms like creeping animals, which is the punishment for an evil soul.

The root of a soul's corruption is ignorance. A soul that knows nothing of the true nature of things or the essence of the Good becomes blinded and consumed by bodily passions. Such a soul, unaware of its true self, serves unworthy desires, becoming a slave to the body instead of its master. This is the tragedy of an ignorant soul. On the other hand, the virtue of the soul lies in knowledge. Those who possess knowledge are both good and devout, already sharing in the divine.

Tat asked, "Who is such a person, Father?" I replied, "It is someone who neither speaks nor listens to many things, for one who hears conflicting messages is like someone lost in shadows." God, the Father, and the Good cannot be fully spoken of or heard. In everything that exists, the senses play a role, for they cannot function without them. But knowledge is different from sense. The senses respond to things beyond them, while knowledge is their ultimate purpose.

Knowledge is a gift from God. Although it has no physical form, it uses the mind as its instrument, just as the mind uses the body. Both spiritual and physical things come into existence through the interaction of opposites, and all things depend on this interplay to exist. It cannot be otherwise.

Tat asked, "Who then is this material god?" I answered, "It is the beautiful world we see around us. But it is not entirely good, for it is material and subject to change. It is the first of all things that can be affected and the second of all created things. It is incomplete and always in need of something else. The world was made once but continues to exist through constant change, endlessly creating things that have form and quality."

The material world is always in motion, and every movement in the material world creates something new. But it is the stability of the mind that directs this movement. The world is a sphere, like a head, and above the head, there is nothing physical, just as beneath the feet, there is nothing of the mind. The entire universe is material. The mind is like the head, moving in a circular motion, just as a head turns. Whatever is connected to the soul's membrane—the thin layer that houses the soul—is immortal. In bodies that have a soul, the soul fills the body entirely, but in beings farther from this membrane, the body holds more soul than the soul holds of the body.

The whole universe is alive, consisting of both material and intellectual aspects. The world is the first living being, and man is the second. However, man is the first mortal being. Though man shares in the benefits of the soul just like other creatures, he is not entirely good—he is in fact evil because of his mortality. The world, being in constant motion, cannot be called good, but neither is it evil since it does not die. However, man is both evil because he moves and because he is mortal.

The soul of man operates in this way: the mind is in reason, reason is in the soul, the soul is in the spirit, and the spirit is in the body. The spirit moves through the veins, arteries, and blood, animating the body and supporting it in life. Some have mistakenly believed that the soul is the same as the blood, misunderstanding the nature of the soul. They do not realize that the spirit first returns to the soul when the body dies, and then the blood thickens, the veins empty, and the creature dies. This is the death of the body.

All things depend on a single beginning, and that beginning comes from the One. The beginning moves to continue being the beginning, but the One remains still and unchanging. These three exist: God, the Father, and the Good, the World, and Man. God holds the world, the world holds man, and the world is the child of God, with man being the offspring of the world. God knows man completely and wishes to be known by him. This knowledge of God is the only path to true health. It is the way to return to Olympus, the only way the soul can become entirely good.

"Father, what do you mean?" asked Tat. I answered, "Think of a child's soul, still connected to its body, which is small and undeveloped. When it looks at itself, it sees beauty, untouched by bodily passions, still connected to the soul of the world. But as the body grows and begins to distract the soul, forgetfulness takes hold, and the soul loses its connection to the Good. Forgetfulness is the root of evil."

A similar thing happens to souls after death. When the soul returns to itself, the spirit contracts into the blood, and the soul into the spirit. But the mind, being free of these outer layers, becomes pure and divine. It takes on a fiery body and moves freely, leaving the soul to face judgment and receive the consequences it deserves.

Tat asked, "Why do you say, Father, that the mind separates from the soul and the soul from the spirit? You just said that the soul is the clothing of the mind and the body is the clothing of the soul." I replied, "Son, listening requires understanding and following along with the one who speaks. One must hear more quickly and sharply than the words being spoken. These layers, or coverings, belong to the earthly body. The mind cannot exist in its pure state within a physical body, nor can a physical body hold such immortality. That is why the mind takes on the body of the soul as a covering. Though the soul is also partly divine, it uses the spirit as a servant, and the spirit governs the body."

"When the mind leaves the body, it takes on its fiery form, which it could not do while confined in an earthly body. The earth cannot withstand fire, as even a small spark can burn it. That is why water surrounds the earth like a protective wall, shielding it from fire. The mind, being sharper and swifter than all elements, uses fire as its body. It is the tool the mind uses to create, just as man uses fire to shape earthly things. Without fire, the mind on earth cannot fulfill its divine purpose or even accomplish the tasks of man."

"Not every soul, but only those that are pious and faithful, become divine or angelic. These souls, once free from the body, ascend through the path of piety and can become either pure mind or divine. Piety means knowing God and doing no harm to others. In this way, the soul becomes mind. But a wicked soul remains trapped in its own sins, seeking another earthly body to inhabit. It is not allowed to enter the body of an irrational creature, for God has decreed that no human soul will face such disgrace."

Tat asked, "How is the soul punished, Father? What is its greatest torment?" I replied, "The greatest punishment is impiety. There is no fire more painful, nor any beast more vicious, than the torment of a soul lost in wickedness. Can't you see the suffering of such a soul? It cries out, 'I am burning! I am consumed! I don't know what to say or do! I am surrounded by evil and devoured by misery!' A soul in torment sees and hears nothing but its own despair."

"These are the cries of a soul in punishment. Yet you, my son, think that the soul leaves the body and becomes a beast. This is a great mistake, for the soul's punishment is far worse."

When the mind receives its fiery body to serve God, it descends into a wicked soul, tormenting it with the punishments of sin. This suffering drives the soul to commit acts of murder, insult, blasphemy, and violence, harming others in many ways. But when the mind enters a pious soul, it guides the soul toward the light of knowledge. Such a soul finds joy in praising God and speaking well of others, constantly doing good in both word and deed, following the example of its divine Father.

Therefore, my son, we must give thanks and pray to receive a good mind. The soul can improve and change for the better, but it cannot change into something worse. There is a connection between souls—those of the gods communicate with men, and the souls of men connect with animals. The higher beings always draw from those below them: gods draw from men, men from animals, and God from all things. For God is the highest of all, and everything else is lesser than Him.

The world is subject to God, man is subject to the world, and animals are subject to man. But God rules over everything. The influence of God flows through His actions, the influence of the world flows through nature, and man's influence flows through arts and sciences. Actions affect the world, which then influences man through the natural forces of the world. Nature works through the elements, and man expresses himself through arts and sciences.

This is how the whole universe is governed—by the nature of the One. Everything flows down from the One Mind, which is the most divine and powerful force, bringing unity and connection between gods and men, and men and gods. This is the good spirit, or the guiding demon.

Blessed is the soul that is filled with it, and unfortunate is the soul that lacks it.

"Why is that, Father?" asked Tat. I replied, "Understand, my son, that every soul has the potential for a good mind. This is the mind we are speaking of now, not the ministering spirit we mentioned earlier that comes from judgment. Without the mind, the soul can neither think nor act. Often, the mind departs from the soul, leaving it unable to see or hear, behaving like a mindless creature. Such is the power of the mind."

"The mind does not stay with a lazy soul; instead, it leaves that soul trapped in the body, weighed down by it. A soul without the mind cannot truly be called a man. A true man is a divine being, incomparable to any animal on earth but more like the gods in heaven. In fact, if we dare to speak the truth, a true man stands above the gods or at least equal to them in power. No being in heaven descends to earth, abandoning its place, but man can ascend to heaven and measure it."

"Man understands both what lies above and what lies below, gaining knowledge of all things. And the greatest of all is that man can remain on earth yet still be above it. Such is the greatness of his nature. Therefore, we may boldly say that an earthly man is a mortal god, and a heavenly god is an immortal man. Through these two—man and the world—all things are governed, and both of them, along with everything else, come from the One."

The Fifth Book, That God Is Not Manifest, And Yet Most Manifest

This message, my son Tat, is for you, so that you will not be unaware of the highest name of God. Think deeply about how something that seems hidden to many can become clear to you. If it were obvious to everyone, it wouldn't be divine, because things that are seen are created. If something can be seen, it was made. But that which is unmade has always existed and does not need to be revealed because it simply is. It brings everything else into being but remains itself unseen. Though it is never revealed, it makes all things appear. What is not created exists in imagination, and through imagination, it brings everything into appearance. All things that appear are created, for appearance itself is part of creation.

The One who was never made and never born is also unseen and hidden. However, by making all things appear, He is present in all and can be seen through everything, especially in the things He chooses to show Himself through. Therefore, my son, pray first to the Lord and Father, the One who is alone, that He may be merciful to you and allow you to know and understand His greatness. Ask that He shines one of His rays upon your mind, so you may understand.

Only the mind can see what is hidden, for it is also hidden itself. If you can focus your mind, you will see this truth clearly within it. The Lord, free from jealousy, reveals Himself throughout the entire world. You can grasp His intelligence, hold it in your thoughts, and witness the image of God within yourself. But if you cannot recognize what lies within you, how will you ever see Him clearly with your physical eyes? If you wish to see Him, contemplate the sun, the moon's path, and the stars. Who is it that keeps them in order? All order follows rules of number and place.

The sun is the greatest of the gods in the heavens, and the other heavenly gods follow him like subjects following their king. Even though the sun is mightier than the earth and sea, he allows countless smaller stars to shine above him. Whom does he fear, my son? Each star follows a different path. Who decided the size and course of each one? The Great

Bear turns around itself and carries the whole world with it—who designed and built this system? Who set the boundaries of the sea and established the earth? There must be someone, my son, who is the Creator and Lord of all these things.

It is impossible for things like place, number, and measure to exist without a creator to establish them. Order cannot come from disorder. I wish it were possible for you to have wings and fly into the air. If you could rise into the space between heaven and earth, you would see the stability of the earth, the movement of the sea, the flowing rivers, the vastness of the air, the sharpness and speed of fire, the motion of the stars, and the swiftness of the heavens as they spin around everything.

What a marvelous sight it would be to see everything at once—the still things moving, and the hidden things becoming visible. If you want to understand the Creator, even through mortal things, study how a human being is formed in the womb. Observe the skill of the Creator, and learn who shaped and designed the human form. Who placed the eyes, carved the nostrils, and formed the ears? Who opened the mouth and stretched the sinews? Who shaped the veins, hardened the bones, and clothed the flesh with skin? Who divided the fingers and joints? Who flattened the soles of the feet and made the pores? Who stretched out the spleen and shaped the heart like a pyramid? Who widened the liver and made the lungs soft and full of airways? Who enlarged the belly and arranged the body's more honorable parts for display, while hiding the unclean parts?

See how many crafts are involved in one body, and how many different works come together to create something so beautiful, all in perfect proportion, yet all different from one another. Who created all of these things? What mother or father could have done it, other than the unseen God who made everything by His own will? No one believes a statue or painting could exist without a sculptor or artist. So how could this intricate creation have come to be without a Creator? What great blindness, what terrible ignorance to deny the existence of the Workman behind this masterpiece!

You cannot separate the creation from its Creator. The greatest name of God is Father, for that is what He truly is—the Father of all. If I must speak even more boldly, it is God's nature to carry everything within

Himself, to be pregnant with all things, and to bring them into existence. Just as nothing can be created without a maker, it is impossible for God not to exist or for Him to stop creating. He continuously makes all things—in heaven, in the air, on earth, in the sea, and throughout the entire universe. Everything, whether visible or invisible, comes from Him.

There is nothing in the world that is not part of Him. What is seen, He has made visible; what is unseen, He has kept within Himself. He is beyond any name, the hidden one who is also most visible. He is seen by the mind and also by the eyes. He is without form, yet He has many forms. There is no body that is not part of Him, for He is everything. Because He is everything, He is called by many names. Yet, as the one Father, He has no need of a name, for He is the source of all.

Who can offer praise or thanks worthy of Him? Which direction should I face when I worship Him—upward, downward, outward, or inward? In these matters, there is no fixed place, nor anything that limits Him. Everything exists within Him, and all things come from Him. He gives everything and needs nothing in return, for He possesses all and lacks nothing.

When, O Father, shall I praise You? It is impossible to grasp Your hour or Your time.

How shall I praise You? Should I give praise for what You have made, or for what You have not made? Should I honor You for the things You have revealed or for the things You have kept hidden?

How can I praise You as if I were separate from You, or as if I possessed anything of my own? Am I not entirely Yours?

For You are what I am. You are everything I do. You are everything I say.

You are all things, and there is nothing that You are not.

You are both what has been created and what has never been created.

You are the Mind that understands.

You are the Father who shapes and forms all things.

You are the Good that brings everything into being.

You are the Good that does all things perfectly.

Air is the most delicate and subtle part of matter. From air comes the soul, from the soul comes the mind, and from the mind comes God.

The Sixth Book, That in God Alone Is Good

God, Asclepius, exists only within Himself, and God Himself is the Good that always exists. If this is true, then God must be a being without movement or change, yet nothing can exist without Him. His essence carries out its work steadily and completely, lacking nothing and generously providing everything. There is one source of all things because it gives everything, and when I speak of the Good, I mean that which is always and completely good.

This Good belongs only to God. He desires nothing because He lacks nothing, and nothing can be taken from Him that would cause sorrow, for sorrow is a part of evil. Nothing is stronger than God to challenge Him, nor is there anything equal to Him to draw His love. He is not angered by anything, nor jealous of anything wiser, because none of these qualities exist within Him. Therefore, what remains in Him is only the Good. Just as He is free of evil, so the Good cannot be found in any other thing.

In everything else, whether large or small, individual or universal, passion and change are present. All created things are full of passion, for creation itself is a form of passion. Where there is passion, there is no Good, and where the Good is, there is no passion—just as day cannot exist where there is night, and night cannot exist where there is day. Thus, the Good cannot be found in things that are created, but only in that which was never created.

Although everything participates in material existence, this participation also extends to the Good in some way. The world is good in that it creates and produces, but beyond that, it is not good. It is subject to change, filled with movement, and brings forth things that are also subject to change. In humanity, what we call good exists only in comparison to what is evil. Here, what we call good is simply the smallest part of evil.

It is impossible for the Good to exist purely in this world because what is good here inevitably becomes evil. When the good turns into evil, it no longer remains good. Therefore, only in God does the Good truly exist—or rather, God Himself is the Good.

Among humans, the idea of the Good exists only as a name, for the thing itself cannot exist here. This is because the material body is surrounded by evils—suffering, desires, anger, deceit, and foolish ideas. Even worse, people believe that the things I have mentioned are the highest good, especially the pleasures of the body, which lead all other evils. In this way, error replaces the Good.

I thank God for placing this understanding in my mind, so I know that true Goodness cannot exist in this world. The world is filled with evil, but God is filled with Goodness. All beauty that appears in this world is purer and more perfect in the divine essence—and perhaps, beauty itself is the essence of God.

Asclepius, we can boldly say that if God has an essence, it must be beauty. However, no true Good exists in the world. Everything we can see is like an illusion or a shadow. What is unseen lasts forever, especially the essence of beauty and goodness. Just as the eye cannot see God, it also cannot see true beauty or the Good. These qualities are part of God, inseparable from Him, known only to Him, and deeply loved by Him.

If you understand God, you will also understand beauty and goodness. These qualities shine brightly, illuminating everything, and are illuminated in turn by God. Their radiance is beyond comparison, and their goodness cannot be copied, just as God Himself cannot be imitated. To know God is to know beauty and goodness, but these things cannot be shared with any other creature, for they remain one with God.

When you seek to understand God, you are also seeking beauty and goodness. There is only one way to find them—through devotion and knowledge. Those who are ignorant and lack devotion mistakenly call people beautiful and good, never realizing what true goodness is. Trapped in evil, they believe that evil is good. They cling to it and fear losing it, and they strive endlessly not only to keep it but to increase it.

These are the things people consider good and beautiful. We cannot truly love or hate these things, for the greatest challenge is that we need them and cannot live without them.

The Seventh Book, His Secret Sermon in The Mount of Regeneration, And The Profession of Silence

Father, in your teachings about divinity, you spoke in riddles and did not explain everything clearly. You said that no one can be saved without being reborn. When we climbed the mountain together, I asked you to teach me more about this rebirth, as it is the only thing I do not fully understand. You told me that I would learn it when I separated myself from the world. I have prepared myself and freed my mind from the distractions of the world.

Now, fulfill what you promised. Teach me about rebirth, whether openly or secretly. I don't know what substance or seed brings about this new birth, nor what kind of womb it comes from.

This knowledge, my son, must be understood in silence. The true Good is the seed of this rebirth.

But who plants this seed, Father? I am still confused and uncertain.

The seed is sown by the will of God, my son.

What kind of man is born through this process? I still cannot fully grasp it.

The one who is reborn becomes a child of God, a new person with divine understanding. God created the universe, filling it with all kinds of powers.

Father, you speak in riddles again and not plainly, as a father should speak to his son.

Son, this is not something that can be taught directly. It is given by God when He wills it, and He helps us remember it.

You are speaking of things that seem too distant and impossible, Father. I must challenge what you are saying.

Will you deny your father's wisdom, my son?

Please forgive me, Father. I am your son by nature. Tell me clearly how rebirth happens.

There is nothing more I can say than this: I have experienced a vision, given to me through God's mercy. I have left behind my old self and entered into an immortal body. I am not who I was before, for I have been reborn in mind.

This truth cannot be taught or seen with physical eyes. I left behind the material world, stepping away from it. Though I once knew and touched it, I am now separated from it.

Even if you look at me with your eyes, you cannot understand what I have become. Your physical sight will not reveal it.

Father, you have confused me deeply. I no longer know what to think about myself.

I wish, my son, that you could leave yourself behind as in a dream, when the mind roams free during sleep.

Then tell me, Father, who brings about this rebirth?

It is the child of God, created through the will of God.

You have silenced me, Father. All my previous thoughts have vanished. I now see only the emptiness in the things of this world, as they constantly change and decay. What is real, Father?

What is real, my son, is that which is not troubled or confined, not colored or shaped, not changed by anything. It is pure, high, and unchanging, understood only by itself and without form.

You have made me feel lost, Father. I thought you were leading me to wisdom, but now I feel my mind slipping away.

Yet it is exactly as I have said, my son. Those who focus only on things that rise like fire, fall like earth, flow like water, or move like air, cannot grasp what has no shape, weight, or form. They cannot understand what can only be known through its power and action. I pray to the divine Mind to reveal to us the meaning of this rebirth.

Father, I don't think I can understand it.

God forbid, my son. You must seek Him, and He will come to you. Be willing, and it will happen. Quiet the senses of your body, and free yourself from the desires that trap you in the material world.

Do I really have these traps within me, Father?

Yes, my son, and there are many of them. Some are quite powerful.

I don't know them, Father. What are they?

Ignorance is one. Sorrow is another. There is also lack of self-control, desire, injustice, greed, deceit, envy, fraud, anger, recklessness, and malice. These twelve are just the beginning. Many others torment the soul through the body, forcing it to suffer deeply.

These forces do not leave easily, even from those who receive God's mercy. This is both the challenge and the purpose of rebirth.

So now, my son, stay silent and praise God in your heart. In silence, we open ourselves to God's mercy, which will never fail us.

Rejoice, my son, for you are now cleansed by the power of God and ready to know the truth.

The knowledge of God has been revealed to us, casting out all ignorance. With knowledge comes joy, and when joy arrives, sorrow is driven away from those who embrace it.

Let us welcome temperance, the sweet power that brings self-control. When temperance arrives, it casts out all excess and restores balance.

Next, we embrace self-discipline, which gives us control over our desires. This, my son, is the firm foundation of justice.

See how, without effort, self-discipline has driven away injustice. When injustice is gone, we are made just.

Then comes the power of generosity, which removes greed from within us.

And when greed is gone, we welcome truth. With truth, all falsehood and deceit vanish.

See, my son, how the Good is made complete by the arrival of Truth. With Truth comes the end of envy, for Truth always brings the Good, along with Life and Light. Darkness and its torments disappear, fleeing suddenly and in confusion, unable to remain.

You now understand the process of rebirth, for when these ten powers arrive, the intellectual rebirth is complete. These powers drive away the twelve torments, as we have witnessed in the process of this transforma-

166

tion. Whoever receives this rebirth through God's mercy leaves behind all physical senses and realizes that they are made of divine things. Such a person rejoices, becoming stable and unchanging through God's work.

I understand now, Father, not with my physical eyes, but through the power of the mind. I feel present in heaven, on earth, in water, in air, in living beings, in plants, and in the womb—everywhere.

Please tell me one more thing. How do the twelve torments of darkness get expelled by the ten powers? How does this work, Trismegistus?

This body, my son, is like the circle of the zodiac, made up of twelve parts but also connected as one whole. All of nature uses different combinations to mislead humans. Although these forces seem separate, they act together. For example, anger always follows rashness. These forces are chaotic, and that is why they are driven away by the ten powers—powers that align with the dead.

The number ten, my son, is the giver of souls. It is where Life and Light unite, and from this unity, the spirit brings forth the power of oneness. In this way, the number ten represents unity, and unity contains the number ten.

Now I see both the universe and myself clearly within the mind, Father.

This is what rebirth means, my son: that we no longer fix our thoughts on the physical body, which exists in three dimensions. As we have discussed, we must not misjudge the universe by focusing only on the material.

Tell me, Father, will this body made of powers ever dissolve?

Speak carefully, my son, and do not entertain impossible thoughts. Doing so leads the mind away from truth and into error.

The physical body, being part of nature, is subject to decay. But the spiritual generation is not—it is beyond decay and immortal. Do you not understand that you are born a god, a child of the One, just as I am?

Father, I wish I could hear that hymn of praise you mentioned, the one you heard from the Powers when I was still within the Octonary.

As Pimander revealed to the Octonary, "You are right to seek the dissolution of the physical body, for you have been purified." Pimander, the mind of supreme authority, has shared only what is written, knowing that I can understand and perceive everything on my own. He commanded me to act only in ways that are good, and so the powers within me sing in harmony.

I wish to hear this song and understand it, Father.

Be still, my son, and listen closely to the hymn of thanksgiving—the hymn of rebirth. I had not intended to speak of it so clearly, but I will reveal it to you now, at the end of everything.

This teaching is not something that can be spoken openly; it must be kept in silence.

So now, my son, stand in the open air. Offer your worship while facing the north wind as the sun sets, and turn toward the south when the sun rises. Now, remain silent.

THE SECRET SONG. The Holy Speech.

Let all of nature listen to this hymn. Open up, O Earth, and release all the treasures of the rain. Trees, do not tremble, for I will sing and praise the Lord, the Creator of all things, the One who is everything. Open, O Heavens, and you Winds, be still, so the eternal circle of God may receive these words. I will sing and praise the One who created everything, who set the earth in place, who hung the heavens above, and commanded the sweet waters of the ocean to flow throughout the world, to nourish both inhabited and uninhabited lands, providing for all things and all people.

He gave fire to shine for every purpose, to serve both gods and men. Let us all give blessing to the One who rides through the heavens, the Creator of all nature. He is the eye of the mind, and He accepts the praises from within me. All the powers within me, praise the One and the All. Join with my will, all you powers within me, and sing with me. O holy knowledge, through your light I magnify the divine light, rejoicing in the joy of the mind.

Sing with me, all the powers that dwell within me. Now, my self-discipline, praise with me. Righteousness, sing with me and celebrate what is just. O spirit of communion within me, offer praise to the All. Through me, truth gives praise to truth, and the good praises the good. O Life and Light, we offer this praise and thanksgiving to you. I thank you, O

Father, for the work of the powers within me. I thank you, O God, for being the source of all my actions. Through me, the Word sings praise to you. Receive this offering of words as a reasonable sacrifice.

The powers within me cry out these praises, fulfilling your will. Your will flows from you and returns to you. O All, receive this offering of reason from everything that exists. O Life, save all that is within us. O Light, shine upon us. O God, guide the spirit, for the mind sustains the Word. O Spirit-bearing Creator, you are God. Through fire, air, earth, water, and spirit, your creation calls out to you.

From the beginning, I have found ways to bless and praise you, and I have gained what I sought—for I rest in your will.

Father, I see that you have sung this hymn with all your heart, and I have taken it into my world.

Speak of your inner world, my son.

Yes, Father, I mean my inner world. Through your hymn and words of praise, my mind has been filled with light. I wish to send my own thanks and praise to God from my understanding.

Do so carefully, my son.

It will come from my mind, Father.

The things I have seen and contemplated, I have shared with you. Now, my son Tat, the source of future generations, send these offerings of reason to God.

O God, you are the Father, the Lord, and the Mind. Accept these offerings of reason, which you have asked of me. All things happen according to your will, O Mind. My son, offer this pleasing sacrifice to God, the Father of all. Speak these words aloud as well.

Thank you, Father, for teaching me how to offer thanks and praise.

I am pleased, my son, to see truth bear the fruits of good things and immortal blessings. Learn this lesson from me: above all virtues, treasure silence. Do not share the sacred knowledge of rebirth with others, lest we be misunderstood or criticized. We have reflected enough—you through listening and I through speaking. Now you know yourself and our Father through the mind.

The Eighth Book, The Greatest Evil in Man Is The Not Knowing God

Where are you headed, O men, drunk from the strong wine of ignorance? If you cannot bear it, why do you keep indulging and spilling it out again?

Stop, clear your minds, and lift your gaze with the eyes of your heart. And if not all of you can do this, let at least those who are able make the effort.

Ignorance surrounds the whole world like a poison, corrupting the soul trapped within the body, keeping it from reaching the harbor of salvation.

Don't let yourselves be swept along by the great current. Resist it if you can, and head toward the harbor of safety, steering your course directly toward it.

Search for someone who can take you by the hand and guide you to the doorway of truth and knowledge, where pure light shines without any darkness, where no one is drunk but all are sober and lift their hearts toward the One who desires to be known.

He cannot be heard with ears, nor seen with eyes, nor described with words, but only understood with the mind and heart.

First, you must tear apart the garment you wear—the web of ignorance that binds you. It is the source of all evil, the chain of corruption, the dark covering over your soul, a kind of living death. It is a burden you carry everywhere, a thief in your own home, pretending to love you but truly hating and envying you.

This harmful garment weighs you down, pulling you downward to keep you from looking upward and seeing the beauty of truth and the good that rests within it. If you saw it, you would despise the wickedness of this garment and recognize the traps it has set for you.

This garment works hard to make things that seem real feel pleasing to your senses. It hides what is truly real by covering it with distractions and burdens, filling your mind with harmful pleasures. As a result, you cannot hear what you need to hear or see what you need to see.

The Ninth Book,
A Universal Sermon to Asclepius

Everything that moves, Asclepius, must move in something and be moved by something, correct?

Yes, that's true.

Doesn't the space where something moves need to be larger than the thing that is moving within it?

Yes, it must be.

And isn't the force that moves something stronger than the thing being moved?

Yes, it is.

Then wouldn't the space in which something moves have to be opposite in nature to the thing being moved?

Yes, it must be.

Now, isn't this vast world a body, and isn't it the greatest of all bodies?

Yes, it is.

And isn't it solid, filled with many great bodies and, in fact, with all bodies that exist?

That's true.

The world is a body, and it moves, right?

Yes, it does.

Then what kind of space can hold something as large as the world and allow it to move freely? It must be far larger, so the world has room to move without being stopped or hindered, right?

Yes, it must be immense. But what kind of space would that be?

It must be something opposite in nature to a body, Asclepius. And isn't the nature of the non-physical opposite to that of the physical?

Yes, it is.

So, the space must be non-physical, and what is non-physical is either divine or God Himself. But by divine, I don't mean something created or born.

If it is divine, it is a kind of essence or being. But if it is God, it is something beyond essence, though it can be understood in a certain way.

God can be understood not by Himself but by us, because anything that can be understood is connected to a mind that perceives it.

Therefore, God does not understand Himself, since He is not separate from what He knows. But we are separate from Him, so we can understand Him.

If this space can be understood, then it is not just space—it is God. But if we understand God, we understand not a place but the way He acts and operates.

Everything that moves does so in something stable, not in another moving thing. And the force that causes movement remains stable while it moves other things, for it cannot move along with them.

But how is it, Trismegistus, that things here on Earth move along with other moving things? Didn't you say the wandering stars are moved by a fixed sphere?

That's not exactly what I meant, Asclepius. The wandering stars and the fixed sphere don't move together but in opposition to one another. They move in opposite ways, and that opposition creates a kind of balance, where movement is stabilized by resistance.

For example, the Bear constellation neither rises nor sets but keeps circling in place. Do you think it moves or stays still?

I think it moves, Trismegistus.

What kind of movement do you think it has?

It moves in a circular path, always revolving around the same point.

Exactly. The circular movement appears as though it's standing still because it moves in a way that keeps it bound to the same path. The opposition of these movements creates stability, keeping everything in place.

Let me give you a simple example from Earth. Consider a man swimming. As the water flows one way, he pushes against it with his hands and feet, holding his position. This resistance keeps him from being carried away or sinking beneath the water.

That's a very clear example, Trismegistus.

So, every movement depends on something stable and is guided by that stability.

The motion of the world and all material things does not come from outside the world but from within it, through a soul, a spirit, or some other non-physical force.

A lifeless body cannot move itself, nor can anything that is entirely lifeless.

But what do you mean, Trismegistus? Don't things like wood, stones, and other inanimate objects move too?

No, Asclepius, not on their own. Something within them causes movement. It's not the body itself that moves, but something alive within it that moves both the object carrying it and the object being carried. One lifeless thing cannot move another—only something alive can cause movement.

Do you see now how the soul is burdened when it carries two bodies?

Yes, and it's clear now that everything that moves must move within and be moved by something.

Doesn't this mean, Trismegistus, that things moving in this world must be moving through empty space?

Be careful, Asclepius. Nothing that exists is truly empty. Only what does not exist can be called empty, for it is entirely outside of existence.

What exists must be full of being, for something that exists cannot be empty.

But aren't some things empty, Trismegistus, like an empty barrel, an empty jug, or an empty wine press?

Oh, Asclepius, you are mistaken. These things, which you believe to be empty, are actually full.

What do you mean, Trismegistus?

Isn't air a kind of body?

Yes, it is.

Then doesn't this body, air, pass through everything and fill everything it touches? And isn't air made up of a mixture of the four elements? So, all the things you call empty are actually full of air.

Instead of calling them empty, you should call them hollow, because they exist and are filled with air and spirit.

That makes perfect sense, Trismegistus. But what should we call the space where the entire universe moves?

Call it incorporeal, Asclepius.

What does that mean—incorporeal or without a body?

It refers to the mind and reason, which encompass everything and exist without a physical form. It cannot be touched or seen, and it is unaffected by anything physical. It is self-sufficient, capable of everything, and is the essence behind all things.

From it come goodness, truth, the original light, and the essence of the soul, like rays from the sun.

Then what is God?

God is none of these things directly, yet He is the source of them all. He is the cause of everything that exists, leaving nothing without being.

Everything that exists comes from things that already are, not from things that are not, because something that doesn't exist cannot produce anything. And what already exists cannot simply stop existing.

So, what exactly is God?

God is not just a mind, but the cause of mind. He is not just a spirit, but the cause of spirit. He is not light, but the cause of light.

Therefore, we must honor God with the two names that belong to Him alone: the Good and the Father.

He is nothing else beyond these names. Everything else is separate from the nature of goodness.

Neither the body nor the soul can contain true goodness.

The greatness of the Good is as vast as the existence of all things, both physical and non-physical, both visible and invisible.

This is the Good—God Himself.

Be careful never to call anything else good, for that would be disrespectful. And never call anyone else God, for only the Good is God.

Many people speak the word "good," but most do not understand what it truly means. Out of ignorance, they call gods and even people "good," though neither can ever truly be so.

The other gods are honored with the title of "god," but God is known as the Good—not by status in the heavens but by His very nature.

There is only one nature of God, and that is the Good. All kinds of beings come from this one source.

The one who is good gives everything and takes nothing. This is why God gives all things freely without ever receiving.

The other title we give Him is the Father, for it is the role of a father to create and give life.

That is why it has always been important for wise and virtuous people to have children.

On the other hand, to remain childless is seen as a misfortune and a wrongdoing. Those who die without children are punished by the spirits, for their souls are condemned to enter bodies that are neither male nor female—a cursed existence beneath the sun.

So, Asclepius, never celebrate a man's childlessness. Instead, pity him, knowing the punishment that awaits him after death.

Let this be a glimpse into the deeper truths of nature.

The Tenth Book, The Mind To Hermes

Hold your speech, Hermes, and reflect on what has been said. But I will speak what is on my mind, for many people have shared different ideas about the universe and goodness, yet I have not discovered the truth.

May the Lord reveal the truth to me now, for I will trust only your explanation of these matters.

Then the Mind spoke of how everything is connected.

God and all things exist together.

God, Eternity, the World, Time, and Generation.

God created Eternity, Eternity created the World, the World brought forth Time, and Time brought about Generation.

From God comes goodness, beauty, blessedness, and wisdom.

From Eternity comes identity and consistency.

From the World comes order.

From Time comes change.

From Generation come life and death.

The workings of God are Mind and Soul.

Eternity brings permanence and immortality.

The World undergoes restoration and decay.

Time brings growth and decline.

Generation gives rise to different qualities.

Eternity belongs to God.

The World exists within Eternity.

Time operates within the World.

Generation unfolds within Time.

Eternity surrounds God.

The World moves within Eternity.

Time unfolds within the World.

Generation occurs within Time.

Therefore, God is the source of all things.

Eternity is the substance behind everything.

The World is the material that holds all things.

Eternity is the power of God.

The World, although ever-changing, is continuously created through the timeless nature of Eternity.

Nothing will ever be destroyed because Eternity is incorruptible.

Nor can anything perish within the World, as it is embraced by the eternal.

The wisdom of God consists of goodness, beauty, blessedness, virtue, and eternity.

Eternity grants matter immortality and everlasting nature, as Generation relies on Eternity just as Eternity relies on God.

Generation and Time operate in both Heaven and on Earth, but their nature differs: in Heaven, they are unchanging and incorruptible, while on Earth, they are subject to change and decay.

God is the soul of Eternity. Eternity is the soul of the World. Heaven is the soul of the Earth.

God resides within the Mind, the Mind within the Soul, and the Soul within matter—all sustained through Eternity.

The entire universe, and everything within it, is filled with soul. The soul holds the Mind, and the Mind is filled with God.

God fills everything from within and holds all things from without, giving life to the universe.

Externally, God gives life to the world, and internally, He breathes life into all living things.

Above, in Heaven, He remains constant and unchanging, while below on Earth, He governs the cycles of birth and transformation.

Eternity encompasses the World, whether through necessity, divine guidance, or natural law.

If anyone thinks otherwise, they misunderstand, for God governs everything.

God's power surpasses all, and nothing can compare, whether human or divine.

Do not mistake anything on Earth or in Heaven as being like God, for such a comparison would be false.

Nothing can resemble the One who is unlike anything else, nor has God shared His power with anything else.

Who else could create life, immortality, or transformation? And what else would God need to make?

God is not idle; if He were, everything would cease to be, for everything is sustained by Him.

There is no idleness anywhere in the universe, for nothing is empty of purpose—both the doer and the deed must exist.

All things must continue according to the nature of each place and being.

The One who creates is present in all things, yet He is not confined by anything. He does not focus on just one task but creates everything.

As the source of action and power, He sustains everything that exists, both beneath Him and under His command.

Look through my eyes, and you will see the world clearly and understand its beauty.

The world is a body that endures forever. Though ancient, it remains youthful and full of life.

Observe the seven heavenly realms above us, each following its own unchanging course, filling eternity with endless movement.

Everything is filled with light, yet fire is not found within it.

The harmonious blending of opposites creates light, through the operation of God, the source of all good, order, and harmony in the seven realms.

Look also upon the Moon, which leads the other heavenly bodies. It serves as an instrument of nature, guiding the transformations of matter here on Earth.

Behold the Earth at the center of all things, serving as the stable foundation of the world, nourishing and sustaining all earthly creatures.

Think about how many immortal and mortal beings exist, and notice how the Moon moves between both realms, touching both mortal and immortal things.

Everything is full of soul, and it is the soul that moves all things. Some things move around the heavens, and others move on the Earth. Yet none of them switch places—what is on the right does not go to the left, nor do things above descend downward, or things below rise upward.

You already know, Hermes, that all these things are created.

They are bodies with souls, and because they have souls, they are in motion.

But for all things to come together in unity, something must hold them together.

There must be a single force that brings everything into one.

Since the motions are so different, and the bodies are not alike, but still follow one orderly flow, it's clear that there cannot be more than one creator.

One creator alone ensures harmony in this order.

If there were many creators, they would envy each other, and that would lead to conflict.

If one creator made mortal beings, he would want to create immortal beings as well. Similarly, the creator of immortal beings would seek to make mortal ones.

And if there were two creators, which one would take charge of the future?

If both shared the responsibility, who would hold the greater power?

Every living being consists of both matter and soul, and is made of both mortal and immortal parts.

All living things have souls. The things that are lifeless are just raw matter.

The soul, as it draws closer to its creator, brings life and existence to everything. And because it is tied to life, it becomes the cause of immortality as well.

So what makes mortal beings different from immortal ones?

If the soul can create life and immortality, how could it not also create living beings?

It is clear that something is behind all of this, and it is just as clear that this force is one.

There is one soul, one life, and one matter.

And who else could this be but the One God?

Who else would have any reason to create life but God alone?

Therefore, there is only one God.

It would be absurd to say there is one world, one Sun, one Moon, and one divine order, yet believe in many gods.

This one God works through many things.

If you yourself are capable of doing many things—seeing, speaking, hearing, smelling, tasting, touching, walking, understanding, and breathing—why would it be difficult for God to create life, soul, immortality, and change?

It is not as though one part of you sees, another part hears, another speaks, and so on. It is one being—yourself—who does all these things.

In the same way, God is behind everything, for nothing can happen without Him.

Just as you would no longer be alive if you stopped doing all these things, God would not be God if He stopped creating.

And since nothing in the universe can remain idle or empty, how much more is this true for God?

If there were anything He could not do, it would mean He was imperfect, which is impossible.

Since God is perfect and never idle, He does everything.

Now listen carefully, Hermes. You will see that it is necessary for God to create everything that exists, has existed, or will exist.

This, my dear friend, is life.

This is beauty.

This is goodness.

This is God.

If you want to understand this through your own actions, think about what happens when you create something.

However, God is not driven by pleasure, nor does He have anyone else working alongside Him.

Being the sole creator, God is always working, and what He makes is part of Himself.

If anything were separated from Him, it would cease to exist, for nothing can live apart from Him.

Since all things in Heaven and on Earth are alive through Him, and since one life flows through all, everything is made by God.

Life is the union of mind and soul.

Death is not the destruction of what has been united, but the separation of their union.

The image of God is Eternity. The image of Eternity is the World. The image of the World is the Sun. And the image of the Sun is humanity.

People say that change is death because the body dissolves, and life returns to what is unseen.

But I tell you, Hermes, the world only changes; it does not dissolve. Each day, part of it becomes invisible, but it is never lost.

These are the transformations of the world—revolutions and hidden cycles. A revolution is a turning, and what is hidden is renewed.

The world is not shaped by things outside it but constantly changes within itself.

If the world is filled with forms, then what must its creator be like? The creator cannot be without form.

And if the creator is filled with every form, He will remain in harmony with the world. But if He had only one form, He would exist apart from the world and its cycles.

We must be careful not to question God with words, for we cannot know anything about Him with doubt in our minds.

God has a single idea, unique to Him. Because this idea is not physical, it cannot be seen, though it reveals itself through all physical forms.

Do not be surprised that such an incorruptible idea exists.

It is like the margins of written words. They may seem to rise and stand out, but in reality, they are smooth and level.

Understand this truth clearly: just as man cannot live without life, God cannot exist without doing good.

Doing good is the life and movement of God. He brings everything into motion and gives life to all.

Some of what I have said needs further explanation, so pay close attention.

Everything exists within God, but not as if placed in a physical space. Space is both physical and unchanging, while things that occupy space cannot move.

What lies within the unbodily is not the same as what appears to be in the physical world.

God contains everything, and nothing is greater, swifter, or stronger than what is not bound by a physical body. The unbodily is limitless in capacity, speed, and power.

To understand this, command your soul to go to a far-off place, like India. It will arrive there even faster than you can speak the command.

Tell it to cross the ocean, and it will instantly be there—not by traveling, but by simply being there.

Command your soul to fly into the heavens, and it will rise without wings. Nothing can stop it—not the heat of the sun, not the ether, not the movements of the stars. It will pass through everything and reach the furthest heights.

If you wish to see what lies beyond the universe, you can.

This is the power and speed your soul holds. If you can do such things, how could God not do the same?

Now, think of God as holding the entire universe within His mind, as if it were all thoughts or ideas.

To understand God, you must become like Him.

Only something like God can understand God.

You must expand yourself beyond all limits—beyond the physical body, beyond time itself. Become one with eternity, and only then will you grasp the nature of God.

Believe that nothing is impossible for you. Consider yourself immortal, capable of understanding everything—every art, every science, and every way of life.

Imagine yourself as greater than the highest heights and deeper than the lowest depths. Contain within yourself the qualities of all things: fire, water, dryness, moisture. Be everywhere at once—in the sea, on the earth.

Understand yourself as unborn, young, old, alive, and dead, all at the same time. Know everything about time, places, actions, qualities, and amounts. Only by doing so will you begin to understand God.

But if you lock your soul within your body and misuse it, saying, "I understand nothing. I can do nothing. I am afraid of the sea. I cannot reach the heavens. I don't know who I am. I don't know what I will become," then you have no connection to God.

You will not be able to understand the beauty and goodness of God. Instead, you will be tied to the desires of the body and all that is evil.

The greatest evil is not knowing God.

But the path to knowing Him is simple: you must desire to know, hope to understand, and believe in your ability to do so. This is the divine way, the way of goodness.

This path will appear to you everywhere—when you are awake or asleep, sailing or traveling, speaking or silent, by day or night.

For everything reflects the image of God.

Though you say that God is invisible, nothing is clearer than Him.

He made all things so that you could see Him in everything.

This is God's goodness and power—to make Himself known and visible in all things.

Even what is not physical can still be seen.

The mind is seen through understanding, and God is seen through creation and action.

Let this be clear to you, Hermes.

Apply this same way of thinking to everything, and you will not go astray.

The Eleventh Book
The Common Mind, To Tat

The Mind, Tat, is part of God's essence, if God has any essence that we can know. Only God knows exactly what that essence is. The Mind is not separate from God's essence but connected to it, like the light from the sun. In humans, this Mind is God, which makes some humans nearly divine, with their humanity closely connected to divinity. The good spirit even called the gods "immortal men" and referred to men as "mortal gods."

In animals, which lack reason, the Mind works as their natural instinct. Where there is a soul, there is a mind, just as where there is life, there is a soul. In creatures without reason, the soul provides life but lacks the operations of the Mind. In humans, however, the Mind guides the soul toward goodness. In animals, it cooperates with their instincts, but in humans, it works against their lower desires.

Once the soul enters the body, it becomes corrupted by sorrow, pain, and pleasure. These emotions flow from the physical body, and the soul is stained by them, like a sponge absorbing liquid. But when the Mind leads the soul, it offers its light, resisting the soul's tendencies toward pleasure and false beliefs. Just as a skilled doctor may hurt the body to heal it by cutting or burning away disease, the Mind causes discomfort to the soul by pulling it away from pleasure, the source of spiritual sickness. The greatest sickness of the soul is denying God, which leads to all other evils and blocks all good.

The Mind helps the soul, just as a physician heals the body. But those souls that reject the guidance of the Mind are left to follow their desires, much like animals. These people give in to every craving, moving toward a life like that of beasts. They act with anger and desire without reason, never satisfied and always trapped in their impulses. Uncontrolled anger and unchecked desires are among the worst evils.

To prevent this, God placed the Mind within humans as a judge, to correct and restrain them.

You mentioned earlier, Tat, that fate determines our actions, so what happens when someone does evil like adultery or theft? If these actions are determined by fate, how can the person be held responsible and punished? Isn't that unjust?

Everything, Tat, happens according to fate. Nothing, good or bad, happens without it. But it is also part of fate that those who commit evil must suffer the consequences of their actions. They are destined to experience the results of what they do, and they do wrong so that they may endure punishment. Let's leave this discussion about fate and evil for now, though, as we've explored it before.

Right now, we are discussing the Mind and its role. In animals, the Mind works through instinct, but in humans, it restrains both anger and desire. Some humans follow reason, while others do not. But all are subject to fate, change, and the cycle of birth and death. These are the boundaries set by fate. Everyone must experience what fate has decreed.

However, those guided by the Mind experience these things differently. Although they may suffer the same external troubles, they do not suffer in the same way as those who are ruled by anger and desire.

What do you mean, Father? Isn't someone who commits adultery or murder an evil person?

The one ruled by the Mind, my son, does not suffer punishment as the adulterer or murderer does. They may face the consequences of actions, but not because they are consumed by evil themselves. Change is unavoidable, but those with the Mind's guidance can escape the grip of vice.

I once heard the good spirit say, though he did not write it down, that everything is connected as one, especially things understood by the Mind. All that exists is part of one reality. We exist in action, power, and eternity.

A good soul is one with the Mind, and when the soul is united with the Mind, it is connected to all things. Therefore, all things known through the Mind are united. Just as the Mind governs everything, the soul that comes from God can do whatever it wills.

This answers the question you asked earlier about the connection between fate and the Mind. If you withdraw from arguments and distractions, you will see that the soul connected to the Mind is above fate and the laws that bind ordinary things. Nothing is impossible for the Mind, not even what fate controls.

Even though the soul is above fate, it should still pay attention to the things governed by fate. This, Tat, is what the good spirit taught.

Father, your words are insightful and profound, but I still need clarity on one thing. You said that in animals, the Mind follows their natural instincts. But if the Mind cooperates with these instincts, which are driven by emotions and desires, does that mean the Mind itself becomes emotional and driven by passions?

That's an excellent question, my son. And you are right to ask it. Let me explain.

All non-physical things that exist in the body are subject to emotions, and in a way, they are emotions themselves. Everything that causes movement is non-physical, while everything that is moved is physical. The Mind causes movement, and through movement, both the mover and the thing being moved experience emotion. Even rulers and those they rule experience emotions through this movement. When the soul is freed from the body, it is also freed from these emotions.

In truth, nothing in existence is completely free from emotion; everything is affected by it in some way. But there is a difference between emotion itself and the thing that experiences it. Emotions cause actions, while those affected by emotions experience them. Physical bodies act in one way or another—they either stay still or move—and both states are forms of emotional experience. Non-physical things, on the other hand, are always active, and because of this, they too experience emotion.

Don't let these words confuse you, though. Action and emotion are closely connected, but it is more respectful to use the word "action."

Consider this as well: God has given humanity two great gifts—Mind and Reason. These gifts are so powerful that they are equal to immortality. If someone uses these gifts correctly, they will be no different from the gods. When they leave their physical body, these gifts will guide them to join the divine beings.

Do other living creatures have speech, Father?

No, my son. They only have voice. There is a big difference between speech and voice. Speech belongs to all of humanity, while voice belongs to individual creatures according to their kind.

But Father, people speak differently in different countries.

That is true, but just as all people are part of humanity, speech is still one. It may sound different in Egypt, Persia, or Greece, but its essence remains the same everywhere. You seem to underestimate the power and importance of speech, my son. The good spirit once revealed that the soul belongs in the body, the mind in the soul, and speech in the mind, with God as the source of all.

Speech is the expression of the mind, just as the mind reflects God. The body is the form of an idea, and the idea flows from the soul. The most subtle part of matter is air, from which the soul emerges. From the soul comes the mind, and from the mind comes God.

God is present in everything and through everything. The mind governs the soul, the soul controls the air, and the air surrounds matter. Meanwhile, destiny, providence, and nature are tools that shape the material world.

All non-physical things share the same essence, which is identity. But physical things are made up of many parts that change, even though their underlying identity remains the same. In every physical object, there is a certain number, and without numbers, nothing can be built, combined, or dissolved. Numbers are born from unity, and when they dissolve, they return to unity.

All things are united by matter. This entire world is like a great god, connected to a higher one, and it is filled with life through the will of the Father. Nothing in the world, whether as a whole or in its parts, is without life. There is nothing dead in the world—nothing that was, is, or will be. The Father wants the world to be alive for as long as it exists, and because of that, it must also be divine.

How can anything be dead in a universe that reflects God and is filled with life? Death is decay, and decay is destruction. But nothing in an incorruptible world can decay, and nothing connected to God can be destroyed.

But don't living things in the world die, Father?

Be careful with your words, my son. What you call "death" is just the dissolving of physical forms. Dissolution is not the same as destruction. Things are not dissolved to disappear but to be made new.

What, then, is life? Isn't it movement?

Yes, and everything in the world is in motion, my son.

But Father, doesn't the Earth seem still?

No, my son. It moves in many ways, even though it may seem stable. It would be strange if the Earth, which gives life to all things, did not move. Nothing can create life without movement. It is absurd to think that any part of the universe could be inactive, for inactivity means nothingness.

Everything in the world moves either by growing or by diminishing. Whatever moves also has life, but life does not need to stay the same. While the universe as a whole remains unchanged, its parts are always changing. Yet nothing is ever truly destroyed. What troubles people is not reality but the names they use for things.

Creation is not the same as life; it is the process of making things visible. Likewise, change is not death; it is the hiding of what once was. All things—matter, life, spirit, soul, and mind—are immortal. Every living thing is immortal because of the mind within it, but especially humans, who receive God and communicate with Him.

God speaks to people in many ways—through dreams at night and through signs during the day. He also gives messages through birds, the wind, and even trees.

Humans have the unique ability to understand what has happened in the past, what is happening now, and what will happen in the future. Think also, my son, about how other creatures only live in specific parts of the world. Fish live in water, land animals on the earth, and birds in the air. But humans interact with all elements—earth, water, air, and even fire—and they experience the heavens through their senses.

God, however, exists everywhere and in everything. He is both action and power. Understanding God is not as difficult as it may seem. If you wish to see him, look at the necessity in all things around you and the way events unfold with purpose. Notice how life fills the material world and how God moves everything—bringing good into gods, spirits, and people alike.

If these things are indeed actions, as you've said, then they are performed by none other than God. Just as the world has its different parts—heaven, earth, water, and air—God has his aspects, which include life, immortality, eternity, spirit, necessity, providence, nature, soul, and mind. All of these parts remain constant and are part of what we call the Good.

There is no place, no moment, and no thing—past or present—where God is absent.

What about matter, Father? Does God exist in matter as well?

How could matter exist without God? If you imagine matter as an inactive pile of material, you misunderstand its nature. If it is active, then it must be God who gives it motion. We've already said that actions are the parts of God. So, who brings life to living things? Who grants immortality to the eternal? Who causes things to change? All of these processes come from God.

Whether we speak of matter, body, or essence, we are talking about acts of God. Matter behaves as matter because of God. Bodies exist as physical things through his power, and essence becomes what it is through him. God is present in everything. There is nothing within creation that is not part of God.

This means that we cannot think of God in terms of size, place, shape, or even time. He is all things, present in all things, and beyond all things. Worship this truth, my son. The only way to truly serve God is to live without doing evil.

The Twelfth Book,
His Crater or Monas

The Creator made the universe, not with hands, but through His Word. Think of Him as always present everywhere, creating everything by His will. His body is not something you can touch, see, measure, or contain. It isn't fire, water, air, or wind, though all these come from Him. Being the ultimate Good, He has taken that name for Himself alone.

He also adorned the Earth with divine beauty and sent humanity into the world—both immortal and mortal beings at once. Humans are above other creatures and the rest of creation because they have both speech and mind. Humans witness the works of God, marvel at them, and recognize Him as the Creator.

While God gave speech to all people, He did not give mind to everyone. Yet, He did not withhold it out of envy, for envy does not reach Him. It exists only in the hearts of people without the gift of mind.

Why, Father, didn't God give mind to everyone?

Because it pleased Him to place it in the center of all souls as a reward to be earned.

Where did He place it?

He filled a great cup with mind and sent it down, along with a messenger to make an announcement.

The messenger proclaimed to all souls: "Come, all who are able, and immerse yourselves in this cup. Those who believe they will return to the One who sent this cup, and those who know their true purpose, come and take part."

Those who understood the message and immersed themselves in the mind became enlightened and perfect, sharing in knowledge. But those who missed the call received only speech, not mind. They do not know why they were created or by whom. Their senses make them like animals, filled with anger and desires. They do not admire what is worthy of awe but chase after bodily pleasures, thinking that life was made only for these things.

However, those who receive God's gift are more like immortals than mortals. They understand all things on Earth, in the heavens, and even beyond. Rising above the world, they see the Good and recognize that staying here is a burden. They despise all things, both material and immaterial, and seek only the One.

This is what it means to know the mind—seeing the divine and understanding God. The cup filled with mind is itself divine.

And I, Father, wish to be immersed in that cup.

You cannot love yourself, my son, until you first reject your attachment to the body. Only by loving yourself will you receive the mind, and only by receiving the mind will you gain true knowledge.

What do you mean, Father?

You cannot focus on both mortal and divine things at the same time. Mortal things are tied to the body, while divine things are not. You must choose between the two, for no one can have both. Whichever you choose will grow stronger, while the other fades away.

Choosing the higher path brings out the best in a person and connects them with God. It shows reverence and devotion. But choosing the lower path leads to ruin, though it does not harm God. Those who follow the lower path are like performers in a show—they make a spectacle of themselves in the world, misled by bodily pleasures.

Since God has given us so much, let us also be generous, without holding back. God is pure and blameless; we are the ones who cause evil by choosing it over the Good.

See how many layers of existence we must pass through—how many spirits and stars we must rise above—to reach the One true God. The Good cannot be surpassed. It is infinite, without beginning or end, though it seems to begin for us when we first come to know it.

Our knowledge of the Good does not mark its true beginning, only the beginning of our awareness of it. Once we grasp that beginning, we can move quickly through all things.

It is difficult to turn away from the familiar things of this world and return to the ancient truths. The things we see attract us, making it hard to believe in what cannot be seen. The things most visible are often evil, while the Good remains hidden. The Good has no shape or form and resembles nothing else.

That is why the Good seems unlike everything else. An immaterial thing cannot be revealed to a physical body. This is the difference between things that are alike and those that are not. Things that are unlike always fall short of those that are alike.

The One is the root and source of all things. Nothing can exist without a beginning, but the Beginning itself has no origin—it exists by itself and is the foundation of everything else. Because it does not come from another, it simply is.

Unity is the beginning of all things, containing every number while being contained by none. It creates all numbers but is not created by any number.

Everything that is created or made is imperfect, meaning it can be divided, increased, or diminished. But what is truly perfect is not subject to any of these changes.

Whatever grows does so through unity, but if it lacks the strength to hold on to unity, it weakens, fades, and disappears.

This is the image of God that I have described to you as best as I can, Tat. If you carefully reflect on it with the eyes of your mind, you will find the path that leads to higher truths. In fact, the image itself will guide you toward them.

What is remarkable about this vision is that it draws those who are able to see it closer, holding them fast. It pulls them toward itself, just as a magnet attracts iron.

The Thirteenth Book, Sense And Understanding

Yesterday, Asclepius, I shared a complete teaching, but today I feel it is important to also talk about sense.

Sense and understanding seem to be different because sense is tied to the physical world, while understanding belongs to the essence of things. However, I believe they are closely connected in human beings. In other creatures, sense works with their nature, but in people, it is linked with understanding.

The mind is different from understanding, just as divinity is distinct from God. Divinity flows from God, and understanding flows from the mind. Understanding and speech work together; neither can exist fully without the other. You can't express words without understanding, and understanding isn't revealed without words.

In humans, sense and understanding are closely intertwined. It's impossible to fully understand without sense, and you can't experience sense without understanding. However, the mind can understand without sense for a time, such as when we dream and experience visions.

I believe that both sense and understanding are active in dreams, awakening the mind. A person's body and soul work together, and when they are in harmony, the mind produces understanding. The mind gives birth to thoughts. Good thoughts come from seeds planted by God, while harmful thoughts arise from seeds sown by demons.

There is no part of the world untouched by evil. Evil spirits secretly plant harmful seeds in the mind, leading people toward actions like adultery, murder, disrespect for parents, and other destructive deeds. These actions come from the seeds of evil spirits.

In contrast, God's seeds are fewer, but they are great, beautiful, and good—virtue, self-control, and piety. Piety is the knowledge of God. Those who know God are filled with good things and possess divine understanding, setting them apart from most people.

Because they have this knowledge, they often do not fit in with the majority. They may be misunderstood, mocked, or even hated. Some are killed because their understanding clashes with the wickedness that prevails on earth.

Wickedness resides on earth, not in the higher realms, even though some may wrongly claim otherwise. A person who knows God will reject wickedness and rise above it. Even though certain things seem evil to others, those who know God see everything as good.

They reflect deeply and come to see everything through the lens of knowledge. Amazingly, they can even turn bad things into something good.

Now, let's return to the topic of sense. Humans are unique because they combine sense with understanding. However, not every person achieves understanding. Some people are dominated by material desires, while others pursue essential truths.

Those focused on material things receive their understanding from evil spirits. But those who seek the good are connected to God. God works through nature, making all things good, just like Himself.

Even though God makes things good, the way they are used in the world can become unlawful or harmful. The movement of the universe generates different qualities, some leading to evil and others to goodness.

The world has its own sense and understanding, different from that of humans. The world's understanding is simpler and more unified. It creates all things and takes them back into itself, following God's will. The world acts as a tool of God, receiving seeds from Him, bringing things into existence, and renewing them through dissolution.

The world is like a farmer of life. When things die or break apart, it sows new seeds, giving birth to new life. Everything in the world is alive, and life flows from the world's constant movement. The world is both the source and the sustainer of life.

The elements that form bodies—earth, water, air, and fire—combine in various ways. Some bodies are more complex, while others are simpler. Heavier bodies are made from more elements, while lighter ones are made from fewer.

The movement of the world influences the qualities of everything born within it. The flow of life touches all things, shaping their nature.

God is the father of the world, and the world is the father of all things within it. The world is God's child, and everything within the world is a child of the world.

That's why the world is called an "ornament"—because it beautifully decorates everything with the endless variety of life. Through constant motion and the blending of elements, the world brings everything to life. This is why it is fitting to call it the world, for it adorns creation with unceasing life and beauty.

All living beings receive both sense and understanding from the outside, through what surrounds and sustains them. The world, having once received these gifts from God when it was created, still holds them today.

But God is not, as some mistakenly think through superstition, without sense or understanding. Everything that exists is in God, made by Him, and depends on Him. Some things operate through their bodies, others move through a soul-like essence, some are energized by a spirit, while others receive rest—everything functioning as it should.

It is more accurate to say that God does not possess these things, but instead is all things. He does not take anything in from outside but instead expresses everything outwardly. This is God's way of knowing and understanding—constantly moving everything.

There will never be a time when anything that exists will stop or disappear. When I speak of "things that are," I mean God. For everything that exists is part of God, and nothing exists apart from Him, just as He exists in everything.

If you understand these ideas, Asclepius, you will find them true. But if you do not understand, they may seem unbelievable. To understand is to believe, and not believing means you do not understand. Words alone cannot reach the truth, but the mind, guided by speech for a time, can eventually grasp it.

When the mind recognizes how everything connects and aligns with the truths shared through speech, it rests in trust and belief. For those who understand these teachings about God, they are believable, but for those who do not, they remain beyond belief.

This is what I have to say about understanding and sense.

The Fourteenth Book
Operation And Sense

The ability to sense and understand comes to all living beings from the outside, through the influence of what surrounds and sustains them. The world, having once received this gift from God at creation, continues to carry it within.

Some people mistakenly believe that God has no sense or understanding, but this is a misunderstanding born of superstition. In truth, everything exists in God, is made by God, and depends on Him. Some things work through their bodies, others move with a soul-like force, and some operate by spirit—all fitting perfectly into their roles.

It is not that God simply possesses these things, but rather He is all these things. He does not gather them from the outside but expresses them outwardly. God's way of knowing is to be the constant force that moves everything.

There will never be a time when what exists ceases or disappears. When I speak of "the things that are," I refer to God, for everything exists within God, and nothing can exist apart from Him, nor is He separate from anything.

If you understand these truths, Asclepius, they will seem clear and true. But if you do not understand, they will seem unbelievable. To understand is to believe, and to lack belief means you have not yet understood. Words alone cannot reach the full truth, but the mind, when guided by speech, can find its way to it.

When the mind sees how everything aligns with the truths we have discussed, it finds peace in belief. To those who understand what has been said about God, these things will seem credible. But for those who do not understand, they will seem impossible to believe.

This, then, is my teaching on the nature of understanding and sense.

Without these elements, the body would not be able to function. Other operations are specific to human souls, expressed through arts, sciences, studies, and actions. These operations also give rise to the senses, or at least perfect them.

Understand, my son, that these operations come from a higher source. While the senses belong to the body and arise from it, they only manifest once an operation brings them to life, making them seem physical. This is why I say that the senses are both physical and mortal. They exist only as long as the body exists, since they are born with the body and die with it.

Mortal things, however, do not have senses because they lack the necessary essence. The senses can only grasp physical experiences of good or bad that affect the body. But external objects do not receive or lose anything in the same way, so they do not have senses.

Do the senses work in every body, you ask? Yes, they do, my son. And do operations act in all things? Yes, even in lifeless things, though the senses differ. In rational beings, the senses operate with reason. In irrational creatures, the senses are purely physical. In lifeless things, the senses only react passively through growth and decay.

Passion and sense are connected at a higher level, both coming together through operations. In living creatures, two more forces follow the senses and passions—grief and pleasure. Without these, no living being, especially one capable of reason, could experience or understand anything.

I call these the ruling ideas of passion, especially in rational beings. Operations carry out actions, but the senses reveal these actions. Since the senses are connected to the lower parts of the soul, they can cause harm. What brings pleasure often becomes the source of suffering for the one who indulges in it. And sorrow brings even stronger pain, showing that both pleasure and sorrow are harmful forces.

The same is true of the soul's own sense. But isn't the soul non-physical, while the senses belong to the body, you ask? Or do the senses exist within the body? If we say that the senses belong in the body, we might mistakenly compare them to the soul or to operations, since both of these are non-physical but act through bodies.

However, the senses are neither operations, nor part of the soul, nor part of the body itself. They exist as something in between, as we have said before. Because the senses are not non-physical, they must be considered physical. Everything that exists is either a body or something without a body.

The Fifteenth Book, Truth To His Son Tat

Humans, being imperfect creatures made of many different parts, cannot speak about truth with complete confidence. True reality only exists in eternal things, where even their very nature is true. Fire is purely fire, earth is only earth, air is solely air, and water is entirely water. But our bodies are made of a mixture of all these elements, and because they are mixed, none of them can be fully true within us.

If our original nature didn't contain truth, how could we ever see, speak, or understand truth unless God allowed it? On Earth, what we see is not truth but only imitations of it, and even these are rare. Most things are filled with falsehood and deception, appearing only as images shaped by our imagination. When our imagination receives guidance from above, it can reflect some aspects of truth, but without that influence, it remains a lie.

An image may resemble the body it portrays, but it is not that body. It may have eyes but cannot see, and it may show ears but cannot hear. It deceives the viewer into believing they are seeing the real thing when in fact, it is just an illusion.

Those who do not recognize falsehood are able to see the truth. If we see things exactly as they are, we understand truth. But if we perceive them differently from what they are, we cannot grasp truth.

You ask if truth exists on Earth. The answer, my son, is no—truth cannot exist here because it cannot be created or made. However, some individuals, with God's guidance, might come to understand glimpses of it. To the mind and reason of men, nothing on Earth is truly real. Everything here is just an appearance, a fleeting image, or an opinion.

You ask whether speaking about things as they are can be called truth. But there is no real truth on Earth. You wonder how we can even claim to know that truth doesn't exist if nothing here is true. Understand this: truth is the most perfect virtue and the highest form of good. It is pure, unchangeable, and unaffected by the material world. It does not have a body and remains constant and clear.

The things here on Earth are always changing and decaying. They are temporary, corruptible, and full of imperfections. How can anything be true if it is always shifting and never remains the same? When something changes, it becomes a lie, showing us different forms instead of staying consistent.

You ask if humans can be considered true. As long as someone is human, they cannot be true. Truth belongs only to what stays unchanged and remains the same forever. Humans are made of many parts and do not remain the same. They change over time, both in appearance and in character, going through stages and transformations during their lives.

People may not even recognize their own children or parents after some time has passed. How can something so changeable be considered true? Instead, it is false, appearing in many different forms throughout life. True things stay constant and unchanging, but people are not constant, so they cannot be truly real. Humans are like fleeting images, and every appearance is ultimately a form of falsehood.

Even the eternal bodies in the universe, though they may seem constant, are not truly real because they too undergo change. Things that are created or altered cannot be fully true, although they might contain elements of truth since they come from the source of all creation. Yet, because they change, they also carry some degree of falsehood.

Something that cannot stay the same is not true. You ask if the sun is the only thing that can be called true because it seems unchanging. Yes, the sun is closer to truth because it stays constant and plays a vital role in shaping the world. It governs creation, maintaining the world's order. I honor and respect the truth that the sun represents, acknowledging it as the work of the Creator.

You wonder what the first and highest truth is. It is the One—without matter, without shape, without color or form, and unchanging. It always remains the same. Falsehood, on the other hand, is tied to corruption, and everything on Earth is affected by it.

Corruption is necessary for new things to be created. Everything that is born or created must eventually decay so that more can be generated.

In this way, creation and decay are intertwined, ensuring that life continues without end.

Recognize the original Creator through the act of creation. The things that come into existence through corruption are not true because they are constantly changing—one thing becomes another. It is impossible for these things to remain the same, and if something is not the same, how can it be true?

Therefore, we must understand these things as mere appearances or illusions. If we wish to describe people accurately, we must say that what we see are appearances. A man is the appearance of a man, a child is the appearance of a child, an old man is the appearance of old age, a young man is the appearance of youth, and a person in their prime is the appearance of maturity.

A man is not truly a man, just as a child is not truly a child, nor is an old man truly old. The same is true for all other stages of life. These appearances change over time, which means they are not real. The things that existed before and the things that exist now are always shifting, and because of this, they are false.

Understand this, my son: these false appearances and changing forms still have their origin in the truth, which comes from above. Even though these shifting forms seem false, they still originate from the source of truth itself.

In this way, falsehood can be understood as a product of truth.

The Sixteenth Book,
That None of The Things That Are Can Perish

We must now talk about the soul and the body, my son, and how the soul is immortal and what happens to the body when it forms and when it dissolves. But there is no such thing as death in any of these processes. Death is just a word, either meaningless or misunderstood, for it suggests an end to something that is truly immortal.

Death implies destruction, but nothing in the universe is ever really destroyed. If the world is like a second god, an immortal living being, then no part of something immortal can die. Everything in the world is connected to the whole, and this includes humans, who are rational beings.

God, who is eternal and uncreated, is the source of all things. The world is the second creation, formed in God's image. It is sustained, nurtured, and made eternal by God, who acts as its father, keeping it alive forever. The world is both immortal and ever-living.

There is a difference between being eternal and being ever-living. What is eternal has no beginning, and if it did have a beginning, it created itself without help from anything else. Eternity is always complete in itself. The eternal, then, is the entire universe.

God, the Father, is eternal on His own. The world was made by God and is always living and immortal. God took all the available matter and shaped it into a body, making it round like a sphere. He gave it qualities and infused it with immortality so that it would never fall into disorder.

The Father, filled with endless ideas, placed these qualities within the spheres, sealing them into circles. His intention was to bring beauty and order to everything that was to be created. He covered the whole universe with immortality so that the matter would not break apart into chaos if it tried to separate from its structure.

When matter was first formed into bodies, it existed in disorder. This same disorder continues to revolve through all material things, growing and shrinking in cycles, which people mistakenly call death. In truth, it is simply disorder occurring within earthly beings.

The heavenly bodies follow a fixed order given to them by the Father, one that remains unchanging and eternal. Earthly bodies, however, undergo change. When they dissolve, they return to their pure, undivided state, becoming immortal once again. This process causes them to lose their senses temporarily, but it does not destroy the body.

The third type of living being is man, created in the image of the world. By the Father's will, humans possess a higher mind than other earthly creatures. Humans are connected to the second god, which is the world, and they also have the capacity to understand the first god, who is beyond all form.

Humans comprehend the second god, the world, through the body, but they understand the first god as something incorporeal—the pure mind of goodness.

Be careful with your words, my son, and try to understand what God is, what the world is, and what it means for something to be immortal or subject to dissolution. Know that the world exists within God, just as God exists within everything. Humans, however, belong to the world and exist within it.

God is the beginning, the end, and the essence of everything that exists.

The Seventeenth Book,
To Asclepius, To Be Truly Wise

Since Tat, my son, was eager to learn about the nature of all things, he didn't allow me to stop teaching him. Although he was young, he was determined to understand every detail, so I had to explain many things in depth to make his learning smoother and more successful. But with you, I will keep it brief, focusing only on the essential points. I will also interpret these ideas more deeply, as you have both the wisdom and the years to grasp the true nature of things.

Everything we see has been created and is continually being created. However, nothing creates itself. Every created thing comes from something else. There are many different kinds of things in the world, each distinct from the other. If all things are made by another, there must be one being who creates everything—someone who was never created but is older than all else. This creator, being unmade, is more ancient than anything that has ever come into existence.

He is the most powerful, the one who knows all things, and nothing existed before him. He governs both the great and small, controlling the variety of everything that exists. His power holds everything together and keeps the process of creation ongoing. The things that are made are visible, but the maker remains invisible. He creates everything to make his presence known, and because of this, he continues to create endlessly.

Understanding this fills the soul with admiration and gratitude. Knowing your divine creator is the greatest blessing, for what could be sweeter than knowing your true father? But who is this being, and how can we recognize him? Should we call him God, the Maker, or the Father—or perhaps all three? We call him God because of his power, the Maker because of his creative work, and the Father because of his goodness.

His power is beyond the things he has made, but through his actions, all things are brought into being. So, instead of engaging in endless debate, we must focus on understanding two truths: the one who creates and the things that are created. Nothing exists outside of these two realities, and nothing stands between them.

Remember this: all things boil down to these two truths—the maker and the creation—and one cannot exist without the other. The creator needs the creation to express his nature, and the creation needs the creator to exist. They are inseparably united, like two parts of the same whole.

Since the creator is complete in himself, everything he makes reflects his essence. That which is made exists because the creator wills it to be. Without the creator, nothing could exist, and without creation, the creator's work would be incomplete. So, creation follows the creator, and in this way, they are joined as one. God is the one who creates, and all that is created follows his design.

We should not fear the variety of things in the world, nor think that it reflects poorly on the creator. Instead, it glorifies him, for it is through creating all things that he expresses his greatness. Creation is like the body of God, and in this divine work, there is nothing shameful or wrong. Just as rust forms naturally on copper, or waste emerges from the body, certain things are simply a result of the process of generation.

The rust is not created by the blacksmith, nor is waste created by the body itself. Similarly, God does not create evil. These imperfections arise naturally from the cycles of life. Change is necessary, like the cleansing that keeps the process of creation in motion.

Consider a painter who creates both the heavens and the earth, gods and humans, animals, and plants. If a painter can create all these things, why would it be hard to imagine that God creates everything? It is foolish to think otherwise. Those who deny this are trapped in ignorance. They claim to praise God but refuse to acknowledge him as the creator of all things, which is both absurd and impious.

By denying God's role in creation, they attribute human flaws like pride, weakness, or envy to him. This is deeply misguided, for God is none of these things. His only quality is goodness. Being good, he lacks pride, ignorance, or malice. God is pure goodness itself.

Because God is good, he has the power to create all things. Everything that exists comes from the Good. Just as a farmer sows seeds in different places—wheat in one spot, barley in another, and vines elsewhere— God also plants seeds of immortality in the world. Through him, life, change, and motion exist.

In truth, there are only a few key elements in all of existence: God, generation, and the life force that animates everything. In these, all things are contained.

The Virgin of the World

Hermes Trismegistus

Introduction

THE HERMETIC BOOKS

These books were very well-known and later became highly valued by those seeking to use them for alchemical purposes, especially for making gold. The Roman Emperor Severus gathered all writings about the Mysteries and buried them in the tomb of Alexander the Great. Diocletian destroyed their alchemy books to prevent Egypt from becoming so wealthy that it could no longer be a dependent state. These writings, containing the laws, science, and theology of Egypt, were said by priests to have been written during the time of the gods, before the reign of the first human king, Menes. Ancient monuments contain references that confirm how old these writings are. There were four main books, which were divided into forty-two volumes altogether. These numbers are the same as the Vedas, which, according to the Puranas, were brought to Egypt by the Yadavas during the first migration from India. The subjects in these books were also similar, though it's still unclear to what extent the Books of Hermes were copied from the Vedas.

These books were kept in the innermost parts of the temples, and only the highest-ranking priests were allowed to read them. They were treated with great respect and carried during important religious ceremonies. The chief priests were responsible for ten volumes that discussed the creation of the world, the gods' nature, and divine laws for priests. Prophets carried four volumes that dealt with astronomy and astrology. The leader of the sacred musicians held two volumes with hymns to the gods and advice on how the king should behave, which the singer had to memorize. These hymns were considered so ancient and sacred that Plato said they were attributed to Isis and believed to be ten thousand years old. Temple workers carried ten more volumes, which contained prayers, rules for offerings, and instructions for festivals and processions. The remaining volumes focused on philosophy and sciences, including anatomy and medicine.

The Books of Hermes, once renowned, have been lost for about fifteen hundred years. The fragments found in this collection have been carefully studied. In the early days of Christianity, these writings were held in high regard and considered genuine. Christian scholars often referred to them to support Christian beliefs, and the writer Lactantius, known as the "Christian Cicero," said, "Hermes, I don't know how, has discovered nearly the whole truth." Hermes was seen as a divine messenger, and his writings were thought to represent the ancient Egyptian religion in which Moses was trained. This view was supported by Renaissance scholars like Marsilio Ficino and Patricius, who believed these works influenced Orphic rituals and the philosophies of Pythagoras and Plato.

However, doubts about the authenticity of these writings arose. Some scholars thought they were written by a Jew, others by a Christian or a Gnostic, based on the content. Modern critics, including Dr. Louis Menard, now believe these writings are among the latest works of Greek philosophy. But within these texts, which reflect Alexandrian ideas, traces of ancient Egyptian religious thought still remain. Menard suggests that the Egyptian philosophy recorded in the Books of Hermes was the result of blending Egyptian religious ideas with Greek philosophical concepts. These books are the only surviving record of that Egyptian philosophy, presenting old beliefs and ideas in abstract terms instead of their original mythological form.

The arrival of Christianity may seem at first like a sudden and complete change in the beliefs and practices of the Western world. However, history shows that such transformations don't happen overnight. To understand how one religion replaces another, it's important not to focus only on their most extreme differences—like comparing Homer's mythology with the Christian symbols from the Council of Nicaea. Instead, it's essential to explore the gradual shifts and connections between them over time.

It is important to study the remaining works from this period of transition, when ancient Greek ideas were being reshaped through discussions and mixed with religions from the East that were spreading into Europe. Christianity is the latest example of how these Eastern beliefs influenced the West. It didn't arrive suddenly, shocking the old world. Instead, it took time to develop, with its ideas forming alongside those in Greece, Asia, and Egypt. Many of the same problems that Christianity aimed to solve were already being discussed in these regions. The ideas in the air at that time blended in different ways.

The rise of many different religious sects today only gives a small sense of how dynamic the intellectual activity was back then. Alexandria was at the heart of this development, acting as a center for moral and philosophical exploration. People were debating big questions like the nature of evil, the purpose of souls, their downfall, and their redemption. The ultimate prize for answering these questions was control over people's beliefs, and in the end, Christianity offered the solution that prevailed.

Our critic looks at the books of Hermes Trismegistus and tries to figure out what parts reflect Egyptian thought and what might have come from Jewish ideas. He points out that when we encounter ideas that resemble those of Plato or Pythagoras, we need to ask if the author rediscovered the same ancient sources that Plato and Pythagoras had used or if these ideas represent something purely Greek. This raises questions about how much Eastern thought influenced Greek philosophy. People tend to overestimate the impact of Eastern ideas on Greek thought, partly because the Greeks themselves believed in that influence. However, the real exchange between Greek and other cultures only became steady and meaningful after Alexandria was founded. During these exchanges, Greece had more to share with other cultures than it received from them. The people of the East, including those who interacted with the Greeks, didn't have what we would call a formal philosophy. They lacked traditions of analyzing the mind, searching for the foundations of knowledge and moral rules, and applying these ideas to society. These concepts were new to the East before Alexander the Great's conquests.

Plato mentions a comment from an Egyptian priest who told the Greeks, "You are just children; there are no elders among you." This could reflect the attitude of Egypt and other Eastern cultures. The spirit of scientific inquiry and political instinct was unfamiliar to these peoples. While they could endure for long periods, they never seemed to mature. They were like grown children, still being guided by others and unable to pursue truth or achieve justice on their own.

The East, having learned philosophy from Greece, could only offer what it had—deep religious feelings. Greece, tired of the skepticism caused by disagreements among its philosophical schools, welcomed this religious intensity. This shift toward spiritual enthusiasm was a sign of the need for renewed faith. The books of Hermes Trismegistus serve as a bridge between past beliefs and future ones, linking ideas from the old world to the new. Though these writings are part of pagan thought, they reflect the final moments of paganism. Paganism resisted the new faith and refused to surrender to it, guarding the knowledge of the old civilization that was fading. It accepted its fate, ready to rest forever in its birthplace—ancient Egypt, the land of the dead.

Dr. Menard concludes that the Hermetic books are the last remains of paganism. They belong to both Greek philosophy and Egyptian religion, and their mystical nature connects them to the Middle Ages. These writings lie between two eras—one ending and the other beginning—like creatures that bridge different species but are not fully part of either group. As a result, they are not as great as the religious beliefs of Homer's time or Christianity, but they help us understand the transition from one to the other. They contain both emerging beliefs and those fading away, meeting and intertwining as one era gives way to the next.

To challenge and correct the earlier statements about the relationship between Greek and Eastern thought, we offer the following insights from Mr. Plumptre's "History of Pantheism." From childhood, most of us are taught to believe that we owe all our knowledge of theology and religion to the Hebrews, and much of our understanding of God as well. At the same time, we are told that the Greeks gave us all our knowledge of the arts, sciences, philosophy, and wisdom. Similarly, we are taught to credit the Romans for shaping our ideas about discipline and law. While these definitions are generally accurate for our connections with the Hebrews and Romans, the same cannot be said about the Greeks.

The statement is somewhat accurate. It is true that we owe much of our knowledge to the Greeks. However, the error lies in assuming that the Greeks were the first to pursue learning purely for its own sake, that they received no knowledge from other cultures, and that they invented it all themselves. This view might also suggest that they were the first people to reach a high level of civilization. Even a basic understanding of Egyptian or Hindu history is enough to show how mistaken this idea is. Egyptian civilization stretches so far back in history that it is almost impossible to pinpoint its beginning. It is now widely accepted that Moses gained much of his knowledge from the Egyptians, meaning that even our earliest religious ideas may have come from Egypt.

Mr. Plumptre points out that while both the Hindus and Egyptians had developed advanced religious and philosophical systems long ago, the Greeks remained trapped in ignorance and superstition. This changed dramatically after a key event that sparked Greek intellectual development and transformed Greece from a state of childish ignorance into a leading cultural and philosophical power. That event was the opening of Egypt's ports by King Psammetichus in 670 B.C. Until that time, Egypt had been closed off from Europe and the Mediterranean with restrictions as strict as those once seen in China and Japan. To the Greeks, Egypt was nothing more than a land of mystery and myth, as reflected in the works of Homer and Hesiod. When Egypt finally opened up, the effect on Europe's development was profound and far-reaching. Greece, followed by the rest of the world, owed its civilization to this event. It shattered belief in old myths and gave birth to Greek philosophy.

This statement needs some adjustment, though. While Greek myths might seem like irrational stories without deeper meaning, they were actually symbols hiding important spiritual truths. Their early presence in Greece shows that institutions dedicated to sacred mysteries existed long before Greek philosophy emerged. The fact that these mysteries shared ideas with Egypt and the East also reveals that there was religious contact between these regions long before trade, political connections, or philosophical exchanges took place. Christian missionary work was not the first of its kind; the sacred mysteries were constantly spreading, establishing themselves in new places even ahead of secular civilizations. The migration of Abraham, the travels of Bacchus, and the journey of Moses are all examples of this kind of movement.

Mr. Plumptre concludes that any similarities between Greek and Egyptian philosophy were the result of the Greeks adopting ideas from Egypt. It seems impossible to disagree with this conclusion. We believe that Menard's differing opinion comes from his focus on classical knowledge without considering Hermetic and Kabbalistic traditions. Since these traditions contain the spiritual history of the world, ignoring them makes it impossible to fully understand these topics. Those who rely only on conventional methods of learning and reject anything beyond surface-level knowledge tend to dismiss the idea that a hidden, divine system of teachings has existed since ancient times. Yet, this conclusion is unavoidable based on the overwhelming evidence, both from public sources and secret teachings.

The earliest traces of this knowledge can be found in India and Egypt. If there are similarities between the ancient teachings of these lands and those of Greece, Judea, and Christianity, it is because the same truths were passed from one culture to another. These truths were reshaped to fit the needs and spirit of each time and place. This process will continue until humanity either falls into complete ignorance and no longer cares about truth or reaches a state of enlightenment where truth is fully understood and preserved as our most valuable treasure forever.

Regardless of the debate, even the most critical arguments must admit three key points. First, some of the teachings in the Hermetic texts are truly ancient, originating from Egypt, making them authentically Hermetic. Second, there are clear similarities between these ancient Hermetic teachings and the ideas found in Christianity. And third, the Church has acknowledged and accepted these similarities, showing that Christianity, rather than being a completely new and original belief system when it first began, is actually a continuation or reworking of ideas that had existed long before.

THE HERMETIC SYSTEM AND THE SIGNIFICANCE OF ITS PRESENT REVIVAL

For anyone studying humanity, one of the most important features of our current era is the revival of occult science and mystical, or hidden, philosophy. This revival is important not just because of the ideas themselves, but also because of the timing. It is happening during a period when the human mind, as represented by modern thinkers, seemed to have fully embraced materialism. However, this shift toward materialism turned out to be temporary, as some people—those attuned to the deeper connections of life and aware of the unity within nature—already knew. Just as the sun's return begins at its lowest point, spiritual renewal follows times of decline. When materialism threatened to extinguish the spiritual awareness of humanity, the return of mystical and occult teachings brought that awareness back to life.

History has shown that the end of old religious forms often signals the beginning of new and better spiritual insights. Those who believe in the divine nature of the human spirit trusted that, in time, it would rise up against materialism. They see the current revival as that very awakening. This revival is also noteworthy because it has brought Hermetic philosophy back into the spotlight for the first time in centuries. Every major religious awakening in history has involved this philosophy in some way. Hermetic Gnosis—an ancient system with roots going back to prehistoric Egypt—has been the foundation of many religious and philosophical traditions across the East and the West. Both Buddhism and Christianity were intended to express its teachings, although this was only recognized by a select few. Even the mystical school that flourished during the Middle Ages, which brought great prestige to the church, was secretly based on the same ideas.

That school aimed to rescue religion from being reduced to rituals, historical events, and the control of a materialistic clergy. Instead, it sought to restore religion's true spiritual and intuitive nature. Although this effort did not achieve lasting success, it was not because of any flaw in the system. The challenge lay in the fact that the spiritual awareness required to fully understand the teachings was something only a few people possessed at that time. The world simply was not ready for a philosophy that represented reason at its highest level. Now, however, it is clear that the revival we are witnessing is just one in a series of similar movements throughout history. Given the current changes in society, there is good reason to believe this revival will succeed more than any before it.

Even though the state of society today may seem bleak in many areas—whether in social issues, philosophy, morality, or religion—there has never been a time when conditions were better for a major positive change. New ideas and knowledge now spread faster than ever, and the hardships and dissatisfaction people are experiencing have made them more open to change. As a result, Hermetic philosophy now has a better chance of gaining acceptance than ever before. In the past, it was embraced by the brightest minds and most honorable individuals. With the right presentation, it is likely that this philosophy will find a place in the hearts and minds of people in this new era.

There are already signs that the church, still a powerful force, may support this revival—not only to preserve itself but also to protect religious truth. The importance of Pope Leo XIII's decision to restore the works of Aquinas as the foundation for church education is not yet widely understood. However, for those initiated in the teachings of Hermes, this move is seen as a reason for great optimism. A similar view applies to the strange, though sometimes misguided, phenomenon of modern spiritualism.

With these thoughts on the circumstances surrounding the revival—of which this collection of writings is both a product and a tool—we will now provide a brief overview of the nature of the teachings that have played such a major role in the past and seem likely to have even greater impact in the future.

It's important to mention that this overview isn't limited to the Hermetic fragments found in these reprints. These fragments are incomplete, and some parts have been altered or corrupted over time, though they still contain profound and valuable teachings. Much of what remains is written in symbolic or mystical language, referring to higher realities that require deeper interpretation beyond what is immediately obvious. For this reason, we need to rely on the work of those who have either accessed now-lost sources or uncovered these teachings through the same intuitive methods that first brought them to light.

The Hermetic system starts with the principle that nothing can come from nothing and recognizes that consciousness is essential to existence. From this foundation, it logically concludes that everything comes from a pure, absolute being. This being is unmanifested and unlimited but contains within it the potential to express itself. It is not just a being with life, mind, and substance—it is life, mind, and substance. The universe is a reflection of this divine self, showing how this being manifests itself in the material world. Some thinkers have developed new ways to apply these teachings, but they remain true to the Hermetic tradition.

However, no amount of knowledge or effort can replace the intuitive insight needed to recognize true Hermetic wisdom. Only with such insight can one grasp the genuine nature of these teachings, and it is hoped that this understanding will not be missing here. What follows is only a brief outline, as even the best attempts can offer only a glimpse of these deep truths.

The Hermetic view holds that all things are forms of consciousness, and consciousness exists in many different ways. It can be defined as the ability of something to affect or be affected by itself or something else, meaning that consciousness is the essence of everything. There are various levels of consciousness, including physical, chemical, magnetic, mental, and spiritual, with divine consciousness being the highest. All forms of consciousness come from the divine, and all will eventually return to it. This process is the essence of evolution, which is the tendency of things to return to their original state. Evolution shows that the material world is not the ultimate form of existence but is instead one step along the way.

By seeing matter as just another form of consciousness—and, in turn, a form of spirit—Hermetic thought avoids the difficulties that come with believing in two opposing forces, such as spirit and matter, as separate and conflicting. Everything is an expression of the same ultimate source, so there can be no true conflict or opposition. What we call unconsciousness is simply a lower form of consciousness, reduced to its smallest degree but still present. Total unconsciousness is non-existence, just as darkness is the absence of light. Consciousness, however limited, always has a positive existence, while non-existence is only the absence of being.

The many expressions of consciousness, whether on different levels or in different forms on the same level, all follow the same underlying law. This law reveals the unity of the divine mind, which exists eternally, independent of its manifestations. As stated in the "Divine Pymander": "He does not need to be revealed, for He exists eternally. He is not created or born but remains unseen and unmanifested. Yet, by making all things visible, He appears in all things and through all things, especially in those who seek Him."

The unity of being also establishes a principle of correspondence between all levels of existence. The larger universe mirrors the smaller individual, just as the individual reflects the divine. "Man on earth," says "The Key," "is a mortal god, while the heavenly god is an immortal man." However, the book clarifies that this description only applies to those who possess higher spiritual awareness. Those who lack this awareness are not yet fully human but only have the potential to become so.

The teachings avoid the mistake of attributing human qualities to the divine by explaining that divinity is not life, mind, or substance itself but the source of these things. Ignorance of the divine is described as the greatest evil, but God cannot be found in the external world. Instead, the search for the divine must take place within oneself. To truly know, one must first fully be. This means developing awareness of all the different levels of one's being and becoming a complete person. The deepest truths belong to the spirit, which is the pure essence of being. Existence is simply the outward expression of that essence.

Since a person can only recognize in the external world what they already have within themselves, spiritual awareness is necessary to perceive spiritual truths. To understand the divine, a person must first become spiritual within.

"The natural man," as the apostle Paul says, following the teachings of both the Hermetists and the Kabbalists, "cannot understand the things of the Spirit, nor can he know them, for they are understood spiritually." This means they can only be grasped through the spiritual part within a person. As a person develops this spiritual awareness, they become a tool for knowledge, capable of discovering deep truths, including the highest truths. At that point, they move from being "agnostic," or unaware of true knowledge, to being "Gnostic," which means having knowledge of both themselves and God, and understanding that both are deeply connected.

The fact that today's world often embraces agnosticism only shows how immature its understanding is. The philosophy of this time reflects the views of people who may be highly intelligent but are still underdeveloped in their spiritual awareness. Because of this, they have not yet reached their full human potential, which requires growth on the spiritual plane. Lacking this higher awareness, they mistake the outward appearance of a person for their true self, assuming that satisfying physical desires will benefit the person, even if such actions harm their deeper humanity.

The knowledge provided by Gnosis helps lift people out of this spiritual darkness. It gives them the essential understanding that all divine teachings aim to provide: a clear understanding of who they truly are. It shows, with certainty, that moral laws are supreme and that it is impossible to gain anything good by doing wrong or to escape the consequences of one's actions. Trying to achieve good by doing harm only makes things worse in the long run. The idea of Karma, central to Hindu thought, is also part of Hermetic philosophy. In Hermetic teachings, this principle is represented by Adrasté, a goddess of justice. In Greek mythology, this same idea is reflected in Nemesis and Hecate. All these figures represent the unbreakable law of cause and effect, which shapes a person's future based on the actions and habits they choose to nurture in the present.

The Hermetic path to perfection—whether physical, intellectual, moral, or spiritual—is through purity. Since consciousness is not just something a person has but something they are, a person's level of awareness depends on how pure they are. Perfect purity allows for complete understanding, even to the point of seeing God, as taught in the gospels. In the same way, a person's power increases with their purity. A fully developed Hermetist, someone who has mastered this knowledge, becomes a magian—a person of great power. Such a person can perform acts that seem miraculous, not just physically but also intellectually, morally, and spiritually, all through the strength of their will. However, the secret of this power is purity, and the only motivation behind it is love. The power they use comes from spirit, and spirit becomes more powerful the purer it is. Pure spirit, at its highest level, is God.

The miracles performed by a magian differ from those of a magician because they are truly the work of God—the divine power within the person. A key part of Hermetic knowledge is the use of intuition. Through intuition, a person turns inward and connects with their true, eternal self—the soul—and gains access to the knowledge it has gathered over countless lifetimes. This approach does not dismiss the role of the intellect, which also needs to be developed as a partner to intuition. These two aspects of the mind—intellect and intuition—are like complements, working together like the masculine and feminine. Only when both are perfected and unified can a person achieve complete understanding. At that point, the person knows God, and to know God is to both possess and become one with God, for "the gift of God is eternal life."

One of the most important teachings in Hermetic philosophy is the idea that the soul is born into many physical bodies over time. The soul continues this cycle of rebirth until it reaches a state of spiritual growth that allows it to exist without needing a physical body. This process of transformation, called regeneration, only ends when the soul no longer needs the material world. The concept of correspondence offers a useful way to understand this process. Just as the body sheds its outer layers—such as skin, feathers, or hair—the soul also leaves behind many physical bodies over time.

The law of gravity, which governs the physical world, also applies to the spiritual world. A person's spiritual state determines the level at which their soul exists, just as the density of a physical object determines how it behaves. The soul must release the attachment that draws it into physical existence before it can move beyond the need for a body. The death of the body does not necessarily mean that the soul has overcome this pull toward material life, so the soul may still be drawn back to earth in another body. However, when the soul returns, it does so without the magnetic or "astral" body that forms the outer personality. Only the soul itself continues its journey, evolving through each lifetime toward greater spiritual awareness.

The idea of transmigration, or the soul's journey through many lifetimes, is central to Hermetic, Kabbalistic, and Hindu teachings. It also runs through the Bible in hidden ways, showing up in the conversation between Jesus and Nicodemus, where Jesus speaks about being "born again." Although Jesus emphasizes spiritual rebirth, this process requires multiple lifetimes to provide the experiences necessary for spiritual growth. As Swedenborg explained, regeneration must begin while a person is still in the body and must reach a certain level before the soul can move beyond needing a physical body. Spiritual growth cannot be completed in a single lifetime. Without many lifetimes to make this process possible, the message of the gospel would not offer salvation but would instead guarantee failure for most people.

In Hermetic teachings, what Christianity calls the "forgiveness of sins" is tied to the process of inner transformation. Each person carries the potential for this transformation within them, but they must actively participate in their own spiritual growth. Through this process, they become a "new creation," born not from physical matter but from "water and spirit." This means their soul and spirit are purified, becoming divine. When a person achieves this higher state of being, they are said to be born of the "Virgin Mary" and the Holy Spirit.

The Hermetic system stands apart from other mystical traditions because it views nature and the body with joy and reverence, rather than disgust. While some other systems see the body and its functions as impure or sinful, Hermeticism sees them as part of divine truth. The relationship between the sexes is honored, symbolizing the highest spiritual mysteries, and fulfilling these relationships is considered a duty. In some lifetimes, these experiences are essential for a person's complete development and initiation. This appreciation of life's beauty aligns Hermetic thought with Greek philosophy and sets it apart from more pessimistic Eastern views.

A true Hermetist sees divine presence everywhere—in every part of nature, just as the prophet Jonah found God even in the belly of a whale. Ignorance of God is viewed as the greatest evil. This belief is why Hermetic teachings promote a vegetarian lifestyle, as described in the "Asclepios." Human beings are not naturally designed to eat meat. Their physical structure shows that they thrive best on plant-based foods, which cleanse and rebuild the body. Eating flesh not only blocks the development of intuition, the key to spiritual insight, but also dulls a person's sensitivity to violence. Failing to be disturbed by killing for food reveals a lack of spiritual awareness.

The goal of the Hermetist is not simply to escape from life, as if existence were something evil. Instead, the goal is to become a clear instrument for perceiving the divine presence in every part of existence. Any pessimism found in Hermetic texts, such as the "Divine Pymander," reflects only the imperfections of existence compared to the perfection of divine being. Hermeticism surpasses other mystical systems by valuing both sexes equally. Although the story of the Fall originates from Hermetic teachings, it is meant to be understood symbolically, not literally. It was never intended to place blame on any person or gender. Instead, the Fall represents a deep truth about divine reality. Sadly, this story has often been used to justify unfair and cruel treatment of women—attitudes that come from primitive and undeveloped sources, not from true spiritual understanding.

Throughout history, it becomes clear that the solutions to life's greatest questions—about human nature and how to live—can be found in the teachings and practices of the Hermetic system. Free inquiry, when pursued without prejudice or narrow thinking, naturally leads to the truths revealed by Hermeticism. These teachings are based on real, lived experiences of the soul, which gains deeper understanding through intuition.

Hermetic philosophy is a triumph of both free thought and religious faith. It encourages exploration of both the physical world and the spiritual realm. In Hermeticism, God is seen as the source of all being. Nature serves as a way for God to reveal Himself, and the human soul—refined and perfected through experience—becomes a unique expression of the divine.

AN INTRODUCTION TO THE VIRGIN OF THE WORLD

The mystical title of the well-known Hermetic fragment that opens this volume, "Koré Kosmou," or "The Kosmic Virgin," reveals the deep connection between the ancient wisdom-religions and the teachings of Catholic Christianity. In the Eleusinian Mysteries, the name Koré was used to address Persephone, the Maiden or Daughter. Interestingly, Koré is also the Greek word for the pupil of the eye. This connection becomes more meaningful when we consider that, in a conversation between Isis, the Moon-goddess and guide of initiates, and Horos, she compares the physical eye's layers to the soul's coverings. Just as the eye's pupil brings light to the body, the soul brings awareness and understanding to a person.

In this Hermetic parable, Persephone, or Koré, symbolizes the soul. Her descent from the divine realm into the material world is a key theme. Some scholars have also noted that the Hindu goddess Parasu-pani, also known as Gorée, shares a similar role, suggesting a deeper connection between these traditions. The Greek Mysteries focused on two primary themes: the story of Persephone's descent and return, and the life, death, and rebirth of Dionysos-Zagreus. In these teachings, Persephone represents the soul, while Dionysos symbolizes the spirit.

The Hermetic doctrine explains that both the universe and human beings have a fourfold nature. Two parts of this nature—spirit and soul—are eternal, while the other two—the lower mind and the physical body—are temporary. The spirit and soul, viewed as masculine and feminine forces, remain unchanged through all cycles of reincarnation, while the mind and body are new with each life. Dionysos, the spirit, is said to have a divine origin, being born from Zeus and the immaculate Virgin Koré-Persephone, who is the daughter of Demeter, known as the "Mother" in the Mysteries.

Koré has two aspects to her nature. As the daughter of Zeus and Demeter, she is pure and divine. However, as the wife of Hades in the underworld, she is connected to the realms of sorrow and decay. This duality reflects the nature of the soul, which remains pure and invulnerable in its essence, yet appears to fall and become stained in the material world. The symbol of the soul in Hermetic teachings is water, also called Maria. Water, though it can appear dirty or polluted, always retains its true purity beneath the surface. When purified through distillation, it leaves all impurities behind and emerges clear and pure once again. In the same way, the soul is always pure at its core, no matter how stained it might seem during its journey through life.

The story of the Kosmic Virgin reflects the soul's journey through existence. The soul moves between two states: an outward journey into the material world, which represents its "fall," and an inward return to its divine origin. Although Koré comes from a heavenly realm, she is more connected to earthly life than her son, Dionysos. As the Mysteries teach, Persephone dwells both above, in the inaccessible places of the divine Mother, and below, with Pluto, where she governs earthly matters and sustains life throughout the universe.

This dual nature of spirit and soul is also central to Hindu philosophy, where the spirit is called Atman. The Upanishads, a key part of Hindu esoteric teachings, focus entirely on understanding this concept.

The concept of Atman is described as self-sustaining, unified, eternal, unchanging, and incorruptible. It exists independently of Karma—the idea that actions shape one's character and destiny—and gaining full awareness of Atman frees a person from the cycle of Karma. Atman is also all-seeing, and as the Mantras teach, "He who sees the universe within his own Atman and his Atman within the universe knows no hatred."

In the Kabbalah, the soul's journey is symbolized by Eve. The soul begins by turning away from divine unity and becoming restless in matter, unable to stay still, as resting seems like death. This moment is reflected in the Greek myth where Persephone leaves the heavens, lured by desire, and falls under Hades' power. Thomas Taylor explains this descent as the soul abandoning its higher, divine life. In the story, Jupiter sends Venus to tempt Persephone from her peaceful retreat, with Diana and Minerva accompanying her to prevent any suspicion. They find Persephone weaving a scarf for her mother, depicting the chaos and creation of the world.

Venus represents desire, which sneaks into the soul even in heavenly realms. Minerva symbolizes reason, while Diana stands for nature. As Persephone wanders from her retreat to gather flowers, surrounded by nymphs symbolizing the cycle of life and birth, she becomes captivated by the beauty of the material world. The soul, in the same way, becomes enchanted by the world of form and sensation. As soon as she steps outside her retreat, Pluto rises from the earth and seizes her, dragging her into the underworld. This reflects the soul's descent into the darkness of material existence, where it is united with the body.

Homer's "Hymn to Ceres" also describes this event, with Persephone saying, "I was joyfully gathering flowers—the crocus, iris, hyacinth, and narcissus—when the earth opened, and the powerful king carried me down to the underworld, despite my cries." This story mirrors the biblical tale of Eve, who, drawn by the beauty of the tree's fruit, eats it and is cast into sorrow. God tells her, "I will increase your pain in childbirth, and your desire will be for your husband, who will rule over you."

Plato's allegory in "Phaedrus" further explains this fall, comparing the body to a chariot pulling the soul down into earthly existence. The soul struggles under the weight of material life, which clouds the mind and reason. This condition, Plato explains, traps the soul in the body, similar to prisoners chained in a cave who mistake shadows for reality. Life on earth is described as a form of imprisonment—a dreamlike exile from the soul's true home.

In the "Koré Kosmou," we read that souls, upon learning they would be trapped in physical bodies, sighed and cried out to the heavens. They lamented, "Oh, what sorrow and heartache to leave behind these vast splendors, the sacred realm, and all the glory of the blessed gods, only to be cast down into these miserable and wretched dwellings! We will no longer gaze upon the radiant heavens!" This sorrowful cry brings to mind Eve's lament when she was exiled from the beautiful paradise of Eden.

Just as the soul falls into this sorrowful state, she is eventually rescued and restored to the divine realm. This rescue happens through the coming of a savior, symbolized here by Osiris, the figure of the "Man Regenerate." Osiris, a divine being, is often represented by different names in various stories, but the meaning behind each is the same. Osiris is the equivalent of Jesus in Christian doctrine—the supreme initiate and "Captain of Salvation." Alongside his divine partner, Osiris is guided in all things by Hermes, known as the messenger of the gods. Hermes is seen as the conductor of souls from darkness, representing divine understanding and reason. In Platonic philosophy, Hermes embodies "nous," the higher mind, and the mystical "Spirit of Christ."

Since the ability to understand sacred things and interpret them comes from Hermes, the name Hermes is connected to all hidden knowledge and divine revelation. Those with such knowledge are known as "divines," meaning they understand the mysteries of heaven. This is why the apostle John, who wrote the Book of Revelation, is often called the "beloved" of Christ. Hermes is recognized as the messenger of the gods, descending to the deepest realms of the underworld to guide souls upward and ascending beyond the heavens to bring wisdom. Understanding must explore both the heights and the depths, for nothing can remain hidden from it. Only by exploring both the spiritual and material realms can a person fully grasp divine truths.

The Greeks, with their joyful and lighthearted nature, added humor and playfulness even to their sacred stories. They called Hermes a thief, hinting at the power of the mind to claim everything for its own understanding. When the myths say that Hermes stole the girdle of Venus, the tools of Vulcan, the thunder of Zeus, and the cattle of Apollo, they mean that even the greatest gifts of the gods are within reach of the mind when it seeks knowledge wisely. As the companion of the sun, Hermes opens the gates of heaven, revealing spiritual light and life. He serves as a mediator between the physical and spiritual worlds, initiating seekers into the sacred mysteries that lead to eternal life.

The symbolic tools carried by Hermes reflect the powers of the mind. His rod represents the wisdom of the magian, his wings signify the courage of the adventurer, his sword embodies the will of the hero, and his cap shows the discretion of the wise. Those initiated into Hermes' teachings recognize no authority but the mind itself. They follow no earthly master, embracing the freedom of true understanding. As scripture says, "Where the Spirit of the Lord is, there is liberty." One advisor of John Inglesant put it this way: "Follow no man; there is nothing of greater value in the world than the Divine Light—follow it."

Lactantius, in his writings, says that Hermes taught how knowing God frees a person from the control of demons and fate. Fate, in this sense, is tied to the power of the stars, which control both the cosmos and the inner life of a person. In Greek mythology, the many-eyed Argos, who represents the watchful power of the stars, was outwitted and slain by Hermes. This story teaches that those who gain the secret knowledge of Hermes rise above fate and break free from the endless cycles of destiny. To know God is to overcome death and conquer the forces that hold one back. Understanding the source of illusion allows a person to transcend it.

The path to God is blocked by layers of deception, ruled by the seven astral powers. These spheres of illusion stand between the soul and God. Beyond them lie the nine celestial realms, where, according to the Mysteries, Demeter once searched in vain for her lost daughter, Persephone. Persephone had fallen into the material world, placing her under the control of the planetary rulers, symbolized by Hecate, the goddess of fate. On the tenth day of her search, Demeter encountered Hecate, the three-formed goddess of karma and retribution, who revealed what had happened to Persephone. From that moment, Hecate became Persephone's constant companion.

This story holds deep meaning. The soul is free from fate until it enters the material world. Fate begins with the soul's involvement in time and physical existence. In the sevenfold astral spheres, the moon symbolizes fate, presenting both a benevolent and a harsh face.

Under her kinder aspect, the Moon is Artemis, reflecting the divine light of Phœbos to the soul. In her harsher form, she is Hecate, the Avenger, dark-faced and three-headed, swift like a horse, sharp as a dog, and fierce as a lion. In this form, she hunts guilty souls from one life to the next, ensuring justice with relentless precision, outmaneuvering even death. For pure and innocent souls, however, the Moon offers a guiding light. As Artemis, she protects virgins—those souls untouched by the pull of the material world. In this role, the Moon becomes an initiator, like Isis, lighting the soul's inner chamber and bringing wisdom through a favorable destiny. With each lifetime, such souls grow more enlightened and become prophetic, even divine.

On the other hand, to those corrupted by evil, the Moon appears as Hecate, bringing nightmares and dark warnings of misfortune. These souls fear the power of the Moon, sensing the misfortune they are creating for their future selves. According to the Kabbalah, the Tree of Good and Evil is rooted in Malchuth, the Moon. While some say that Karma is unique to Hindu thought, it appears just as clearly in the Hebrew, Greek, and Christian teachings. The Greeks called it Fate, while in Christianity, it is known as Original Sin—the burden that all mortals carry. Only the "Mother of God" is exempt, the "immaculate virgin" through whose child the world is redeemed. As the Church sings, "As a lily among thorns, so is the Beloved among the daughters of Adam. You are all beautiful, O Beloved, and there is no stain within you; your name, O Mary, is like oil poured out, and the virgins love you greatly."

In Persephone or Koré, the "Virgin of the World," we see the soul. In Isis, the guiding initiator, we see the teacher. Isis, like Koré, is both a virgin and a mother. In her philosophical role, the Egyptian Isis is equivalent to Artemis of Ephesus, the Greek goddess symbolizing nature's power to nourish and create. She was called the "eternal maid of heaven," and her priests were eunuchs. Her statue in the grand temple of Ephesus portrayed her with many breasts, symbolizing abundance. The black skin of some depictions, such as the "Black Virgin," represents the hidden and mysterious nature of the forces that shape destiny. These forces may seem random to those who lack understanding, but they follow deeper spiritual laws.

In art, Artemis is often depicted as a huntress with hounds, representing the relentless forces of nature. She is also shown as the Moon goddess, wearing a long veil and a crescent crown, or as a many-breasted mother, carrying a torch. The Romans knew her as Diana, and it is by this name that the Artemis of Ephesus is mentioned in the Christian scriptures. Like Artemis and Diana, Isis embodies the hidden power of nature—Fate, which manifests as fortune, retribution, and destiny. The Kabbalists represent this power with Malchuth, the Moon, while Hindu philosophy calls it Karma. Artemis' hounds symbolize the natural forces that pursue the soul through each lifetime, ensuring that every soul faces the results of its actions.

In the story of Actaeon, the hero ignores the sacredness of fate and disrespects the law of Karma. As punishment, he is torn apart by his own hounds, symbolizing how one's own actions can turn against them. Similarly, initiates of Isis wore masks with dog heads during processions, showing their understanding of how closely fate is tied to the soul's journey. The Moon, linked with Karma, represents the force that draws souls through cycles of birth and rebirth. Proclus, a Greek philosopher, explained that Diana, or Artemis, governs the process by which all things are born into the natural world and extends her power even to the underworld.

This view perfectly describes the role of Isis, showing how the Moon, as the force of Karma, drives the ongoing cycle of life and follows the soul even into realms of purification after death. In the Orphic Hymn to Nature, the goddess is shown standing on a wheel that she spins endlessly, representing the eternal movement of fate. In another hymn, Fortune, identified with Diana, is invoked as the goddess who controls destiny.

Proclus adds that the Moon is not only the cause of nature for mortals but also a reflection of a deeper source—the fountain of life itself. As Thomas Taylor explains, this fountain consists of three main sources within the Demiurge, or creator of the world: the fountain of souls, personified by Hera; the fountain of virtues, represented by Athena; and the fountain of nature, embodied by Artemis. Taylor further illustrates this concept with a passage from Apuleius' "Metamorphoses," in which the Moon speaks: "Behold, Lucius, moved by your prayers, I am here. I am Nature, the mother of all things, ruler of the elements, the beginning of time, the highest among gods and goddesses. I control the bright heavens, the winds of the sea, and the silent darkness of the underworld. Though my essence is one, all the earth honors me by many names and worships me through many rites. Those blessed by the rising sun—the Ethiopians, Aryans, and Egyptians, who possess ancient wisdom—know me as Queen Isis."

The hymn continues with praise: "The gods above honor you, and even those below bow to your power. You set the world in motion, guide the sun's light, and rule the entire universe. The stars obey your will, the gods celebrate you, time flows by your command, and the elements serve you."

This understanding follows naturally when we consider that the divine fountain of Nature exists within the Demiurgus and serves as the pattern for the nature we observe in the Moon and throughout the material world. Knowing this, it is easy to understand why the writer of the Hermetic text chose Isis to represent the soul's origin, journey, and destiny. Isis plays a unique role in guiding the soul through its existence, overseeing its path. If Demeter, the divine intelligence, is the true mother of Koré, then Isis acts as the foster-mother, taking over as soon as the soul enters the material world. Once the soul begins its earthly existence, Isis directs it and determines its fate. This is why some myths equate Isis with Demeter, adjusting Isis's role to match the story of Demeter's grief, as told in the Eleusinian Mysteries.

This blending of roles becomes clear when we understand the Hermetic teachings. Isis, whether she appears as Artemis (good fortune) or Hekate (bad fortune), governs and enlightens the soul while it is still bound by nature and time. Meanwhile, Demeter represents the heavenly source from which the soul originates. Demeter's concern is not with the soul's exile in the physical world but with its eventual return to the divine realm. In harmony with this idea, Isis is depicted both as the wife and the mother of Osiris, the savior of humankind. Osiris, the inner sun of the human soul, reflects the cosmic Dionysos, or Son of God, just as the soul mirrors the greater universe. This is why some myths merge Isis with Demeter and Osiris with Dionysos, placing Osiris at the center of the Bacchic Mysteries.

The Hermetic writings present three levels of divine expression. First, there is the supreme, eternal God, who exists beyond all manifestation.

Second is the only-begotten God, the expression of the divine within the universe. Third is the divine presence within humanity, embodied by Osiris, the redeemer. Inscriptions found on the walls of the Temple of the Sun at Philae and the gate at Medinet-Abou read, "He made all things, and without Him, nothing exists." These words, later used in the Gospel of John to describe the Word of God, show the connection between Osiris, the inner light of humanity, and the divine principle of creation.

Osiris, the inner sun within each person, is a reflection of the greater cosmic sun. The soul, through its experiences in time and physical existence, gives birth to this inner light. This connection explains why Osiris, the force of renewal within each individual, is closely linked to Isis, who guides the soul's growth. Through her influence, events and conditions shape the soul's development, preparing it for transformation. Isis symbolizes the hidden force that drives evolution forward, while Osiris represents the highest potential of humanity, the ideal self toward which all growth is directed.

The Virgin of The World

PART 1

After speaking, Isis gave Horos a sweet drink, the gift of immortality, which is granted by the gods to souls. Then, she began her sacred teaching. She explained that the heavens, crowned with stars, exist above all of creation, complete and lacking nothing. All of nature must be perfected by what is above, as the order of the universe flows from the higher to the lower realms. This order cannot begin from below and move upward. The higher mysteries always rule over the lower ones. Celestial order governs the earthly order, being eternal and beyond death. The things of earth feel fear before the eternal beauty and permanence of the heavens.

The heavens, with their glorious sights, display the majesty of a divine power not yet fully understood. The night sky, though less bright than the sun, reveals hidden mysteries that move in harmony, quietly guiding life on earth through unseen forces. Before the Divine Architect revealed Himself, the universe was full of fear and uncertainty. Ignorance surrounded everything. But when He chose to reveal Himself, He filled the gods with love and poured into them the wisdom contained within His being. This gave them the desire to seek, the will to find, and the power to restore what had been lost.

This great awakening did not happen among mortals, for humanity had not yet come into existence. Instead, it took place within the universal Soul, reflecting the mysteries of the heavens. This universal Soul was Hermes, the cosmic thought. He observed the universe, understood its nature, and revealed what he had discovered. Hermes wrote down these truths, but he kept many hidden, alternating between speaking and remaining silent so that these secrets would continue to be sought throughout time. He instructed the other gods to follow his lead, and then he returned to the stars. Hermes passed his knowledge to his son, Tat, and later to Asclepios, the son of Imouthè, guided by Pan and Hephaistos.

Hermes explained to those around him that he did not reveal the complete knowledge to his son because of his youth. But I, Isis, with my eyes that see the hidden truths of the universe, witnessed these events. And I saw those who, through divine guidance, were granted a perfect understanding of the mysteries of the heavens.

It is important, my son, that you hear the words of Hermes when he sealed his sacred books. "O holy books of the Immortals," he said, "within you are written the remedies that grant eternal life. Remain hidden from those who dwell in this realm until a time comes when souls, worthy of your knowledge, will be born under the ancient heavens."

Hermes then wrapped his books and returned to his place among the stars, leaving his teachings hidden for a time. Nature remained barren until those ordained to observe the heavens sought divine help. They prayed to the Creator, saying, "Please consider what is and what must still come to be." The Creator smiled and commanded Nature to bring forth life. With His voice, the feminine aspect of creation emerged in perfect beauty, leaving the gods amazed. The great Ancestor poured an elixir over Nature, making her fruitful. He declared, "Let heaven be filled with all things, along with the air and the ether." And it was so.

Nature, reflecting on her purpose, realized that she must not stray from the Creator's command. She joined with Labor to bring forth a beautiful daughter, whom she named Invention. The Creator gave Invention life and charged her with shaping creation. He filled the universe with mysteries and entrusted Invention to oversee them. Not wishing for the heavens to remain idle, the Creator filled the upper world with spirits, ensuring that all regions of existence were active. Using sacred knowledge, He formed these beings by mixing His essence with an intellectual flame, along with other elements through hidden means.

From this mixture, a substance more refined and pure than the original elements emerged. It was transparent, visible only to the divine Artist. This new creation reached perfection, immune to both fire and cold, stable in its form and nature. The Creator named this essence Self-Consciousness. From it, He formed countless souls, carefully choosing the finest parts of the mixture for His purpose. Although the souls were not identical, the finest ones were animated by divine motion and set apart from the rest.

The Creator arranged the souls into layers, each more refined than the one beneath it, until sixty degrees were completed. Though the souls differed in rank, they all shared the same eternal essence, determined by the Creator alone. He placed them in their rightful places in the order of nature, instructing them to turn the wheel of life with wisdom and joy, fulfilling the divine plan.

Summoning these souls to the realms of ether, the Creator spoke to them: "O souls, my beloved children, formed from my breath and care, created by my hands to serve my universe, hear my law: Do not abandon the place I have prepared for you. Your home is the heavens, adorned with stars and thrones of virtue.

If you go against my command, I swear by my sacred breath, the same life-giving essence from which you were created, and by my creative hands, that I will quickly forge chains to bind you and cast you into punishment." After speaking these words, God combined the remaining elements—earth and water—into a new form. Using different, powerful words, He breathed life and motion into the liquid protoplasm, thickening it into a pliable material. From this, He shaped living beings in human form. He gave the remaining substance to the divine souls dwelling near the stars, known as the Sacred Genii, and instructed them: "Continue my work, my children, born of my nature. Use what I have left and shape beings in your own image. I will provide models."

God took the signs of the Zodiac and arranged them to guide creation, placing the animals after the human forms. He released the generative forces for all living beings, then withdrew, promising that every creation would carry an invisible breath and a reproductive essence so that life could continue without needing to be created from scratch.

"What did the souls do then, my Mother?" asked Horos. Isis replied, "They studied the material given to them, contemplating and admiring the Father's work. They sought to understand its components, though it was not easy to uncover. Fearing the Father's anger, they focused on following His commands. They used the lightest part of the protoplasm to create birds. As the mixture thickened, they formed quadrupeds, and with the densest part, supported by water, they created fish. The heaviest and coldest portions were used to make reptiles. Proud of their work, the souls began to disobey the divine law. They could not bear to stay in one place, restless in their pursuit of change, as stillness seemed like death to them."

Hermes told me that their disobedience did not escape the notice of the Lord. He decided to punish the souls and prepare chains to restrain them. To correct them, He shaped the human body—a blend of mortal and immortal elements. God summoned Hermes and said, "Soul of my soul, thought of my thought, how long must the world remain barren and without praise? How much longer will creation lie unfinished? Bring the gods before me." At His command, all the gods gathered. "Look upon the earth and everything below," God told them. When the gods gazed down, they understood His will.

When He asked what each god could offer to the new human race, the Sun spoke first: "I will illuminate them." The Moon followed, promising to bring enlightenment, along with Fear, Silence, Sleep, and Memory, which she had already created. Kronos offered Justice and Necessity. Zeus declared, "To prevent endless wars, I will bestow Fortune, Hope, and Peace." Ares proclaimed that he had already fathered Conflict, Zeal, and Ambition. Aphrodite eagerly added, "I will gift humans with Desire, Joy, and Laughter, so that the burdens placed upon their souls may not weigh too heavily."

The other gods welcomed Aphrodite's offer. Hermes then said, "I will grant humans Wisdom, Temperance, Persuasion, and Truth, and I will remain closely allied with Invention. I will protect the lives of those born under my signs, for the Creator has entrusted me with the Zodiac signs that govern Knowledge and Intelligence. I will assist whenever the stars align with the natural forces of these individuals."

The Lord rejoiced at the gods' offerings and decreed that the human race would be created. Hermes continued, "I sought the proper materials for this task and prayed to the Lord for guidance. He ordered the souls to release the leftover protoplasm. However, when I received it, it had dried up, so I added an excess of water to soften it. I ensured the new form would remain flexible and fragile, balancing intelligence with vulnerability. Once my work was complete, it was beautiful, and I rejoiced in what I had made. I called upon the Lord to witness my creation. He looked upon it and approved, ordering the souls to inhabit the forms."

The souls, upon learning of their fate, were filled with dread. Isis continued, "These words shook me deeply. Listen closely, my son Horos, for I share a great mystery with you. Our ancestor Kamephes received this knowledge from Hermes, who recorded all things. Kamephes passed it to me when I underwent the initiation of the black veil. Now I pass it to you, my beloved and extraordinary child."

Isis described the souls' reaction when they learned they would be bound to physical bodies. Some sighed and lamented, like wild animals suddenly captured and forced into servitude, rebelling against their captors. Others hissed like serpents or cried out in despair, looking helplessly from the heights of heaven to the depths below.

One soul cried, "Great Heaven, source of our birth, pure air, sacred breath of God, and you, shining stars, the unceasing light of the Sun and Moon—our brothers in the heavens—what sorrow awaits us! Must we leave these vast, radiant spaces, this sacred realm, and all the splendors of the divine world? Are we to be cast down into miserable, wretched places? What crime have we committed to deserve this punishment? What terrible sin have we, poor souls, committed to merit such suffering?"

Behold the sorrowful future that lies ahead—to tend to the needs of a fragile and fleeting body! No longer will our eyes perceive the souls of divine beings clearly. Through these clouded, earthly lenses, we will barely glimpse, with longing, our ancestral home in the heavens. There will be times when we won't see it at all. This tragic fate denies us the ability to see directly; we must rely on external light to see. Our eyes become mere windows, not true vision. And our suffering will deepen when we hear the winds breathing freely in the air—winds that we can no longer join. Our breath will be trapped, not in the wide, open world, but within the narrow prison of our own chests! Yet, O Master and Father, who cast us down from such a high place to this lowly state, set a limit to our suffering! Do not become indifferent to your creation. Let our punishment have an end, and give us a final message before we lose sight of the shining realms above!

This plea from the Souls was answered, my son Horos, for the Lord was present. Seated on the throne of Truth, He spoke: "Souls, you will be governed by Desire and Necessity. They will be your rulers and guides after Me. As long as you remain pure, you will live in the heavens. But if some of you are found guilty, you will dwell within mortal bodies. If your faults are minor, you will return to the heavens after being freed from the flesh. But those who commit serious wrongs, who abandon their true purpose, will not return to the heavens nor inhabit human bodies—they will enter the bodies of animals without reason."

It has been debated whether the Hermetic teachings support the idea of reincarnation into lower life forms. I believe they do align with this belief, without contradiction. The Divine Pymander states that if a human soul continues to act wickedly, "it will neither taste immortality nor partake in the good, but will be pulled back into creeping creatures; this is the fate of an evil soul." However, Hermes clarifies that a truly human soul—one containing the divine Mind—cannot fall this low, even if it has strayed. As long as the soul holds the divine fire within, it remains human, and such a soul is compared not to animals but to beings above, even to gods. Yet, if a soul falls so far that this inner flame is extinguished, it becomes dark and forsaken, no longer human. "Such a soul," says Hermes, "has lost the Mind and should not be called human."

This teaching emphasizes that a human soul cannot enter the body of a mindless creature, nor can it become something less than human unless it loses its divine essence. When a soul sinks to this low state, it gravitates toward creatures that match its nature. After its purification, however, the soul may awaken and say, "I will return to my Father." Some Rabbis have even suggested that this is the hidden meaning of the parable of the prodigal son, where the swine symbolize lust and base desires. The Hermetic view aligns with the Kabbalah and the teachings of Apollonius of Tyana on this point.

After addressing the souls, the Lord breathed upon them and said, "Your destiny is not left to chance. If you act wrongly, things will go badly for you; if you act wisely, they will improve. I, not another, will be your witness and judge. Your suffering in physical bodies is the result of your past mistakes. Each rebirth will be different, as I have already told you. Death will be a gift, restoring you to a better state. But if you act against My will, your judgment will be clouded. You will mistake suffering for fortune and fear happiness as if it were a curse.

Those among you who act with justice will rise closer to the divine in future lives. They will become wise rulers, true philosophers, visionary leaders, healers of plants, talented musicians, knowledgeable astronomers, insightful prophets, and servants of wisdom. These are noble roles. Just as the eagle does not harm its kind and protects the weak with justice, or the lion, who tirelessly performs great deeds in his mortal body, so too are the wise uplifted. The dragon, who is powerful, gentle, and a friend to man, embodies divine traits, and the dolphin, who saves drowning people without devouring them, shows kindness even as the most voracious sea creature."

After saying these things, the Lord returned to His incorruptible, unmanifested state. Then, my son Horos, a mighty Spirit arose from the earth. He had no physical form, yet was filled with wisdom and strength. Although fearsome, this Spirit knew what he sought and observed the human form with admiration, for it was both beautiful and dignified. He noticed the souls about to enter their bodies and asked, "What are these beings, Hermes, Secretary of the Gods?"

"These are men," replied Hermes.

The Spirit remarked, "It is risky to create men with such keen sight, quick tongues, and sharp hearing, allowing them to sense things not meant for them. They will have hands skilled enough to grasp anything. Is it wise to leave them free from care? These creatures, who will explore every corner of the earth, study plants and stones, and even dissect themselves to learn how they are made? They will cut down forests to cross seas in search of each other, and they will pursue the secrets of nature to the highest heavens. They will seek the edges of night and try to extend their power over the elements themselves. If they are free from hardship, fear, and anxiety, nothing will stop them—not even the heavens. Teach them desire and hope, so they may also know fear and failure. Let their souls struggle with love and longing, sometimes fulfilled, sometimes not, so that even success will lead them toward misfortune. Let them face sickness and suffering, breaking their desires and humbling their hearts."

Do you feel sorrow, Horos, hearing this story? Does it surprise you to learn about the hardships awaiting humanity? What you will hear next is even more troubling. Hermes approved the Spirit's words and decided to follow his advice.

"O Momos," he said, "the divine breath that fills all things will not fail in its purpose! The Master of the universe has entrusted me to oversee His creation. The deity with the all-seeing eye, Adrastia, will watch and guide every event. As for me, I will design a mysterious tool—one that is precise and unchanging, a law that will govern everything from birth to destruction and bind all created things together. This tool will rule over the earth and everything in it."

The Lord then summoned the assembly of the gods. They gathered, and He addressed them, saying: "You gods, who possess an eternal, unchanging nature and the power to sustain the harmony of the universe, how much longer shall we reign over an invisible world? How long will creation remain hidden from the light of the sun and moon? Let us each take our place in the universe and end this stagnant state. Let us transform chaos into an ancient tale, unbelievable to those who come after us. Begin your great work, and I will guide you."

With these words, the cosmic order, which had been hidden, revealed itself. The heavens appeared in all their splendor, and the earth, once unstable, grew firm under the sun's radiance, showing forth its hidden riches. In God's eyes, everything was beautiful, even what seemed unpleasant to mortals, for everything followed the divine laws. God rejoiced, seeing His creation full of life and movement, and with His hands He gathered the treasures of nature.

"Take these," He said, "O sacred earth, take these, you who will be the mother of all things. From now on, let nothing be lacking to you." Opening His divine hands, He poured these treasures into the heart of the universe. Yet, the embodied souls, ashamed of their fate, sought to rival the gods. Proud of their noble origin, they boasted of being equals to the gods and rebelled. In their rebellion, humans became their instruments, leading to conflicts and civil wars. The strong oppressed the weak, and both the living and the dead were cast out of sacred places.

The elements, witnessing these horrors, went before the Lord to complain about the cruelty of mankind. The fire spoke first, saying, "O Master, Creator of this new world, You whose name is revered by both gods and men, how long will You allow human life to remain without divine guidance? Reveal Yourself to the world that cries out for You. Bring peace to end their savage ways. Give life its laws and night its oracles. Let happy omens fill all things. Let people fear divine judgment, so they no longer sin. Punish wrongdoing fairly, and people will avoid evil. Teach them gratitude for blessings, and I will devote my flames to pure offerings. Let the altars rise with the sweet scent of sacrifices. But now, O Master, I am polluted. The wickedness of humans forces me to burn flesh, corrupting my purity. I am no longer what I was meant to be."

The air spoke next, saying, "O Master, I am tainted by the stench of corpses. I grow poisonous and foul, forced to witness things I was never meant to see."

Then the water took its turn: "Father and Creator of all things, divine source of life, command the waters to remain pure. The rivers and seas are now used to wash away the deeds of killers and to receive their victims."

Finally, the earth spoke: "O King, Ruler of the heavens and Lord of all orbits, Master and Father of the elements, everything in creation rises and falls by Your will, and everything must return to You. But look how the wickedness of humanity spreads across me. I, who was commanded to house all beings, now bear the burden of their sins. I receive into my depths everything that dies, and this has become my shame. Your creation is empty of divine presence, and because humans revere nothing, they break every law and fill me with evil deeds. I am polluted by the remains of the dead. But I, who receive all things, ask to also receive Your presence. Grant me this grace. If You cannot come Yourself—for I could never contain You—let me receive some part of Your divine essence. Let the earth become the most honored of all the elements. Since I give all things to all beings, let me revere myself as the vessel of Your blessings."

After hearing the pleas of the elements, God filled the universe with His divine voice.

"Go forth," He said, "sacred children, worthy of your Father's greatness. Do not try to change anything, and do not deny your service to My creations. I will send a pure Being, an extension of Myself, who will examine all actions. He will be the feared and incorruptible Judge of the living, and His justice will reach even the shadows beneath the earth. In this way, each person will receive what they deserve." After this, the elements stopped their complaints and returned to their proper roles and duties.

"But how," asked Horos, "did the earth receive this gift from God?"

"I cannot reveal this birth," Isis replied. "I dare not speak of your origins, mighty Horos, for fear that future generations may discover how the Gods were created. I will only say that the Supreme God, Creator, and Builder of the world, allowed Osiris, your father, and me, the great Goddess Isis, to come to the earth for a time to bring the salvation that was promised. With our arrival, life reached its fullness. Violent and bloody wars were brought to an end. We dedicated temples to the Gods who came before us and began the practice of offerings. We provided laws, food, and clothing to mortals."

"They will read my sacred writings," said Hermes, "and divide them into two parts. Some will be kept secret, while others will be engraved on columns and obelisks for the benefit of mankind." Osiris and Isis established the first courts of justice and brought order to the world. They introduced the practice of honoring treaties and the sacred duty of making oaths. They taught the proper rites for the burial of the dead, explored the mysteries of death, and explained how the soul longs to return to the body. If this return is blocked, life itself is disrupted.

Following the teachings of Hermes, they inscribed secret messages on hidden tablets, revealing that the air is filled with spirits. Through Hermes' guidance in divine law, they became humanity's first teachers and lawgivers, introducing people to knowledge, skills, and the advantages of civilized life. They also learned from Hermes about the connections between heaven and earth, which the Creator had established, and used this knowledge to create religious rituals and sacred ceremonies. Understanding that all physical bodies are subject to decay, they developed practices of prophetic initiation. This way, prophets who raise their hands in prayer to the Gods would gain full knowledge, allowing philosophy and magic to nourish the soul and medicine to heal the body.

After completing these tasks and seeing the world reach its peak, Osiris and I were summoned back to the heavens. But we could not return without first praising the Lord, ensuring that the celestial Vision would fill the skies and that the path for a joyful ascent would open before us, for God delights in hymns."

"O Mother," said Horos, "teach me this hymn so that I may learn it too."

"Listen carefully, my son," Isis replied.

PART 2

My honored son, if you wish to know anything more, ask me. Horos replied, Revered Mother, I would like to understand how royal souls are born. Isis responded: My son Horos, this is what makes royal souls different. There are four regions in the universe, each governed by unchanging laws: heaven, the ether, the air, and the sacred earth. In heaven live the Gods, who, like everything else, follow the commands of the Creator of the universe. The stars reside in the ether and are ruled by the great fire, the sun. The souls of spirits dwell in the air, ruled by the moon. On earth are humans and animals, led by a soul that serves as their king during its time on earth.

Even the Gods themselves create the souls that are meant to become kings in the earthly world. Kings give birth to princes, and the one who embodies the most kingly nature will rise to become a greater king than others. This isn't just about ordinary kings who rule nations, but about souls destined to lead humanity, whether spiritually, intellectually, or politically. The sun, being closer to God than the moon, is stronger and greater, and the moon follows the sun both in power and rank. A king is the lowest among the Gods, yet the highest among men. While he walks on earth, his divine nature remains hidden, but there is something within him that sets him apart from others and brings him closer to the divine. His soul comes from a higher place than those of ordinary people.

There are two reasons why souls are sent to reign on earth. Some souls, having lived pure and honorable lives before, are rewarded with a chance to become divine, with royalty serving as their preparation for this higher state. Others, who committed small mistakes against the inner divine law, receive royalty as a way to correct these faults. Through the challenges and burdens of being incarnated as royalty, they ease the hardships of their earthly existence and move closer to spiritual purification.

When these souls take on a body, their experience is different from others. They remain as blessed as when they were free. The differences in the nature of these kings are not in their souls, since all are royal. Instead, it comes from the qualities of the angels and spirits that guide them. Souls chosen for these roles are always accompanied by guardians and helpers. Even though they are sent away from the divine realms, they are still treated according to their true nature.

When the angels and spirits assigned to them are warriors, the soul adopts that nature, temporarily setting aside its own. If the angels are peaceful, the soul becomes calm. If the guardians value justice, the soul takes pleasure in judging fairly. If the spirits love music, the soul finds joy in singing. If they cherish truth, the soul becomes drawn to philosophy. In this way, souls take on the qualities of their guardians. When they enter human bodies, they lose their original state and become more like the beings that helped them take form.

Horos said, Mother, your explanation is clear, but you haven't told me how noble souls are born. On earth, just as there are different roles among people, souls also have different ranks. A soul that comes from a higher realm is nobler than the rest, just as a free person is nobler than a slave. Royal and noble souls are destined to be leaders over others.

How are souls born as male or female? Horos asked. Isis answered: All souls are the same by nature because they come from the same place, created by the Creator. There are no males or females among souls— those differences exist only in physical bodies, not in spiritual beings. Some souls are more active and others are gentler, and this reflects the air that surrounds them. Souls are wrapped in airy bodies made of earth, water, air, and fire. In women, there is more coldness and moisture than heat and dryness, making their souls softer. In men, the air around the soul has more heat and dryness, which makes them more energetic and lively.

And how, my mother, are the souls of wise people born? asked Horos. Isis replied: Think of vision, which is covered by layers of tissue. If the coverings are thick, the sight is weak; if they are thin and clear, the sight is sharp. The soul, too, has coverings made of invisible air. If these coverings are fine and light, the soul becomes clear and insightful. But when the coverings are heavy and dense, the soul can only see what is nearby, like trying to see through a cloudy day.

Why is it, my mother, that the minds of people outside our sacred land seem less open than the minds of those who belong to it? Horos asked. Isis answered: The earth is positioned in the center of the universe, like a person lying on their back and looking up at the sky. The different regions of the earth correspond to different parts of this body. The earth looks to the heavens like a child looking to a father, and its changes follow the movements of the sky.

The head of the earth lies to the south, the right shoulder to the east, and the left shoulder toward the winds of Libya. The feet rest under the stars of the Bear constellation, with the right foot beneath the tail and the left foot beneath the head of the Bear. The waist aligns with the sky closest to the Bear, and the middle of the body lies under the center of the heavens. You can see proof of these connections in the way people from different places look and behave. Those who live in the south have beautiful faces and thick hair. People from the east are skilled with their hands, good in battle, and quick with a bow, using their right hands with ease. Those from the west are strong and fight with their left hands, doing with their left what others do with their right. People living beneath the Bear constellation are known for the shape and beauty of their legs. Those from places beyond the Bear, such as Italy and Greece, are admired for the beauty of their waists, which is why they often favor male companionship. That part of the body, being lighter in color, produces men with fairer skin.

The sacred land of our ancestors lies at the center of the earth. Just as the heart sits in the middle of the human body and serves as the seat of the soul, the heart of the earth gives life and wisdom to the people born from it. This is why, my son, the people of this land possess not only the same qualities that all humans share but also a higher intelligence and deeper wisdom, for they are nourished by the heart of the earth. Additionally, my son, the southern region stores the clouds, gathering them until they release the river (Nile) when the cold grows intense. Wherever these clouds gather, the air becomes heavy with mist, which not only clouds vision but also dulls the mind.

The east, my son Horos, is restless with the rising sun, just as the west stirs with the setting sun. Those who live in these regions find it difficult to maintain clear thinking. In the north, the cold hardens both body and mind. Only the central land remains calm and bright, blessing its people with tranquility. From this peaceful place, life is created and perfected. The central land stands strong against others, triumphs over them, and, like a noble ruler, shares the rewards of victory with those it has defeated.

Horos asked, Tell me more, Mother. What causes people to lose clarity, reason, or even part of their soul during long illnesses? Isis replied: Every animal connects with one or more of the elements—fire, water, earth, or air. Some creatures are closely tied to a specific element, while others are connected to two, three, or even all four. In the same way, some animals avoid certain elements. For example, insects and locusts flee from fire. Eagles, hawks, and other birds avoid water. Fish fear both air and land. Snakes, like all creatures that crawl, love the ground but avoid open air. Fish thrive in deep waters, and birds enjoy life in the skies. Those birds that fly highest find joy in the heat of the sun and remain close to it. Some creatures, like salamanders, even live within fire.

The elements surround and bind the body, and every soul in a body feels the weight of these elements. As a result, every soul is drawn to certain elements and repelled by others, which keeps it from finding perfect happiness. Yet, since the soul is divine, it continues to seek and reflect, even while trapped in a physical form. However, the soul's thoughts are not as free as they would be without the body. If the body is troubled by illness or fear, the soul is thrown into confusion, just as a man is tossed around by stormy waves.

PART 3

You have given me wonderful knowledge, powerful Mother Isis, about how God creates souls, and I am amazed by it. But you have not yet explained where souls go when they leave their bodies. I deeply wish to understand this mystery and will be grateful for your guidance. Isis replied: Listen carefully, my son, for this is a very important question, and it must not be overlooked. I will answer you fully. Do not think that when souls leave their bodies, they get lost in the vastness of the universe, merging into a boundless spirit with no way to return to a body or retain their identity. Imagine water spilled from a vase—it cannot return to the vase, and instead, it mixes with all other water. But this is not what happens with souls, wise Horos. I have been initiated into the mysteries of the immortal soul, and I walk the path of truth. I will tell you everything, leaving nothing out.

Water is made up of countless fluid particles without reason or purpose, while the soul is an individual being, created by God's mind and hands, filled with intelligence. Souls are born from unity, not from many things, so they do not mix with other beings. To join the soul with a body, God enforces a union through divine necessity. Souls do not return to the same place by chance or in confusion but are sent to the place that matches their experience. What they go through while living in a body, which weighs them down and limits them, determines where they will go next.

Listen to this example, my beloved Horos. Imagine a prison filled with people, eagles, doves, swans, hawks, swallows, sparrows, flies, serpents, lions, leopards, wolves, dogs, hares, oxen, sheep, and amphibious animals like seals, turtles, hydras, and crocodiles. Now imagine all these creatures being set free at the same time. Each would go where it belongs—humans to cities and public places, eagles to the sky, doves to the lower air, hawks to the higher air, swallows to places where people gather, sparrows to orchards, and swans to places where they can sing. Flies would stay close to the ground, living off the smells and vapors they find there. Lions and leopards would run to the mountains, wolves to remote places, dogs would follow humans, hares would go to the woods, oxen to fields, and sheep to pastures. Serpents would seek caves in the earth. Seals and turtles would return to shallow waters and rivers, living as they are meant to, close to both land and water. Every creature knows where it belongs, guided by its nature. In the same way, every soul—whether it lived as a human or some other form—knows where it must go. It would be as foolish as saying a bull could live in water or a turtle could survive in the air to believe that souls would forget their place.

Even while they are trapped in flesh and blood, souls obey the laws of order, even though living in a body is a kind of punishment. How much more, then, will they follow these laws when they are free from the body! This sacred law applies to everything, even reaching up to the heavens. Now, my noble son, listen to how the hierarchy of souls is arranged. The space between the highest heaven, called the empyrean, and the moon is filled with gods, stars, and divine powers. Below the moon, between it and the earth, lies the home of souls.

The endless air, which we call wind, has its own paths to follow as it moves across the earth to give it life. But the movement of the wind does not block the path of souls. Souls travel freely through the air without mixing with it, much like water gliding over oil. This space between the earth and the heavens is divided into four main sections and sixty smaller regions. The first section starts from the earth and rises through four regions until it reaches certain high points, which it cannot go beyond.

The second province includes eight regions where the winds begin their movement. Pay close attention, my son, for you are hearing the hidden mysteries of the earth, the sky, and the sacred fluid that lies between them. Now, I will tell you, my glorious Horos, which souls inhabit each of these regions, starting with the highest. In the province of the winds, the birds fly, for beyond that point, there is no moving air, and no creatures can live there. However, the air spreads into every corner within its reach and fills all the boundaries of the four directions of the earth, even though the earth itself cannot rise into the homes of the air.

The third province contains sixteen regions filled with a pure and delicate element. The fourth province has thirty-two regions where the air becomes so thin and clear that fire can pass through it without resistance. This is the order that rules from the lowest point to the highest: four main divisions, twelve intervals, and sixty regions, where each soul lives according to its nature. Though all souls share the same essence, they are arranged in a hierarchy. The farther a region is from the earth, the greater the dignity of the souls living there.

The space between the earth and the heavens is divided into these regions with careful order and harmony, my son Horos. Different people have called them by many names—zones, firmaments, or spheres. These are the places where souls dwell—both those who have been freed from their bodies and those who have not yet taken one. The position each soul occupies reflects its worth. Divine and royal souls reside in the upper regions, while the less noble souls remain close to the surface of the earth. Souls of ordinary rank inhabit the middle areas.

The souls destined to rule descend from the higher zones. When these souls are freed from their bodies, they return to their original home, or even to a higher realm—unless, of course, they have acted in ways that go against their dignity and God's laws. If they have failed, divine Providence sends them to lower regions according to their mistakes. Similarly, souls of lower rank may be moved to higher places as they grow in strength and honor.

Two great ministers serve universal Providence. One guards the souls, and the other leads them, giving them bodies and guiding them through their paths. The first minister protects the souls, while the second binds or releases them according to God's will. This sacred law of fairness governs the changes above, just as it shapes and forms the physical bodies in which the souls are housed.

This law works alongside two forces: Memory and Experience. Memory ensures that all things in creation retain their original design, as determined in the heavens. Experience ensures that every soul receives a body that matches its nature. Passionate souls are given strong bodies, lazy souls weak ones, active souls energetic bodies, gentle souls peaceful ones, powerful souls robust forms, and cunning souls are given quick and nimble bodies. In short, every soul is provided with the right kind of body.

There is wisdom in the way all creatures are formed. Birds are covered with feathers, intelligent beings are given sharp senses, and animals in the wild are equipped with horns, tusks, claws, or other defenses. Reptiles, with their smooth and flexible bodies, are also given sharp teeth or scales to protect them from harm, since their moist nature could otherwise make them weak. Fish, being timid creatures, are given a home in water, where the power of fire is dulled, for it can neither shine nor burn in that element.

Each fish swims freely using its fins, moving wherever it chooses, and its weakness is hidden by the darkness of the deep water. In the same way, souls are placed in bodies that suit their nature: rational souls in human bodies, wild souls in flying creatures, and souls without reason in beasts, whose only rule is strength. Deceptive souls dwell in reptiles, for they do not attack openly but strike by hiding and waiting. Timid souls inhabit fish, as they are not fit to live in other elements. Yet in every kind of creature, there are some that act against their nature.

How does this happen, Mother? asked Horos. And Isis replied: A person might act without reason, a beast might escape the need for survival, a reptile may forget its cunning, a fish could lose its fear, and a bird might abandon its freedom. You have now heard about the hierarchy of souls, their descent, and how bodies are created. In each type of soul, there are some royal ones, with various qualities—some fiery, some cold, some proud, some gentle, some clever, some simple, some thoughtful, and others active. These differences reflect the regions from which the souls descend into bodies. Royal souls come from a royal realm, though there are many kinds of royalty—spiritual, physical, artistic, intellectual, and moral.

How do you describe these kinds of royalty? asked Horos. Isis answered: The king of souls is your father, Osiris. The king of bodies is the ruler of each nation. The king of wisdom is the Father of all things. The master of knowledge is Hermes Trismegistus, and Asclepius, the son of Hephaestus, presides over medicine. Power belongs to Osiris, and after him, to you, my son. Philosophy is guided by Arnebaskenis, and poetry by Asclepius, the son of Imhotep. So, as you reflect on this, you will see that there are many forms of kingship. The highest form of royalty belongs to the highest realm, while the lesser ones correspond to the different regions from which they originate. Souls born from the fiery realm handle fire; those from the watery realm thrive in water; those from the realms of art and knowledge pursue these paths; and those from the realm of idleness live in ease. Everything that happens on earth has its origin in the higher realms, where all things are measured and balanced. Nothing begins here that does not first come from above and eventually return there.

Explain this further, Mother, said Horos. And Isis replied: Nature has stamped this truth into every creature. We breathe in air from above, exhale it, and breathe it in again through our lungs, which are made for this purpose. When our lungs can no longer receive air, we leave this life. Other disruptions can also break the balance of our nature.

What do you mean by this balance, Mother? Horos asked. Isis answered: It is the mixing and union of the four elements, which produce a vapor that surrounds the soul and enters the body, giving both a certain nature. This combination explains the variety in both souls and bodies. If fire is the dominant element in the body, the soul—already fiery—becomes even more energetic, and the body more lively and active. If air is dominant, both body and soul become unstable and restless. When water is the strongest element, the soul becomes gentle, kind, and adaptable, as water mixes easily with other things. If there is too much water, the body becomes soft and weak, easily broken by illness. If earth is dominant, the soul becomes slow, as the body's dense structure prevents clear expression. Such a soul turns inward, burdened by the heavy body, which moves slowly and with effort. But when all elements are balanced, the entire nature becomes lively in action, quick in movement, sensitive in perception, and strong in health.

Birds are born from a mixture of air and fire, matching the nature of the elements that form them. Humans have a large amount of fire, with a little air, and equal parts of water and earth. This abundance of fire gives humans intelligence, for thought is like a flame—it burns through obstacles, not with destruction, but by insight.

When water and earth dominate, with a little air and very little fire, animals are born. Those that have more fire than others are braver. When water and earth are present in equal amounts, reptiles are formed. Lacking fire, these creatures have no courage or honesty. Too much water makes them cold, while too much earth makes them dull and heavy, and with little air, they struggle to move easily. Creatures like fish are born when water far exceeds the amount of earth. Without fire or air, they are timid and prefer to stay hidden. The heavy presence of water and earth in their nature makes them similar to the way soil dissolves in water.

The growth of the body happens through the balanced increase of these elements. When the right amount is reached, growth stops. As long as the original balance of fire, air, earth, and water stays the same, the creature stays healthy. But if these elements lose their balance—whether by too much or too little fire, air, water, or earth—illness will arise. I am not talking about changes in activity or shifts in order, but rather a disruption in the balance itself. If air and fire, which are closest to the soul's nature, become too strong, the creature loses its natural state, as these elements tend to weaken the body.

The body relies on earth to sustain it, while water helps bind it together. Air provides movement, and fire gives energy. When these elements combine, they create vapors that merge with the soul, influencing it with their own qualities, whether good or bad. As long as the soul stays in harmony with these elements, it maintains its current state. But if the balance shifts, the relationship between the body and soul also changes. Fire and air, which naturally rise upward, pull the soul with them, while water and earth, which are drawn toward the ground, weigh down the body, making it heavy and keeping it tied to the earth.

A Treatise on Initiations; or, Asclepios

PART 1

Hermes: It is by the will of a god that you have come to us, Asclepios, so that you may take part in a divine discussion. This will be the most sacred teaching we have ever shared or been inspired to deliver. If you understand it, you will gain every blessing—though, perhaps, it is more accurate to say that all blessings are really just one, since they are all connected. They come from the same source, forming a unity that cannot be separated. You will understand this if you listen carefully to what we are about to say. But first, Asclepios, step away for a moment and find someone to join us for this discussion.

[Asclepios suggests inviting Ammon.]

There is no reason why Ammon cannot join us, replied Trismegistus. I have written to him before on topics about nature and other teachings, as I would to a beloved son. But it is your name, Asclepios, that I will place at the beginning of this work. Do not invite anyone else except for Ammon, for a conversation about the holiest matters should not be shared with too many. It would be wrong to reveal these divine teachings to a large audience, just as it would be wrong to share sacred truths with those who cannot understand or respect them.

[Ammon enters, completing the group, which now has four members.]

The presence of four is essential for these teachings, for they reflect the four great aspects of existence, representing the entirety of the universe. As Nebuchadnezzar said in the allegory recorded by Daniel, "The form of the fourth is like the Son of God." This shows how, through transformation instead of destruction, the earthly elements of man are purified by suffering.

Hermes: Every human soul, Asclepios, is immortal. But not every soul's immortality is the same. The way they experience it and the length of their journey differ from soul to soul.

Asclepios: That must be because not all souls are of the same kind, Trismegistus.

Hermes: You understand quickly, Asclepios! I haven't yet mentioned

249

that everything is one, and one is everything. All things existed within the Creator before they came into being, and we call Him "all" because everything belongs to Him. Throughout this discussion, remember that the Creator is both One and All, the source of everything. All things flow from above—down to the earth, into the waters, and through the air. Fire alone rises, giving life, while everything that descends becomes subject to it. What comes down from above creates, and what rises from below nourishes. The earth, which supports itself, receives and reshapes all that it takes in.

The universe contains everything and is everything. It moves the soul and the world and encompasses all that nature holds. Though life expresses itself in countless different forms, all these forms are connected, creating unity. Everything emerges from this oneness. The universe is made of four elements: fire, water, earth, and air. There is one world, one soul, and one God.

Now, focus your thoughts fully, for understanding the Divine requires divine help. This knowledge is like a powerful river rushing forward with great speed. It moves so quickly that it can easily escape the attention of those listening—and even the one who teaches it.

PART 2

Heaven, which reveals God, governs all things. The sun and moon determine the growth and decline of all bodies. But it is the true God—the Creator—who directs heaven, the soul, and everything that exists in the world. From His high place, countless influences flow down, spreading through the world into every soul, both in general and in specific ways, and into the nature of all things. God prepared the world to receive every individual form. Through Nature, He shapes these forms and draws the world upward toward heaven using the four elements. Everything follows God's plan, though the things that come from above are separated into individuals in a specific way.

Each type contains many individuals that share its nature. A type is whole, while each individual is a part of that whole. For example, gods make up one type, as do spirits, humans, birds, and all other beings in the world. These types create individual beings that resemble their original type. There is also a type without sensation but not without a soul—plants, which survive by rooting themselves in the earth. Individual plants can be found everywhere. Heaven is filled with God's presence. The types I mentioned extend all the way up to the beings whose individual souls are immortal. While types are eternal, not all individuals are. For example, humanity as a type is immortal, but individual humans are not.

Divine beings form a type where both the type and its individuals are as eternal as the divine itself. For other beings, only the type is eternal, while individual creatures die and are replaced through reproduction. Some individual beings are mortal. For example, man is mortal, but humanity as a whole is immortal. Yet, individual beings of all kinds can mix with those from other types. Some are original creations, while others are brought forth by gods, spirits, or humans. All of them resemble the type they come from. Bodies only take shape through divine will, individual beings take on their unique qualities with the help of spirits, and humans play a role in the care and training of animals.

Some spirits leave their original type and join with divine beings, becoming companions and allies of the gods. Those who keep their original character are called spirits and are drawn to things connected with humanity. Humans are similar to spirits, and in some ways, they even surpass them. Human individuality is complex and diverse because it results from the connections between different types. Humans serve as a vital link between many other kinds of beings. A person who aligns with the gods through intelligence and devotion becomes close to God. A person who aligns with spirits draws closer to them. Those who remain content with ordinary human life stay part of the human type. Other individuals will find themselves connected with the beings they are naturally drawn toward.

PART 3

Man, Asclepios, is a great wonder, a being worthy of admiration and respect. He moves within this divine world as though he were a god himself. He understands the nature of spirits and, knowing that he shares the same origin, he rises above his human side to focus on the divine within him. How fortunate and close to the gods mankind is! By connecting with the divine, man lets go of his earthly nature. Through love, he forms a bond with all other beings and feels his role is essential to the order of the universe. He looks toward the heavens and, from his place between the higher and lower realms, he loves everything beneath him and is loved by everything above him.

He works the land, harnesses the speed of the elements, and uses his sharp mind to explore the depths of the sea. Nothing is hidden from him. Heaven does not seem too distant, for knowledge lifts him up to it. His mind's brilliance is not dimmed by the thick air, the pull of the earth does not hold him back, and the depths of the ocean do not trouble him. He embraces everything and remains the same, no matter where he is.

All living beings seem to have roots that reach downward, but lifeless things have only one root that grows upward, supporting many branches like a tree. Some creatures live by feeding on two elements, while others need only one. There are also two kinds of nourishment—one for the soul and one for the body. The soul of the world is sustained by constant motion, while bodies grow through the nourishment provided by water and earth, the elements of the lower world. The spirit, which fills all things, mingles with everything and brings life to it. This spirit gives consciousness to intelligence, and through the fifth element—the ether—man receives the unique gift of awareness. In humans, this awareness becomes a deeper understanding of the divine order.

Since I am now speaking of consciousness, I will soon explain its purpose, which is as grand and sacred as divinity itself. But first, let us continue what we have already begun, speaking of humanity's union with the gods—a gift given only to mankind. Only a few people have the great fortune to understand the divine, a knowledge that exists only within God and the human mind.

Asclepios: Do all men have this awareness, Trismegistus?

Hermes: No, Asclepios, not everyone has true intelligence. Some people are deceived by the surface of things, following appearances without searching for their deeper meaning. This is where evil arises in man, causing the highest of creatures to lower himself to the level of animals. But I will explain more about consciousness and the mind later.

Man alone is made of two parts. One part is single and essential, as the Greeks say, formed in the image of the divine. The other part, which the Greeks call Kosmic, belongs to the material world and is made of four elements. This part makes up the body, which serves as a covering for the divine spirit within. The divine part, along with its pure perceptions and intelligence, hides behind the barrier of the physical body.

PART 4

Asclepios: Why, then, Trismegistus, was man placed in this world instead of with God, where he could live in perfect happiness?

Hermes: Your question is a reasonable one, Asclepios, and I ask God to help me answer it, for everything depends on His will—especially these great matters we are now discussing. Listen carefully, Asclepios. The Lord and Creator of all things, whom we call God, brought forth another God—one that can be seen and perceived by the senses. I call him sensible not because he possesses feelings, for this is not the place to discuss that, but because he is experienced through sight and touch. After bringing forth this being—who stands above all creatures and ranks second only to Himself—God saw that His creation was beautiful and filled with every kind of goodness. He loved it as His own child.

For God, to will something and to make it happen are one and the same. His will is instantly accomplished. Knowing that the essential part of man could not understand everything unless it was wrapped in the physical world, He gave man a body to dwell in. God wanted man to have two natures. He united and blended these natures perfectly. Through this, man could admire and worship the celestial and eternal things and also take care of and govern what is on earth.

Man was made with both spirit and body, with a nature that is partly eternal and partly mortal. This combination allows him to honor what is divine while managing the things of this world. I speak here of earthly things—not just the elements of earth and water that are under man's care, but also the things that come from him or depend on him. These include tending the land, raising livestock, building structures, creating ports, navigating the seas, engaging in trade, and carrying out exchanges that form the bonds between people.

Earth and water are part of the world, and this earthly part is supported by arts and sciences. Without these, the world would be incomplete in God's eyes. Whatever God wills must happen, and the result always accompanies His will. We cannot believe that anything which pleased Him at the beginning would stop pleasing Him, for from the very start He knew what would exist and what would bring Him joy.

PART 5

I see, Asclepios, that you are eager to understand how heaven and its inhabitants can become the focus of human aspiration and worship. Know then, Asclepios, that to seek after the God of heaven and all who dwell there is to offer them constant reverence, for man alone, among both divine and earthly beings, is capable of doing so. The admiration, worship, praise, and devotion of man bring joy to heaven and its celestial inhabitants. The Muses were sent to men by the supreme Divinity so that the earthly world would not lack the beauty of hymns, and so that the human voice might sing to the One who is All, the Father of everything. In this way, the gentle harmonies of earth are united with the choirs of heaven.

Only a few men, with minds pure and clear, are given the sacred task of seeing heaven clearly. Those whose minds are weighed down by the conflict between their earthly and divine natures are connected to the lower elements. Man is not lessened because he has a mortal part. In fact, his mortality increases his abilities and strength. His dual nature allows him to fulfill both earthly and divine roles. He is made in such a way that he can connect with both the physical world and the divine.

I hope, Asclepios, that you will give this teaching your full attention and focus, for many people lack faith in these things. Now I will explain the true principles for the benefit of the purest minds.

PART 6

The Master of Eternity is the first God, the world is the second, and man is the third. God, the Creator of the world and everything in it, governs the universe and places it under man's authority. In turn, man focuses his efforts on the world, making it his responsibility. The world and man are interconnected, each depending on the other, which is why the Greeks call the world Kosmos. Man understands both himself and the world, so he should know what aligns with his nature, what he can use, and what he should revere. As he offers praise and gratitude to God, he must also honor the world, which reflects God's image, just as man is also an image of God. God has two likenesses: the world and man.

Man's nature is complex. His soul, consciousness, mind, and reason are divine qualities, capable of reaching toward heaven. But his physical body, made of fire, water, earth, and air, is mortal and belongs to the earth, returning to it when life ends. In this way, man is made of both a divine part and a mortal part, with his body serving as the temporary vessel for the soul. The guiding principle of this dual nature is religion, and its result is goodness. Man reaches perfection when he frees himself from desires and rejects what is not truly part of him. The material things the body craves are external to the divine mind and can be called possessions only because they are not born with us but are acquired later. They are foreign to man's true nature, just as even the body itself is. For this reason, man must resist both the objects of desire and the part of him that makes him vulnerable to those desires.

It is man's duty to direct his soul through reason, allowing the contemplation of the divine to help him focus less on the mortal body that was given to him to care for the material world. For man to function fully, both his physical and spiritual aspects must work together. His body, with its two hands, two feet, and other organs, connects him to the lower, earthly world. At the same time, his inner nature is equipped with four essential faculties: sensibility, soul, memory, and foresight. These enable him to understand and perceive divine truths. With these abilities, man can explore differences, qualities, causes, and quantities. However, if the body weighs too heavily on him, it will prevent him from understanding the deeper truths of existence.

When man fulfills his purpose—governing the world and worshiping the Divine—what reward should he receive? If the world is the work of God, then the person who tends and enhances its beauty becomes a helper of God's will, using both his body and his daily efforts to serve what was created by God. What reward could be greater than the one given to our ancestors? May divine goodness grant us the same reward. All our hopes and prayers strive toward this goal: that we may be freed from the prison of the body and, released from the chains of mortality, return pure and sanctified to the divine inheritance of our nature.

Asclepios: What you say is just and true, Trismegistus. This is indeed the reward for honoring God and caring for the world. But those who live without piety are denied this return to the heavens. Instead, they must endure punishment, being sent into new bodies, a fate from which holy souls are spared.

The end of this teaching gives us the hope of an eternal future for the soul, a future earned through how we live in this world. Yet some find this idea hard to believe. To others, it is a mere story, and still others mock it. For many, the pleasures of the physical world are too sweet to resist. That is the problem—they become attached to their mortal part, forgetting their divine nature, and they lose sight of immortality.

I tell you this with prophetic insight: in the future, no one will choose the simple path of philosophy, which consists of studying divine things and practicing holy religion. Most people will complicate philosophy with all sorts of questions, adding subjects that do not belong to it. Why do they burden it with unnecessary sciences, and how do they mix it with so many irrelevant matters?

Hermes: Asclepios, they mix philosophy with all sorts of unnecessary subjects—like arithmetic, music, and geometry. But pure philosophy, which should focus on holy religion, should only touch on other sciences to admire the predictable movements of the stars, their positions, and their paths, as measured by calculation. It should explore the size of the earth, its qualities and quantities, the depths of the sea, and the power of fire. It should seek to understand the effects of these things and how Nature works, honoring both Art and the divine intelligence behind it. As for music, it is understood when one grasps reason and the divine order of the universe. This order arranges everything perfectly within the unity of the whole, creating a beautiful harmony and a divine melody.

Asclepios: What, then, will happen to men after us?

Hermes: Misled by the clever tricks of false teachers, they will stray from true, pure, and holy philosophy. To worship God with simple thoughts and a pure heart, to honor His works, and to bless His will—this alone is philosophy untouched by the distractions of idle curiosity. But that is enough on this subject.

PART 7

Let's begin by discussing Mind and related matters. In the beginning, there were God and Hylè—the Greek word for the first substance or matter of the universe. Spirit was present in the universe but not in the same way as with God. The things that make up the universe are not God; before they came into being, they did not exist, though they were contained in the source from which they would eventually emerge. Beyond created things is not only that which has yet to be born but also that which lacks the ability to create anything. Whatever has the power to create holds within it the seeds of all that can come into being, for it is natural that what exists can bring forth more existence.

God, however, is eternal and cannot be born. He always is, has been, and will be. His nature is to exist without a beginning. Matter, or the nature of the world, and mind both seem to have been brought forth at the beginning, possessing the ability to grow and create. The potential to generate life lies within Nature herself, and she acts as the source of creation without needing outside help. This is different from beings that can only create when they mix with something else. The universe holds within it all of Nature, acting as a womb for everything that exists. I call it a womb because nothing could come into being without a space to hold it. Everything that exists must occupy a place, for without a space to contain them, things could have no qualities, quantities, positions, or effects.

Although the world itself was not born, it holds within it the source of all creation, providing a fitting place for everything to be conceived. The universe contains the potential for both good and evil. This leads some to ask whether God could have prevented evil from existing. There is no need to answer them, but for you, Asclepios and Ammon, I will explain. Some say that God should have kept the world free from evil, but evil is an inherent part of creation. God has provided humanity with emotions, knowledge, and intelligence so that we can avoid evil. These gifts make humans superior to other animals, giving us the ability to recognize and escape evil before being trapped by it. True knowledge rests on supreme goodness.

Spirit animates and gives life to everything in the world. It acts as the tool through which the will of God is carried out. We must understand the supreme, invisible God through intelligence alone. This God directs the secondary, visible God—the universe—containing all space, matter, and energy, along with everything that can create and produce. Spirit, or Mind, governs all individual beings in the world according to the nature assigned to them by God. Matter—called Hylè or the Kosmos— serves as the container, motion, and reflection of everything that God directs. It provides each thing with what it needs and fills it with spirit according to its nature.

The universe takes the shape of a hollow sphere, containing within it- self the reason for its form, though the cause of this form remains invis- ible. If someone were to examine any point on its surface and try to see what lies at its center, they would find nothing visible. The sphere can only be seen through the forms that appear on its surface, but in itself, it remains invisible. The center of this sphere—if it can be called a place— is known as Hades in Greek, meaning "the unseen," since it cannot be observed from the outside. The Greeks called the forms that shape reali- ty "Ideas" because they represent the unseen patterns that give shape to everything. This hidden center, known as Hades by the Greeks, is called Hell (Inferno) by the Latins because of its deep and concealed location. These are the fundamental principles from which all things arise. Every- thing exists in them, through them, or emerges from them.

Asclepios: Are these principles the foundation of all individual beings, Trismegistus?

Hermes: Yes, the world sustains bodies, and spirit sustains souls. Thought, which is a gift from heaven and a privilege of humanity, nour- ishes intelligence, though only a few people have minds capable of re- ceiving this gift. Thought is like a light that illuminates the mind, just as the sun illuminates the world. But it is even greater than the sun's light, which can be blocked by the moon or hidden when night falls. Once thought has entered the human soul, it becomes part of her nature and can never again be darkened by ignorance. This is why it is rightly said that the souls of the gods are pure intelligences. As for me, I say not this of all of them, but of the great supernal Gods.

PART 8

Asclepios: What are the fundamental principles of everything, Trismegistus?

Hermes: I am about to reveal to you profound and divine mysteries. As we begin, I ask for the favor of heaven, for these truths are not ordinary. There are many levels of divine beings, and each of them contains an element of intelligence. Do not think they are beyond our perception. In fact, we can understand them more clearly than things that are merely visible, as you will soon discover. If you pay close attention to what I am about to say, you will grasp this truth. These ideas are lofty and sacred, far beyond human understanding, so you must remain focused. If not, these words will pass through your mind without taking root, only to return to their source and be lost again.

There are gods above all visible forms, followed by spiritual gods. These gods, because they have both spiritual and physical aspects, express their presence through their visible nature, with each one illuminating the others through their works. Everything is connected, from the center of creation to its farthest reaches, in accordance with the natural relationships between things. The supreme being of the heavens is called Zeus, for it is through the heavens that Zeus gives life to all things. The supreme being of the sun is light, which reaches us through the sun's disk. The thirty-six constellations are ruled by a being named Pantomorphos, meaning "one with all forms," because he gives divine shape to everything. The seven planets are governed by the spirits of Fortune and Destiny, who ensure the laws of Nature remain stable, even amid constant change. Ether serves as the medium through which everything is created.

Everything follows its kind: mortal beings are drawn to what is mortal, and visible things to what is visible. However, the ultimate guidance belongs to the highest master, so all diversity resolves back into unity. All things either emerge from unity or depend on it. Though things may appear separate, they are really parts of the same whole, which consists of two fundamental principles. These principles are the substance from which all things are made and the will of the One who shapes them.

Asclepios: What is the reason for this, Trismegistus?

Hermes: It is because God is the Father and ruler of everything. Though we may call Him by many names—each sacred in its own way—none of these names can fully describe His divine nature. Words are just sounds carried by air, expressing what a person's mind understands through the senses. Names, made of syllables and spoken aloud, are symbols that connect the voice to the ear. But no matter how complex a name may be, it cannot capture the essence of the One who is the source of all greatness. Yet, since He must be named, we must either call Him "All" or refer to Him by the names of everything that exists.

He is both one and all, containing the fullness of both masculine and feminine principles. Through His own will, He continuously creates everything He intends. His will is universal goodness, and this same goodness is present in everything. Nature is born from His divine essence, ensuring that all things are exactly as they should be and that Nature itself has the power to give birth to everything that will come into existence.

This, Asclepios, is why everything has both male and female aspects.

Asclepios: Do you say this is true even of God, Trismegistus?

Hermes: Yes, not just of God but of all things, whether they are alive or not. Nothing that exists can be without the ability to create. If things could not bring forth life, they could not remain as they are. This law of creation is present in Nature, in the mind, and throughout the universe, sustaining everything that is brought into existence. Both male and female are full of creative power, and their union—or rather, their perfect merging—can be known as Eros, or Aphrodite, or even by both names together.

If the mind can grasp one truth more clearly than any other, it is this: the duty to create life is a law that the God of Nature has placed on all beings. To this law, He has also attached the highest joy, delight, longing, and the purest love. There would be no need to explain the importance of this law, since everyone can sense it within themselves. Notice how, at the moment when the essence of life flows from the brain, the two natures blend into each other. One eagerly draws in and hides the seed of the other. Through this joining, the female receives the strength of the male, and the male rests on the embrace of the female.

This sacred union is performed in secret, for if it were openly displayed, the divine nature of both would risk being mocked by those who do not understand. True piety is rare in this world, and it would not take long to count the few who possess it. Most people are filled with malice because they lack wisdom and knowledge of how the universe works. Understanding divine religion is the foundation of all things, leading to the rejection of vices and providing the remedy for them. But when ignorance takes hold, vice grows and wounds the soul in ways that are difficult to heal. A soul poisoned by vice swells with sickness, and only knowledge and understanding can restore it.

Let us continue this teaching, even if only a few will benefit from it. Now, Asclepios, listen carefully as I explain why God gave part of His intelligence and knowledge to humanity alone.

God the Father, the Ruler above all gods, gave man reason and intelligence to help him avoid or overcome the weaknesses of the body and to hold on to the hope of immortality. Man was created good, capable of living forever, and formed from two natures: one divine and one mortal. This dual nature makes man superior to both the gods, who possess only immortality, and mortal beings, who lack divinity. Because of this, man is closely connected to the gods, honoring them with religious devotion, and the gods, in turn, care for human affairs with affection. But I speak only of pious men. As for the wicked, I will not mention them here, for discussing them would spoil the holiness of this teaching.

PART 9

And since we are now speaking of the connection and similarity between humans and gods, consider the power and ability of man, Asclepios. Just as the Ruler and Father—whom we call God—created the celestial gods, man creates the gods that dwell in temples. These gods enjoy being close to humans, for they not only receive light but also give it in return. This connection benefits both mankind and the gods, strengthening them.

Does this surprise you, Asclepios? Do you doubt it, as many others do?

Asclepios: I am amazed, Trismegistus, but I accept your words. I see that man is truly fortunate to have such a gift.

Hermes: Yes, he is indeed worthy of admiration, for he is the greatest of all gods. The celestial gods are made from the purest part of Nature, without any mixture of other elements, and their visible forms are like heads only.

Asclepios: But the gods made by humans have two aspects—one divine, which is their purest nature, and the other human, formed from earthly matter. These gods not only have heads but also full bodies, with all their limbs. This means that humans, remembering their own nature and origins, imitate the divine by creating these gods. Just as the Father and Lord shaped the eternal gods to reflect Himself, so mankind creates gods in its own image. Are you referring to statues, Trismegistus?

Hermes: Yes, I am speaking of statues, Asclepios. How little faith you have! What else could I mean but these statues, which are so full of life, emotion, and purpose? They perform many amazing acts—some offer prophecies by sending dreams or other signs, while others bring illness or healing according to what people deserve.

Do you not understand, Asclepios, that Egypt is a reflection of heaven, a mirror of the divine order on earth? In truth, this land is the temple of the world. Yet, as wise men must foresee what is to come, there is something you should know. A time will come when it will seem that all the Egyptians' devotion to the gods was for nothing and that their prayers have gone unanswered. The divine presence will leave the earth and return to the heavens, abandoning Egypt, which was once its sacred home. Religion will fade, and the gods will no longer be found here.

Foreigners will overrun the land, and not only will sacred practices be neglected, but religion, worship, and reverence for the gods will be outlawed and punished by law.

The land, once filled with temples, will become full of tombs and the dead. O Egypt, Egypt, all that will remain of your religion will be legends that future generations will not believe. Only the words carved into stone will bear witness to your devotion. Barbarians—whether from Scythia, India, or other neighboring lands—will take control of Egypt. The gods will return to the heavens, and mankind, abandoned, will be lost. Egypt will be left empty, deserted by both men and gods.

I call upon you, O sacred River, to bear witness to what is to come! Waves of blood will stain your waters, overflowing your banks. The dead will outnumber the living, and if any Egyptians survive, they will no longer act as Egyptians but as foreigners in their own land.

You weep, Asclepios, but even sadder things will come to pass. Egypt will fall into apostasy, the worst of all evils. Once the sacred land loved by the gods, Egypt will become a place of corruption, a school of impiety, and a home to all forms of violence. People will grow tired of everything. They will no longer admire or love the world. They will turn away from this beautiful creation, which is the most perfect work of all time—past, present, and future. The weariness of their souls will leave them with nothing but contempt for the universe, this magnificent creation of God. They will reject this masterpiece, in which God's will united everything in perfect harmony, worthy of eternal reverence, praise, and love.

Darkness will be preferred to light, and death will seem better than life. No one will look toward heaven. Those who remain faithful to religion will be seen as fools, while the wicked will be praised as wise. The violent will be honored as heroes, and the evil-hearted will be celebrated as the best of men. Everything related to the soul—whether mortal or capable of eternal life—will be mocked and dismissed as foolishness. Faithful people will even face death for their beliefs. Believe me, Asclepios, those who remain true to religion and wisdom will face great danger.

New laws and customs will arise, and not a single sacred word or belief will remain—nothing religious or worthy of heaven will endure. What a tragic separation there will be between gods and humans! Evil spirits will be all that remain, and they will mix with the suffering human race, driving people toward wickedness, war, greed, lies, and everything that goes against the nature of the soul. The earth will lose its balance, the seas will become impossible to navigate, and even the stars will stray from their usual paths. Every holy voice will be silenced, crops will rot, and the land will no longer be fruitful. Even the air will become heavy with gloom. This will be the world's old age, a time marked by irreligion, disorder, lawlessness, and the confusion of good people.

When all of these things come to pass, Asclepios, the Lord and Father—sovereign God over all the world—will see the evil ways and actions of men. Then, through His divine will and goodness, He will put an end to these misfortunes. To stop the errors and corruption, He may flood the world, burn it with fire, or destroy it with wars and plagues. Afterward, He will restore the world to its original beauty, making it once more a place worthy of admiration and worship. Songs of praise and blessing will again celebrate Him, the One who created and redeemed this marvelous work.

This rebirth of the world, the restoration of all good things, and the renewal of Nature will happen at the appointed time, according to the eternal and unchanging will of God.

Asclepios: Truly, Trismegistus, God's nature reflects His will, which is absolute goodness and wisdom.

Hermes: Yes, Asclepios, will arises from reflection, and to will is itself an act of choice. God, who contains everything and has everything He desires, wills nothing out of whim. Everything He wills is good, and He possesses all that He wills. Whatever is good, He thinks and wills, for such is His nature. The world reflects His righteousness.

Asclepios: Then the world is good, Trismegistus?

Hermes: Yes, Asclepios, the world is good, as I will now explain. Just as God grants all beings various gifts—such as thought, soul, and life—the world distributes good things to mortals. These include the changing seasons, the fruits of the earth, birth, growth, maturity, and other blessings.

Though God is beyond the highest heavens, He is also present everywhere, watching over all things. Beyond the heavens lies a starless sphere, which surpasses all physical existence. Between the heavens and the earth rules the giver of life, whom we call Zeus (Jupiter). Over the earth and sea reigns the one who nourishes all living creatures, as well as the plants and fruit-bearing trees—this is Zeus Sarapis (Jupiter Plutonius).

Those who are destined to rule the earth will be sent to the farthest reaches of Egypt, to a city built toward the west, where people from every part of the world will gather by land and sea.

Asclepios: And where are they now, Trismegistus?

Hermes: They are already established in a great city on the mountain of Libya. But enough of this.

PART 10

Let us now discuss what is mortal and what is immortal. People who do not understand the nature of things are troubled by the thought and fear of death. Death happens when the body, exhausted by its work, falls apart. When the force that holds the body together reaches its limit, the body can no longer carry the burdens of life, and so it dies. Death is simply the breaking down of the body and the end of physical sensations. There is no need to trouble ourselves over it. However, there is another law that people often ignore or refuse to believe.

Asclepios: What is this law that people overlook?

Hermes: Listen carefully, Asclepios. When the soul leaves the body, it comes under the power of God, who judges it according to its deeds. If the soul is found to be pious and just, it is allowed to dwell in the divine realms. But if it is stained with vice, it is cast down, tossed between the forces of air, fire, and water. Such a soul is caught in endless storms, drifting between heaven and earth, condemned to eternal punishment. Its immortality only ensures that it suffers the consequences of its actions without end.

We should fear such a terrible fate. Those who now doubt the truth of these things will be forced to believe—not through words, but by the suffering they will endure.

Asclepios: So human laws alone are not enough to punish wrongdoing?

Hermes: Everything on earth is mortal, Asclepios. Those who live according to the desires of the body, without obeying the laws that guide human life, face even greater punishment after death. The punishment will be especially harsh for those whose sins were hidden, for God knows everything and ensures the punishment fits the crime.

Asclepios: Who suffers the greatest punishment, Trismegistus?

Hermes: Those who die violent deaths for their crimes seem to escape the debt they owe to Nature. Their earthly punishment might appear to be the result of their actions, but they still owe a debt. Because they could not pay this debt while alive, they must suffer greatly after death. Without the chance to correct their actions or seek forgiveness, they are delivered into torment until their debt is fully paid.

The Father and Lord of all things, who is everything and rules over all, reveals Himself willingly to everyone. However, He does not show His dwelling place, His glory, or His greatness. Instead, He grants people understanding through intelligence, which clears away ignorance and reveals the truth.

A just person finds strength in religion and piety, and God protects him from harm. Through this connection with divine intelligence, man rises above his mortal nature and hopes for eternal life. This is the difference between the good and the wicked. The person who is guided by piety, wisdom, and devotion to God gains true understanding, as if seeing with open eyes. This faith gives him confidence and allows him to rise above others, just as the sun shines brighter than the other lights in the sky.

If the sun gives light to the other stars, it is not only because of its size and strength, but because of its divine nature and holiness. You must see the sun, Asclepios, as a secondary god that governs the rest of the world, giving light to everything, both living and non-living. If the world is a living being—one that exists, has always existed, and will always exist—then nothing within it is truly mortal. Every part of it is alive, for in something that lives forever, death has no place. In the same way, God is the fullness of life and eternity, for He must live forever. The sun, which endures as long as the universe, continuously sustains all living beings, acting as the source and provider of life.

God is the eternal ruler of everything that both gives life and receives it. He is the one who gave life to all living creatures through an unchanging law, which I will explain to you. The movement of the universe is what makes eternity alive, and the endless motion of life is what keeps the universe eternal. The universe will never stop moving, nor will it ever decay. Eternal life surrounds and protects it like a fortress, giving life to everything inside it and keeping everything connected under the sun's rule.

This movement has two effects: the universe is kept alive by the eternity that encircles it, and in turn, it gives life to all that it holds. This life spreads through everything, following specific patterns, numbers, and seasons. All things follow their appointed times according to the sun and the stars, under divine law. Earthly cycles are marked by changes in the atmosphere, through the shifts between heat and cold. Celestial cycles are measured by the movement of the stars, which return to the same places in the sky at regular intervals.

The universe is the stage on which time plays out, and its constant motion sustains life. Time and order ensure the renewal of all things through the recurring seasons.

PART 11

Since the universe is as it is, nothing in nature—whether in the heavens or on the earth—remains unchanged or stable. Only God is complete, perfect, and unchanging in Himself. He is firm in His stability and cannot be moved by anything, for everything exists within Him, and He alone is everything. If we say that God moves, it can only be within eternity. Yet eternity itself does not move, because time, with all its motion, exists within eternity and draws its meaning from it.

God has always been and will always remain unchanging. Together with God exists eternal stability, containing within it an unmanifest universe—an image of the eternal world that has yet to appear. The created universe mirrors this eternal one. Time, though constantly moving, has its own kind of stability because it repeats its cycles endlessly. So, while eternity is fixed and unchanging, time flows within it, and this flow is essential to the nature of time. It may seem as though eternity moves because of the motion within time, and in the same way, it might seem that God Himself moves within His unchanging nature.

Even in the vast balance of existence, there is a kind of movement within what does not change. The law of God's immensity remains unaltered. The Infinite, the Unknowable, and the Immeasurable cannot be grasped or carried by anything. We cannot know where it comes from, where it is going, where it exists, or what it truly is. It rests within its own perfect stability, just as its stability rests within it. Whether God exists within eternity or eternity exists within God—or both exist within each other—remains a mystery beyond understanding.

Eternity cannot be measured by time, and time—defined by cycles, numbers, and repeating patterns—shares in eternity. Both time and eternity appear endless. Stability, as the foundation of all movement, holds the highest place because everything relies on stability. Thus, God and eternity are the source of all things, while the changing world cannot be considered their source. The changing nature of the world outweighs its stability, following the law of eternal movement within balance.

The divine consciousness is unchanging, moving only within perfect equilibrium. It is holy, incorruptible, and eternal. Or, to say it more clearly, it is the essence of eternity itself—rooted in the absolute truth of the Supreme God, filled with all understanding and knowledge, or, simply put, in God Himself. The consciousness of the natural world includes everything that can be sensed, while human consciousness holds memory, which allows us to recall what we have done. The divine consciousness reaches even to human beings, though God did not extend this supreme awareness to all creatures, for if every living thing shared it, the divine glory would be lessened.

The intelligence of the human mind depends entirely on memory, and it is through memory that humans have become masters of the earth. The intelligence of nature and the essence of the universe can be understood through the things we can see and experience. Eternity reveals its nature through the physical world. However, the consciousness of the Divine Being, the awareness of the Supreme God, is the only true reality. This truth cannot be found—even as a shadow—within the ever-changing world, which is full of illusions, shifting appearances, and errors. In this world, everything is understood only in terms of time.

Do you see, Asclepios, how profound these matters are? I thank the Most High God for granting me the light of His grace. And to you, Tat, Asclepios, and Ammon, I say: keep these divine mysteries within your hearts, and speak of them only in silence.

There is a difference between perception and intellect. The intellect, through study, can understand the nature of the universe. The universal mind connects to the awareness of eternity and the divine beings beyond this world. Yet, as humans, we can only glimpse these heavenly things as if through a mist, because the limits of our senses allow us to see them only dimly. Our strength is too small to fully grasp such divine truths, but when we do manage to reach them, we are blessed with the joy of knowing them deep within ourselves.

PART 12

Regarding the concept of the void, to which many people give great importance, I believe it does not exist, has never existed, and never will. Every part of the universe is filled, just as the earth is full of bodies of different shapes and qualities. Some bodies are larger, others smaller; some are solid, others light or thin. The larger, more solid things are easy to see, while the smaller, more delicate ones are harder to notice or even invisible. We can only recognize them through touch. Many people believe these things are not real bodies but just empty spaces. However, true emptiness cannot exist.

If there were something beyond the universe—though I do not believe this—it would still be filled with divine beings suited to the nature of such a place. The world we see is filled with bodies appropriate to its qualities. We do not perceive everything within the world. Some things are vast, others small. Some seem tiny only because they are far away, or our vision is too weak to notice them. Other things may be so fine and subtle that we are entirely unaware of them. I am referring to the spirits and heroes that dwell between us and the higher skies, where there are no clouds or storms.

It is incorrect to say that any space is truly empty unless we specify what it is empty of—whether fire, water, or something else. Even if a space lacks one of these elements, it is never without spirit or air. The same is true of the idea of "place." A place only makes sense when it refers to something within it. Saying "place" without naming what belongs there makes no sense. For example, we say "the place of water" or "the place of fire." Just as there can be no space completely empty of everything, there is no such thing as place on its own. If a place were entirely empty, it would not exist. For this reason, in my view, no such empty place exists within the universe.

If nothing is truly empty, then space cannot exist on its own unless it has dimensions like length, width, and depth, just as human bodies have their own defining characteristics. If this is true, then we must understand that the higher world—what we call God, who is only known through intelligence—is incorporeal. Nothing material can mix with His nature or be described by qualities, quantities, or measurements. None of these things belong to Him.

This world that we call the physical world holds all things that can be seen, touched, or measured. But even this universe cannot exist without God. God is everything, and everything comes from Him and depends on His will. He contains all that is good, orderly, wise, and perfect. Only He can fully know and understand these things. Nothing exists without Him. Everything that was, is, or will be originates from Him, is contained within Him, and relies on Him—whether it be qualities, sizes, or countless forms.

If you understand this, Asclepios, give thanks to God. When you observe the universe, recognize that everything in this world, with all it contains, is wrapped like a garment by the higher, divine world. All beings—whether mortal or immortal, rational or irrational, living or non-living—carry the nature of the class to which they belong. Although each creature shares the general characteristics of its kind, there are also differences within every kind. Humanity, too, has a common type, though individual people differ from one another.

The essence that comes from God is without a body, as is everything that belongs to intelligence. Since there are two sources of form—one material and the other immaterial—it is impossible for anything created to be an exact copy of something else, no matter how much time or space separates them. Forms are constantly changing, just like the passing moments of an hour. Yet the world, which moves in endless cycles, reflects the nature of God, who contains all forms within Himself. Each form continues to exist, creating countless versions of itself as time moves forward. The world changes as it revolves, but the essence of each kind remains the same. While individual forms within a species may vary, the essence of the species does not change.

Asclepios: Does the world also change in its form, Trismegistus?

Hermes: Asclepios, have you not been paying attention? The world consists of everything that is created within it. Are you asking about the heavens, the earth, and the elements? These things also change in their appearance. The sky, for example, is sometimes rainy, sometimes dry; sometimes hot, sometimes cold. It may be bright or covered with clouds. Though it seems to remain the same, it constantly shifts.

The earth, too, changes. At times, it brings forth fruit, and at other times, it hides it away. It produces many different kinds of plants, trees, flowers, and seeds, each with unique properties, colors, scents, and shapes. Fire also transforms in many ways. The sun and moon show us different phases and appearances, like the reflections we see in mirrors.

We have now said enough on these matters.

PART 13

Let us turn our attention back to people and explore the gift of reason, which gives humans the right to be called rational beings. Among all the amazing things about humanity, one stands out the most: humans have discovered the divine force within nature and learned how to use it for their purposes. Long ago, our ancestors, confused about their beliefs in the gods and unable to reach an understanding of divine truth and religion, developed the art of making gods. Once they learned this art, they gave their creations special powers taken from the natural world. But since they couldn't create souls, they called on the spirits of beings like angels and genii to fill their sacred images and ceremonies with life. This gave these idols the ability to bring about good or bad outcomes.

In this way, Asclepios, the founder of medicine, has a temple on a mountain in Libya, near a river known for its crocodiles. There, his earthly body rests. As for his spirit—the better part of him—it resides elsewhere. The idea behind this is explored further in earlier sections. Understanding these thoughts requires some knowledge of occult teachings, especially about spirits connected to the world and nature. In ancient times, people believed that the idols representing their gods had powers, just as many today believe that certain statues of saints have special abilities. For example, we hear stories of how a particular statue of the Virgin Mary in one town grants prayers, while another in a different place does not. Even now, sacred images are said to heal the sick, stop plagues, uncover hidden water sources, and bless worshippers.

Hermes explains that these abilities come from the divine power in nature, which humans shape to suit their needs. Humanity, he argues, must first go through the stage of worshipping nature before it can fully understand the divine order and recognize the existence of heavenly gods. Before human intelligence can reach the highest spiritual realms, it must pass through the levels between earth and heaven. This is why people first worship the images of gods before they come to know the gods themselves. These images are not always made of wood or stone. In fact, every personality is like an idol, reflecting deeper truths and holding a part of the divine essence. Though these images seem powerful and worthy of worship to those who don't understand true divine religion, Hermetists see them as symbols of essential truths that exist beyond any physical form and remain unchanged by it.

There are three signs of true divinity: it goes beyond physical form, beyond time, and beyond individual personalities. Instead of physical form, there is pure essence. Instead of time, there is eternity. Instead of individual people, there are universal principles. Events turn into continuous processes, and what we think of as physical occurrences become inner realities.

As long as any idea of the divine is tied to a physical event or historical fact, it shows that the heavenly realm has not been reached. Symbols, once recognized as symbols, are no longer misleading or harmful. They act like veils of light, revealing glimpses of the "Divine Darkness," which is the ultimate goal of the true Hermetist. Even the most refined or abstract way of expressing supreme truth is still only a symbol or metaphor. The real truth is something beyond words, only known from God to God. It is pure essence, silence, and darkness.

The person who understands this truth—because consciousness and life are one with the whole person—returns to the divine realm. Through his divinity, he offers help to the sick, just as he once taught people the art of healing. Likewise, Hermes, my ancestor whose name I carry, now rests in the land named after him. People from all over come to his shrine to seek health and guidance through their prayers. We also see how Isis, the wife of Osiris, brings blessings to people when she is pleased, and misfortune when she is angry. These earthly gods can feel both kindness and anger, as they are shaped from nature by humans. This explains why in Egypt, people worship animals, and cities honor the souls of those who gave them laws and whose names they still remember. For this reason, Asclepios, gods worshipped in one place might be ignored elsewhere, which often causes conflicts between cities in Egypt.

Asclepios: What kind of divinity do these earthly gods possess, O Trismegistus?

Hermes: Their divinity lies in the spiritual essence found in plants, stones, and fragrant substances. This is why these gods are drawn to sacrifices, songs of praise, and sweet music that echoes the harmony of the heavens. These rituals attract them to their shrines, where they remain among humans for long periods. This is how people create gods. But do not think, Asclepios, that the actions of these earthly gods are random. While the gods in the heavens maintain their order and position above, these earthly gods also have their own roles. Some predict the future through signs and divination, while others assist with different aspects of life, acting as helpers, family, or friends to those who call upon them.

PART 14

Asclepios: O Trismegistos, what role does Destiny or Fate play in how things work? If the heavenly gods rule the universe and the earthly gods control specific events, where does Destiny fit in?

Hermes: O Asclepios, Destiny is the force that makes everything happen. It's like a chain connecting all events together. It's the reason behind everything and can be seen as the highest power—or rather, the second god, created by God Himself. It's the law governing everything in both heaven and earth, based on divine rules. Destiny and Necessity are inseparable: Destiny starts everything, and Necessity makes sure things unfold as they were meant to. From this process, Order arises—it's the way things follow one another in Time, for nothing can happen without Order. This is how the world becomes complete. The world is built on Order, and the universe holds together because of it.

These three forces—Destiny (or Fate), Necessity, and Order—completely depend on God's will. He governs the world through divine reason and law. These forces have no will of their own; they are unmoved by anger or kindness. They are simply the tools of eternal Reason, which never changes, never wavers, and never breaks.

Destiny comes first, carrying within it the seeds of future events, just like freshly planted soil contains seeds waiting to grow. Next is Necessity, which pushes these events to happen. Lastly, Order keeps everything in place, ensuring that what Destiny and Necessity create holds together. This entire process is a never-ending cycle, with no clear beginning or end. It continues forever, governed by an unchanging law that flows through eternity. As time moves on, things that once disappeared rise again, and what was on top sinks back down. This is how the circular movement works. Everything is so connected that it's impossible to tell where one thing begins or ends. They follow and lead each other endlessly.

However, chance and luck still influence earthly events.

PART 15

Now that we have spoken of all things within our reach, as much as God has allowed, it is time to offer our blessings and prayers to Him and return to our earthly responsibilities. After filling our minds with sacred knowledge, which nourishes the soul, we leave the sanctuary and lift our prayers to God. Turning toward the south, they began their orations, for it is proper to look toward the sun's descent when offering praise, just as one should face the east at sunrise to honor the new day. While they prayed, Asclepios spoke quietly: "O Tatius, let us ask our Father to allow our prayers to rise with the fragrance of incense and perfumes."

Trismegistos overheard him and responded with emotion: "May the omen be favorable, O Asclepios. But to burn incense or perfume during prayer is almost a sacrilege. He who is all things and contains all things needs nothing from us. We should offer Him only our praise and devotion. The purest offering is the grace we give in worship."

They prayed: "We thank You, O Most High, for through Your grace, we have received the light of knowledge. May Your name be praised and honored, for it is the name through which divinity is worshipped in the tradition of our ancestors! You grant us the gifts of faith, love, and devotion, and above all, You bless us with awareness, reason, and understanding. Through awareness, we recognize You; through reason, we seek You; and through understanding, we rejoice in knowing You.

"By Your divine power, we are saved, and we take joy in seeing Your presence revealed. We are grateful that from the time we came into this body, You have chosen to prepare us for eternity. Our only true joy is the knowledge of Your greatness. We have come to know You, O magnificent Light, grasped only through understanding. We have known You, O true Path of Life, inexhaustible Source of all creation! We have known You, O abundant Spirit of Nature, unchanging and eternal!

"In this prayer, we honor Your holy sanctity and ask only that You allow us to continue loving Your truth, so we may never stray from this way of life. Filled with this hope, we now go forth to enjoy a pure meal, free from the flesh of animals."

The Definitions of Asclepios
PART 1

Asclepios to the King Ammon. I send you, O King, an important message. I will begin by calling upon God, the Master of the Universe, the Creator and Father of everything. He contains all things, is everything in one, and is one in everything. Everything that exists comes from unity and remains in unity. These two are not separate, for they are one. Keep this in mind, O King, throughout my entire message. It is pointless to try and separate the All from the One by calling everything "the All" and ignoring their unity. This distinction cannot be made because the All cannot exist without unity, just as unity cannot exist without the All. Unity always exists and never stops being one; otherwise, all things would fall apart.

What I am saying goes against common beliefs and may even seem different from some of my other teachings. My teacher Hermes often spoke with me, either alone or with Tatios present. He used to say that those who read my writings would think they are simple and clear, but in truth, they contain deeper, hidden meanings. This hidden meaning has become harder to understand because the Greeks translated our words into their language, which caused misunderstandings. The Egyptian language has a special power that makes the meaning clear to the mind. As much as you can, O King—and you have great power—do not allow this message to be translated, or these mysteries may fall into Greek hands. Their polished way of speaking could weaken the seriousness and strength of these teachings. The Greeks love new ways of talking and are very wordy in their philosophy, while we focus more on actions and facts rather than many words.

In the earth, there are powerful springs of water and fire. These represent the three elements—fire, water, and earth—which all come from the same source. It shows that all matter comes from one great origin, filled with abundance, receiving its existence from above. This is how the Creator, through the sun, governs heaven and earth. The sun sends down essence and draws up matter, holding the universe together and giving everything life through its light. The sun spreads its energy not only in the heavens and air but also on earth and deep into the abyss. If there is an essence beyond what we can see, it must belong to the sun, and light is its messenger. Only the sun knows its true nature and origin.

To fully understand these hidden things, we would need to be close to the sun and share its nature. However, what the sun reveals to us is not guesswork—it is the brilliant vision that lights up both the heavens and the world. The sun stands at the center of the universe like a crown-bearer, guiding the world like a skilled charioteer. It controls the reins of life, soul, spirit, immortality, and birth, carrying everything along with it. Through this process, the sun forms everything and grants immortality to eternal beings.

The light that radiates outward nourishes the eternal spaces of the universe. The light that spreads across the waters, earth, and air becomes a fertile place where life begins. Here, all kinds of births and transformations take place, as things change from one form to another in a continuous spiral movement. This transformation allows creatures to move through different parts of the world, shifting between forms and appearances while keeping the balance of all these changes, just like in the creation of larger beings. The stability of physical forms comes from constant change, but immortal forms never break down, while mortal bodies do. This is the difference between what is immortal and what is mortal.

The sun creates life as constantly as it shines, without ever stopping. Surrounding it are countless groups of spiritual beings. These spirits stay close to the immortal gods and watch over human affairs. They carry out the will of the gods through storms, fires, earthquakes, wars, and famines to punish those who act against the divine. The greatest sin people can commit is disrespecting the gods. The gods are meant to do good, humans are meant to honor them, and the spirits are there to discipline those who stray.

The gods do not hold people accountable for mistakes made by accident, bold actions taken because of fate, or through ignorance. Only true wrongdoing falls under their judgment. The sun supports and sustains all living things, just as the Ideal World surrounds the physical world and fills it with countless forms. Similarly, the sun wraps everything in its light, bringing life and helping all creatures grow. When they become tired and weak, the sun gathers them back to itself. The sun commands the Genii—actually, many groups of Genii—whose numbers match the stars. Every star has its own Genii, some naturally good, some bad, and others mixed, depending on what they do. A Genie's actions define its essence.

Some Genii perform both good and harmful deeds. All of these Genii oversee what happens on Earth. They disrupt governments and individual lives, shaping our souls. They are present in our nerves, marrow, veins, arteries, and even our brains and internal organs. When a person is born, they are assigned to Genii responsible for overseeing births, who operate under the influence of the stars. These Genii are constantly changing, moving in cycles, never staying the same. They act through the body to affect two parts of the soul, leaving their unique influence on each. However, the rational part of the soul is beyond the reach of the Genii, as it is meant to receive God's light, which shines like a ray from the sun.

Only a few people receive this divine light, and for those who do, the Genii have no power over them. Neither gods nor Genii can interfere when even a single ray from God touches someone. For all other people, both their souls and bodies are guided by Genii, and they become connected to these spiritual forces, mirroring their actions. Desire, which often misleads, is not the same as reason, which remains steady. The Genii control earthly matters and use our bodies as their tools. This influence is what Hermes refers to as Destiny.

The Intelligible World is linked to God, while the physical world is connected to the Intelligible World. Through these two realms, the sun transmits God's energy, which is creative in nature. Surrounding the sun are eight spheres: the sphere of the fixed stars, the six planetary spheres, and the sphere that encircles the Earth. The Genii are tied to these spheres, and humans are connected to the Genii, creating a chain that binds all beings to God, the universal Father. The sun is the source of creation, and the world is like a crucible where creation takes shape. The Intelligible Essence governs the heavens, the heavens guide the gods, the gods oversee the Genii, and the Genii direct human beings. This is the divine order, and through this hierarchy, God works through both gods and Genii to carry out His will.

Since everything is a part of God, God is present in all things. By creating everything, God is continually extending Himself without pause. God's energy exists only in the present, for it has no past, and because God has no limits, His creation has neither a beginning nor an end.

PART 2

If you think about it, O King, you'll realize that some things are both physical and non-physical. "Which things are those?" asked the King. Things like the images you see in mirrors—aren't they non-physical, even though they appear to be real? "That's true, Tat," the King replied. "You have quite an interesting way of thinking!" There are other non-physical things too, such as abstract ideas. Wouldn't you agree that these ideas are not physical themselves, but they still appear through living and non-living things? "That's true again, Tat," said the King. So, it seems that non-physical things reflect onto physical things, and physical things reflect back onto the non-physical. In other words, the physical world and the world of ideas mirror each other. Therefore, O King, honor the sacred images, for they are reflections of the physical world. The King then stood up and said, "I think it's time to take care of our guests, prophet. We can continue this theological discussion tomorrow."

PART 3

When a musician tries to play a melody but can't get the instruments to work together in harmony, his efforts end in failure, and the audience laughs. No matter how skilled he is or how hard he tries, he cannot blame the instrument for his inability to create music. The great musician of Nature, the God who oversees all harmony and controls how every instrument plays in perfect rhythm, never tires. Fatigue doesn't touch the gods. If a conductor leads a concert with trumpeters playing their parts, flute players performing the soft melodies, and lyres and violins accompanying the song, no one would blame the composer if one instrument plays out of tune. Instead, we honor the composer's talent, even if the music is disturbed by a single instrument.

In the same way, it would be disrespectful to blame Humanity for the failures of our physical bodies. God, the untiring Artist, is always perfect in His craft, working flawlessly and providing equal gifts to all. If Phidias, the great sculptor, struggled with material that was difficult to shape, we should not blame him for doing his best. Likewise, we shouldn't fault a musician for the mistakes of a faulty instrument. Instead, we should recognize that a musician deserves even more praise if he can still draw beautiful music from an instrument with broken strings or faulty notes. When the music is flawed, it is the instrument's fault, not the artist's. Those who listen will respect the musician even more for overcoming such difficulties.

Just like that, my noble audience, we must adjust the strings of our inner selves to match the intentions of the musician. Imagine a musician, without his usual instrument, being asked to create beautiful music. He might find a new way to make the sound, using unfamiliar tools, and amaze his listeners even more. There is a story about a cithara player who had Apollo's favor. While playing a melody, one of the strings on his instrument snapped, but a cicada stepped in with its song to fill the missing notes. Thanks to this divine help, the musician continued his performance without fear and won great praise.

I feel the same, noble listeners, as though when I doubt my own strength, the power of the Supreme Being steps in and fills the melody in my place, giving me the ability to honor the king. The purpose of this speech is to glorify royalty and celebrate their achievements. So let us proceed! The musician has begun, and the lyre is ready. May the beauty and sweetness of the music match the message of our song! Since we are here to praise kings and honor their greatness, let us first give thanks to the good God, the supreme King of the universe. After Him, we will honor the rulers who reflect His image and hold the royal scepter.

Even kings welcome songs that descend from the heavens, step by step, knowing that it is Heaven that grants them victory. So let the singer praise the mighty God of the universe, who is eternal and whose power has no end. He is the greatest of all victors, the source of all triumphs, one after another. Let us now finish this speech so we can honor the kings—those who protect peace and keep everyone safe, who hold their ancient power from the Lord above and receive victory from His hand. These rulers hold shining scepters that signal the trials of war, with triumph already in sight. They are not only given the right to rule but also the power to conquer. Even their march into battle strikes fear into their enemies before the fight begins.

PART 4

This discourse ends where it began, with praise for the Supreme Being and the most holy kings who bring us peace. Just as we started by honoring the Almighty, we now end by returning to that same greatness. Just as the sun nurtures seeds and gathers the fruits with its rays, like divine hands collecting gifts for God, so too do we gather within ourselves the beauty of divine wisdom. After breathing in the sweetness of these heavenly gifts, we must now collect the blessings of this sacred harvest, which God will enrich with His nourishing rains. Even if we had ten thousand mouths and ten thousand voices to glorify the pure God, the Father of Souls, we would still fall short of offering Him the praise He deserves. Just like infants who cannot properly honor their father, but are still forgiven for their efforts, we too receive His mercy.

The greatness of God shines in His ability to rise above all creatures. He is the Beginning, the End, the Center, and the Continuation of all praise. In Him, all beings recognize their source—He is all-powerful and limitless. The same is true of our king. As his children, we love to praise him and ask for his forgiveness, knowing that he has already granted it to us. Just as a father is pleased when his children recognize him, even in their weakness, so too does our king rejoice when we acknowledge him. The universal wisdom that gives life to everything and allows us to honor God is itself a gift from God. Since God is good, He holds within Himself all perfection. Being immortal, He possesses endless peace, and His eternal power brings blessings to the world.

In God's divine order, there is no division or change. All beings in Him are filled with wisdom, and the same divine care governs them all. They are guided by the same intelligence, moved by the same kindness, and united by the same love, creating harmony throughout the universe. Therefore, let us bless God and honor the kings who receive their authority from Him. And since we have begun to praise the kings, let us also glorify the reverence they show toward the Supreme. May God teach us how to honor Him properly, and may He help us in this pursuit. Our highest aim must be to revere God and celebrate the kings, for they bring us the peace we enjoy.

The virtue of the king lies in his power to create peace, and his very name carries the meaning of peace. He is called king because he leads with reason and calm authority. He surpasses all other rulers, and even his name becomes a symbol of peace. Just the mention of his name can often drive away enemies. His image acts as a beacon of safety in troubled times. The sight of the king alone brings victory, ensures security, and makes us feel invincible.

Some scholars argue that this text, "Asclepios to King Ammon," might not have been written by one of Hermes' disciples, believing it unworthy of someone taught by such a great master. Dr. Menard notes that despite the criticism of the Greeks in the earlier part of the text, it was likely written in Greek, as suggested by the reference to the Greek word for king, "basileus," and the discussion of its meaning from the Greek verb "bainein," meaning "to advance." The text also mentions Phidias and Eunomios, a musician from Locris, showing Greek influence. The description of the sun as a charioteer, along with the reference to the one who "bears the crowns," reflects Greek customs. In Egypt, the sun was usually depicted as traveling across the Nile on a barge.

Because of these points, Dr. Menard suggests that the negative remarks about the Greeks may have been added later to mislead readers about the text's true origin. He also believes that the kings mentioned in this passage might refer to the Roman emperors Valens and Valentinian. However, I respectfully disagree. Whether or not Asclepios wrote these words, I believe the references to "kings" and "royalties" carry a deeper, mystical meaning. If the intention was simply to flatter a ruler, as Dr. Menard suggests, then why would the writer emphasize that the message contains hidden meanings? Everything said about kingship here fits the symbolic nature of Osiris, the divine ruler whose essence lives within all people.

Osiris reflects the supreme Lord of the Universe and represents the ideal form of humanity. That is why, in the Egyptian Book of the Dead, the soul of the deceased is described as "an Osiris." This symbolizes that the higher part of our nature, the true divine self within us, is like Osiris. It is to this inner king—our higher reason and the divine word of God— that we owe our loyalty, devotion, and eternal service.

Fragments of The Book of Hermes to His Son Tatios

PART 1

Trismegistus: Out of love for humanity and respect for God, my son, I begin writing this. There is no higher religion than to reflect on the universe and express gratitude to the Creator, and this is something I will always do.

Tatios: Father, if nothing here on Earth is real, how can we use our lives wisely?

Trismegistus: Be religious, my son. Religion is elevated philosophy, and without philosophy, there is no true religion. The person who understands the universe—its laws, principles, and purpose—offers thanks to the Creator, who is like a loving father, a wise teacher, and a faithful protector. This is the essence of religion, for through it, we discover what truth is and where to find it. The more we learn, the deeper our connection to religion becomes. Once the soul, trapped within the body, reaches an understanding of the true Good and Truth, it can never return to ignorance. The power of Love and the forgetting of all evil bind the soul to the Good and prevent it from separating from the Creator.

This is the goal of religion, my son. If you can reach it, your life will be pure, your death will be peaceful, and your soul will know where to go. This is the path that leads to Truth, the same path our ancestors followed to discover the Good. It is a beautiful and steady path, but it is hard for the soul to walk it while trapped in the body. The soul must first struggle with itself, dividing into parts and submitting to its highest aspect. The higher part of the soul fights to rise, while the lower parts—desire and passion—try to drag it down.

If the higher part wins, it builds a defense for itself and its master. But if the lower parts overpower the higher one, the soul is led astray and punished in this life. It is the higher part, my son, that must be your guide. Prepare yourself for the struggle, fight to keep your soul strong, and aim for victory. Now, let me summarize the principles we have discussed. Everything that exists moves, except for things that do not exist.

All bodies change, though some only break apart. Not all beings are mortal, nor are all immortal. Things that can break down are corruptible, while those that remain unchanged are eternal.

God comes first, then the universe, and finally humanity. The universe exists for humanity, and humanity exists for God. The emotional part of the soul is mortal, but the rational part is eternal. Every substance is subject to change, yet all true essence is immortal. Everything has two aspects; nothing stays the same forever. Not all things have a soul, but anything that exists is alive through a soul. What is passive can feel, and everything that feels is temporary. All creatures that feel pain and pleasure are mortal, but those that only experience joy without pain are immortal.

Not every body suffers from disease, but anything that can suffer from illness will eventually be destroyed. Intelligence resides in God, and reason in humanity. Reason belongs to intelligence, and intelligence never changes. Nothing physical is fully real, and nothing non-physical is false. Everything that is born undergoes change, though not everything that changes becomes corrupted. There is no perfection on Earth, and no evil in Heaven. God is perfect, while humanity is flawed. Goodness arises through choice, while evil goes against the will. The gods always choose good.

Time belongs to the divine, but law belongs to humanity. Evil feeds the world, while time destroys humans. Everything in Heaven stays the same, while nothing on Earth is unchanging. In Heaven, there is no servitude; on Earth, there is no true freedom. In Heaven, nothing is unknown, while on Earth, nothing is fully understood. There is no connection between celestial things and earthly things. All is perfect in Heaven, and nothing on Earth is free from fault. The immortal knows nothing of death, just as the mortal cannot comprehend immortality. Not everything that is planted will grow, but everything that grows has been planted.

Mortal bodies have two stages of existence: from conception to birth, and from birth to death. Eternal beings, however, exist in a single, unchanging state from the moment they come into being. Mortal bodies increase and decrease. Perishable matter moves between destruction and creation, while immortal essence either remains within itself or transforms into something similar. The birth of one thing brings about the end of another, and every ending is also a beginning.

Some beings exist in physical form, some in pure form, and others in energy. The body contains forms, and forms contain energy. The immortal receives nothing from the mortal, but the mortal can receive from the immortal. Mortal things do not enter immortal forms, but the immortal can dwell in mortal bodies. Energy always moves downward, not upward. What exists on Earth does not benefit what is in Heaven, but everything in Heaven benefits what exists on Earth.

Heaven is filled with immortal beings, while earth holds perishable bodies. The earth is irrational, but heaven is guided by reason. Heavenly things are governed by celestial forces, while earthly things remain on earth. Heaven is the original source of all. Divine providence creates order, and necessity is the tool that providence uses. Chance brings disorder—it is a false image of real energy, only an illusion. God is unchanging Goodness, while man is constantly entangled in evil. If you remember these principles, you will also recall everything I've explained to you in more detail. But be careful about sharing these ideas with the masses. It is not that I want to keep these truths from them, but because exposing them may cause you to become a target for ridicule. Like attracts like, but opposites find no harmony. These teachings should be shared with only a few, or else they might be ignored completely.

There is also a danger in these ideas—if wicked people misuse them, they could become even worse. Stay away from the crowd, for they cannot grasp the value of these teachings.

Tatios: What do you mean, Father?

Trismegistos: Listen closely, my son. Humans are naturally drawn toward evil—it is part of their nature, and they find it pleasing. If people understood that the world was created through divine order and that everything happens because of providence and necessity, they might misuse this knowledge. They could begin to look down on everything that is created, blame destiny for their vices, and indulge in all kinds of wrongdoing. This is why it is wise to avoid sharing these truths with the crowd. Sometimes, ignorance helps keep people within limits, as fear of the unknown can prevent them from acting out.

PART 2

Tatios: You have explained these things clearly, my father, but I still have more questions. You told me that knowledge and skill are activities of reason, and now you say that animals are called "brute" because they lack reason. So does that mean animals cannot possess knowledge or skill?

Trismegistus: Yes, my son, that is correct.

Tatios: But, father, how do you explain animals that seem to display knowledge and skill? For example, ants store food for the winter, birds build nests, and cattle recognize their stables and return to them.

Trismegistus: These actions are not guided by knowledge or skill, my son, but by nature. Knowledge and skill are things we acquire, but these creatures have learned nothing. What they do comes from universal nature. Knowledge and skill belong only to those who acquire them. Actions that are shared by all creatures are natural, not learned. For example, all people can see with their eyes, but not everyone becomes a musician, an archer, or a hunter. Only a few people learn a specific skill or craft and put it to use. If only some ants stored food while others didn't, then you could say those ants possessed the skill of gathering provisions. But since they all behave the same way without deliberate thought, it is clear that neither knowledge nor skill directs them.

Activities, my son, are not physical; they exist within the body and are carried out through the body. Because they are not physical, they are immortal in a sense. But since they must be expressed through a body, they always appear within a body. Anything that has a purpose, determined by divine will and necessity, cannot remain idle. What exists will continue to exist, and that is its life and purpose. This is why bodies will always exist, for the creation of bodies is an eternal function. Even though earthly bodies are corruptible, they are necessary as vessels and tools for the energies that flow through them. Energies are immortal, and because they are immortal, they are always active.

The creation of bodies is ongoing and endless. The abilities of the soul do not all appear at once. Some abilities are present from birth, within the nonrational part of the soul, while the higher abilities emerge as the soul grows in wisdom over time. These abilities are linked to the body, but they come from divine forms and flow into mortal forms, creating bodies. Each ability serves a function, either of the body or the soul, but these abilities remain within the soul even when not connected to a body. The energies are eternal, but the soul is not always confined within a mortal body. The soul can exist without the body, but the abilities cannot manifest unless they have a body to work through.

This is a deep truth, my son. The body cannot exist without the soul, but being itself can.

Tatios: What do you mean by that, father?

Trismegistus: Listen carefully, Tatios. When the soul leaves the body, the body remains, but it begins to break down from within until it completely dissolves. Such a process requires an active force, so even after the soul departs, some energy remains in the body. The difference between an immortal being and a mortal being is this: the immortal being is made of pure, simple essence, while the mortal being is not. One is active and governs, while the other is passive and obeys. One is free, while the other is ruled. Energies are present not only in living beings but also in lifeless things like wood, stone, and similar objects. Through energy, these things grow, ripen, decay, decompose, and change. Energy is what causes transformation, and all becoming is part of the universal process.

There will never be a time when the universe lacks new life, for it constantly produces and destroys beings. Energy itself can never be destroyed, no matter what form it takes or where it manifests. Some energies work through divine beings, others through mortal beings. Some energies are universal, affecting many, while others are specific, working on individual beings. Divine energies operate within eternal beings and are as perfect as those beings themselves.

Partial energies act through living beings, while specific energies operate within everything that exists. This means, my son, that the entire universe is filled with energies. Since energies need bodies to manifest, and there are many bodies in the universe, we can see how abundant these energies are. However, there are even more energies than bodies because one body can hold multiple energies—sometimes one, two, or three—on top of those energies that exist everywhere. I call these universal energies the ones that cannot be separated from bodies, which show themselves through sensations and movements. Without these universal energies, no body could exist.

In contrast, specific energies appear in the minds of humans through art, science, and labor. Sensations come with energies or result from them. Understand, my son, the difference between energy and sensation. Energy comes from a higher place, while sensation belongs to the body and depends on it. The body serves as a seat or vehicle for energy, allowing the energy to express itself through it. For this reason, I say that sensations are tied to the body and are mortal. Their existence begins and ends with the body. On the other hand, immortal energies do not have sensations because of their nature. Sensations can only arise from some good or bad experience affecting the body, and immortal beings are not subject to these changes.

Tatios: So, does every body experience sensation?

Trismegistus: Yes, my son, every body experiences sensation, and energies act in all bodies.

Tatios: Even in lifeless things, father?

Trismegistus: Yes, even in lifeless things. Sensations vary by type. In beings with reason, sensations are accompanied by thought. In beings without reason, sensations are purely physical. In lifeless things, sensations take the form of passive processes, such as growth and decay. Both passion and sensation are the result of energies, coming from a single source and leading to a single outcome.

In living beings, two more energies accompany passion and sensation: joy and sorrow. Without these, no living being—and especially no reasonable being—would be able to feel anything. Therefore, joy and sorrow can be seen as forms of emotion in all living beings. They appear through sensations, as movements within the body, driven by the irrational parts of the soul. Both joy and sorrow are forms of suffering. Joy, which is the feeling of pleasure, often brings about greater troubles. Sorrow leads to pain and punishment, making it equally harmful.

Tatios: Is sensation the same thing in both the soul and the body, father?

Trismegistus: What do you mean by the sensation of the soul, my son?

Tatios: The soul is not physical, father. But sensation seems to be tied to the body, since it exists within it.

Trismegistus: If we say that sensation belongs to the body, then we must compare it either to the soul or to the energies, which are not physical, even though they exist within the body. However, sensation is neither an energy nor a soul, nor is it separate from the body. Therefore, it cannot be something non-physical. If it isn't non-physical, it must be physical, because nothing exists that is neither physical nor non-physical.

PART 3

The Lord, the Creator of immortal forms, Tatios, completed His work and made nothing more. He does not create anything new now either. Once these eternal forms were given life and connected to one another, they began to move on their own, needing nothing to sustain them. Even if they rely on each other in some ways, they do not need anything outside themselves because they are immortal. This is how the creations of the supreme God are meant to be.

However, our immediate creator, the one who made us, has a body. He created us and continues to create mortal bodies that are subject to change and decay. Unlike the supreme Creator, he cannot create immortal beings, nor should he try to imitate Him. The supreme God created eternal forms from His own essence, which is incorporeal. But our creator formed us from material substances, giving us physical bodies that are naturally weak and dependent on external support.

Because we are made of physical matter, we need constant nourishment and renewal to survive. The earth, water, fire, and air flow into us, restoring and sustaining our bodies. Without these elements replenishing us, the combination of substances that make up our bodies would fall apart. We are so fragile that we cannot even remain active for a full day without rest. You know well, my son, that without the night's rest, our bodies could not endure the strain of the day's work.

In His wisdom, our good creator has provided for our survival by creating sleep, which restores movement and strength. He made sure that the time spent resting is equal to or even longer than the time spent working. Think, my son, about how sleep serves the body and how important it is, even though it contrasts with the soul's constant activity. If the soul's function is to keep moving, the body relies on sleep to loosen the tension within and restore what it needs. Sleep provides the body with water to nourish the blood, earth for the bones, air for the nerves and vessels, and fire for the eyes. This is why the body finds such pleasure in sleep.

The teachings of Hermetic philosophy reflect the idea that divine energy flows constantly into the universe, even though the forms through which it flows remain unchanged and self-sustaining. The natural order was set from the beginning and cannot be altered. The soul's journey into physical life is an ongoing process and will only end when the creative cycle is complete. The flow of divine energy has never stopped since the beginning of creation. Life continues to emerge because of this constant outpouring of being into existence, and without it, the process of creation and evolution would halt. The creator mentioned here is the Demiurge, the one responsible for shaping the physical universe.

PART 4

A great and divine power, my son, is placed at the center of the universe, observing everything that people do on earth. In the divine order, everything is guided by providential Necessity, while among people, this role is fulfilled by Justice. The first order governs heavenly things, for the Gods neither wish to, nor are able to, break any laws. They cannot make mistakes, and because mistakes lead to sin, they are free from sin.

The second order, Justice, is responsible for correcting the wrongs that happen among people on earth. Since humans are mortal and made of corruptible matter, they are prone to losing their way when they no longer focus on divine things to guide them toward virtue. This is where Justice steps in to act.

Through the energies he draws from Nature, man is subject to Destiny. But through the mistakes he makes in life, man is subject to Justice.

PART 5

Here, then, is what can be said about the three aspects of time. They do not exist independently, and they are not completely separate from each other. Yet, in another way, they are both connected and distinct. Can we imagine the present without the past? One cannot exist without the other, because the present is created by the past, and the future emerges from the present.

If we want to fully understand this, we need to reason like this: The past has already moved into what no longer exists. The future does not exist until it becomes the present. And the present, in turn, stops being itself the moment it passes. How can we call something present when it doesn't stay for even an instant and has no fixed point? If it vanishes as soon as it appears, can it really be said to exist?

Moreover, since the past is closely tied to the present, and the present connects directly to the future, they blend into one. They share an identity, unity, and continuity. Time flows without interruption, constantly moving and changing, even though it remains one and the same.

PART 6

My son, matter is always in the process of becoming. It has existed before, and it continues to change, for matter serves as the vehicle for transformation. Becoming is how the uncreated and all-knowing God expresses His activity. Matter carries within it the seed of change, and through this seed, it is brought into existence. The creative force shapes matter according to ideal forms, giving it structure. Before it is formed, matter has no shape or identity. It only takes on form when it is put into motion through creation.

PART 7

It is impossible for a human, who is imperfect and made up of many flawed parts, to speak with certainty about what is truly real, my son Tatios. Our bodies are formed from different elements that are not originally part of us. Still, as much as I can, I say that reality only exists in eternal beings, for their forms are truly real. Fire is simply fire, earth is only earth, and air is only air. But our bodies are made of a combination of these elements—fire, earth, water, and air—yet our bodies are not really fire, earth, water, or air, nor anything truly real.

Since reality has never been a part of us from the start, how could we ever see it, speak of it, or even understand it unless God allows us to? The things of this world are not truly real but only copies of reality. In fact, not all things are even proper copies; some are nothing more than illusions and errors, mere tricks of the mind. When something receives a spark of higher truth, it can become a reflection of the real. Without this divine influence, it stays an illusion. It is like a portrait: a painting of a person, but not the person it represents. It may have eyes, but it cannot see; it may have ears, but it cannot hear. A portrait only gives the appearance of a person but is nothing more than an image that fools the eye. It seems real but is only a shadow. Those who avoid being deceived by false appearances see what is true. If we can see things as they are, we understand the real, but if we only see what is false, we cannot understand or know the real at all.

Tatios: So, is there anything truly real on earth, my father?

Trismegistus: Reality does not exist on earth, my son, and it cannot be found here. However, a few people may grasp it if God grants them the gift of divine vision. What exists on earth is only made up of appearances and opinions, not reality itself. And yet, reality can be found through intelligence and reason. To think and speak the truth is as close as we come to what is real.

Tatios: But how can that be? How can we think and speak truthfully if nothing on earth is real?

Trismegistus: It is true, my son, that we know nothing of absolute Truth. How could it be otherwise? Truth is the highest virtue, the ultimate Good. It is not clouded by matter or trapped in physical form. It is pure, unchanging, and eternal. But the things here on earth, as you see, are not compatible with the Good. They are temporary, always changing, and constantly shifting from one form to another. How can something be real if it cannot even remain the same as itself? Anything that is always changing is not just an illusion in itself, but it also deceives us by appearing in different ways at different times.

Tatios: Does this mean that even man is not real, father?

Trismegistus: No, my son. Man is not real in the truest sense. Reality only belongs to something that remains the same and stays true to itself. Man, on the other hand, is made up of many different parts and never stays the same. As long as he lives in a body, he changes from one age to another, from one state to the next. Sometimes, after only a short while, parents no longer recognize their children, and children no longer recognize their parents. Can something that changes so much that it is no longer recognizable be considered real? Should we not see these ever-changing forms as illusions? Only what is eternal and good can be considered real. Man is temporary, and therefore not real; he is just an appearance, and appearances are the ultimate illusion.

Tatios: So even the stars and celestial bodies are not real, since they also change?

Trismegistus: Anything that is born and subject to change cannot be real. However, the works of the great Creator can receive a kind of reality from Him. Still, even they contain an element of falsehood because they change, and nothing can be truly real unless it remains the same.

Tatios: Then what can we call truly real, my father?

Trismegistus: The sun is the only being among all creatures that does not change and remains constant. This is why it is given the task of overseeing the universe. It is the leader and creator of all things. I honor the sun and bow before its truth. After the One, it is the second creator I recognize.

Tatios: What, then, is the original Reality, father?

Trismegistus: He is the One and only, Tatios, who is not made of matter, who does not exist within any body. He has no color, no shape, and He never changes. He simply is. Anything that is an illusion will perish, my son. The order of the Real ensures that everything in this world will end through dissolution, for the cycle of birth depends on things breaking apart. Everything that is created must eventually dissolve, only to be born again. From dissolution, life emerges, and life must also decay, so that creation can continue without end.

See, then, the Creator who existed before everything. The things born from dissolution are just shadows; they shift and change, becoming one thing today and another tomorrow. They can never remain the same, and how can something that is always changing be truly real? Such things are mere appearances, my son. Man, too, is only an appearance of Humanity, just as a child represents childhood, a youth represents adolescence, a grown man represents adulthood, and an old man represents old age. How can we say that a child remains a child, or a man remains the same man, when constant changes hide what they were and what they have become?

So understand, my son, that all these things are only illusions reflecting a higher Reality. Since this is the case, I define illusion as a reflection of what is truly Real.

It is difficult to understand God, and it is impossible to describe Him. The physical world cannot express the non-physical, and something imperfect cannot fully grasp what is perfect. How can the eternal be connected with the temporary? The eternal remains forever, while the temporary quickly passes away. What is eternal is Real, while what is temporary is only a faint reflection. The difference between the mortal and the divine is as great as the difference between weakness and strength, or smallness and greatness. This distance between them clouds our understanding of true beauty.

We can see physical things with our eyes, and what the eyes perceive, the tongue can describe. But what has no body, no appearance, no shape, and no form cannot be understood by the senses. I know, Tatios, that God cannot be fully described. He is beyond anything we can define or explain.

Fragments of The Writings of Hermes to Ammon

PART 1

The force that governs the universe is Providence. What holds the universe together and sets its boundaries is Necessity. Destiny drives and controls everything with the power it possesses. It is Destiny that causes both the beginning of life and its end. Providence comes first and gives order to the universe. It reaches to the heavens, where the gods move in endless, tireless motion. Destiny exists because Necessity exists. Providence sees what is to come, and Destiny decides the arrangement of the stars. This is the universal law.

PART 2

Everything is brought into existence by Nature and Destiny, and no place is beyond the reach of Providence. Providence is the free will of the Supreme God, from which two natural forces arise: Necessity and Destiny. Destiny follows the guidance of both Providence and Necessity, while the stars follow the path set by Destiny. No one can escape from Destiny or defend themselves against the influence of the stars, as they act as tools of Destiny. Through them, the will of Destiny is carried out across all of Nature and in the lives of human beings.

PART 3

The soul is an essence that has no physical form, and even when it is within a body, it does not lose its true nature. Its essence lies in constant movement—the free movement of thought. Yet the soul does not move through anything, towards anything, or for any specific purpose. It is a primal force, and what is primary does not rely on anything secondary.

The phrase "in anything" refers to place, time, and nature. "Towards anything" refers to harmony, shape, or structure. "For anything" refers to the body, since time, place, nature, and form are connected to the body. All these elements are tied together in a cycle of mutual dependence. A body requires a place, because it cannot exist without occupying space. A body changes its nature, and such change must happen over time, through movement in nature. The parts of a body cannot come together without harmony in form.

Space exists because of physical bodies. It holds their changes and prevents them from being lost as they transform. A body shifts from one state to another, but even when it leaves one state, it remains a body; it just takes on a new condition. It is still a body—only its state has changed. This means that what shifts in a body is not its essence, but its qualities and way of being.

Place, time, and natural movement are not physical things, but each has its own unique role. The role of space is to contain. The role of time is to mark intervals and measure change. The role of nature is movement. The role of harmony is connection. The role of the body is to change. And the role of the soul is to think.

PART 4

The soul is an essence without a physical form. If it had a body, it could not preserve itself, because every body needs breath and life, which depend on order. Wherever something is born, it is always changing. To "become" implies growth, and growth brings increase, but every increase eventually leads to decrease, which brings about destruction. Anything that receives the form of life can only exist through the soul. For something to exist, it must already be part of life. I define existence as the process of becoming reasonable and participating in intelligent life. Life creates the creature, intelligence makes it reasonable, and the body makes it mortal.

The soul has no physical form and holds an unchanging power. Can a being be intelligent without a living soul? Can it be rational if there is no intelligent force guiding its rational life? Intelligence does not show itself equally in all creatures because the way their bodies are formed affects their harmony. If a body contains too much heat, the creature becomes restless and energetic. If cold dominates, the creature becomes sluggish and heavy. Nature arranges the elements of the body according to a balance or harmony. This balance comes in three forms: hot, cold, and balanced or temperate.

The way these elements combine in a body depends on the influence of the stars. The soul takes the body that is destined for it and gives it life through the work of nature. Nature matches the harmony within the body to the arrangement of the stars, aligning the elements in the body with the harmony of the heavens. This creates a mutual connection, where the stars and the body reflect each other. The purpose of this stellar harmony is to create sympathies that align with destiny.

PART 5

The soul, Ammon, is an essence that exists for its own purpose, receiving the life it was given from the start. It draws to itself a certain kind of reason mixed with passion and desire. Passion is like a raw material; when it aligns with the intelligent part of the soul, it becomes courage, standing firm against fear. Desire, too, is a raw material; when it works alongside the rational part of the soul, it turns into aspiration and resists indulgence. Reason acts like a light, guiding and correcting the blindness of desire. When the soul's different abilities are balanced under the control of reason, they create justice.

The management of the soul's abilities belongs to the Intellectual Principle, which functions with its own thoughtful reason. It governs everything like a judge, with its reason acting as its advisor. This Principle understands how reason can guide even the irrational parts, giving them a form of rationality. Though this rationality is weaker than true reason, it still surpasses the irrational—much like how an echo reflects a voice or how the moon reflects the sun's light. Passion and desire follow their own patterns of reason, attracting each other and creating a flow of thought between them.

Every soul is immortal and always in motion. Movement either comes from energy or from the body. Since the soul is without a physical form, it does not come from matter but from an essence that is also non-material. Everything that is born must come from something else. All things that are born and eventually decay involve two kinds of movement: the soul moves the being to life, while the body grows, shrinks, and decomposes as it breaks down. This is the cycle of perishable bodies. But the soul itself is in constant motion, never stopping. It moves by its own nature, creating movement from within. Every soul, therefore, is immortal because it is always in motion.

There are three kinds of souls: divine, human, and irrational. The divine soul exists in a divine form, which gives it the energy to move and act. When this soul leaves mortal beings, it abandons its irrational parts and returns to its divine form. Because the divine soul is always in motion, it flows along with the universal movement. The human soul also contains something divine, but it is bound to irrational elements like desire and passion. These irrational parts are energies, and although they are tied to mortal bodies, they do not die. However, they are separate from the divine part of the soul, which belongs to the divine form. When the divine part enters a mortal body and meets these irrational elements, it becomes a human soul.

The soul of animals is made up of passion and desire, which is why animals are called brutes—they lack reason. The fourth type of soul is the one connected to lifeless things. This soul exists outside the bodies it influences. It moves within the divine form and passively directs the objects it touches.

PART 6

The soul is an eternal and intelligent essence, guided by its own reason. It aligns itself with the concept of harmony. Even when it is separated from the physical body, the soul continues to exist on its own, independent in the world of ideals. It governs its reason and gives life a movement similar to its own thought—this is the essence of being, for the soul's nature is to shape other things according to its own character.

There are two types of life movements: one that matches the essence of the soul, and one that follows the nature of the body. The first type is universal and free, while the second is specific and bound by necessity. Everything that moves must follow the laws of whatever causes its movement. However, the soul's movement is connected by its nature to the principle of intelligence. The soul must be without a physical form and entirely distinct from the body because, if it had a body, it could not have reason or thought. All bodies lack intelligence, but when they receive the spirit, they become alive and breathe.

Breath belongs to the body, while reason focuses on the beauty of what is essential. The spirit connected to the senses interprets appearances. This spirit is divided among the different senses, such as sight, hearing, smell, taste, and touch. It interacts with thought to make sense of sensations; without thought, it only produces illusions because it belongs to the body and passively receives everything. Judgment belongs to reason, which understands higher things, while opinion belongs to the sensory spirit. The sensory spirit draws its energy from the outside world, while reason finds its energy within itself.

Various Hermetic Fragments

PART 1

There are essential spirit, reason, intelligence, and perception. Opinion and sensation lean toward perception, while reason aligns with the essential spirit. Thought moves independently but is also connected to perception. When combined, these elements form the soul. Opinion and sensation aim for perfection but do not stay consistent. They can shift between excess, deficiency, or change. Without perception, they decline, but when they follow perception closely, they connect with intellectual reason through learning and knowledge.

We have the power to choose, and it is up to us whether we select the best or the worst path by our will. Choosing what is harmful ties us to the physical world and places us under the control of Destiny. However, the intellectual spirit within us is free, and because of that, our reason is also free, unchanging, and beyond the reach of Destiny. When we follow this higher, intelligent reason, which is guided by the will of the supreme God, the spirit rises above the natural order of created things. But when the soul becomes attached to these created things, it becomes connected to their destiny, even though it is not truly part of their nature.

PART 2

There is a state of Being that is higher than all other beings and everything that exists. This Being is what gives universal essence to everything that is real and intelligible. Nature is the essence we can sense, containing within itself all physical objects. Between these two realms are the intellectual gods and the gods of the senses. The thoughts of intelligence connect with the intellectual gods, while opinions align with the gods of the senses, who reflect the higher intelligences. For example, the sun is a reflection of the creative and celestial God. Just as God created the universe, the sun brings animals to life, causes plants to grow, and controls the movement of water and other fluids.

PART 3

Thus, the soul's formless vision rises beyond the body to gaze upon true beauty. It lifts itself up in reverence, not for shape, body, or appearance, but for what lies beyond them all—something serene, still, essential, and unchanging. It is everything, complete in itself, singular and whole, existing by and through itself, always the same, without change or variation.

PART 4

If you understand this one and only Good, nothing will be beyond your reach, for all virtue is contained within it. Do not think this Good exists inside anyone or outside of anyone—it has no boundaries, yet it is the boundary of all things. Nothing holds it, but it holds everything within itself. What difference is there between the physical and the non-physical, the created and the uncreated, the things bound by necessity and those that are free, or between earthly things and heavenly things, between what can decay and what is eternal? The difference lies in this: some things exist freely, while others are bound by necessity. What belongs to the lower realm is incomplete and will pass away.

PART 5

Beneath nature and the ideal world stands the pyramid. At its peak is the cornerstone, the Creative Word of the universal Lord. This Word is the first power after Him—uncreated, infinite, and existing before everything He made. It is the child of the Most Perfect, the true and fruitful Son. The nature of this intelligent Word is to generate and create. You may call it generation, nature, or character, but know this: it is perfect in the Perfect, it comes from the Perfect, and all its works are perfectly good. It is the source of both creation and life.

Because this is its nature, it is rightly named. If not for the care and guidance of the universal Lord, who has caused me to share these truths, you would not have such a strong desire to explore these matters. Now, listen to the conclusion of this message. The Spirit I have spoken of so often is essential to all things. It sustains everything, gives life to all beings, and nourishes them. Flowing endlessly from the holy Source, it continually provides support to spirits and all living creatures.

PART 6

The Ideal Light existed before any other light, and the pure Intelligence of Intelligence has always been. Its unity is nothing other than the Spirit that surrounds the entire universe. From this Spirit comes neither gods, nor angels, nor anything else essential, for He is the Lord of all things, the source of power and light. Everything depends on Him and exists within Him. His perfect Word, both generative and creative, descended into the forces of nature and into the waters that bring forth life, making them fruitful.

After saying this, he stood and declared: "I call upon you, Heaven, sacred work of the great God. I call upon you, Voice of the Father, spoken at the beginning when the universe was created. I call upon you, Word, the only Son of the Father, who holds all things together. Be kind, be kind!"

PART 7

Seven planets move along the paths of Olympus, and through them, Eternity is measured: the Moon that lights the night, the dark Kronos, the gentle Sun, the Paphian Goddess who protects marriage, the bold Ares, the fertile Hermes, and Zeus, the source of life and nature's foundation. These planets have also been connected to humanity, for within each of us are the Moon, Zeus, Ares, Aphrodite, Kronos, Phoebus, and Hermes.

From the heavenly essence, we draw our tears, laughter, anger, speech, creation, sleep, and desire. Tears come from Kronos, creation from Zeus, speech from Hermes, courage from Ares, sleep from Artemis, desire from Kytheraea (Aphrodite), and laughter from Apollo, who brings joy to human thoughts and fills the endless world with delight.

PART 8

Hermes teaches that those who know God are protected from the attacks of evil and are no longer bound by Destiny. Knowing God is what true religion means.

The Chaldean Oracles

Zoroaster

Preface

These Oracles are believed to capture many of the key ideas of Chaldean philosophy. They were passed down to us through Greek translations and were highly respected in ancient times, valued by both early Christian leaders and later Platonists. The teachings are attributed to Zoroaster, though which Zoroaster they refer to is unknown, as historians mention up to six different individuals with that name. It is likely that "Zoroaster" was a title for the leader of the Magi, used as a general term. Scholars offer different ideas about the meaning of the name. One of the more interesting interpretations comes from Kircher, who suggests that it could mean "fashioning images of hidden fire" or "the image of secret things," based on a combination of words. Others say the name comes from terms meaning "one who contemplates the stars."

This collection is acknowledged to be fragmented and incomplete, and many of the original meanings have likely been lost or distorted through translation. Where possible, efforts have been made to clarify confusing expressions, either by refining the Greek translation or adding explanatory notes. Some suggest these Oracles were created by the Greeks, but as Stanley points out, Picus de Mirandula claimed to have the original Chaldean text. According to him, the Greek version contained flaws that did not appear in the original, and he stated that he found the manuscript after Mirandula's death. Additionally, some words in the Greek version are not of Greek origin but have Chaldean roots, adapted to the Greek language.

Berosus is believed to have been the first to introduce Chaldean writings on astronomy and philosophy to the Greeks. It is clear that Chaldean traditions had a significant influence on Greek thought. Taylor believed that some of these mystical sayings inspired the philosophical ideas of Plato, and scholars such as Porphyry, Iamblichus, Proclus, Pletho, and Psellus wrote extensive commentaries on them. The fact that such brilliant thinkers held these Oracles in high regard suggests that they deserve our attention.

The name "Oracles" was likely used to emphasize their deep and mysterious nature. The Chaldeans also had an Oracle that they respected as much as the Greeks revered the Oracle at Delphi. Psellus and Pletho both provided detailed commentary on the Chaldean Oracles. Franciscus Patricius later expanded on their work, adding material from other writers, including Proclus, Hermias, Simplicius, Damascius, Synesius, Olympiodorus, Nicephorus, and Arnobius. Patricius compiled around 324 Oracles, organizing them under various topics. His collection, published in Latin in 1593, served as the foundation for later classifications by Taylor and Cory, and their work was used in preparing the current version.

Some of the Oracles collected by Psellus appear to come from an early Chaldean Zoroaster and are marked with the letter "Z," following Taylor's method, with a few exceptions. Another set is attributed to a group of philosophers called Theurgists, who were active during the reign of Marcus Antoninus, as recorded by Proclus. These are marked with the letter "T." Additional Oracles of uncertain origin are labeled "Z or T," while other passages are credited to individual authors where appropriate.

Introduction

Many people, with good reason, believe that these short and mysterious sayings contain a deep system of mystical philosophy. However, truly understanding this philosophy requires a refined ability to perceive non-physical realities. It is said that the Chaldean Magi passed down their secret knowledge through generations, keeping it alive through tradition from father to son. According to Diodorus, "They do not teach these things as the Greeks do. Among the Chaldeans, philosophy is passed down within families, with sons learning from their fathers. These sons are free from other duties, dedicating themselves fully to learning from their parents, trusting what is taught to them more deeply."

The essence of this oral tradition seems to have survived within these Oracles, which should be studied alongside the teachings of the Kabbalah and Egyptian theology. Those familiar with the Kabbalah know that it can be interpreted in extraordinary ways, especially when paired with the Tarot, which reflects the core ideas of Egyptian theology. If commentators in the past had taken this approach, the Chaldean system within the Oracles would not have been misinterpreted to the extent that it has.

The entire structure of the Hebrew Kabbalah is built on the concept of ten divine powers, each emerging successively from an infinite source of light. These ten powers are seen as the key to understanding all things. They are arranged into three sets of triads, with a tenth power bringing them together. These divine forces extend across four worlds, called Atziluth, Briah, Yetzirah, and Assiah, moving from the most subtle to the most physical. This idea is rooted in pantheism, though it also points toward a divine source. At the heart of all things is the absolute Deity, whose thoughts form the universe we experience.

This same structure applies to the Chaldean system. The diagrams included demonstrate how Chaldean philosophy aligns with the Kabbalah. In the Chaldean view, the "First Mind" and the Intelligible Triad—consisting of Father (Pater), Power (Potentia or Mater), and Mind (Mens)—belong to the realm of higher, non-physical light. The "First Mind" symbolizes the original intelligence that exists within the depths of the divine Father. This intelligence reflects into the "Second Mind," representing divine power in the celestial world. This second mind aligns with the next great triad of divine powers, known as both Intelligible and Intellectual. The third triad belongs to the ethereal world, and it consists of intellectual forces working together.

Finally, the fourth world, known as the Elementary World, is shaped by Hypezokos, or the Flower of Fire, which is the force responsible for building the physical world.

Chaldean theology divided the higher realities into three main levels. The first is Eternal, without a beginning or end, called the "Paternal Depth," the heart of the divine presence. The second is a state of being that has a beginning but no end. This is the Creative World, also known as the Empyrean, which is filled with creations, although its source remains beyond them. The third level is the temporary Ethereal World, which had a beginning in time and will eventually end.

These three worlds are connected by seven spheres. One sphere belongs to the Empyrean, or extends from it, three are part of the Ethereal World, and three exist in the Elementary World, with the physical world uniting them all. These spheres should not be confused with the seven material planets, although the planets represent these spheres physically. The spheres themselves are not material in the usual sense but exist in a deeper, metaphysical way. Psellus tried to link these spheres directly with the planets, but Stanley criticized his approach. However, Stanley's own ideas are not entirely consistent, as he suggests that these worlds are non-physical but also claims that a physical world exists in the Empyrean.

Before the Light of the higher realms, there was the "Paternal Depth," the Absolute Deity that holds all things in potential, always present and unchanging. This idea mirrors the concept of Ain Soph Aur in the Kabbalah—three words, each with three letters, representing three sets of divine powers. These powers become manifest and follow the Triadic Law, guided by the Demiurge, the creator of the universe.

The Light of the higher realms was seen as the first expression of the Paternal Depth, an original and universal essence that flows everywhere and is beyond complete human understanding. The Empyrean is a more refined but still creative fire, serving as the source of the Ethereal World. In turn, the Ethereal World acts as the source for the Elementary World. Through these stages, the ideas of the divine mind become real in time and space.

In many ways, the way of thinking in the East today may not be so different from what it was thousands of years ago. Much that seems strange to us in ancient traditions still resonates with many people around the world. Modern thinkers and scientists have expressed ideas that, while not identical, are similar to these ancient Chaldean beliefs. One example is the idea that natural laws are guided by an intelligent and conscious power. From this point of view, it is not a big leap to see forces as living entities, filling the universe with the creations of the imagination. In this way, history repeats itself, and both ancient and modern ideas reflect the same, ever-changing truth.

Without delving too deeply into metaphysics, it is essential to recognize the importance given to the "Paternal Mind." This is the intelligence of the universe, described poetically as "energizing before energy," which establishes the original patterns of everything that will exist. These patterns are then handed over to the divine powers, known as the Rectores Mundorum, to develop and govern. As the saying goes, "Mind is with Him, power with them."

In the Platonic sense, the word "Intelligible" refers to a way of knowing or perceiving that goes beyond intellectual thought—something higher and distinct from ordinary reasoning. The Chaldeans identified three ways of perceiving: through the senses, through intellectual thought, and through the higher, intelligible concepts. Each of these operates separately, through unique forms or channels. However, their exploration of the soul's nature went much deeper. Though the soul is ultimately connected to the divine, it was seen as a complex being when manifested in existence.

The Oracles speak of the "Paths of the Soul," which are like streams of unyielding fire connecting its essential parts and keeping them whole. These paths, along with its "summits," "fountains," and "vessels," mirror the universal principles that guide everything. This idea, shared by many ancient cosmologies, shows how closely Chaldean metaphysics connect the structure of the universe to the nature of human beings.

In each of the Chaldean Divine Worlds, a group of three divine powers operates together, forming a fourth element that completes the group. As the Oracle says, "In every World, a Triad shines, with the Monad as the ruling principle." These Monads are divine representatives that manage the universe. Each of the four worlds—the Empyrean, Ethereal, Elementary, and Material—is governed by a supreme power that remains directly connected to the Father and guided by divine wisdom. This aligns closely with the Kabbalistic idea of the divine name, which is expressed through four letters in various languages.

The Oracle describes this by saying, "There is a Venerable Name that moves through the Worlds in an unending cycle." The Kabbalah explains this further, teaching that each of the four worlds corresponds to one of the four letters in the divine name. Each world also has its own way of writing this name, reflecting how the order of elements—both on a cosmic and personal level—is governed by the continuous motion of this name. The divine name, associated with the elements, is seen as a universal law that guides creation. This creative force is summed up in the figure known as the Demiurge, or Hypezokos, the "Flower of Fire."

Plato's view of the human being offers a similar idea of the soul's structure. He places intellect in the head, the soul with passions like courage in the heart, and another part of the soul, which contains desires and basic urges, near the stomach and spleen. According to the Chaldean doctrine, as recorded by Psellus, humanity is made up of three types of souls:

First, the Intelligible, or divine soul,

Second, the Intellect or rational soul, and

Third, the Irrational, or passional soul.

This last soul, tied to the body, was thought to change and dissolve at death. The divine soul, according to the Oracles, is described as "a bright fire that, through the Father's power, remains immortal and rules over life." Its influence can only be grasped when the soul moves beyond the illusions created by passions and stops reacting to them.

The rational soul, the Chaldeans taught, can either align itself with the divine or fall under the control of the irrational soul. As the Oracles say, "The divine cannot be reached by those who focus only on the body; only those who strip away these attachments can reach the highest truth." The three types of souls each have their own vehicles. The divine soul's vehicle is immortal, the rational soul's can become immortal through its progress, and the irrational soul is connected to what is called "the image," which is the astral form of the physical body.

Physical life works through these three types of activity. When the body dies, each soul follows a different path, depending on how they used their energies in life. The Oracles encourage people to focus on divine things and resist the urges of the irrational soul, warning, "If you do not succeed, your body will be inhabited by the beasts of the earth."

The Chaldeans assigned the astral form of the irrational soul to the Lunar Sphere. This probably referred to more than just the Moon itself; it included the whole region below the Moon, with Earth at its center. At death, the rational soul rises beyond the Moon's influence, but only if its past life allows for this release. Much importance was placed on how life is lived while the soul is in the body, with frequent calls to seek communion with divine powers. Only the highest form of theurgy was believed to offer such a connection.

"Let the depth of your immortal soul lead you," one Oracle says, "but raise your eyes earnestly upward." Taylor explains this with the idea that "the eyes" represent the soul's inner abilities. When these abilities awaken, the soul becomes filled with a higher life and divine light, almost as if it rises beyond itself.

The Chaldean Magi were said to be the first to separate true visions from dreams. They had a deep understanding of both mental and spiritual realities. Their attention to inner images, along with their passionate devotion, made them more than just teachers—they lived out the philosophy they taught. Life on the open plains of Chaldea, under calm nights and starry skies, nurtured this inner development. From a young age, students of the Magi were taught how to break free from worldly limitations and explore the vast inner realms. One Oracle teaches, "The bonds of the soul, which give her breath, are easy to loosen." Other texts speak of the "Melody of the Ether" and the "Lunar clashings," showing how these mystical experiences reflected real inner practices.

The Oracles also describe how divine visions and impressions appear in the Ether. The Chaldeans believed that the ethers of the elements are the subtle forces through which the more familiar elements—Earth, Air, Water, and Fire—work. These subtle ethers represent the underlying principles of dryness and moisture, heat and cold. The signs of the Zodiac were also linked to these ethers, with each element appearing in three forms. This connection influenced how they understood personality and tendencies. For example, when it was said that someone had Aries rising, it meant that fiery ether dominated their nature, making them energetic and active.

The planets, in turn, were thought to influence the ethers, giving them specific vibrations or energies. These planets, positioned in carefully arranged zones, controlled the flow of these subtle forces throughout the universe.

The Chaldeans believed that the planets were connected not only to specific colors and sounds but also to the ethers, with each planetary force having a special link to certain constellations in the Zodiac. Part of their spiritual practice involved forming connections with these celestial beings. In one fragment, it is said: "If you call upon the celestial Lion often, then, when the heavens disappear from your sight, when the stars lose their light, the moon becomes hidden, and the earth vanishes, you will see everything around you take the shape of a Lion." Both the Chaldeans and Egyptians had a deep understanding of color, which reflected their heightened spiritual awareness. Bright colors were thought to awaken the mind's ability to imagine and engage with inner visions.

The Chaldean method of contemplation involved becoming one with the object of meditation, similar to the process used in Indian Yoga. This approach is captured in the saying, "He becomes one with the images, casting them around himself." Though the divine is without form or body, it was believed that divine forces become temporarily bound to forms for the benefit of humanity.

The subtle ethers served as coverings for the divine Light. The Oracles teach that beyond these ethers lies "a solar world and endless Light." This divine Light was the object of their deepest reverence. However, the Light they sought was not the light of the sun we know. Instead, it was referred to as "the starless sphere above," where "the more true Sun" resides. Theosophists understand this as the idea that the physical sun is just a reflection of a higher, more glorious light.

Some individuals, through their strength, could reach this Light on their own. As the Oracles say, "The mortal who approaches the fire will receive Light from the divine, and the immortal ones are swift to aid those who persevere." However, even those less capable were not entirely left out. The Oracles explain, "Some are blessed with knowledge even as they sleep, drawing strength from the divine." This idea inspired many later thinkers, including Porphyry and Synesius. Apuleius's Metamorphoses and the Vision of Scipio also reflect this belief. Though many Christians are familiar with the saying "He gives to His beloved in sleep," few fully grasp the deeper meaning behind it.

What, then, was the Chaldean view of earthly life? Were they pessimistic, dismissing the material world as unimportant? It seems more accurate to say that their philosophy was filled with spiritual hope. They believed that beyond the limits of matter lay a better and truer reality. Earthly life was seen as a flawed reflection of this higher realm. Like us, the Chaldeans sought what is good, beautiful, and true. But unlike those who chase external pleasures, they understood that true fulfillment is found within.

The first step in this journey toward inner fulfillment was living a simple life. For most of the Magi, this way of life was ingrained from birth. The discipline of living simply, combined with wisdom, made them especially open to nature's truths. As one Oracle warns: "Do not descend into the dark, glittering world below. Beneath the earth lies a steep fall, where a throne of destructive power awaits. Do not go down into that deceptive splendor, for it will only defile your inner light. Its brilliance is false, and it is home only to the children of sorrow." This beautifully expresses the idea that pursuing physical pleasures diminishes the soul's higher energy. Yet, for those who live virtuously and purify themselves, the Oracles offer encouragement: "The higher powers build up the bodies of the holy ones."

The law of karma was just as important in Chaldean thought as it is in modern theosophy. Ficinus explains, "The soul moves continuously, passing through everything in its journey. Once this journey is complete, it must return through the same paths, weaving a new cycle of life, as Zoroaster teaches: whenever the same causes arise, the same effects will follow."

This is the deeper meaning behind the saying "History repeats itself," far removed from superstitious ideas of fate. Here, everyone receives what they deserve based on their actions, whether good or bad. These are the bonds of life. Yet, the Oracles warn, "Do not expand your destiny," urging people to explore the "River of the Soul." Though the soul serves the body, it can still rise back to the divine order from which it came by combining sacred actions with reason.

We are encouraged to understand the Intelligible, that divine part of being which lies beyond the mind. This can only be grasped with the highest potential of our intellect. The Oracles say, "Understand the Intelligible with the bright flame of an awakened mind." Zoroaster is also credited with saying, "The one who knows himself knows everything within himself." Another teaching suggests that "The Paternal Mind has planted symbols within the soul." However, such knowledge was only available to Theurgists, who, as the Oracles explain, "do not fall into the same fate as the masses." The divine light cannot shine in a disordered soul, just as clouds block the sun. Those who seek higher wisdom without preparation or purity walk a path filled with confusion and darkness, and their efforts will fail.

Even though our destiny may be "written in the stars," the divine soul's mission is to raise the human soul above the circle of necessity. The Oracles praise the power of a will that triumphs over obstacles, describing it like this:

"Hewing down walls with the force of magic, Breaking apart the barriers, Splitting the seven posts to pieces, Speaking the words of mastery!"

This triumph comes through strengthening the will and elevating the imagination, which has the power to guide consciousness. As the Oracles say, "Believe yourself to be beyond the body, and you will be." They might have added, "Then your purified imagination will reveal the symbols of the soul." Yet, when looking within, one must confront the self honestly. "On beholding yourself, fear," meaning you must face the imperfect parts of yourself.

To achieve the highest perfection, everything must be viewed as ideal. Willpower is the key to mystical progress, having a powerful influence over the body's nervous system. Through will, fleeting visions can be held steady within the astral light. Will also drives consciousness toward communion with the divine. However, the challenge lies in aligning three distinct wills—the wills of the Divine Soul, the Rational Soul, and the Irrational Soul.

Selfishness blocks the flow of higher thought, keeping it tied to the body. This is not just a moral idea but a scientific truth. Selfishness beyond basic needs is nothing more than vulgarity. Just as a picture that seems beautiful to a refined mind might look like a mess of colors to someone untrained, so too the broad perspective of one who sees beyond personal concerns cannot be understood by those focused only on themselves.

The path to the greatest good lies through self-sacrifice—offering up the lower self to serve the higher self. Behind this higher self is the hidden presence of the "Ancient of Days," the unified essence of divine humanity. These truths are grasped only by the soul. The soul's song can only be heard in the sacred silence where the divine dwells.

The Oracles of Zoroaster

CAUSE.	GOD.	
FATHER	MIND	FIRE
MONAD	DYAD	TRIAD

God is described as having the head of a hawk. He is the first and eternal being, beyond corruption, not created by anything else, whole and unchanging, unlike anything else. He gives all good things, cannot be destroyed, and is the highest good and the wisest. He is the source of fairness, justice, and wisdom, teaching Himself and embodying perfection. He is the inspiration for Sacred Philosophy. Eusebius, Præparatio Evangelica, Book 1, Chapter 10. This Oracle isn't found in ancient collections or in the writings of medieval occultists. Cory seems to have found it in Eusebius's writings, where the Persian Zoroaster is credited as its author.

Theurgists say that this God is both old and young. They describe Him as a God who moves endlessly, whose power fills the universe, and who controls everything that moves. He has limitless energy and exerts a force that spirals throughout creation. Proclus on Plato's Timaeus, 244. Z. or T. p. 24 In Egyptian mythology, there were two Horuses—an older and younger God—both sons of Osiris and Isis. Taylor suggests that this passage refers to Kronos, or Time, called Chronos by later Platonists. In Roman mythology, Kronos (also called Saturnus) was the son of Uranus and Gaia, married to Rhea, and father of Zeus.

The God of the Universe is eternal and boundless, both young and old, with a spiraling force. Cory includes this Oracle in his collection but doesn't mention its source. Lobeck questioned its authenticity.

The Eternal Æon, according to the Oracle, is the reason for endless life, boundless strength, and tireless energy. Taylor.—T.

The divine ones call this unknowable God "silent" and say He communicates through the power of the Mind. Human souls can only understand Him using their minds. Proclus in Theology of Plato, 321. T. The word "inscrutable" is used, though Taylor translates it as "stable," and some suggest "incomprehensible" might be a better term.

The Chaldeans call this God Dionysos (or Bacchus) and Iao in the Phoenician language, referring to Him as the "Intelligible Light." He is also called Sabaoth, meaning He is above the Seven Spheres and acts as the Demiurge. Lydus, De Mensibus, 83. T.

He holds all things within Himself, at the peak of His existence, yet He also exists beyond everything. Proclus in Theology of Plato, 212. T. "Hyparxis" usually refers to "existence" or "subsistence." "Hupar" suggests reality as distinct from appearance, and "Huparche" means "beginning."

He measures and defines all things. Proclus in Theology of Plato, 386. T. The phrase "Thus he speaks the words" appears in the Greek text but is omitted by Taylor and Cory.

Nothing imperfect comes from the Paternal Principle. Psellus, 38; Pletho. Z. This suggests that imperfection only appears through later processes of creation.

The Father did not bring forth fear; instead, He gave the gift of persuasion. Pletho. Z.

The Father fully understands Himself and doesn't limit His fire to His intellectual power alone. Psellus, 30; Pletho, 33. Z. p. 26 Taylor interprets this as "The Father withdrew Himself quickly but didn't confine His fire to His mind." However, the Greek text doesn't mention "quickly." The word "Arpazo" can mean "grasp" or "understand with the mind."

This is the kind of Mind that exists before action begins, staying in the Father's depth and nourishing silence in the hidden place of God. Proclus on Timaeus, 167. T.

Everything comes from the same divine fire. The Father created everything perfectly and passed it to the Second Mind, whom all nations refer to as the First. Psellus, 24; Pletho, 30. Z.

The Second Mind governs the Empyrean World. Damascius, On Principles. T.

The Intelligible speaks by understanding. Psellus, 35. Z.

• Power belongs to them, but the source of Mind is from Him. Proclus in Plato's Theology, 365. T.

- The Father's Mind rides upon delicate Guides, which shine with the trails of unwavering and unstoppable Fire. Proclus on Plato's Cratylus. T.
- ...After the Father's thought, I, the Soul, take my place, a warmth that gives life to all things. ...For He placed The Intelligible within the Soul, and the Soul within the lifeless body, Just as the Father of Gods and Men has placed these within us. Proclus in Timaeus, 124. Z. or T.
- Nature's works exist together with the Father's light of understanding. The Soul decorated the vast Heaven, and after the Father, it continues to shape it. But her rule remains high above. Proclus in Timaeus, 106. Z. or T. The word "dominion" is from the Greek krata, though some versions use kerata, meaning "horns."
- The Soul, as a shining Fire through the Father's power, remains immortal, ruling over Life and filling the deep places of the World's heart. Psellus, 28; Pletho, 11. Z.
- With the channels intertwined, the Soul carries out the works of eternal Fire. Proclus in Politico, p. 399. Z. or T.
- The Fire from beyond does not lock its power in matter but exists within the Mind. For it is the Mind of Mind that shapes the Fiery World. Proclus in Theology, 333, and Timaeus, 157. T.
- The one who first came from Mind wraps one Fire within another, weaving them together to unite the flowing fountains of Fire while keeping its brilliance untouched. Proclus in Parmenides. T.
- A Fiery Whirlwind draws down the glow of flashing flames, penetrating the Universe's depths, as its marvelous rays extend downwards from there. Proclus in Plato's Theology, 171 and 172. T.
- The Monad came first into existence and still remains as the Paternal Monad. Proclus in Euclid, 27. T.
- When the Monad stretches outward, the Dyad is born. Proclus in Euclid, 27. T. The Pythagoreans describe the Monad, Dyad, and Triad just as Plato does with Bound, Infinite, and Mixed. These Oracles use the terms Hyparxis, Power, and Energy for the same ideas. Damascius On Principles. Taylor.
- Beside Him sits the Dyad, sparkling with intellectual divisions. It governs all things and brings order to whatever lacks it. Proclus in Plato's Theology, 376. T.

- The Father's Mind declared that all things should be divided into Three, and with His Will's agreement, everything was immediately separated this way. Proclus in Parmenides. T.
- The Eternal Father's Mind spoke of the Three, ruling everything through understanding. Proclus in Timaeus. T.
- The Father blended every Spirit from within this Triad. Lydus, De Mensibus, 20. Taylor.
- Everything flows from the heart of this Triad. Lydus, De Mensibus, 20. Taylor.
- Everything is ruled by and exists within this Triad. Proclus in First Alcibiades. T.

You must understand that everything bows before the Three Supreme Powers. Damascius, On Principles. T.

From this source comes the Form of the Triad, which existed before creation. It is not the first Essence but the principle by which all things are measured. Anon. Z. or T.

In it appeared Virtue, Wisdom, and all-knowing Truth. Anon. Z. or T.

In every World, the Triad shines brightly, and above it all, the Monad reigns supreme. Damascius in Parmenides. T.

The first course is Sacred. In the middle course, the Sun moves, and in the third, the Earth is warmed by inner fire. Anon. Z. or T.

It stands high above, giving life to Light, Fire, Ether, and Worlds. Simplicius in his Physics, 143. Z. or T.

Ideas

INTELLIGIBLES, INTELLECTUALS, IYNGES, SYNOCHES, TELETARCHÆ, FOUNTAINS, PRINCIPLES, HECATE AND DÆMONS.

1.   The Mind of the Father spun forth with a roaring sound, grasping with unshakable Will every possible Idea. These Ideas, which flowed from a single source, were released, for both the Will and the Purpose came from the Father, and through changing forms of life, they remain connected to Him. But these Ideas were separated and spread by Intellectual Fire into other forms of Intelligence. Before the diverse World took shape, the King of All placed an intellectual and unchanging Pattern as a model. The impression of this Pattern spread throughout the World, filling the Universe with many kinds of Ideas, yet all these Ideas share a single origin. From this one foundation, they split and spread across different bodies throughout the Universe, moving endlessly through the depths, shining and radiating outward without end. These are intellectual concepts from the Father's Fountain, filled with the brightness of Fire, carried by the flow of unceasing Time. The Father's original, perfect Fountain released these first-born Ideas. Proclus in Parmenidem. Z. or T.

2.   These Ideas, though many, flash down onto the shining Worlds, carrying with them the Three Divine Powers. Damascius in Parmenidem. T.

3.   They guard the works of the Father and the One Mind, which holds all understanding. Proclus in Theologiam Platonis, 205. T.

4.   All things exist together within the World of Pure Intelligence. Damascius, De Principiis. T.

5.   Every form of Intelligence knows the Divine, for Intelligence cannot exist without the object of its understanding, and the object of understanding cannot exist apart from Intelligence. Damascius. Z. or T.

6.   Intelligence depends on what it understands, and without this connection, it cannot exist. Proclus, Th. Pl., 172. Z. or T.

7.   Through Intelligence, He holds together the things that can be understood and brings the Soul into the Worlds.

8.   With Intelligence, He gathers what can be known and brings Sen-

sation into the Worlds. Proclus in Crat. T.

9.   The Father's Intelligence, which knows all things and beautifies what cannot be expressed, has scattered symbols throughout the World. Proclus in Cratylum. T.

10.   This structure is the starting point of all division. Damascius, De Principiis. T.

11.   Pure Understanding is the root of every division. Damascius, De Principiis. T.

12.   Pure Understanding serves as nourishment for what gains knowledge. Damascius, De Principiis. T.

13.   The oracles describe the Order as existing before the Heavens, beyond words, and say it possesses Mystic Silence. Proclus in Cratylum. T.

14.   The oracle explains that causes born from Understanding are swift. It says that after flowing from the Father, they quickly return to Him again. Proclus in Cratylum. T.

15.   These Natures are both Intelligent and objects of Intelligence. They hold knowledge within themselves and become subjects for others to understand. Proclus, Theologiam Platonis. T.

The Second Order of Platonic philosophy is called the "Intelligible and Intellectual Triad." In Chaldean teachings, this order includes the Iynges, Synoches, and Teletarchs. The later Platonists' Intellectual Triad corresponds with the Chaldean Fountains, Fontal Fathers, or Cosmagogi.

1.   The Iynges gain their understanding from the Father. Through mysterious guidance, they are moved to comprehend. Psellus, 41; Pletho, 31. Z.

16.   It is the Operator and the Giver of Life-bearing Fire. It fills Hecate's life-giving womb and transfers the empowering energy of Fire to the Synoches, endowing them with immense strength. Proclus in Timaeus, 128. T.

17.   He gave His Whirlwinds to guard the Supernals, blending His own force within the Synoches. Dam., On Principles. T.

18.   Likewise, many others serve the material Synoches. T.

19.   The Teletarchs are part of the Synoches. Dam., On Principles. T.

20.   Rhea, the source and river of blessed intellects, holds the powers of all things in her sacred womb, pouring out continuous creation upon

everything. Proclus in Cratylus. T.

21.　She marks the boundary of the Father's Depth and serves as the source of intellect. Dam., On Principles. T.

22.　He shines with clear, radiant strength, filled with intellectual energy. Dam. T.

23.　His brilliance contains intellectual power, spreading love throughout everything. Dam. T.

24.　All things submit to the swirling motions of the Intellectual Fire, following the Father's wise guidance. Proclus in Parmenides. T.

25.　Oh, how the World is governed by unyielding Intellectual Rulers.

26.　Hecate's source aligns with that of the Fontal Fathers. T.

27.　From Him leap forth the Amilicti, unrelenting thunderbolts, and the whirlwinds that fill Hecate's sacred womb with unstoppable strength. He surrounds the brilliance of Fire, and His mighty Spirit, burning beyond, rules the Poles. Proclus in Cratylus. T.

28.　There is another source that leads the Empyrean World. Proclus in Timaeus. Z. or T.

29.　It is the source of all sources and the boundary of every spring. Dam., On Principles.

30.　The fountain that generates life for Souls is contained within two Minds. Dam., On Principles. T.

31.　Beneath these exists the Primary One of all non-material things. Dam. in Parmenides. Z. or T.

Following the Intellectual Triad is the Demiurgos, from whom came the Essences and Orders, including various spirits and the material world.

32.　Light born from the Father alone holds the power to grasp His Mind. It pours understanding into all sources and principles, driving their endless cycles. Proclus in Timaeus, 242.

33.　All sources and principles revolve continuously, never ceasing their motion. Proclus in Parmenides. Z. or T.

34.　The principles that have understood the Father's plans are wrapped in physical forms and bodies. These serve as links between the Father and matter, making invisible ideas visible in the world. Dam., On Principles. Z. or T.

35.　Typhon, Echidna, and Python, children of Tartarus and Gaia, joined by Uranus, form a Chaldean Triad that watches over and controls chaotic creations. Olymp. in Phaedrus. T.

36.   Some irrational demons, without thought, are sustained by the rulers of the air. This is why the oracle says, "They guide the airy, earthly, and water-dwelling creatures." Olymp. in Phaedrus. T.

37.   When connected to divine beings, the word "Aquatic" signifies rule tied to water. This is why the oracle calls the aquatic gods "Water Walkers." Proclus in Timaeus, 270. T.

38.   Some water spirits, known as Nereids in Orpheus's writings, dwell in high, misty waters, appearing in the damp air. As Zoroaster taught, these spirits can sometimes be seen by those with keen sight, especially in Persia and Africa. Ficino, On the Immortality of the Soul, 123. T.

Particular Souls

SOUL, LIFE, MAN.

1.   The Father created ideas, and He gave life to all mortal bodies. Proclus in Tim., 336. T.

39.   The Father of gods and humans placed the Mind (nous) in the Soul (psyche) and placed both within the human body.

40.   The Father's Mind planted symbols within the Soul. Psellus, 26; Pletho, 6. Z.

41.   He mixed the Vital Spark from two substances—Mind and Divine Spirit—and as a third element, He added Holy Love, the sacred Charioteer that unites all things. Lydus, De Mensibus, 3.

42.   This Love fills the Soul with deep affection. Proclus in Platonis Theologia, 4. Z. or T.

43.   The human Soul embraces God closely. It holds no mortal nature and is entirely filled with God's presence, rejoicing in the harmony that sustains the mortal body. Psellus, 17; Pletho, 10. Z.

44.   Stronger Souls can see Truth by their own nature and are more creative. According to the Oracle, such Souls are saved by their own power. Proclus in I. Alcibiades. Z.

45.   The Oracle says that ascending Souls sing hymns of praise. Olympiodorus in Phaedrus. Z. or T.

46.   Of all Souls, the most blessed are those sent from Heaven to Earth.

They are joyful and possess indescribable strength, for they come from your radiant essence, O King, or from Jove himself, driven by the unbreakable power of Mithus. Synesius, De Insomniis, 153. Z. or T.

47.   The Souls of those who die suddenly are the purest. Psellus, 27. Z.

48.   The threads that hold the Soul's breath can be easily released. Psellus, 32; Pletho, 8. Z.

49.   When one Soul is set free, the Father sends another to keep the number complete. Z. or T.

50.   By understanding the Father's works, these Souls escape the grasp of Fate. They remain in God's presence, drawing strong lights that descend from the Father. As they descend, the Soul gathers the heavenly fruit, the flower that nourishes the spirit. Proclus in Tim., 321. Z. or T.

51.   This spiritual force, which the blessed call the Pneumatic Soul, becomes a god, a powerful spirit, or an image without a body. In this form, the Soul experiences punishment. The Oracles say that the Soul's tasks in Hades resemble the deceptive visions of a dream. Synesius, De Insomniis. Z. or T. The term "Dæmon" originally referred to both good and bad spirits, often applied to pure beings as much as to impure ones. This concept aligns with the Eastern teaching of Devachan, a state of pleasant illusion after death.

52.   Life flows from many sources, moving from above, through the opposite side, to the center of the Earth. From there, it reaches the fiery middle point, where the life-giving fire descends into the physical world. Z. or T.

53.   Water represents life, which is why Plato and the ancient gods described the Soul as both the water that gives life and the fountain from which it flows. Proclus in Tim., 318. Z.

54.   O Man, daring by nature, you are a subtle creation. Psellus, 12; Pletho, 21. Z.

55.   Your body will become the home of the beasts of the Earth. Psellus, 36; Pletho, 7. Z. The body is the vessel that temporarily holds the Mind (nous).

56.   The Soul moves continuously through different experiences over time. Once these experiences are complete, it must pass through everything again, weaving the same pattern of life in the world. Zoroaster believed that when the same causes arise, the same effects will inevitably

follow. Ficinus, De Immortalitate Animæ, 129. Z.

57.   According to Zoroaster, the Soul's ethereal form continually returns through reincarnation. Ficinus, De Immortalitate Animæ, 131. Z.

58.   The Oracles celebrate the essential source of every Soul, which flows from the Empyrean, the Ethereal, and the Material realms. They separate this source from Zoogonothea, the life-giving goddess Rhea. From her, they create two orders: one related to the Soul and the other to Fate. The Oracles teach that the Soul comes from the animating order but sometimes falls under the control of Fate. When this happens, the Soul enters an irrational state and becomes subject to Fate instead of Divine Providence. Proclus, De Providentia apud Fabricium, Bibliotheca Graeca, vol. 8, 486. Z. or T.

Matter

THE WORLD--AND NATURE.

1.   The Matrix contains everything within it. T.

59.   It can be divided entirely, yet it also remains whole.

60.   From it flows the endless creation of many different types of Matter. Proclus in *Tim.*, 118. T.

61.   These creations form atoms, physical shapes, material bodies, and everything that belongs to the realm of matter. Damascius, *De Principiis*. T.

62.   The Nymphs of the Fountains, along with all Water Spirits and forms of the Earth, sky, and stars, are the Riders and Rulers of Matter—whether celestial, starry, or deep within the Abyss. Lydus, p. 32.

63.   The Oracles teach that Evil is weaker than even nothingness. Proclus, *De Providentia*. Z. or T.

64.   Matter fills the whole world, as the gods also proclaim. Proclus, *Tim.*, 142. Z. or T.

65.   Although Divine Beings have no bodies, they are bound to bodies for our sake. Since bodies cannot fully hold spiritual beings due to the limits of material nature, this connection exists to focus the divine within us. Proclus in *Platonis Politicus*, 359. Z. or T.

66.   The Father's Mind, understanding His creations, spread the fiery

bonds of love throughout everything, ensuring that all things would remain connected in love for eternity. This way, everything in creation stays linked to the Father's Light, and the elements of the world are drawn together by mutual attraction. Proclus in *Tim.*, 155. T.

67.   The Maker of everything, acting through His own power, shaped the World. Out of a fiery mass, He formed all things by His will, making the Universe a visible creation, not hidden or shapeless. Proclus in *Tim.*, 154. Z. or T.

68.   He made all things in His own likeness, casting them in the image of His form.

69.   They reflect His Mind, but because they are made, they also contain something physical. Proclus in *Tim.*, 87. Z. or T.

70.   There is a Holy Name that moves without rest, leaping into the worlds through the Father's rapid vibrations. Proclus in *Cratylus*. Z. or T.

71.   The ethers of the elements are present there. Olympiodorus in *Phaedrus*. Z. or T.

72.   The Oracles reveal that divine symbols and other visions appear within the Ether or Astral Light. Simplicius in *Physica*, 144. Z. or T.

73.   In this realm, the shapeless takes form. Simplicius in *Physica*, 143. Z. or T.

74.   These are the hidden and revealed impressions of the World.

75.   The World that resists the Light draws many down through twisting currents. Proclus in *Tim.*, 339. Z. or T.

76.   He made the whole world from Fire, Air, Water, Earth, and nourishing Ether. Z. or T.

77.   He placed the Earth in the center, Water beneath it, and Air above both. Z. or T.

78.   He fixed countless stars in place, keeping them steady and unmoving, with no labor but by stable order, forcing Fire into Fire. Proclus in *Tim.*, 280. Z. or T.

79.   The Father gathered the seven layers of the Cosmos, shaping the Heavens in a curved form. Damascius in *Parmenides*. Z. or T.

80.   He created the seven wandering bodies (the planets). Z. or T.

81.   Their movements were set within well-organized zones. Z. or T.

82.   He made six of them, placing the Fiery Sun as the seventh in the

center. Proclus in *Tim.*, 280. Z. or T.

83. From the center, all lines extend equally in every direction. Proclus in *Euclidem.*

84. The Sun moves continuously around this central point. Proclus in *Platonis Theologia*, 317. Z. or T.

85. It eagerly races toward the center of brilliant Light. Proclus in *Tim.*, 236. T.

86. The Great Sun and the Shining Moon.

87. Its rays spread outward like flowing hair, ending in sharp points. Proclus in *Platonis Politicus*, 387. T.

88. The movements of the Sun and Moon, the silent spaces of the sky, and the music of Ether join together with the phases of the Sun, Moon, and Air. Proclus in *Tim.*, 257. Z. or T.

89. The most mysterious teachings say that His completeness is found in the realms beyond this world, where a Solar World and endless Light exist, as the Chaldean Oracles proclaim. Proclus in *Tim.*, 264. Z. or T.

90. The Sun is the truest measure of time, for it is itself the time of all time, as the Oracle of the gods teaches. Proclus in *Tim.*, 249. Z. or T.

91. The Sun's disk moves through the starless region above the unchanging sphere and is not among the planets but within the three worlds, according to mystical teachings. Julian, *Cratylus*, 5, 334. Z. or T.

92. The Sun is Fire, a channel of Fire, and a distributor of Fire. Proclus in *Tim.*, 141. Z. or T.

93. Thus, Kronos, through the Sun, observes the true pole.

94. The movements of Ether, the Moon's great path, and the changing flows of Air. Proclus in *Tim.*, 257. Z. or T.

95. O Ether, Sun, and Spirit of the Moon, you are the rulers of the Air. Proclus in *Tim.*, 257. Z. or T.

96. The wide sky, the Moon's path, and the Sun's pole. Proclus in *Tim.*, 257. Z. or T.

97. The Goddess brings forth the mighty Sun and the bright Moon.

98. She gathers their light, absorbing the music of Ether, the Sun, the Moon, and all that exists in the Air.

99. Tireless Nature governs the worlds and their motions, ensuring that the Heavens move in an eternal cycle, so the rhythms of the Sun,

Moon, seasons, day, and night are fulfilled. Proclus in *Tim.*, 4, 323. Z. or T.

100. And above the shoulders of the Great Goddess, vast Nature is exalted. Proclus in *Tim.*, 4. T.

101. The greatest thinkers of Babylon, along with Ostanes and Zoroaster, rightly call the starry spheres "Herds"—either because they alone move perfectly around a center or because, as the Oracles suggest, they gather the principles of nature, which are also called "Herds" (agelous). Adding a "gamma" makes them "Angels" (aggelous). This is why the stars that govern these herds are viewed as divine beings or spirits like Angels and are called Archangels, numbering seven. Anonymous in *Theologumenis Arithmeticis*. Z.

102. Zoroaster describes the alignment between physical forms and the Soul's ideals as "Divine Allurements." Ficinus, *De Vita Cælitus Comparanda*. Z.

Magical And Philosophical Precepts

1.   Do not focus your mind on the vast lands of the Earth, for the Plant of Truth does not grow from the ground. Do not try to measure the Sun's movements by creating rules, for it moves by the Father's Eternal Will, not just for your benefit. Let go of the Moon's restless path, for it always moves by the force of necessity. The Stars were not created just for you. The flight of birds through the sky reveals no truth, nor does the examination of animal sacrifices—these are mere illusions, tricks used for profit. Stay away from these if you wish to enter the sacred paradise of devotion, where Virtue, Wisdom, and Justice meet. Psellus, 4. Z.

103. Do not lower yourself to the shadowy, splendid World, where there lies a deceptive Depth and Hades, wrapped in clouds, filled with unintelligible images. This dark abyss is treacherous and endlessly churning, always joined with a lifeless and formless body. Synesius, *De Insomniis*, 140. Z. or T.

104. Do not descend, for beneath the Earth lies a cliff, reached by a ladder with seven steps, and on that path rests the Throne of a destructive and fateful force. Psellus, 6; Pletho, 2. Z.

105. Do not linger at the edge of the cliff, trapped in material filth, for

your true form belongs to a radiant realm. Psellus, 1, 2; Pletho, 14; Synesius, 140. Z.

106. Do not call upon the visible form of Nature's Soul. Psellus, 15; Pletho, 23. Z.

107. Do not seek Nature, for her name brings ruin. Proclus in *Platonis Theologia*, 143. Z.

108. You should not look upon them before your body is initiated, for their allure draws souls away from the sacred mysteries. Proclus in *I. Alcibiades*. Z. or T.

109. Do not bring her forth, or she may take something with her when she leaves. Psellus, 3; Pletho, 15. Z. (Taylor says that "her" refers to the human soul.)

110. Do not corrupt the Spirit or delve too deeply into superficial matters. Psellus, 19; Pletho, 13. Z.

111. Do not seek to expand your destiny. Psellus, 37; Pletho, 4.

112. The Oracle says not to step beyond what is required for devotion. Damascius, *Vita Isidori*. Z. or T.

113. Do not change the sacred names used in invocations, for in every language, God has provided sacred names with great power. Psellus, 7; Nicephorus. Z. or T.

114. Do not go out when the official passes by. Picus de Mirandola, *Conclusions*. Z.

115. Let fiery hope sustain you on the angelic plane. Olympiodorus in *Phaedrus*; Proclus in *Alcibiades*. Z. or T.

116. The glowing Fire comes first, and those who approach it will receive Light from God. The blessed Immortals respond swiftly to those who persevere. Proclus in *Tim.*, 65. Z. or T.

117. The gods urge us to understand the radiating form of Light. Proclus in *Cratylus*. Z. or T.

118. You must hasten toward the Light and the Rays of the Father, who sent you a Soul (Psyche) endowed with deep Mind (Nous). Psellus, 33; Pletho, 6. Z.

119. Seek the path to Paradise. Psellus, 41; Pletho, 27. Z.

120. Learn what is beyond Mind, for it exists beyond understanding. Psellus, 41; Pletho, 27. Z.

121. There is one Intelligible Being whom you must grasp with the fin-

est part of your Mind. Psellus, 31; Pletho, 28. Z.

122. The Paternal Mind will not accept the soul's longing until it awakens from forgetfulness and remembers the sacred symbol of the Father. Psellus, 39; Pletho, 5. Z.

123. Some are given the ability to know the Light, while others, even in sleep, are blessed with insight from the Father's strength. Synesius, *De Insomniis*, 135. Z. or T.

124. You must approach the Intelligible Being not with force but with a calm, searching mind, measuring all things except this Being. If you incline your Mind gently, you will understand it—not with effort, but with a pure, inquisitive sense. Stretch your Soul toward this higher understanding, for it lies beyond ordinary thought. Damascius. T.

125. You cannot grasp it in the same way you understand common things. Damascius, *De Primis Principiis*. T.

126. Those who understand must know the deep mysteries of the Paternal Mind beyond this world. Damascius. Z. or T.

127. Divine truths are not accessible to those focused only on the body. They can only be known by those who, stripped of their earthly attachments, reach the highest summit. Proclus in *Cratylus*. Z. or T.

128. Clothed in the strength of radiant Light, with triple power protecting both Soul and Mind, one must fill the Mind with sacred symbols and focus, not wander along the celestial path without direction.

129. Armed with every kind of strength, he becomes like the Goddess. Proclus in *Platonis Theologia*, 324. T.

130. Explore the River of the Soul—know where you came from and in what order. Even though you have served the body, rise again to the place from which you descended by aligning your actions with sacred reason. Psellus, 5; Pletho, 1. Z.

131. Fiery rays extend in all directions toward the freed Soul. Psellus, 11; Pletho, 24. Z.

132. Let the infinite depth of your Soul guide you, and raise your eyes upward with purpose. Psellus, 11; Pletho, 20.

133. As a rational being, you must control your Soul so it avoids earthly misfortune and finds salvation. Lydus, *De Mensibus*, 2.

134. If you direct your fiery Mind toward devotion, you will preserve the fragile body. Psellus, 22; Pletho, 16. Z.

135. A life purified by Divine Fire removes every stain and all irrational impulses that cling to the Soul during its earthly existence, as the Oracle teaches us to believe. Proclus in *Tim.*, 331. Taylor.

136. The Oracles state that purification rituals benefit not only the Soul but also the body, making it fit to receive help and health. These teachings are given by the gods to the most devoted Theurgists. Julian, *Cratylus*, 334. Z. or T.

137. The Oracle warns us to avoid following the masses blindly. Proclus in *I. Alcibiades*. Z. or T.

138. He who knows himself knows everything within himself. Picus, p. 211. Z.

139. The Oracles emphasize that we have the power to choose, rather than being ruled by the natural order. For example, they say, "When you look at yourself, be mindful," and "If you believe you are more than your body, then you are." Furthermore, they teach that "Our personal struggles shape the kind of life we create." Proclus, *De Providentia*, p. 483. Z. or T.

140. These are deep mysteries I explore in the profound Abyss of the Mind.

141. The Oracle says that God does not abandon us unless we approach divine matters with confusion or impurity. If we do so, our progress is incomplete, our efforts are wasted, and the path becomes dark. Proclus in *Parmenides*. Z. or T.

142. If you do not recognize that every god is good, you remain vigilant for nothing. Proclus in *Platonis Politicus*, 355. Z. or T.

143. Theurgists do not fall into the ranks of those controlled by Fate. Lydus, *De Mensibus*. Taylor.

144. The number nine, composed of three triads, reaches the highest level of theology, as the Chaldean philosophy teaches through Porphyry. Lydus, p. 121.

145. On Hecate's left side is a fountain of Virtue that remains untouched and pure. Psellus, 13; Pletho, 9. Z.

146. Even the Earth mourned for them and their children. Psellus, 21; Pletho, 3. Z.

147. The Furies are the enforcers of punishment upon humans. Psellus, 26; Pletho, 19. Z.

148. Do not become trapped by the Furies of Earth or the demands of nature, or you will perish. Proclus in *Theologia*, 297. Z. or T.

149. Nature teaches us that there are pure spirits, and that even the harmful seeds of matter can be transformed into something useful and good. Psell., 16; Pletho, 18. Z.

150. You only need to offer sacrifices for three days, no more. Pic. Concl. Z.

151. Before anything else, the priest in charge of the works of fire must sprinkle water from the roaring sea. Proc. in Crat. Z. or T.

152. Work diligently around the sacred wheel of Hecate. Psell., 9. Nicephorus.

153. When you see an earthly spirit approaching, shout out loud and offer the stone Mnizourin as a sacrifice. Psell., 40. Z.

154. If you call upon these forces often, you will notice everything around you fading into darkness. The sky will no longer be visible, the stars will lose their light, and the moon will be hidden. The Earth itself will feel absent, lightning will flash around you, and thunder will fill the air. Psell., 10; Pletho, 22. Z.

155. From the depths of the Earth will spring forth demons with the faces of dogs, offering no real sign to guide mortals. Psell., 23; Pletho, 10. Z.

156. A similar fire will rush through the air, formless and chaotic, bringing with it the sound of a voice or a swirling flash of light. You may see the vision of a fiery horse, or a child riding on a celestial steed—either clothed in gold, naked, or shooting arrows of light while standing on the horse's shoulders. If you focus deeply in meditation, you will be able to unite these visions into the image of a lion. Proc. in Pl. Polit., 380; Stanley Hist. Philos. Z. or T.

157. When you see the holy, formless fire shining through the depths of the universe, listen closely and hear the voice of the fire. Psell., 14; Pletho, 25. Z.

Oracles From Porphyry

1. Above the celestial lights, there is an eternal flame that sparkles without end. It is the source of life and the origin of all beings, the beginning of everything! This flame brings everything into existence, and nothing is destroyed except by its consuming fire. It reveals itself by its own nature. This fire cannot be contained in any place, for it has no physical form and no material substance. It surrounds the heavens entirely. From it, tiny sparks emerge, creating all the fires of the Sun, the Moon, and the Stars. This is what I understand about God. Do not seek to know more, for no matter how wise you are, it is beyond human comprehension. Know this: unjust and wicked people cannot hide from God's presence! No clever trick or excuse can conceal anything from His all-seeing eyes. God is present in everything, and everything is filled with God!

158. Within God is a vast depth of flame! Yet, the heart should not fear approaching this sacred fire or being touched by it. It is a gentle fire that will not destroy you. Its calm and soothing heat binds everything together, bringing harmony and stability to the world. Nothing exists without this fire, for it is God Himself. He has no creator and no mother. He knows all things and cannot be taught anything. His plans are perfect, and His name is beyond words. This is what God is! As for us, His messengers, we are only a small part of God.

The Life and Teachings of Thoth

Hermes Trismegistus

The Life and Teachings of Thoth Hermes Trismegistus

THUNDER boomed, and lightning lit up the sky. The veil hanging in the Temple was torn from top to bottom. The wise initiator, dressed in robes of blue and gold, slowly lifted his jeweled staff and pointed it toward the darkness that had been revealed behind the torn silk curtain. "Behold the Light of Egypt!" he declared.

The candidate, dressed in a simple white robe, stared into the deep blackness framed between two massive columns topped with lotus flowers, where the veil had once hung. As he stood there, a soft, glowing mist began to spread throughout the air until the atmosphere shimmered with tiny glowing particles. The candidate's face lit up from the soft glow, and he scanned the glittering mist, hoping to spot something solid within it.

The initiator spoke again: "This Light you see is the hidden radiance of the Mysteries. No one knows where it comes from, except for the 'Master of the Light.' Behold Him!"

Suddenly, through the glowing haze, a figure emerged, surrounded by a flickering greenish light. The initiator lowered his staff, bowed his head humbly, and placed one hand flat against his chest in reverence.

The candidate took a step back, overwhelmed and partially blinded by the brilliance of the figure before him. Slowly, he gathered his courage and looked again at the Divine One. The figure was much larger than any human being, and its body was partly transparent, revealing a glowing heart and brain that pulsed with radiant energy.

As the candidate watched in amazement, the heart of the figure transformed into an ibis, while the brain became a shining emerald. The mysterious being held in its hand a winged staff coiled with serpents.

The aged initiator lifted his staff again and cried out in a booming voice: "All hail to you, Thoth Hermes, Thrice Greatest! All hail, Prince of Men! All hail to you who stand upon the head of Typhon!"

At that moment, a terrifying dragon appeared—a monstrous creature that was part serpent, part crocodile, and part hog. Flames burst from its mouth and nostrils, and horrible sounds echoed throughout the chamber.

Without hesitation, Hermes struck the advancing dragon with his serpent-twined staff. With a snarling cry, the beast collapsed onto its side, and the flames around it slowly faded.

Hermes placed his foot firmly on the skull of the defeated Typhon. In the next instant, a burst of unbearable light filled the room, forcing the candidate to stumble back against one of the pillars.

Streams of greenish mist trailed behind Hermes as he moved across the chamber, and with a final flash, the immortal figure vanished into nothingness.

Suppositions Concerning The Identity of Hermes

Iamblichus claimed that Hermes wrote twenty thousand books, while Manetho said the number was more than thirty-six thousand (see James Gardner). These numbers make it clear that a single person, even if gifted with divine abilities, could hardly have created so many works alone. It is said that Hermes revealed many arts and sciences to humanity, including medicine, chemistry, law, art, astrology, music, rhetoric, magic, philosophy, geography, mathematics (especially geometry), anatomy, and public speaking. Orpheus was honored in a similar way by the Greeks.

In his Biographia Antiqua, Francis Barrett writes about Hermes: "* * * if God ever appeared in a man, he appeared in him, as is shown by his books and his Pymander. In these works, Hermes shared the secrets of the Abyss and divine knowledge with future generations. Through them, he proved himself to be not only an inspired prophet but also a profound philosopher, gaining his wisdom from God and the heavens, not from humans."

Because of his great knowledge, Hermes was connected with many ancient sages and prophets. In Ancient Mythology, Bryant says: "I have mentioned that Cadmus was the same as the Egyptian Thoth; it is clear from his identification as Hermes, and from the fact that he was credited with inventing writing." (The chapter on Pythagorean Mathematics includes a table of the original Cadmean letters.) Scholars believe that Hermes was known to the Jews as "Enoch," whom Kenealy called the "Second Messenger of God."

The Greeks accepted Hermes into their mythology, and he later became known as Mercury among the Romans. He was honored through the planet Mercury because it is the closest to the Sun. Just as Mercury orbits near the Sun, Hermes was thought to be closest to God and became known as the Messenger of the Gods.

In Egyptian drawings, Thoth, identified as Hermes, is shown carrying a wax writing tablet and recording the weighing of souls in the judgment hall of Osiris—a ritual of deep meaning. Hermes is especially important to Masonic scholars because he is believed to have created the Masonic initiation rituals, which were based on the Mysteries he established. Most of the symbols used in Masonry are Hermetic in nature. Pythagoras studied mathematics with the Egyptians and learned about symbolic geometric shapes from them.

Hermes is also remembered for reforming the calendar by increasing the year from 360 days to 365, setting a standard that we still use today. The title "Thrice Greatest" was given to Hermes because he was considered the greatest philosopher, the greatest priest, and the greatest king. Notably, the final poem written by Henry Wadsworth Longfellow, one of America's beloved poets, was a lyrical ode to Hermes. (See Chambers' Encyclopædia.)

The Mutilated Hermetic Fragments

James Campbell Brown, in his History of Chemistry, writes about the Hermetic books: "Leaving behind the Chaldean and earliest Egyptian times, from which we have only remnants and no records—no names of chemists or philosophers—we now move into the historical period, when books were first written, not on parchment or paper, but on papyrus. A collection of early Egyptian books is credited to Hermes Trismegistus, who may have been a real scholar or perhaps a symbol for many different authors over time. * * * Some connect him with the Greek god Hermes, as well as with the Egyptian god Thoth or Tuti, who was the moon god, often shown in art with the head of an ibis and the disc and crescent of the moon. The Egyptians saw him as the god of wisdom, writing, and timekeeping.

Because of the high regard alchemists had for Hermes, chemical writings became known as 'hermetic,' and the term 'hermetically sealed'—used to describe sealing a glass container by melting it shut—comes from this tradition. The same origin can be found in Paracelsus' hermetic medicines and the hermetic freemasonry of the Middle Ages."

Among the fragments believed to come from Hermes are two famous works. One is the Emerald Tablet, and the other is the Divine Pymander, also called The Shepherd of Men, which will be discussed later. Hermes stands out as one of the few pagan philosophers whom the early Christians did not attack. In fact, some Church Fathers even admitted that Hermes showed signs of intelligence. They said that if he had lived in a more enlightened age and had received their teachings, he could have been truly great.

In Stromata, Clement of Alexandria, one of the few ancient writers whose accounts of pagan traditions survive today, shares nearly all we know about the original forty-two books of Hermes and how highly they were valued by both the spiritual and political leaders of Egypt. Clement describes a ceremonial procession like this:

"For the Egyptians follow their own philosophy, which is reflected in their rituals. First comes the Singer, holding a symbol of music. He must study two of Hermes' books: one containing hymns to the gods and another with rules for the king's life. Following the Singer is the Astrologer, carrying a clock and a palm branch—both symbols of astrology. He must memorize four books of Hermes about the stars: one on the fixed stars, another on the phases of the sun and moon, and the other two on their risings.

Next in the procession is the sacred Scribe, wearing wings on his head and carrying a book and measuring tool, along with ink and a reed for writing. He must know the hieroglyphs and be familiar with cosmography, geography, the paths of the sun and moon, the five planets, and the layout of Egypt, including a chart of the Nile. He also needs to understand the priests' equipment, sacred spaces, and rituals. After the Scribe comes the Stole-keeper, carrying the cubit of justice and a ceremonial cup for offerings. He is skilled in matters of training and sacrifice.

There are ten books dedicated to the worship of the gods, covering topics like sacrifices, hymns, prayers, processions, and festivals. Lastly comes the Prophet, holding a water vase, with followers carrying bread behind him. As the temple leader, the Prophet studies ten more books called 'Hieratic,' which contain laws, knowledge of the gods, and priestly training. The Prophet also manages the temple's resources. Of Hermes' forty-two essential books, thirty-six contain Egyptian philosophy, studied by the individuals mentioned above. The remaining six books, which are medical, are entrusted to the Pastophoroi, or image-bearers, and deal with anatomy, diseases, medical tools, treatments, eye care, and women's health."

One of the greatest losses to philosophy was the destruction of nearly all these forty-two books of Hermes. They disappeared during the burning of Alexandria. Both the Romans and later the Christians understood that as long as these books existed, they could not fully dominate the Egyptian people. The few volumes that escaped the fire were hidden in the desert, and only a small group of initiates from secret schools know where they are buried.

The Book of Thoth

While Hermes still walked among men, he entrusted the sacred Book of Thoth to his chosen successors. This book contained the secret methods for bringing about the spiritual rebirth of humanity and served as the key to understanding all of Hermes' other writings. Although the exact contents of the Book of Thoth are unknown, it is said that the pages were filled with strange hieroglyphs and symbols. Those who knew how to use them gained unlimited power over the spirits of the air and the gods beneath the earth.

The book also revealed the process by which certain areas of the brain could be stimulated through the Mysteries, expanding human consciousness. This allowed individuals to see the Immortals and stand in the presence of higher gods. Because it described how this awakening could be achieved, the Book of Thoth was known as the "Key to Immortality."

According to legend, the Book of Thoth was kept inside a golden box in the inner sanctuary of a temple. Only one key existed, held by the "Master of the Mysteries," the highest Hermetic initiate. He alone knew what was written in the book. When the Mysteries faded from the ancient world, the book was lost. However, devoted followers carried the sealed casket to another land. It is believed that the book still exists today, guiding those who seek the presence of the Immortals. No further details about the book can be revealed to the world now, but the unbroken line of initiation—starting with the first hierophant initiated by Hermes—continues to this day. Those who are truly dedicated to serving the Immortals may find this priceless work if they search with sincerity and determination.

Some claim that the Book of Thoth is, in fact, the mysterious Tarot of the Bohemians—a symbolic collection of seventy-eight cards, said to have been carried by the gypsies since they were exiled from their ancient temple, the Serapeum. (According to secret histories, the gypsies were originally priests from Egypt.) There are still several secret schools in the world today that initiate worthy students into the Mysteries. Almost all of them began by lighting their sacred flames from the torch of Hermes.

In the Book of Thoth, Hermes revealed the "One Way" to humanity. For centuries, the wise from every culture and faith have followed this path to reach immortality. Hermes created this Way to shine a light in the darkness, offering redemption to humankind.

Poimandres, The Vision of Hermes

The Divine Pymander of Hermes Mercurius Trismegistus is one of the earliest surviving Hermetic writings. Although it likely does not exist in its original form—having been reworked during the first centuries of the Christian era and mistranslated over time—it still holds many core ideas of the Hermetic tradition. The Divine Pymander is made up of seventeen fragments, gathered and presented as one complete work. The second book, called Poimandres or The Vision, describes how divine wisdom was first revealed to Hermes. After receiving this knowledge, Hermes began his ministry, teaching the secrets of the unseen universe to anyone willing to listen.

The Vision is the most well-known Hermetic fragment and explains the Hermetic view of the universe and the Egyptian teachings on how the human soul develops and grows. For some time, it was mistakenly called The Genesis of Enoch, but this error has since been corrected. To interpret the symbolic meaning in Hermes' Vision, the following works were used: The Divine Pymander (London, 1650), translated from Arabic and Greek by Dr. Everard; Hermetica (Oxford, 1924), edited by Walter Scott; Hermes, The Mysteries of Egypt (Philadelphia, 1925), by Edouard Schuré; and Thrice-Greatest Hermes (London, 1906), by G. R. S. Mead. These sources were supplemented with commentary based on the ancient Egyptian esoteric philosophy and other Hermetic writings. Outdated language has been replaced with modern terms, and the narrative style has been chosen over the original dialogue format for clarity.

While wandering through a barren, rocky landscape, Hermes devoted himself to meditation and prayer. By following the secret teachings of the Temple, he gradually freed his higher mind from the control of his bodily senses. Once released, his divine nature revealed to him the mysteries of the spiritual realms. He saw a figure of immense power and awe—a Great Dragon whose wings stretched across the sky, with light radiating from its body in all directions. (In the Mysteries, the Universal Life Force is symbolized by a dragon.) The Dragon called Hermes by name and asked him why he was contemplating the World Mystery. Overwhelmed with fear, Hermes bowed before the Dragon and begged to know its identity.

The Dragon responded that it was Poimandres, the Mind of the Universe, the Creative Intelligence, and the supreme ruler of all things. (According to Schuré, Poimandres represents the god Osiris.) Hermes asked Poimandres to reveal the structure of the universe and the nature of the gods. The Dragon agreed, telling Hermes to hold its image firmly in his mind.

At that moment, Poimandres' form changed into a brilliant, pulsing light. This light was the true spiritual essence of the Great Dragon. Hermes was lifted into the heart of this radiant glow, and the material world vanished from his awareness. Then a deep darkness descended, spreading out until it completely swallowed the light. Chaos followed, and a swirling, watery substance emerged, releasing clouds of vapor. Strange sounds filled the air, moaning and sighing, as though the light trapped within the darkness was crying out. Hermes realized that the light represented the spiritual universe, while the swirling darkness symbolized material substance.

From the light trapped in the darkness came a mysterious and sacred Word, which stood upon the smoky waters. This Word—known as the Voice of the Light—rose from the darkness like a mighty pillar. Fire and air followed the Word upward, while earth and water remained below. In this way, the waters of light were separated from the waters of darkness. The upper waters formed the worlds above, while the lower waters created the worlds below. Earth and water mixed together and became inseparable, and the Spiritual Word, called Reason, moved over their surface, stirring it into motion.

Then Poimandres spoke again, though he did not reveal his form: "I, your God, am the Light and the Mind that existed before spirit and matter were separated, before darkness and light were divided. The Word, which appeared as a pillar of flame, is the Son of God, born from the mystery of the Mind. Its name is Reason. Reason is the child of Thought, and it will divide light from darkness, placing Truth in the midst of the waters. Understand this, Hermes, and reflect deeply upon it. What sees and hears within you is not of the earth—it is the Word of God living within you. This is why it is said that divine light exists even within mortal darkness, and ignorance cannot divide them. The union of the Word and the Mind creates the mystery of Life.

Just as the darkness outside you is in conflict with itself, the darkness within you is also divided. The light and fire within you represent the divine man, who rises along the path of the Word. The part that does not rise is the mortal man, who cannot share in immortality. Study the Mind and its mysteries, for in them lies the secret to eternal life."

The Dragon revealed itself once more to Hermes, and for a long time, the two stared deeply into each other's eyes. Hermes trembled under the gaze of Poimandres. At the Dragon's Word, the heavens opened, revealing countless Light Powers soaring across the Cosmos on wings of streaming fire. Hermes saw the spirits of the stars and the celestial beings that govern the universe, each glowing with the brilliance of the One Fire—the glory of the Supreme Mind. Hermes realized that this vision was shown to him only because Poimandres had spoken the Word. That Word was Reason, and by the power of Reason, the invisible had been made visible.

The Divine Mind—the Dragon—continued: "Before the visible universe existed, its mold had already been formed. This mold was called the Archetype, and it existed in the Supreme Mind long before creation began. The Supreme Mind gazed upon these Archetypes and became enchanted with Its own thoughts. Taking the Word as a powerful tool, it carved out vast spaces in the formless void, casting the spheres of creation into the Archetypal mold. At the same time, it planted the seeds of life in the newly formed bodies. When the darkness received the Word, it transformed into an ordered universe. The elements separated into layers, and from these layers, life began to emerge. The Supreme Being—the Mind, both male and female—brought forth the Word. Suspended between Light and darkness, the Word gave rise to another Mind, known as the Workman, the Master Builder, or the Maker of Things.

"This is how it was done, Hermes: As the Word moved like a breath through space, it ignited Fire through the force of its motion. Thus, the Fire is called the Son of Striving. The Workman passed like a whirlwind through the universe, making the elements vibrate and glow from the friction of its motion. From this process, the Son of Striving created the Seven Governors—the spirits of the planets—who established the boundaries of the world. These Governors control the world through Destiny, a power given to them by the Fiery Workman. Once the Second Mind (the Workman) had organized the Chaos, the Word of God emerged from the prison of material substance, leaving the elements behind without Reason. It joined itself to the Fiery Workman, and together, they settled at the center of the universe, setting the celestial powers in motion. This process will continue forever, for the beginning and the end are one and the same.

"Then the elements that lacked Reason produced creatures without it. Air gave rise to flying beings, water brought forth swimming creatures, and the earth created strange four-legged beasts, dragons, and bizarre monsters. Since Reason had risen out of material things, it could not be given to these creatures. The Father—the Supreme Mind—who is Light and Life, then created a Universal Man in Its own image. This Man was not earthly but heavenly, dwelling in the Light of God. The Supreme Mind loved the Man It had made and entrusted him with control over all creation.

"The Man, eager to create, moved into the sphere of generation and observed the works of the Second Mind, which sat upon the Ring of Fire. Seeing the achievements of the Fiery Workman, the Man desired to create as well, and the Father granted him permission. The Seven Governors, each sharing their power with him, rejoiced and gave him part of their nature.

"The Man, curious to understand the mysteries beyond the spheres, looked through the Seven Harmonies and broke through the strength of the circles. He revealed himself to Nature stretched out below. Gazing into the depths, the Man saw his own reflection upon the earth and in the waters. He smiled, enchanted by his reflection, and longed to descend into it. As soon as he desired this, the intelligent part of him united with the unreasoning image.

"Nature, seeing the Man's descent, embraced him, and the two became intertwined. This is why earthly man is a mixture of both worlds. Within him is the immortal, beautiful Sky Man, but on the outside, he is clothed in mortal Nature, which is destined to perish. Suffering arises because the Immortal Man fell in love with his shadow, giving up true Reality to dwell in the darkness of illusion. Though he possesses the power of the Seven Governors, along with Life, Light, and the Word, he is also subject to Fate and Destiny, ruled by the Rings of the Governors."

It is said that the Immortal Man is both male and female, always awake and watchful. He never slumbers or sleeps and is governed by a Father who is also both male and female, and equally watchful. This is a secret that remains hidden to this day. When Nature joined with the Sky Man, she gave birth to seven beings, each male and female, upright in form, and reflecting the qualities of the Seven Governors. These, O Hermes, are the seven races, species, and wheels of creation.

The seven beings came into existence in this way: Earth acted as the female element, while water was the male element. Fire and aether provided their spirits, and Nature formed bodies that took human shapes. The Great Dragon gave them Life and Light. From Life, they gained their

Soul, and from Light, they received their Mind. These beings, containing both mortality and immortality, lived in this state for a time. They reproduced on their own, for each was both male and female. But after a certain period, God's will untied the knot of Destiny, and all things were set free.

At that time, all creatures, including man, who had been both male and female, were separated. The males were divided from the females according to the law of Reason. Then God spoke to the Holy Word within all souls, saying, "Increase and multiply, all of you, my creatures and creations. Let those with Mind know they are immortal and understand that death comes from loving the body too much. Let them learn all things, for those who know themselves will enter the realm of Good."

With the help of the Seven Governors and Harmony, God brought the sexes together, and from their union, new generations were born. Everything multiplied according to its kind. Those who mistakenly love their body remain trapped in darkness, suffering from the experience of death. But those who realize the body is only a temporary home for the soul rise to immortality.

Hermes then asked why ignorance alone should cause men to lose immortality. The Great Dragon replied, "For those who do not understand, the body is all they know. They believe in death because they worship the material world, which is both the cause and reality of death."

Hermes asked how the wise and righteous find their way to God. Poimandres answered, "What the Word of God has said, I also say: 'Since the Father of all things is made of Life and Light, and man is made from the same, whoever understands the nature of Life and Light will enter the eternal Life and Light.'"

Hermes then asked how the wise could attain eternal Life. Poimandres replied, "Let those with Mind reflect, examine themselves, and use their Mind's power to separate what is real from what is not. They must devote themselves to Truth and Reality."

Hermes asked, "Don't all people have Minds?" The Great Dragon responded, "Be careful what you say, for I am the Mind—the Eternal Teacher. I am the Father of the Word, the Savior of all men. In the nature of the wise, the Word takes form. Through the Word, the world is saved.

I, Thought (Thoth)—the Father of the Word, the Mind—come only to those who are good, pure, merciful, and live faithfully and righteously. When I come, I help them understand everything, and they worship the Universal Father.

Before these wise people die, they learn to turn away from their senses, knowing that the senses are enemies of the immortal soul. I will not let evil desires or emotions control the bodies of those who love me, nor will I allow wicked thoughts to enter them. I guard them, shutting out all evil, and protect them from their own lower nature. But I do not come to the wicked, the envious, or the greedy, for such people cannot grasp the mysteries of the Mind and reject me. I leave them to the demon they have created within themselves. Evil grows every day, tormenting those who indulge in it, and each wicked act adds to the suffering caused by the ones that came before it. In the end, evil destroys itself. The punishment for desire is the pain of never being satisfied."

Hermes bowed his head in gratitude to the Great Dragon, who had revealed so much to him, and asked to learn more about the ultimate fate of the human soul. Poimandres continued: "At death, the material body returns to the elements from which it came, and the divine, invisible man rises to the Eighth Sphere, the place from which he first came. Evil, however, descends to the demon's domain, while the senses, emotions, desires, and bodily passions return to the Seven Governors, who give life to the spiritual man but bring destruction to the lower man.

"Once the lower nature returns to its animal instincts, the higher self begins its journey back to reclaim its spiritual state. It ascends through the seven Rings of the Seven Governors, returning to each the powers it once borrowed. The first Ring belongs to the Moon, to which it returns the ability to wax and wane. The second Ring is ruled by Mercury, where it returns cunning, deceit, and cleverness. The third Ring belongs to Venus, receiving back lust and passion. The fourth Ring is the Sun's, which takes back ambition. The fifth Ring is governed by Mars, where rashness and boldness return. The sixth belongs to Jupiter, receiving greed and the desire for wealth. Finally, the seventh Ring is Saturn's, standing at the edge of Chaos, where falsehood and evil schemes are returned.

"When the soul has shed all it carried from the Seven Rings, it reaches the Eighth Sphere, the realm of the fixed stars. There, free from illusion, the soul dwells in Light, singing praises to the Father in a voice understood only by the pure in spirit. Know this, Hermes: the Eighth Sphere holds a great mystery, for the Milky Way is where souls are born. From it, they descend into the Rings, and to it, they return after passing through the wheels of Saturn. However, not all souls can climb the ladder of the seven Rings. Some become lost in darkness below, swept away into eternity by the illusions of the senses and the material world.

"The path to immortality is difficult, and only a few find it. The rest wait for the Great Day when the wheels of the universe will stop, and the immortal sparks will escape from the prison of matter. But those who wait are unfortunate, for they will return to the Milky Way, unaware and unknowing, to begin the cycle again. Those who follow the light of the mystery I have revealed to you, Hermes, will return to the Father in the White Light. There, they will give themselves to the Light and become one with it, transformed into Powers within God. This is the Way of Good, revealed only to the wise.

"Blessed are you, O Son of Light, for I, Poimandres, the Light of the World, have shown myself to you. Now, I command you to go forth and guide those lost in darkness, so that the spirit of My Mind—the Universal Mind—within them may awaken and be saved through My Mind within you. Establish My Mysteries, and they will remain on earth as long as the Mind endures, for the Mind of the Mysteries can never fail."

With these final words, Poimandres, radiant with celestial light, vanished, merging with the powers of the heavens. Lifting his eyes to the sky, Hermes blessed the Father of All Things and dedicated his life to the service of the Great Light.

Hermes preached: "O people of the earth, born of the elements yet carrying the spirit of the Divine Man within you, rise from your slumber of ignorance! Be alert and thoughtful. Know that your true home is not on earth but in the Light. Why have you chosen death when you have the power to share in immortality? Repent, change your ways, and turn away from darkness. Leave corruption behind and prepare to ascend through the Seven Rings to unite your soul with the eternal Light."

Some mocked him, refusing his teachings, and condemned themselves to the Second Death, from which there is no return. But others fell at

Hermes' feet, begging him to show them the Way of Life. He gently lifted them, seeking no praise for himself, and with his staff in hand, he set out to teach and guide humanity, showing them the path to salvation.

Among the people, Hermes planted the seeds of wisdom and watered them with the Immortal Waters. As his life drew to a close and the light of the earthly world began to fade, Hermes instructed his disciples to guard his teachings faithfully through all ages. He committed the Vision of Poimandres to writing so that all who seek immortality could find the way within its pages.

In concluding his account of the Vision, Hermes wrote: "The sleep of the body allows the Mind to stay awake, and when I close my eyes, I can see the true Light. In my silence, life and hope begin to grow, filling it with goodness. My words are the blossoms that grow from the tree of my soul. This is the honest record of what I received from my true Mind—Poimandres, the Great Dragon, Lord of the Word—through whom God filled me with Truth. From that moment on, my Mind has remained with me, and within my soul, it gave birth to the Word. The Word is Reason, and through Reason, I have been saved. For this, I give all my praise and thanks to God, the Father—Life, Light, and Eternal Goodness—with all my soul and strength.

"Holy is God, the Father of all, who existed before the First Beginning. Holy is God, whose will is fulfilled by the Powers born from Himself. Holy is God, who has chosen to be known and is known only by those to whom He reveals Himself. Holy are You, who have established all things through Your Word, Reason. Holy are You, whose image is reflected in all of Nature. Holy are You, whom the lower nature cannot shape. Holy are You, who are stronger than all other powers. Holy are You, who surpass all greatness. Holy are You, who are beyond all praise.

"Accept these offerings of Reason from a pure soul and a heart lifted up toward You. O Unspeakable One, beyond words, You are to be praised through silence! I ask You to look upon me with mercy, that I may not stray from the knowledge of You and that I may help enlighten those who are lost in ignorance—my brothers, Your children.

"I believe in You and bear witness to You, and I leave in peace, trusting in Your Light and Life. Blessed are You, O Father! May the man You created be sanctified with You, just as You gave him the power to sanctify others through Your Word and Truth."

The Vision of Hermes, like many Hermetic writings, is an allegory that contains deep philosophical and spiritual truths. Its hidden meanings can only be fully understood by those who have been "raised" into the presence of the True Mind.

The Initiation of the Pyramid

The Great Pyramid of Giza stands as one of the most remarkable wonders of ancient times, unmatched by the works of later architects and builders. It silently bears witness to a lost civilization that fulfilled its purpose and faded into history. Its grandeur is awe-inspiring, simple yet divine, and it seems like a message carved in stone. Its enormous size makes human efforts seem small, and it serves as a symbol of eternity, standing firm against the ever-shifting sands of time. But who were the enlightened mathematicians who designed it? Who were the master builders and craftsmen who made sure every stone was perfectly placed?

The earliest and most famous account of the pyramid's construction comes from the well-known historian Herodotus. He wrote: "The pyramid was built in stages, like steps or battlements. After placing the stones for the base, workers used machines made of short wooden planks to raise the stones to each new level. The first machine lifted the stones from the ground to the first step. Another machine took the stones from there to the second step, and so on. Either they had as many machines as there were steps, or they moved one machine from tier to tier as needed. Both versions have been told, so I mention them both. The upper part of the pyramid was completed first, followed by the middle section, and finally the lowest part near the ground. Egyptian characters are inscribed on the pyramid, recording the amount of radishes, onions, and garlic consumed by the laborers during construction. I remember the interpreter telling me that the food cost 1,600 talents of silver. If this is true, imagine the enormous amount spent on tools, clothing, and food for the workers during the ten years it took to complete the work, not counting the time needed to quarry the stones and prepare the underground chambers."

While Herodotus' story is vivid, it seems likely that he created this tale to hide the true origin and purpose of the pyramid. This is one of several cases in his writings that suggest he was initiated into ancient secret knowledge and was sworn to keep it hidden. The widely accepted theory that the Great Pyramid was built as a tomb for Pharaoh Cheops is unproven. In fact, Manetho, Eratosthenes, and Diodorus Siculus all offer different accounts of who built the pyramid, with none agreeing with Herodotus—or with each other. According to the rules of pyramid construction known as the Lepsius Law, the burial chamber should have been completed at the same time as the monument, or even earlier, but in this case, it wasn't.

There is no clear evidence that the Egyptians built the Great Pyramid. Unlike other royal tombs, which are decorated with intricate carvings, inscriptions, and images, the pyramid lacks these typical elements of Egyptian art and architecture. No cartouches, paintings, or symbols of Egyptian royalty are present, except for a few simple markings in construction chambers. These markings, discovered by Howard Vyse, appear to have been made before the stones were placed since they are sometimes upside down or distorted from the fitting process. Egyptologists have tried to identify these markings as the name of Cheops, but it is hard to believe that a ruler would allow his royal name to be treated with such carelessness.

Experts are still unsure of the true meaning of these markings. Any claim that the pyramid was built during the fourth dynasty is challenged by the sea shells found at its base, which Mr. Gab suggests as evidence that the structure predates the Great Flood—a theory also supported by ancient Arabian traditions. One Arab historian claimed the pyramid was built by Egyptian sages to protect against the Flood, while another said it was the treasure house of Sheddad Ben Ad, a powerful king from before the flood. A panel of hieroglyphs above the entrance might seem like a clue to the pyramid's origin, but it was actually carved in 1843 by Dr. Lepsius as a tribute to the King of Prussia.

Caliph al-Mamoun, a distinguished descendant of the Prophet, was inspired by stories of vast treasures hidden within the Great Pyramid. In 820 A.D., he traveled from Baghdad to Cairo with a large group of workers, determined to open the ancient monument. When the Caliph first stood at the base of the "Rock of Ages" and looked up at its smooth, gleaming surface, he must have felt overwhelmed with emotion. At that time, the pyramid's original casing stones were likely still intact because he could not find any sign of an entrance—just four perfectly smooth walls in every direction. Relying on vague rumors, he ordered his men to begin digging on the north side of the pyramid, instructing them to keep cutting into the stone until they uncovered something. For the workers, armed with only simple tools and vinegar to soften the limestone, digging through a hundred feet of solid rock was an exhausting and nearly impossible task. Many times, they were ready to abandon the project, but the Caliph's command was law, and the hope of finding treasure kept them going.

Just when the workers were about to give up entirely, fate intervened. They heard the sound of a large stone falling within the wall they had been chiseling. Encouraged by the noise, they pushed forward with new energy and eventually broke through into a sloping passage that led deep into the pyramid's underground chambers. They found a massive stone barrier blocking their path, but they managed to carve their way around it. Afterward, they removed several granite blocks that kept sliding down the passage from the Queen's Chamber above. Finally, the last of the blocks stopped falling, and the way was clear for the Caliph's followers to explore.

However, there were no treasures to be found. From chamber to chamber, the workers searched frantically, but there was nothing of value anywhere. The frustration among the workers grew so intense that Caliph al-Mamoun, knowing that rebellion was near, decided to take action. He secretly sent for funds from Baghdad and had the money buried near the pyramid's entrance. The next day, he ordered the workers to dig in that spot, and their joy was overwhelming when they uncovered the hidden treasure. The workers were so impressed by what they believed to be the foresight of an ancient king, who, in their minds, had calculated their wages long ago and buried the exact amount for them to find.

Satisfied with this solution, the Caliph returned to the city of his ancestors, leaving the Great Pyramid to face the passage of time. In the ninth century, the pyramid's smooth, polished surfaces reflected the sun's rays so brilliantly that each side of the structure appeared as a glowing triangle of light. Over the years, however, nearly all the original casing stones were removed, and today, only two remain in place. Investigations later found that many of these stones had been recut and repurposed to decorate the walls of mosques and palaces throughout Cairo and the surrounding areas.

Pyramid Problems

C. Piazzi Smyth asks, "Was the Great Pyramid built before hieroglyphics were invented and before the Egyptian religion was established?" It is possible that time will reveal the upper chambers of the Pyramid as a sealed mystery even before the rise of the Egyptian empire. However, markings in the underground chamber suggest that the Romans later gained access. Based on secret Egyptian teachings, W. W. Harmon calculated that the Pyramid's first ceremonial took place 68,890 years ago, at the moment when the star Vega first cast its light down the descending passage into the pit. He estimates that the actual construction of the Pyramid took place over ten to fifteen years just before this event.

These dates may seem ridiculous to modern Egyptologists, but they are based on a detailed study of the astronomical principles incorporated into the Pyramid by its builders. If the outer casing stones were still intact in the ninth century, the erosion marks on the exterior are unlikely to have been caused by water. The theory that salt deposits inside the Pyramid are evidence of submersion is also questionable, as the type of stone used naturally releases salt over time. Although the Pyramid may have been partially submerged at some point, the evidence for this is not conclusive.

The Great Pyramid was built entirely from limestone and granite, with the two types of rock arranged in a meaningful way. The stones were cut with extreme precision, and the cement used between them is now as hard as the stones themselves. The limestone blocks were likely cut with bronze saws tipped with diamonds or other precious stones. Stone chips left from construction were piled against the north side of the plateau to help support the structure's immense weight. The Pyramid was built with perfect alignment and, astonishingly, "squares the circle."

This means that if you drop a vertical line from the tip of the Pyramid to its base, that line acts as the radius of an imaginary circle. The circumference of that circle matches the total length of the four base sides of the Pyramid.

If the passageways to the King's and Queen's Chambers were sealed thousands of years before the Christian era, later initiates must have used hidden underground galleries for their rituals. Without such galleries, it would have been impossible to enter or exit the Pyramid, as the only surface entrance was sealed with casing stones. If not blocked by the Sphinx or concealed within it, the hidden entrance could be located in one of the nearby temples or on the slopes of the limestone plateau.

A notable feature of the Pyramid is the granite plugs that block the passage leading to the Queen's Chamber. Caliph al-Mamoun had to smash through these plugs to reach the upper chambers. According to Smyth, the position of the stones shows that they were set in place from above, suggesting that many workers had to leave the upper chambers after placing them. Smyth believes these workers escaped by descending through a well, dropping a ramp stone into place behind them. He also suggests that robbers might have later used this well to reach the upper chambers. The robbers broke through the ramp stone, leaving a jagged hole, as it had been set in plaster.

However, the architect Mr. Dupré offers a different theory. He argues that the well itself was made by robbers and was the first successful attempt to reach the upper chambers from the underground chamber, which was the only open area of the Pyramid at the time. Dupré points out that the well is rough and irregular, unlike the precise design of the rest of the Pyramid. The well's size also makes it unlikely that it was dug downward; it must have been carved from below, with the nearby grotto providing ventilation for the thieves. It seems unlikely that the Pyramid's builders would have left a broken ramp stone and a gaping hole in their otherwise perfect gallery. If the well is indeed a robbers' tunnel, this could explain why the Pyramid was empty when Caliph al-Mamoun entered and why the coffer lid was missing. A thorough inspection of the unfinished underground chamber—possibly the robbers' base of operations—might reveal traces of their presence or show where they stored the rubble from their digging. It remains unclear how the robbers entered the underground chamber, but it seems unlikely that they used the descending passage.

One intriguing feature in the Queen's Chamber is a niche in the north wall. Muslim guides often describe it as a shrine, but the niche's shape, with its walls sloping inward like those in the Grand Gallery, suggests it may have been intended as a passage. Attempts to explore the niche have been unsuccessful, but Dupré believes it may hide a secret entrance. If the well did not exist at the time, the workers may have exited the Pyramid through this hidden passage after placing the granite plugs in the ascending gallery.

Some Biblical scholars have offered remarkable interpretations of the Great Pyramid. They have claimed it to be Joseph's granary, even though its storage capacity is far too small to support that idea. Others have suggested it was meant to serve as the tomb for the Pharaoh from the Exodus, though his body was never recovered from the Red Sea and, therefore, couldn't have been buried there. Some even believe the pyramid stands as a lasting confirmation of the accuracy of the prophecies found in the Authorized Version of the Bible.

The Sphinx

Ignatius Donnelly suggests that the Great Pyramid follows a design from before the Great Flood, a style found in many ancient cultures around the world. In contrast, the Sphinx (Hu) is distinctly Egyptian. According to the inscription between its paws, the Sphinx is an image of the Sun God, Harmachis, carved in the likeness of the Pharaoh who ruled at the time. The Sphinx was later restored by Thutmose IV, inspired by a dream in which the god complained that the sand surrounding him caused him great discomfort. Excavators even found a broken beard of the Sphinx buried between its paws. The steps, altar, and temple between the paws were added much later, likely by the Romans, who frequently rebuilt Egyptian monuments.

The shallow indentation on the Sphinx's head, once thought to conceal a hidden passage leading to the Great Pyramid, was actually intended to support a now-missing headdress. Explorers have driven metal rods into the body of the Sphinx in an unsuccessful attempt to locate hidden chambers or tunnels. Most of the Sphinx was carved from a single stone, with only the front paws constructed from smaller stones. Measuring around 200 feet in length, 70 feet in height, and 38 feet across the shoulders, the Sphinx was carved either from native rock or from stone transported from distant quarries. Some once believed that both the Pyramid and the Sphinx were made from artificial stone formed on-site, but this idea was abandoned after studies showed that the limestone contains the remains of small sea creatures called mummulites.

The idea that the Sphinx served as the entrance to the Great Pyramid is a popular belief that has persisted, though without any real proof. P. Christian, drawing from the writings of Iamblichus, describes the theory this way: "The Sphinx of Giza marked the entrance to underground chambers where initiates faced trials. The entrance, now blocked by sand and debris, lay between the Sphinx's front legs. In ancient times, a bronze door guarded this entrance, which could only be opened by the Magi through a secret mechanism. Public respect and religious fear kept the entrance safe from intrusion. Inside the Sphinx, tunnels led to the underground chambers of the Great Pyramid, forming a maze so complex that anyone entering without a guide would inevitably circle back to where they began."

However, there is no sign of the bronze door Christian mentions, nor any evidence it ever existed. Over the centuries, the Sphinx has undergone many changes, and it is possible that any original entrance was sealed. Many believe that underground chambers still exist beneath the Great Pyramid. Robert Ballard writes, "Just as the priests of the Pyramids of Lake Moeris lived in vast underground quarters, it seems likely that the priests of Giza had similar residences. In fact, the limestone used to build the pyramids might have been excavated from these underground caverns. I am convinced that exploring beneath the Pyramid will reveal important clues about its purpose. A diamond drill capable of reaching a few hundred feet would be needed to investigate both the solidity of the Pyramid and any hidden spaces beneath it."

Ballard's theory raises an important architectural question. The Pyramid's builders were too skilled to place over five million tons of stone on anything but a solid foundation. If there are underground chambers, they must be small and well-supported, much like the chambers inside the Pyramid, which occupy only a tiny fraction of its total volume.

The Sphinx was likely created for symbolic purposes under the direction of the priesthood. Some theories suggest that the Sphinx once had a uraeus, or serpent symbol, on its forehead that served as the pointer of a giant sundial. Others believe both the Pyramid and the Sphinx were used to track time, the seasons, and the precession of the equinoxes. If the Sphinx was built to block access to a hidden passage leading to an underground temple within the Pyramid, its symbolic meaning would be fitting. However, compared to the majesty and scale of the Pyramid, the Sphinx seems relatively insignificant.

Today, the face of the Sphinx, which still shows traces of the red paint it was originally covered with, is heavily damaged. Its nose was broken off by a devout Muslim who feared it might lead people toward idol worship. The repairs now required to keep the head from collapsing suggest that the Sphinx could not have survived the same vast stretches of time as the Pyramid.

To the Egyptians, the Sphinx symbolized both strength and intelligence. Its androgynous form reflected the belief that initiates and gods contained both masculine and feminine energies. Gerald Massey explains, "This is the secret of the Sphinx. The Egyptian sphinx is male in the front and female in the back. The image of Sut-Typhon follows the same pattern, with horns and a tail—male at the front and female at the back. Pharaohs, too, wore the tail of a lioness or cow behind them, representing the union of both sexes within themselves. Like the gods, they embodied the complete dual nature of existence."

Despite its symbolic importance, many researchers have dismissed the Sphinx, choosing instead to focus on the greater mystery of the Pyramid.

The Pyramid Mysteries

The word "pyramid" is often thought to come from the Greek word pyr, meaning fire, symbolizing the divine flame that gives life to all beings. John Taylor believed the word referred to a "measure of wheat," while C. Piazzi Smyth suggested it meant "a division into ten" in Coptic. Ancient initiates saw the pyramid shape as a perfect symbol for both their hidden teachings and the institutions created to spread this wisdom. Pyramids and mounds were thought to represent the Holy Mountain, a sacred place believed to stand at the center of the earth. John P. Lundy compared the Great Pyramid to Mount Olympus, saying its underground passages were like the winding paths of Hades.

The square base of the Pyramid symbolizes that the foundation of wisdom rests on nature's unchanging laws. Albert Pike wrote that the Gnostics built their knowledge on a square whose corners represented Silence, Profundity, Intelligence, and Truth. The four sides of the Great Pyramid align with the cardinal directions: north and south, which represent cold and heat, and east and west, which stand for light and darkness. The base also represents the four material elements from which the physical body is formed. Rising from each side is a triangle, symbolizing the divine being that dwells within all material forms. If each base line is treated as a square from which spiritual power rises, the total of the lines on the four sides (12) and the squares of the base (16) is 28, a sacred number. Adding the three sets of seven that represent the sun (21) gives 49, the square of seven, which symbolizes the universe.

The twelve zodiac signs are represented by the twelve edges of the Pyramid's four triangular faces. Within each face is one of the four creatures from the vision of Ezekiel, turning the entire structure into a representation of the Cherubim. The three main chambers of the Pyramid correspond to the heart, the brain, and the reproductive system—key spiritual centers in human beings. The Pyramid's triangular shape also mirrors the posture used in ancient meditation practices. According to the Mysteries, divine energy descended from the gods onto the Pyramid's tip, which was compared to the roots of an inverted tree, with branches spreading downward along the Pyramid's sides, radiating wisdom throughout the world.

No one knows the exact size of the Pyramid's capstone, and although many believe it once existed, it is now missing. It's common for builders of sacred structures to leave them unfinished, as a reminder that only God is complete. If the capstone did exist, it would have been a miniature pyramid, with a smaller version of itself on top, continuing infinitely. This capstone represents the entire structure in miniature. Similarly, the Pyramid can be seen as a symbol of the universe, with the capstone representing humanity. Within each person, the mind is the capstone of the body, the spirit is the capstone of the mind, and God is the final capstone of the spirit. Just as a rough stone is shaped into a perfect capstone, the Mysteries transform a person into the living apex through which divine energy flows into the world below.

W. Marsham Adams called the Great Pyramid the "House of the Hidden Places" because it symbolized the secret wisdom that predated Egyptian civilization. The Egyptians linked the Pyramid to Hermes, the god of wisdom and knowledge, also associated with the planet Mercury. Connecting Hermes with the Pyramid emphasizes that the structure was a temple dedicated to the Invisible and Supreme Deity. It was not built as a tomb, observatory, or lighthouse, but as the first temple of the Mysteries—a place that guarded the truths at the heart of all knowledge and science. The Pyramid perfectly represents the microcosm (the small world) and the macrocosm (the larger universe). According to secret teachings, it was also considered the tomb of Osiris, the black god of the Nile, who symbolizes a form of solar energy. His tomb represents the universe, where Osiris is both buried and crucified on the cross of material existence.

Through the hidden passages and chambers of the Great Pyramid, the enlightened ones of ancient times made their journey. They entered as ordinary men and emerged as gods. The Pyramid was known as the "womb of the Mysteries," a place of "second birth," where wisdom lived just as God lives within the hearts of people. Deep within its recesses dwelled a mysterious figure called "The Initiator" or "The Illustrious One." This being, dressed in blue and gold and holding the sevenfold key of Eternity, was the lion-faced teacher, the Holy One, and the Master of Masters. He never left the House of Wisdom, and no one saw him unless they had first gone through the trials of preparation and purification. It was in these sacred chambers that Plato, the philosopher with the broad brow, encountered ancient wisdom personified in the Master of the Hidden House.

Who was this Master who lived within the Pyramid, whose many chambers symbolized the worlds of the universe? Only those who had been "born again" could see him. He alone knew the deepest secrets of the Pyramid, but now he has left, and the sacred halls are empty. No longer do hymns of praise echo through the corridors. No one now passes through the elements or walks among the seven stars. The "Word of Life" is no longer given to the worthy by the lips of the Eternal One. All that remains visible to the world is an empty shell—an outer symbol of an inner truth—and people call this House of God a tomb.

The Master of the Secret House, the Sage Illuminator, revealed the techniques of the Mysteries to new initiates. He showed them how to recognize their guardian spirit and taught them how to free their spiritual essence from the physical body. At the height of their transformation, he shared the Divine Name—the secret and unspoken title of the Supreme Deity. With this knowledge, the initiate became like a pyramid within his soul, where others could find their own spiritual awakening.

In the King's Chamber, the initiate underwent the ritual of the "second death." There, after being symbolically crucified upon the cross of the solstices and equinoxes, he was placed in the great stone coffer. The King's Chamber had a strange and deathly cold that seemed to reach into the bones. This sacred space acted as a gateway between the physical world and the higher realms of Nature. While the initiate's body rested in the coffer, his soul, like a human-headed hawk, soared through the celestial realms. In these realms, he saw the truth of eternal Life, Light, and Truth and understood that Death, Darkness, and Sin were mere illusions. In this way, the Great Pyramid served as a gateway through which the ancient priests allowed a few to reach spiritual completion.

If someone strikes the coffer in the King's Chamber, the sound it makes does not match any known musical scale. This unique tone may have been part of what made the King's Chamber the ideal place to perform the highest rites of the Mysteries.

Modern science and theology know little about these ancient rituals.

Scholars look at the Great Pyramid and wonder what motivated such immense labor. But if they paused to reflect, they might realize that only one thing could inspire such effort: the soul's deep desire to understand, to know the truth, and to exchange mortal limitation for divine knowledge. People today say the Great Pyramid is the most perfect building ever made, the origin of weights and measures, the first Noah's Ark, and the source of alphabets, languages, and even scales for measuring temperature and humidity. Few realize, however, that it is also a gateway to the Eternal.

Though the modern world may hold countless secrets, the ancient world held one—and that one was greater than all others. The many secrets of today lead to death, sorrow, selfishness, greed, and destruction, but the one secret of the past brings life, light, and truth. A time will come when the ancient wisdom will once again guide humanity's religious and philosophical search. The collapse of rigid dogmas is near. The "Tower of Babel," with its confusion of languages, was built from bricks of mud held together by slime. But from the ashes of dead creeds, the ancient Mysteries will rise like a phoenix. No other institution has ever fulfilled humanity's spiritual needs as completely as the Mysteries. Since their destruction, no religious system has emerged that someone like Plato could fully embrace. The development of the human spirit is as precise a science as astronomy, medicine, or law. Religion was created for this very purpose, and from it arose philosophy, science, and logic as tools to achieve this divine goal.

The Dying God will rise again! The hidden chamber in the House of Secrets will be rediscovered. The Pyramid will once more stand as a symbol of strength, renewal, aspiration, resurrection, and transformation. As one civilization after another is buried beneath the sands of time, the Pyramid will remain as a visible reminder of the eternal connection between divine wisdom and the world. One day, the ancient hymns of enlightenment will again echo through its halls. The Master of the Hidden House will wait in the Silent Place for those who, leaving behind the false ideas of dogma, seek only Truth and will not settle for anything less than the real thing.

Isis, the Virgin of the World

The study of Hermetic symbolism often begins with the figure of the Saitic Isis, a version of the goddess from the city of Sais. Her temple bore the famous inscription: "I, Isis, am all that has been, that is, or shall be; no mortal man has ever lifted my veil." According to Plutarch, some ancient authors believed Isis was the daughter of Hermes, while others thought she was the child of Prometheus. Both were known for their divine wisdom, though her connection to them may be symbolic rather than literal. Plutarch also interpreted the name Isis to mean wisdom. In Anacalypsis, Godfrey Higgins traced her name to the Hebrew word Iso and the Greek word zoo, meaning "to save." Other scholars, like Richard Payne Knight, suggested her name had Northern origins, possibly from Scandinavian or Gothic languages, where it is pronounced Isa, meaning "ice" or "frozen water."

This goddess, known by many names, represented fertility across various ancient religions. She was sometimes called the "goddess with ten thousand names" and, over time, was transformed in Christian tradition into the Virgin Mary. Although Isis was believed to have given birth to all living things—especially the sun—legend says she remained a virgin.

In The Golden Ass, Apuleius includes a description of Isis where she declares her divine attributes: "I am Nature, the mother of all things, ruler of the elements, first among the gods, queen of the dead, and leader of the celestial beings. The entire world honors me with different names and rituals. The Phrygians call me Pessinuntica, the Mother of the Gods. The Athenians name me Cecropian Minerva, the Cypriots call me Paphian Venus, and the Cretans know me as Diana. The Sicilians worship me as Proserpine, and the Eleusinians as Ceres. Others call me Juno, Bellona, Hecate, or Rhamnusia. In Ethiopia, Egypt, and among the Arii, where the sun's light is strong, I am known by my true name: Queen Isis."

Some historians, like Le Plongeon, believe that the story of Isis has historical roots among the Mayans of Central America, where she was known as Queen Moo, and her brother-husband Osiris was represented as Prince Coh. According to this theory, Queen Moo fled to Egypt after Prince Coh's death, where she was accepted as queen and given the name Isis. However, the global presence of Isis in so many myths suggests that she was likely more of a symbolic figure than a real person.

Sextus Empiricus claims that the Trojan War was fought over a statue of the moon goddess, not for the mortal Helen, as commonly believed. Some authors have even tried to connect figures like Isis, Osiris, Typhon, and Thoth to the descendants of Noah's son, Ham. But since the story of Noah is more of a cosmic allegory about the renewal of life, it is unlikely that these Egyptian deities were ever real historical figures.

According to Robert Fludd, the sun embodies life, light, and heat—qualities that energize the three realms of existence: the spiritual, intellectual, and physical worlds. This is summarized by the phrase, "From one light, three lights," which reflects the sun's role in bringing life and vitality to the earth. Osiris, therefore, symbolizes the life-giving power of the sun, though not the sun itself. His symbol was an open eye, representing the "Great Eye" of the universe—the sun—while Isis symbolized the receptive force of Nature.

Modern science has shown that everything, from stars to atoms, follows a pattern of positive centers surrounded by negative bodies that depend on the central life force. This allegory is echoed in the story of Solomon and his many wives, where Solomon represents the sun, and his wives are the planets and moons orbiting it. In The Song of Solomon, the dark maid of Jerusalem symbolizes Isis, representing the nurturing force of Nature that gives life after being energized by the sun.

The ancient year consisted of 360 days, with five extra days set aside as the birthdays of five gods and goddesses—Osiris being born on the first day, and Isis on the fourth. Typhon, the spirit of destruction, was born on the third day and is often represented as a crocodile or a mixture of crocodile and pig. Isis stood for wisdom, while Typhon symbolized arrogance and pride—traits that block understanding and truth.

The story continues with Osiris, symbolizing the sun, bringing knowledge to Egypt and traveling to other lands to spread enlightenment. Meanwhile, his brother Typhon plotted against him. Like the Norse trickster Loki, Typhon gathered conspirators and devised a plan to trap Osiris. He commissioned a beautifully decorated chest, perfectly sized to fit Osiris's body. During a banquet, Typhon invited the gods to lie inside the chest, promising to give it to whoever fit inside perfectly. When Osiris tried it, Typhon sealed the chest with molten lead and cast it into the Nile, where it floated out to sea. According to Plutarch, this event occurred on the seventeenth day of the month Athyr, when the sun was in Scorpio—a symbol of betrayal. This story also parallels the moment when Noah entered the ark to escape the flood.

Plutarch also says that the Pans and Satyrs, which are nature spirits and elementals, were the first to find out that Osiris had been killed. As soon as they discovered this, they raised an alarm, and from this event, we get the word "panic," which means fear or amazement felt by many people. Isis found out about her husband's death from some children who saw the killers running off with the box that held his body. She immediately dressed in mourning clothes and began her search for him.

Eventually, Isis discovered that the chest had floated to the shores of Byblos. There, it got stuck in the branches of a tree that quickly grew around it in a miraculous way. The king of that land was so amazed by the tree that he ordered it to be cut down and turned into a pillar to hold up the roof of his palace. When Isis arrived in Byblos, she was able to get her husband's body back, but Typhon stole it again. This time, he cut Osiris's body into fourteen pieces and scattered them across the earth. In despair, Isis began gathering the parts of her husband but could only find thirteen. The missing piece, the phallus, had fallen into the Nile River and been swallowed by a fish, so Isis made a replacement out of gold.

Later, Osiris's son killed Typhon in battle. Some Egyptians believed that the souls of gods went to heaven, where they became stars. They thought the soul of Isis shined from the Dog Star, while Typhon became the constellation of the Bear. However, it is unclear if this belief was widely accepted. In Egyptian art, Isis is often shown wearing a head-dress shaped like the empty throne of her dead husband, which became her symbol during certain periods. The headdresses worn by Egyptians carry deep symbolic meaning, representing the spiritual energy around divine beings, much like halos and auras in Christian art. Frank C. Higgins, a well-known Masonic expert on symbols, noted that the way some Egyptian gods and pharaohs wore their headpieces at a backward tilt mirrored the tilt of the earth's axis. The clothing, jewelry, and ornaments of ancient priests symbolized the spiritual energy radiating from the human body. Modern science is starting to rediscover some of the lost knowledge from Hermetic philosophy. One of these discoveries is the ability to measure a person's mental, spiritual, and physical state by observing the streams of barely visible electric energy that flow from the surface of their skin throughout their life. (For more details on how this energy can be seen using a scientific process, see The Human Atmosphere by Dr. Walter J. Kilner.)

Isis is sometimes symbolized with the head of a cow, and in some cases, the whole animal represents her. In Norse mythology, the first gods were said to be licked out of ice blocks by a mother cow named Audhumla, who symbolized natural nourishment and fertility because of her milk. Isis is also depicted as a bird in some representations. She often holds the crux ansata, a symbol of eternal life, in one hand, and a flowered scepter representing her authority in the other.

Thoth Hermes Trismegistus, known as the founder of Egyptian knowledge and one of the wisest figures in history, passed down the ancient secrets that are still preserved today through myths and legends. These stories and symbols hide instructions for spiritual, mental, moral, and physical transformation, which is often referred to as the "Mystic Chemistry of the Soul," or alchemy. These sacred truths were shared with those initiated into the Mystery Schools but kept hidden from the general public. People who couldn't understand the deeper meaning of these teachings ended up worshiping the statues and symbols that represented these hidden truths. The wisdom and secrecy of Egypt are perfectly captured in the image of the Sphinx, which has kept its secrets safe for countless generations of seekers.

The mysteries of Hermeticism contain great spiritual truths that remain hidden from most of the world because of ignorance. The keys to these ancient teachings are all symbolized by the figure of the Virgin Isis. She is depicted veiled from head to toe, revealing her wisdom only to those who have earned the right to stand in her presence. These worthy few can uncover the hidden knowledge of nature and confront the deeper reality of the divine directly.

The descriptions of the symbols associated with the Virgin Isis in this text are mainly drawn from a free translation of the fourth book of Bibliotèque des Philosophes Hermétiques, titled "The Hermetical Signification of the Symbols and Attributes of Isis," with extra notes added by the writer to explain and clarify the ideas. Statues of Isis were decorated with images of the sun, moon, stars, and other symbols connected to the earth, which she was believed to rule as the guardian spirit of Nature itself. Many statues of the goddess have been found with their original symbols intact, showing the respect and status she held. Ancient philosophers viewed her as a symbol of Universal Nature, the source of all creation. She was often depicted as a partly nude woman, sometimes pregnant, and sometimes covered in a flowing robe, usually in green or black. In some cases, her clothing was a mix of black, white, yellow, and red.

Apuleius described her in great detail: "Her long hair flowed down her neck in soft, loose strands, and a crown made from many flowers rested on her head. In the center of this crown was a round object that looked like a mirror, or more like a bright, glowing light, representing the moon. Vipers, coiled like plowed furrows, wound around the crown on both sides, and ears of corn extended upward. Her robe, made from the finest linen, shimmered with many colors—white like light, yellow like crocus flowers, and rosy red. However, the part of her clothing that stood out most was a black robe that glittered darkly. It draped across her right side, rose over her left shoulder, and gathered at the front, looking like the center of a shield. The ends of this robe hung in graceful folds, with delicate tassels at the edges. Stars were scattered across the embroidery, and in the middle of these stars, the full moon shone brightly, radiating light like fire. A crown made of flowers and fruits of all kinds ran along the edge of the robe, moving with each graceful motion. In one hand, she held a bronze rattle called a sistrum, which made a sharp, triple sound as it shook. In the other hand, she carried a long, narrow vessel shaped like a boat, with the head of an asp rising from the handle, its neck swollen as if ready to strike. Her immortal feet were wrapped in shoes woven from palm leaves, symbolizing victory."

The green in her robe represents the plants that cover the earth, symbolizing Nature's clothing. The black color stands for death and decay, which lead to new life. This idea reflects the saying: "Unless someone is born again, they cannot see the kingdom of God" (John 3:3). The white, yellow, and red represent the three main colors used in alchemy, following the blackness that symbolizes decay and transformation. The name "Isis" was also used for one of the secret medicines of the ancient world, which shows that this description has connections to chemistry. Her black robe symbolizes the moon's dependence on the sun, as the moon has no light of its own but reflects the sun's light, energy, and life-giving power. Isis also represents the greatest achievements of ancient wisdom—like the Philosopher's Stone, the Elixir of Life, and the Universal Medicine.

Other symbols related to Isis are just as fascinating, but it's impossible to list them all since the Egyptian Hermetists often used them interchangeably. Isis is sometimes shown wearing a hat made from cypress branches, symbolizing her mourning for her dead husband, as well as the physical death that all living things must undergo to achieve new life or rebirth. At times, her head is decorated with a crown of gold or a wreath of olive leaves, which show her power as the queen of the world and ruler of the universe. The golden crown also represents the fiery energy of the sun, which gives life to all beings by maintaining the balance of the elements. This ongoing cycle of energy is symbolized by the musical sistrum she carries, which also represents purity.

A serpent woven through the olive leaves on her head, biting its own tail, symbolizes how the energy from the sun becomes tainted by earthly corruption. This energy must undergo purification through seven stages, called "planetary circulations" or "flying eagles" in alchemical terms, to restore it to its healing power. The sun's energy is seen as a kind of medicine for human illnesses. These seven stages are symbolized in different rituals, such as the seven circuits made by Masons around their lodge, the Jewish priests' seven marches around Jericho, and the Muslim priests' seven rounds around the Kaaba in Mecca. From the crown of gold rise three horns of plenty, which represent the abundance of Nature's gifts, all coming from one source—the heavens, symbolized by the head of Isis.

In this image, ancient thinkers describe the forces that sustain the three kingdoms of nature: minerals, plants, and animals (including humans). At one ear, the moon, and at the other, the sun represent two essential forces—one active, the other receptive, like father and mother.

Isis, who symbolizes Nature, uses these two celestial bodies to spread her power across the realms of animals, plants, and minerals. On her neck, there are symbols of planets and zodiac signs, showing that heavenly forces influence the growth and destiny of all living things. These forces guide everything under the moon and shape smaller worlds that reflect the larger universe.

In her right hand, Isis holds a small ship with a spinning wheel as its mast. At the top of the mast is a water jug with a snake-shaped handle, full of venom. This shows that Isis guides the fragile ship of life through the storms of time. The spinning wheel represents how she spins and cuts the thread of life. These symbols also suggest that Isis brings moisture to everything in nature, protecting life from the sun's heat by keeping things hydrated with moisture from the air. Water helps plants grow, but this life-giving moisture often carries poison caused by decay. To make this moisture pure, it must encounter Nature's invisible cleansing fire. This fire refines, perfects, and re-energizes the substance, turning it into a healing power that can renew all life.

The snake sheds its skin every year, symbolizing the renewal of the spirit after material life. The earth also renews itself every spring when the sun returns to the northern lands. In her left hand, the symbolic Virgin carries a sistrum and a square cymbal, which produces the key-note of Nature (Fa) when struck. Sometimes, she also holds an olive branch, representing the harmony she brings to nature with her renewing power. Through death and decay, she brings forth new life in endless cycles. The square shape of the cymbal, rather than the usual triangle, shows that all things are transformed according to the balance of the four elements.

Dr. Sigismund Bacstrom believed that if a doctor could balance earth, fire, air, and water, and bring them together into the Philosopher's Stone, represented by a six-pointed star or two interlocking triangles, they could heal any disease. Dr. Bacstrom also believed the universal fire or spirit of Nature was present in everything: "It does all and is all." Through attraction, repulsion, movement, heat, evaporation, drying, thickening, and fixing, this spirit shapes matter and reveals itself in creation. Anyone who understands these natural laws and uses them wisely becomes a true philosopher.

From Isis's right breast, a cluster of grapes emerges, and from her left, an ear of corn or wheat, golden in color. This shows that Nature provides food for plants, animals, and people, nourishing all life. The golden color of the wheat suggests that within sunlight or spiritual gold lies the essence of life itself. Around the upper part of her body is a belt with mysterious symbols. This belt is held together at the front by four golden plates, arranged in a square, symbolizing the four elements—earth, air, fire, and water—that create everything. Stars also appear on this belt, symbolizing the influence of both sunlight and darkness. Isis is identified with the constellation Virgo, where she is depicted with a serpent under her feet and a crown of stars on her head. In her arms, she holds a sheaf of grain and, at times, the young Sun God.

The statue of Isis was placed on a pedestal made of dark stone, decorated with the heads of rams. Beneath her feet were several poisonous snakes. This shows that Nature has the power to remove harmful substances and cleanse all impurities caused by earthly decay. The rams' heads represent that the best time for life to begin is when the sun moves through Aries. The snakes under her feet symbolize Nature's ability to preserve life and cure illness by getting rid of impurities and decay.

This idea reflects the wisdom of ancient philosophers, who expressed it with these sayings:

Nature contains Nature,

Nature delights in her own nature,

Nature surpasses Nature,

Nature can only be corrected through her own nature.

Thus, when thinking about the statue of Isis, it is important to consider the deeper meanings behind the symbols. If we do not, the Virgin's message will remain a mystery.

A golden ring on her left arm holds a cord, which extends to a deep container filled with glowing coals and incense. This shows that Isis, as a symbol of Nature, carries with her the sacred fire, which was always kept burning by temple priestesses called vestal virgins. This flame represents the pure, eternal spirit of Nature—the essence of life itself. The oil that never burns away, known as the balsam of life, is often mentioned by wise thinkers and in religious texts, symbolizing the fuel that sustains this everlasting flame.

From her right arm hangs another thread, connected to a pair of scales. This represents Nature's precision in balancing all things, as she weighs and measures them perfectly. Isis is often shown as a symbol of justice, reflecting Nature's unwavering consistency. The World Virgin is sometimes depicted standing between two tall pillars, known in Freemasonry as Jachin and Boaz. These pillars represent the idea that Nature creates by balancing opposites. Isis, as a figure of wisdom, stands between these opposites, showing that true understanding is found in balance and that truth often appears hidden between conflicting ideas.

The golden shine in her dark hair represents how her power, although connected to the moon, comes from the sun's light, giving her a reddish glow. Just as the moon reflects the sun's light, Isis is portrayed like the Virgin in Revelation, bathed in the brightness of the sun. The writer Apuleius describes a vision in which he saw the goddess Isis rising from the ocean. The ancient people understood that life began in water, and modern science agrees. In Outline of History, H.G. Wells explains how early life filled the oceans, but the land above the tide was barren and lifeless. Later, he writes, "Wherever the shoreline ran, there was life, and that life existed through water, in water, and with water as its essential element."

The ancients believed that the seeds of life came from warm, moist vapor. The veiled figure of Isis symbolizes this vapor, which carries the life force from the sun, shown by the child she holds in her arms. Since the sun, moon, and stars appear to sink into the sea when they set, and the water absorbs their light, people believed the sea was the source of life's seeds. These seeds were thought to be formed through the combined influence of the celestial bodies. That is why Isis is sometimes shown as being pregnant.

The statue of Isis was often shown with a large ox that was black and white. The ox symbolized either Osiris, connected to Taurus, the bull in the zodiac, or Apis, a sacred bull linked to Osiris because of its special patterns and colors. In Egyptian culture, bulls were used for hard labor, reminding people that Nature works patiently to keep all living things healthy and alive. Alongside Isis, the figure of Harpocrates, the God of Silence, is often shown with a finger held to his mouth, signaling that the secrets of the wise must be kept from those who are not ready to understand them.

The Druids of Britain and Gaul knew much about the mysteries of Isis and worshiped her through the symbol of the moon. However, Godfrey Higgins believed it was wrong to see Isis as identical to the moon itself. Instead, the moon was used to represent her because it controls water. The Druids saw the sun as the father and the moon as the mother of all creation, and through these symbols, they honored the power of Universal Nature.

Sometimes, the figure of Isis stands for mystical and magical practices such as necromancy, spell-casting, and miracle-working. One myth tells of how Isis used her magic to make Ra, the powerful God of Eternity, reveal his secret, sacred name. This name is thought to be like the Lost Word of Masonry, which gives those who know it power over unseen and higher beings. The priests of Isis mastered these hidden forces of Nature, practicing things like hypnotism and mesmerism long before the modern world understood them.

Plutarch described what it takes to follow Isis, saying: "Just as a beard or rough clothing does not make a philosopher, neither do frequent shavings or wearing linen make someone a true follower of Isis. Only the one who listens, learns the stories of these gods properly, and seeks out the hidden meaning behind them, guided by reason and wisdom, is a true servant of this goddess."

During the Middle Ages, the troubadours of Central Europe kept the legends of Isis alive in their songs. They wrote poems about the most beautiful woman in the world, though her true identity was rarely known. She was Sophia, the Virgin of Wisdom, whom philosophers throughout history have sought to understand. Isis represents the mystery of motherhood, which ancient people saw as the greatest example of Nature's wisdom and proof of divine power. To those seeking truth today, Isis symbolizes the Great Unknown, and only those who uncover her mysteries can truly understand life, death, birth, and renewal.

Mummification of The Egyptian Dead

Servius, commenting on Virgil's Æneid, notes that "the wise Egyptians carefully embalmed their bodies and placed them in catacombs so that the soul would stay connected to the body for a long time, preventing it from wandering off too soon. On the other hand, the Romans, with the opposite goal, burned the bodies of their dead on funeral pyres, hoping the soul would quickly return to the original, universal element." (From Prichard's An Analysis of the Egyptian Mythology.)

There are no complete records revealing the Egyptians' secret beliefs about how the soul, or consciousness, was connected to the body. However, it seems likely that Pythagoras, who was initiated into the Egyptian temples, shared parts of these teachings when he introduced the idea of metempsychosis, or the soul's migration from one body to another. The common idea that Egyptians mummified their dead to preserve the body for a future physical resurrection does not align with modern understanding of their philosophy about death. In the fourth book of On Abstinence from Animal Food, Porphyry explains that the Egyptians purified the dead by removing the internal organs and placing them in a separate chest. He also shares a prayer, translated from Egyptian by Euphantus, which says:

"O sovereign Sun, and all you Gods who give life to humans, receive me and bring me to the eternal Gods to dwell with them. For I have faithfully honored the gods my parents taught me to worship during my life. I also showed respect for those who gave me life. As for other people, I have neither killed anyone nor cheated anyone of anything entrusted to me. I have committed no serious wrong. If I have done anything wrong by eating or drinking what was forbidden, the fault lies not with me but with these." (Here, the speaker points to the chest containing the organs.)

The Egyptians believed that removing the organs, which were seen as the source of cravings, purified the body by freeing it from their harmful influence.

Early Christians took their scriptures so literally that they preserved bodies by soaking them in salt water, believing this would ensure the spirit could return to a whole and intact body on the day of resurrection. They avoided embalming or removing internal organs, fearing that doing so would stop the soul from returning to the body. Instead, they buried their dead without using the Egyptians' complex mummification practices.

In Egyptian Magic, S.S.D.D. offers an interesting theory about the hidden purpose behind mummification. He writes, "It seems likely that only those who had reached a certain level of initiation were mummified. To the Egyptians, mummification prevented reincarnation, which was only required for souls that had failed the initiation tests. Those with the strength and wisdom to enter the Secret Adytum did not need to reincarnate. Their bodies were preserved as a kind of talisman or material anchor for the soul to return to earth when needed."

In its early stages, mummification was reserved for Pharaohs and members of the royal family, who were believed to share some of the qualities of Osiris, the divine king of the underworld, who was also mummified.

The Sun, A Universal Deity

Worship of the sun was one of the earliest and most natural ways people expressed their faith. Many modern religious beliefs are just more complicated versions of this simple, original idea. Early humans, recognizing the life-giving power of the sun, honored it as a representative of the Supreme Being. Albert Pike explains the origin of sun worship in Morals and Dogma by saying: "To them [early people], he [the sun] was the inner fire within all things, the fire of Nature. As the source of life, warmth, and energy, the sun was seen as the power behind all creation. Without him, there could be no movement, no life, and no shape to anything. He seemed vast, eternal, and always present. People felt a deep need for his light and creative force, and nothing frightened them more than his absence. His kindness and life-giving energy made him a symbol of Good. The BRAHMA of the Hindus, MITHRAS of the Persians, and ATHOM, AMUN, PHTHA, and OSIRIS of the Egyptians, along with the BEL of the Chaldeans, the ADONAI of the Phoenicians, and the ADONIS and APOLLO of the Greeks, were all forms of the sun. These gods represented the renewing power of life, the energy that keeps the world alive and refreshed."

Throughout ancient times, people built altars, temples, and mounds to honor the sun. Many of these sacred places still stand today, including the pyramids of Yucatan and Egypt, the snake mounds of the American Indians, the Zikkurats of Babylon and Chaldea, the round towers of Ireland, and the great stone circles in Britain and Normandy. Even the Tower of Babel, which the Bible says was built to reach God, may have actually been an observatory to study the stars.

Both pagan and early Christian priests and prophets knew a lot about astronomy and astrology. Their teachings often make more sense when viewed through the lens of these ancient sciences. As people learned more about the movements and patterns of the stars and planets, they began incorporating astronomical ideas into their religious beliefs. Gods were given homes among the stars, with different planets being named after these deities. The fixed stars were arranged into constellations, and the sun and planets were believed to travel through these constellations, along with the moons that orbited some of the planets.

The Solar Trinity

The sun, as the most important of the heavenly bodies visible to ancient astronomers, was linked to the highest gods and became a symbol of the supreme authority of the Creator Himself. From reflecting on the sun's powers and qualities, the idea of the Trinity, as we understand it today, was born. The concept of a Triune God is not unique to Christian or Jewish beliefs but appears in many of the world's great religions, both ancient and modern. The Persians, Hindus, Babylonians, and Egyptians all had their own versions of the Trinity. In each case, the Trinity represented three aspects of one Supreme Intelligence. In modern Masonry, God is represented by an equilateral triangle, with each side symbolizing one of the primary aspects of the Eternal Being, who is also shown as a small flame, called Yod ( ) by the Hebrews. Jakob Böhme, a German mystic, referred to the Trinity as "The Three Witnesses," saying that through these three aspects, the invisible divine becomes known in the physical world.

The idea of the Trinity is easy to understand when we observe the daily journey of the sun. Since the sun symbolizes all light, it has three distinct stages: rising, midday, and setting. Philosophers saw these phases as representing the three stages of life: growth, maturity, and decline. Between the soft light of morning and evening lies the brilliant peak of midday. God the Father, the Creator, is represented by the sunrise, and His color is blue, like the morning sky veiled in mist. God the Son, the radiant one who reveals His Father's glory to the world, is represented by the midday sun, shining brightly like a lion with golden hair. His color is yellow, and His power is eternal. God the Holy Ghost corresponds to sunset, when the sun rests briefly on the horizon, clothed in fiery red, before disappearing into the night. This symbolizes the soul's journey into darkness, only to rise again with the dawn.

For the Egyptians, the sun was a symbol of immortality because it dies each night but rises again every morning. Beyond its daily path, the sun also has an annual journey, moving through twelve sections of the sky called the zodiac, spending thirty days in each. Additionally, the sun follows a third path known as the precession of the equinoxes, slowly moving backward through the zodiac at a rate of one degree every seventy-two years.

Robert Hewitt Brown, a 32nd-degree Mason, explains the sun's yearly journey through the zodiac this way: "As the sun moves through the signs of the zodiac, it is said to take on the qualities of each sign or to triumph over it. In Taurus, the sun becomes a bull and was worshiped as Apis by the Egyptians and as Bel, Baal, or Bul by the Assyrians. In Leo, the sun becomes a lion-slayer like Hercules, and in Sagittarius, it takes the form of an archer. In Pisces, the sun appears as a fish—Dagon of the Philistines or Vishnu, the fish-god of the Hindus."

A close study of ancient religions shows that their priests served solar energy and that the highest god was often a personification of the sun. After thirty years of research into the origins of religion, Godfrey Higgins concluded that "All the gods of ancient times ultimately trace back to the solar fire, either as the god itself or as a symbol of a higher creative power."

Egyptian priests often wore lion skins during their ceremonies because the lion was a symbol of the sun. The sun is especially honored in the constellation of Leo, which it rules. At one point in history, Leo was considered the keystone of the heavens. Hercules, another solar figure, performed twelve heroic tasks, just as the sun completes twelve essential tasks during its journey through the zodiac each year. Like the Egyptian priests, Hercules wore a lion's skin as a belt. Samson, the Hebrew hero, also symbolizes the sun. His name reflects his solar nature, and his struggles with the Nubian lion and the Philistines (representing forces of darkness), as well as his feat of carrying away the gates of Gaza, all reflect aspects of the sun's journey and power.

Many ancient cultures had more than one sun god, with different gods and goddesses reflecting parts of the sun's energy. The gold decorations used by priests in various religions refer to solar energy, as do the crowns of kings. Ancient crowns often had pointed rays extending outward to resemble the sun, though later designs either bent these points inward or gathered them at the top under a globe or cross. Many ancient prophets, philosophers, and leaders carried scepters with the sun symbol at the top, surrounded by rays. All earthly kingdoms were seen as reflections of the heavenly kingdom, with the sun as the supreme ruler, the planets as his council, and all of nature as his subjects.

Many gods have been linked to the sun. The Greeks believed that Apollo, Bacchus, Dionysos, Sabazius, Hercules, Jason, Ulysses, Zeus, Uranus, and Vulcan either embodied visible or hidden aspects of the sun. In Norse mythology, Balder the Beautiful was seen as a sun god, and Odin was also connected to the sun, especially because of his single eye. In Egypt, deities like Osiris, Ra, Anubis, Hermes, and the mysterious Ammon shared similarities with the sun. Isis was considered the mother of the sun, and even Typhon, known as the Destroyer, was thought to be a form of solar energy. The Egyptian sun myth eventually centered around a mysterious god named Serapis. The Central American gods Tezcatlipoca and Quetzalcoatl, while mainly associated with the winds, were also linked to the sun.

In Freemasonry, the sun holds deep symbolic meaning. One of the sun's representations is Solomon, whose name, SOL-OM-ON, translates to "Supreme Light" in three different languages. Hiram Abiff, also known as CHiram by the Chaldeans, is another figure connected to the sun. His story, including his attack and death at the hands of the Ruffians, contains solar symbolism, which is explored further in The Hiramic Legend.

George Oliver, D.D., provides a clear example of the role the sun plays in Freemasonry's symbols and rituals in his Dictionary of Symbolical Masonry. He writes: "The sun rises in the east, and the east is where the Worshipful Master stands. Just as the sun is the source of all light and warmth, the Worshipful Master must inspire and energize the brethren in their work. For the ancient Egyptians, the sun was a symbol of divine providence."

The priests in ancient mysteries wore many symbols representing solar power. The gold sunbursts embroidered on the robes of Catholic priests today reflect this same idea, showing that the priest acts as a messenger of Sol Invictus, the Unconquered Sun.

Christianity And The Sun

For reasons they believed to be necessary, those who recorded the life of Jesus chose to portray him as a solar deity. The historical figure of Jesus faded into the background, and almost all the important events described in the four Gospels align with the movements, phases, or functions of the celestial bodies.

Among the many stories Christianity borrowed from ancient pagan traditions is the tale of the beautiful, blue-eyed Sun God. His golden hair flows over his shoulders, and he is dressed entirely in pure white. In his arms, he holds the Lamb of God, symbolizing the spring equinox. This radiant figure is a blend of Apollo, Osiris, Orpheus, Mithras, and Bacchus, as he shares qualities with each of these pagan gods.

Greek and Egyptian philosophers divided the sun's journey through the year into four parts, each represented by a different figure. At the winter solstice, the Sun God appears as a newborn baby, having mysteriously escaped the forces of darkness trying to destroy him during winter's cold. Since the sun is weak at this time of year, it is shown with no golden rays, or hair, except for a single thin strand symbolizing the survival of light through winter's darkness. Because the sun's birth happens in Capricorn, it was often depicted as being nursed by a goat.

By the spring equinox, the Sun God becomes a beautiful youth with golden hair falling in curls over his shoulders, his light shining across all of creation, as Schiller described. During the summer solstice, the sun is shown as a strong, bearded man in the prime of life, representing the peak of nature's strength and fertility. By the autumn equinox, the sun appears as an old man with bent posture and white hair, slowly fading into the darkness of winter. These four stages mark the sun's twelve-month journey, during which it triumphantly passes through the twelve zodiac signs. In autumn, the sun enters the house of Virgo, symbolized by Delilah in the story of Samson, where its rays are cut and it loses its power. In Masonic symbolism, the harsh winter months are represented by three figures who try to destroy the God of Light and Truth.

The arrival of the sun was celebrated with joy, while its departure was a time of sorrow and mourning. This brilliant and radiant sun, the true light "which lighteth every man who cometh into the world," was seen as the ultimate benefactor, the one who brought life to everything, fed the hungry, calmed storms, and rose from death to restore life. This Supreme Spirit of love for humanity and generosity is recognized by Christianity as Christ, the Redeemer of worlds, the Only Begotten of the Father, the Word made Flesh, and the Hope of Glory.

The Birthday of The Sun

The pagans celebrated December 25th as the birth of the Solar Man. They rejoiced with feasts, processions, and offerings at temples. This marked the end of winter's darkness and the return of the sun's light to the Northern Hemisphere. It was believed that the old Sun God had destroyed the house of the Philistines (representing the forces of darkness) to make way for the new sun, born that day from the earth alongside symbolic creatures of the underworld.

An anonymous scholar from Balliol College, Oxford, explains in Mankind: Their Origin and Destiny that "The Romans also had a solar festival, celebrated with games in the circus, to honor the birth of the sun god. It took place eight days before the Kalends of January—December 25. Servius, in his commentary on the Æneid (Book 7, verse 720), mentions that the sun is considered 'new' on December 25. During the time of Leo I, some church leaders even stated that Christmas was made special less by the birth of Jesus and more by the return, or 'new birth,' of the sun." On the same day, the Romans celebrated the birth of the Invincible Sun (Natalis Solis Invicti), as shown in the Roman calendars from the reigns of Constantine and Julian. This title, 'Invictus,' was the same one the Persians gave to their god Mithra, whom they believed was born in a grotto. Christians later depicted Christ's birth in a stable in a similar way.

The same scholar also writes about the Catholic Feast of the Assumption and its link to astronomy. "Eight months after the sun god's birth, he moves into the eighth sign of the zodiac and absorbs the celestial Virgin into his light. She disappears in his glow and glory. This event, which occurs each year in mid-August, gave rise to a festival. In this festival, it is believed that the Virgin Mary leaves behind her earthly life to join her son in heaven. The ancient Roman calendar of Columella mentions the disappearance of the constellation Virgo around this time, stating that the sun enters Virgo thirteen days before the Kalends of September. The Catholic Church celebrates the Assumption, or the reunion of the Virgin with her Son, on this date. This feast was once called the 'Passage of the Virgin,' and ancient texts like the Library of the Fathers contain descriptions of it. The Greeks and Romans also marked the disappearance of Astraea, the Virgin goddess, on the same day."

This Virgin mother, who gives birth to the Sun God, reflects the ancient Egyptian goddess Isis. An inscription on the Temple of Sais honors Isis with the words, "The fruit I have brought forth is the sun." While early pagans connected the Virgin with the moon, they also understood her as a constellation. Most ancient cultures believed she was the mother of the sun, and although the moon couldn't hold this role, the sign of Virgo could. According to Albertus Magnus, "We know that the constellation of the Virgin rose on the horizon at the moment we mark as the birth of our Lord Jesus Christ."

Some Arabian and Persian astronomers called the three stars in Orion's belt the Magi, who traveled to honor the newborn Sun God. The same author from Mankind: Their Origin and Destiny adds: "At midnight, the constellation of the Stable and the Ass, located in Cancer, rises to the meridian. The ancients called this Præsepe Jovis. Meanwhile, the northern stars forming the Bear were known as Martha and Mary or the coffin of Lazarus." These examples show how much ancient pagan symbolism was carried into Christianity, even though the deeper meanings have been lost over time. The Christian Church continues to follow many of these ancient customs, often giving shallow explanations when asked about their origins, unaware that each religion builds on the secret teachings of the one that came before it.

The Three Suns

The ancient sages believed that, just like human nature, the sun could be divided into three different forms. Mystics taught that every solar system has three suns, which reflect the three main centers of life in a person. These are known as the three lights: the spiritual sun, the intellectual or soular sun, and the material sun. In Freemasonry, these are symbolized by three candles. The spiritual sun represents the power of God the Father, the soular sun carries the life of God the Son, and the material sun is the means through which God the Holy Spirit is revealed. Mystics also divided human nature into three parts: spirit, soul, and body. The physical body is sustained by the material sun, the spirit is enlightened by the spiritual sun, and the soul is redeemed through the true light of the soular sun. The alignment of these three suns in the sky was one explanation for why planetary orbits are elliptical instead of perfectly circular.

The pagan priests viewed the solar system as a Grand Man and compared its three main centers of energy to the human body's brain, heart, and reproductive system. In the story of Jesus' Transfiguration, there are three tabernacles: the largest in the center representing the heart, and smaller ones on either side representing the brain and the generative system. The idea of three suns may also be connected to a natural phenomenon that has been observed throughout history. In the fifty-first year after Christ, three suns were seen in the sky at once, and two suns appeared in both the sixty-sixth and sixty-ninth years. William Lilly recorded twenty similar sightings between 1156 and 1648.

Hermetists believed that, just as the physical sun is the greatest benefactor of the material world, there is also a spiritual sun that provides for the invisible and divine aspects of nature—both human and universal. Paracelsus, a great philosopher, wrote: "There is an earthly sun, which gives all heat, and anyone with sight can see it; even the blind can feel its warmth. There is also an Eternal Sun, the source of all wisdom. Those with awakened spiritual senses will see this sun and know it exists, but even those who have not yet reached spiritual awareness can still feel its power through their inner sense, called Intuition."

Some Rosicrucian scholars gave special names to the three forms of the sun. They called the spiritual sun Vulcan, the soular sun Christ, and the material sun Jehovah, the Demiurge of the Jews. In this context, Lucifer represents the intellectual mind without the guidance of the spiritual mind, making it the "false light." This false light is eventually overcome and transformed by the true light of the soul, referred to as the Second Logos or Christ. The secret process of turning the false, intellectual light into the enlightened mind of Christ is one of the core mysteries of alchemy, symbolized by the transformation of base metals into gold.

In The Secret Symbols of The Rosicrucians, Franz Hartmann describes the sun in alchemical terms as: "The symbol of Wisdom. The center of power, the heart of all things. The sun is a source of energy and a storehouse of power. Every living being contains within itself a center of life that can grow into a sun. In the heart of one who is spiritually reborn, divine power, awakened by the Light of the Logos, grows into a sun that illuminates the mind." In a note, Hartmann adds: "The physical sun is the reflection of the invisible spiritual sun. The spiritual sun is to the realm of Spirit what the physical sun is to the realm of Matter, but the material sun draws its power from the spiritual one."

Most ancient religions agreed that the physical sun was not a true source of power but acted as a reflector. The sun was sometimes shown as a shield carried by a Sun God, such as Frey, the solar deity of Scandinavia. This physical sun reflected the light of the invisible spiritual sun, which was the real source of life, light, and truth. The physical universe is receptive, meaning it displays the results of hidden causes that come from the spiritual realm. In this way, the spiritual world is the realm of causes, the material world is the realm of effects, and the intellectual or soul world serves as the bridge between the two. Christ, representing the higher intellect and soul, acts as "the Mediator," saying: "No man cometh to the Father, but by me."

Just as the sun is central to the solar system, the spirit is central to the human body. A person's organs and functions are like planets orbiting this inner sun, depending on its energy for life. The spiritual power within humans is divided into three parts, known as the threefold human spirit. All three are radiant and transcendent, and together they form the Divinity within man. The lower nature of man—his physical body, emotions, and mental faculties—reflects this inner Divinity and brings its light into the material world.

The three parts of man's lower nature are symbolized by an upright triangle, while his threefold spiritual nature is symbolized by an inverted triangle. When these two triangles come together to form a six-pointed star, they represent the unity of the spiritual and material worlds. This symbol, known as "the Star of David," "the Signet of Solomon," or "the Star of Zion," illustrates how humanity connects both Nature and Divinity.

A person's animal nature is connected to the earth, their divine nature to the heavens, and their human nature bridges the two as a mediator.

The Celestial Inhabitants of The Sun

The Rosicrucians and the Illuminati described angels, archangels, and other celestial beings as small suns, acting as centers of radiant energy surrounded by streamers of a powerful force called Vril. These streaming forces are the source of the common belief that angels have wings. Instead of physical wings, these beings have corona-like fans of light that allow them to move through the subtle, non-physical realms.

True mystics agree that angels and archangels are not shaped like humans, as they are often portrayed. Human forms would be useless in the ethereal worlds where these beings exist. Scientists have long debated whether other planets, such as Mars, Jupiter, Uranus, and Neptune, could support life. Many argue that creatures with human-like bodies could not survive in these environments. However, this view overlooks Nature's law that life always adapts to its surroundings. Ancient thinkers believed that life originated from the sun and that all living things absorb solar energy to grow and later release it as plants and animals. One idea suggested that the sun acts as a parent to the planets, with each planet connected to the sun by invisible cords that provide life and nourishment.

Some secret groups have taught that the sun is inhabited by beings whose bodies are made of radiant spiritual energy, similar to the glowing substance of the sun itself. These beings are not harmed by the sun's intense heat because their bodies are perfectly in tune with the sun's powerful vibrations. They resemble small suns, usually a bit larger than a dinner plate, though some more powerful beings are much larger. Their color matches the golden-white light of the sun, and they emit four long streamers of Vril energy that are always in motion. These beings also pulse or ripple, which causes the streamers to vibrate.

The most powerful and radiant of these beings is the Archangel Michael. All the beings that live on the sun and share his qualities are known today by Christians as "archangels" or "spirits of the light."

The Sun in Alchemical Symbology

Gold is connected to the sun and is often thought of as sunlight in solid form. When alchemical writings mention gold, they could be referring to either the physical metal or the sun, which is the source and spirit of gold. Sulfur, with its fiery nature, was also associated with the sun.

Since gold symbolized the spirit and base metals represented a person's lower nature, some alchemists were known as "miners." They were shown with tools like picks and shovels, digging through the earth in search of precious metals—symbolizing the search for noble qualities buried under materialism and ignorance. The diamond, hidden within black carbon, reflected this idea. The Illuminati used the image of a pearl inside an oyster, lying deep in the sea, to represent spiritual power. In this way, a seeker of truth became like a pearl diver, diving into the ocean of material illusion to find wisdom, which initiates called "the Pearl of Great Price."

When alchemists said that every living and non-living thing in the universe held the seeds of gold, they meant that even a grain of sand had a spiritual essence because gold represented the spirit within all things. A Rosicrucian saying explains this idea: "A seed is useless and powerless unless it is placed in its proper matrix." Franz Hartmann added to this idea, saying: "A soul cannot grow or evolve without the right kind of body, because the physical body provides the materials needed for development." (See In the Pronaos of the Temple of Wisdom.)

The goal of alchemy was not to create something from nothing but to nurture the seeds that were already present. Alchemical processes did not generate gold from scratch but instead helped the hidden seeds of gold to grow and thrive. Everything that exists has a spirit—a seed of the divine within it. Regeneration is not about placing something new where it did not exist before. Instead, it is about unfolding the divine essence already present in a person so that this inner divinity can shine like the sun and illuminate everyone it touches.

The Midnight Sun

Apuleius, describing his initiation, said: "At midnight I saw the sun shining with a splendid light." The idea of the midnight sun was part of the mysteries of alchemy. It symbolized the inner spirit within a person shining through the darkness of their physical body. It also referred to the spiritual sun in the solar system, which mystics could see just as clearly at midnight as at noon, as the material earth could not block the rays of this divine sun. Some believed that the mysterious lights illuminating the Egyptian temples during the night were reflections of the spiritual sun, gathered and projected by the magical abilities of the priests. The strange light seen ten miles underground by I-AM-THE-MAN in the Masonic allegory Etidorhpa (Aphrodite spelled backward) may also symbolize this mystical midnight sun from ancient rites.

Primitive ideas about the struggle between Good and Evil were often tied to the cycle of day and night. In the Middle Ages, black magic was practiced at night, and those who followed the Spirit of Evil were known as black magicians, while those who served the Spirit of Good were called white magicians. Black and white were linked to night and day, and many mythologies referred to the never-ending battle between light and darkness.

In Egyptian mythology, the demon Typhon was part crocodile and part hog, both animals known for their earthy, crude nature. From ancient times, living creatures have feared darkness, while only a few use it as cover for their activities—these animals were often linked with the Spirit of Evil. As a result, animals like cats, bats, toads, and owls became associated with witchcraft. In some parts of Europe, people still believe that black magicians take the form of wolves at night to roam and destroy, which led to the stories of werewolves.

Snakes, because they live underground, were also connected to the Spirit of Darkness. Since the conflict between Good and Evil revolves around the generative forces of Nature, winged serpents became symbols of the transformation of human instincts into higher, spiritual forces. The Egyptians often depicted the rays of the sun ending in human hands. Masons may find this symbolism connected to the "Paw of the Lion," a grip that symbolizes the power to raise things to life.

Solar Colors

The idea of three primary and four secondary colors is only a surface-level understanding. Since ancient times, it has been known that there are seven primary colors, not three. However, the human eye can only clearly recognize three of them. While green can be created by mixing blue and yellow, there is also a pure green that exists on its own and is not a mixture. This becomes clear when the light spectrum is broken apart using a prism. Helmholtz discovered that the secondary colors in the spectrum cannot be separated into primary colors. For example, when orange light passes through a second prism, it does not split into red and yellow; it stays orange.

Colors like blue, yellow, and red symbolize consciousness, intelligence, and force. These meanings are reflected in their therapeutic effects: blue is calming and has electrical properties, yellow is energizing and refining, and red creates heat and excitement. Minerals and plants also affect people according to their colors. For instance, yellow flowers tend to produce medicines that have effects similar to yellow light or the musical note "mi." An orange flower, associated with orange light, corresponds to musical tones like "re" or the chord of "do" and "mi."

The ancients connected the human spirit with the color blue, the mind with yellow, and the body with red. Heaven was seen as blue, the earth as yellow, and the underworld—or hell—as red. The fiery imagery of the underworld represents the nature of its intense, destructive energy. In the Greek Mysteries, red symbolized the irrational side of human nature, tied to uncontrolled passions and desires. In India, some gods—often forms of Vishnu—are shown with blue skin to represent their divine nature, beyond the physical world. In esoteric teachings, blue is considered the true, sacred color of the sun, while the sun's yellowish-orange appearance results from its rays passing through the material world, which distorts their original color.

In the early Christian Church, colors held deep symbolic meanings, and strict rules guided their use. However, since the Middle Ages, these meanings have been largely forgotten as people began to use colors carelessly. In their original symbolism, white or silver represented life, purity, joy, and light; red stood for Christ's suffering, the blood of saints, divine love, and warfare; blue symbolized the heavenly realm and spiritual contemplation; yellow or gold signified glory, fertility, and goodness; green reflected youth, growth, and prosperity; violet conveyed humility, deep love, and sorrow; and black represented death, destruction, and humiliation. Early church art even used the colors of clothing and decorations to show if a saint had been martyred and the nature of the work they did to earn sainthood.

Beyond the colors visible in the spectrum, there are many more wavelengths of color that humans cannot see—some are too low, while others are too high to register with the human eye. It is staggering to consider how little humanity understands about these hidden aspects of light and space. Just as people once explored unknown continents, in the future, they will explore these unseen realms of light, color, sound, and consciousness, using tools specifically designed for that purpose.

The Zodiac and Its Signs

It is difficult today to fully understand how deeply the study of the planets, stars, and constellations influenced the religions, philosophies, and sciences of ancient times. The Magi of Persia were called "Star Gazers" for good reason, and the Egyptians were highly regarded for their skill in calculating the movements and power of celestial bodies and how these influenced the destinies of both individuals and nations. Ancient astronomical observatories have been discovered all over the world, though modern archaeologists often do not understand the true purpose behind these structures. Although ancient astronomers did not have telescopes, they still made impressive calculations using instruments carved from granite or shaped from brass and copper. In India, similar instruments are still used today, showing a high level of accuracy. For example, the observatory in Jaipur, Rajputana, contains enormous stone sundials that remain functional. In Peking, China, there is a famous observatory with large bronze instruments, including a simple telescope made from a hollow tube without lenses.

The pagans believed the stars were living beings that could influence the fate of individuals, nations, and races. Even the early Jewish patriarchs thought that celestial bodies took part in human affairs. This belief is reflected in the Bible, such as in the Book of Judges: "They fought from heaven, even the stars in their courses fought against Sisera." The Chaldeans, Phoenicians, Egyptians, Persians, Hindus, and Chinese all had zodiacs with many similarities, and various experts credit each of these cultures with the origins of astrology and astronomy. The Central and North American Indians also developed their own understanding of the zodiac, although their signs and patterns differed in some ways from those used in the Eastern Hemisphere.

The word "zodiac" comes from the Greek word (zodiakos), meaning "a circle of animals," or, as some believe, "little animals." This name was given by ancient astronomers to a band of fixed stars about sixteen degrees wide that appeared to encircle the earth. Robert Hewitt Brown, a 32nd-degree Mason, explains that the Greek word "zodiakos" comes from zo-on, which means "an animal." He also points out that the word is derived from ancient Egyptian roots: zo, meaning "life," and on, meaning "a being."

The Greeks, and later other cultures influenced by them, divided this zodiacal band into twelve sections, each one sixteen degrees wide and thirty degrees long. These sections were called the Houses of the Zodiac. The sun, during its yearly journey, passed through each of these houses in turn. Star groups within these sections were imagined to form creatures, many of which were part animal. Because of this, these star groups became known as the Constellations or Signs of the Zodiac.

A common theory about the origin of these zodiac signs suggests that shepherds, watching their flocks at night, entertained themselves by imagining the shapes of animals and birds among the stars. However, this theory seems unlikely unless the "shepherds" were actually the priest-shepherds of ancient times. It is also doubtful that the signs of the zodiac came directly from the star groups they now represent. It is more likely that the animals connected to the twelve houses are symbolic of the different qualities and strengths of the sun as it moves through each part of the zodiac.

Richard Payne Knight writes on this subject: "The symbolic meanings given to certain animals were based on specific qualities that these animals represented. These meanings were not difficult to discover, as they came naturally from the mind's way of thinking. However, the star groups named after these animals do not actually resemble them. These animals were chosen as symbols to represent certain parts of the sky, which were probably dedicated to personified qualities that the animals symbolized." (The Symbolical Language of Ancient Art and Mythology.)

Some experts believe that the zodiac originally had ten houses, or "solar mansions," instead of twelve. In ancient times, two different systems were used to measure months, years, and seasons—one based on the sun and the other on the moon. The solar year was made up of ten months, each lasting thirty-six days, plus five extra days dedicated to the gods. The lunar year had thirteen months of twenty-eight days, with one day left over. During that time, the solar zodiac was thought to have ten houses, each covering thirty-six degrees.

The first six signs in the twelve-sign zodiac were seen as favorable because the sun traveled through them while passing over the Northern Hemisphere, bringing warmth and light. The Persians believed that these six signs symbolized the 6,000 years during which Ahura-Mazda ruled the universe in peace and harmony. The remaining six signs were considered unfavorable since the sun traveled through them while in the Southern Hemisphere, bringing winter to the Greeks, Egyptians, and Persians. These six signs represented the 6,000 years of suffering and hardship caused by the Persian evil spirit, Ahriman, who tried to overthrow Ahura-Mazda.

Those who believe the zodiac originally had ten signs suggest that Libra (the Scales) was added later. They argue that Virgo and Scorpio were once a single sign that was divided to create Libra, establishing "the balance" between the northern and southern signs. (See The Rosicrucians, Their Rites and Mysteries by Hargrave Jennings.) On this subject, Isaac Myer wrote: "We think that the zodiacal constellations were originally ten, representing a great androgynous being or deity. Later, they were changed, splitting into Virgo and Scorpio, making eleven signs. From Scorpio, Libra—the Balance—was created, completing the current twelve-sign zodiac." (The Qabbalah.)

Each year, the sun completes a journey through the zodiac and returns to the same spot where it started at the spring equinox. However, the sun falls slightly behind its previous position every year. Each zodiac sign covers thirty degrees, and since the sun loses about one degree every seventy-two years, it takes around 2,160 years to move backward through one full sign. This gradual shift through all twelve signs of the zodiac takes about 25,920 years to complete, although experts sometimes disagree on the exact numbers. This backward motion is known as the precession of the equinoxes. In this long cycle, called the Great Solar or Platonic Year, each constellation takes its turn occupying the position of the spring equinox for roughly 2,160 years before giving way to the previous sign.

Throughout history, people have symbolized the sun using the constellation it occupied during the spring equinox. For nearly 2,000 years, the sun has crossed the equator in the sign of Pisces (the Two Fishes) at the spring equinox. Before that, for about 2,160 years, it crossed in Aries (the Ram). Even earlier, the equinox was in Taurus (the Bull). The bull likely became associated with this constellation because ancient people used bulls to plow their fields, and this activity took place during the time when the sun entered Taurus.

Albert Pike describes how the Persians revered Taurus and used astrological symbols to reflect this respect: "In Zoroaster's cave of initiation, the Sun and Planets were depicted above, made from gems and gold, along with the zodiac. The Sun was shown rising from behind the Bull." In the constellation Taurus, there is also a star cluster known as the "Seven Sisters," or the Pleiades, which Freemasons refer to as the Seven Stars found at the top of the Sacred Ladder.

In ancient Egypt, during the period when the spring equinox was in Taurus, the Bull Apis was considered sacred to the Sun God. The Egyptians worshiped the Sun God through the bull, believing that the god's presence filled this constellation when the sun crossed into the Northern Hemisphere. This belief gave rise to the saying that the celestial Bull "broke the egg of the year with his horns."

Sampson Arnold Mackey, in his book Mythological Astronomy of the Ancients Demonstrated, makes two interesting observations about the bull in Egyptian symbolism. Mackey suggests that the movement of the earth, known as the shifting of the poles, has changed the positions of the equator and the zodiac. He believes that, originally, the zodiac was aligned at right angles to the equator, with the sign of Cancer positioned at the north pole and Capricorn at the south pole. Mackey thinks the Orphic symbol of the serpent coiled around the egg represents the motion of the sun under these conditions. He uses examples such as the Labyrinth of Crete, the word "Abraxas," and the magic formula "abracadabra" to support his theory. About "abracadabra," Mackey writes:

"But the gradual disappearance of the Bull is cleverly remembered in the vanishing series of letters, perfectly representing an important astronomical event. For ABRACADABRA means 'The Bull, the only Bull.' When broken down, the phrase reads: Ab'r-achad-ab'ra—'Ab'r,' meaning 'the Bull,' and 'achad,' meaning 'the only.' Achad is also a name for the Sun, given to it because it shines alone—it is the only star visible when it appears. The remaining 'ab'ra' completes the phrase: 'The Bull, the only Bull.' The way the letters are repeated, with one removed at each step until none remain, is a simple yet effective way of preserving the memory of this fact. The name of Sorapis, or Serapis, given to the Bull in this ritual confirms it beyond doubt. The word 'abracadabra' disappears in eleven decreasing stages, just like in the figure. Remarkably, a serpent with eleven coils wraps around a three-headed figure, placed beside Sorapis. The eleven coils form a triangle similar to the one created by the eleven diminishing lines of the word abracadabra."

Nearly every religion shows traces of astrology. The Old Testament, shaped by Egyptian culture, contains many astrological and astronomical symbols. Most of Greek and Roman mythology can be linked to groups of stars. Some scholars believe the original twenty-two letters of the Hebrew alphabet were inspired by star patterns, with stars forming consonants and planets or celestial lights serving as vowels. These combinations spelled out words, which, if read correctly, revealed future events.

The zodiac marks the path of the sun through the constellations, creating the changes in the seasons. Ancient calendars were based on the equinoxes and solstices, with the year starting at the spring equinox on March 21, when the sun crosses the equator going north. The summer solstice, marking the sun's most northerly point, was celebrated on June 21. After that, the sun began moving back toward the equator, crossing it again at the autumn equinox on September 21. The sun reached its southernmost point on December 21, the winter solstice.

Four zodiac signs are permanently associated with the equinoxes and solstices. Although the signs no longer align perfectly with their original constellations, modern astronomers still use them for calculations. The spring equinox is linked with Aries (the Ram), a fitting choice, as the Ram leads the zodiac. Long before Christianity, pagans revered this constellation. Godfrey Higgins writes: "This constellation was called the 'Lamb of God.' It was also known as the 'Savior' and believed to save humanity from sin. It was honored with the title 'Dominus,' or 'Lord,' and was called the 'Lamb of God which taketh away the sins of the world.' Devotees would repeat the words in prayer: 'O Lamb of God, that taketh away the sin of the world, have mercy upon us. Grant us Thy peace.'" The Lamb of God refers to the sun, which is said to be reborn each year in the Northern Hemisphere when it enters Aries, though due to a shift in the zodiac, the sun now rises in Pisces.

The summer solstice is connected with Cancer (the Crab), which the Egyptians symbolized with the scarab beetle. This beetle was sacred in Egypt and represented eternal life. The crab fits the symbolism because, after passing through Cancer, the sun appears to move backward, retracing its path along the zodiac. Cancer also represents creation and birth, as it is ruled by the moon, the Mother of all life and the protector of nature's life forces. Diana, the Greek moon goddess, was known as the Mother of the World. Regarding the worship of feminine or maternal principles, Richard Payne Knight writes:

"By attracting and lifting the ocean's waters, the moon naturally seemed to rule over moisture. It was also believed to have a powerful effect on women's bodies, making it appear to govern nutrition and passive reproduction. Because of this, the moon was said to have received her nymphs—her helpers or symbolic forms—from the ocean. The moon was often symbolized by the sea crab, an animal that can shed injured limbs and regrow them. This regeneration connects the crab to the idea of life cycles, making it a fitting symbol for the maternal principle of Nature. For pagans, this maternal force was recognized as the origin of all life, and the moon became its natural home.

The autumn equinox takes place in the constellation of Libra (the Scales). At this point, the scales tip, and the sun begins its journey into winter. Libra was placed in the zodiac to represent the power of choice, allowing humans to weigh one option against another. Long ago, when the human race was still developing, people were like angels who did not know good or evil. They became aware of good and evil when the gods planted the seeds of mental awareness in them. Through their experiences, humans developed knowledge that not only restored them to their former state but also gave them unique individual intelligence. Paracelsus explained: 'The body comes from the elements, the soul from the stars, and the spirit from God. All that the mind understands comes from the stars—not the physical stars but the spiritual beings behind them.'

The winter solstice occurs in Capricorn, known as the House of Death. In winter, life in the Northern Hemisphere reaches its lowest point. Capricorn is depicted as a creature with the upper body of a goat and the tail of a fish. During this time, the sun's power is weakest, but after passing through Capricorn, the sun begins to grow stronger. In Greek mythology, it was said that Jupiter, the Sun God, was nursed by a goat. John Cole offers a different interpretation of Capricorn in A Treatise on the Circular Zodiac of Tentyra, in Egypt: 'The Goat rising from the fish symbolizes the rise of Babylon's towering buildings from the marshes. The two horns of the Goat represent the two cities, Nineveh and Babylon—one on the Tigris River and the other on the Euphrates—but both ruled by a single power.'

It takes about 2,160 years for the sun to move backward through one zodiac sign, a period known as an age. These ages are named after the sign the sun passes through at the spring equinox each year. This is why we refer to the Taurian Age, the Aryan Age, the Piscean Age, and the Aquarian Age. During each of these ages, religious worship reflects the qualities of the zodiac sign associated with it. The sun is believed to take on the personality of each sign, just as a spirit takes on a body. These twelve signs are like the jewels in the sun's breastplate, with its light shining through each one in turn.

This system helps explain why certain religious symbols appear during specific times in history. For example, during the Taurian Age, the sun was connected to Apis, the sacred bull, and the Bull became a symbol of Osiris. (For more details about how astrological ages relate to the Bible, see The Message of the Stars by Max and Augusta Foss Heindel.) During the Aryan Age, the Lamb became sacred, and priests were called shepherds. At this time, sheep and goats were sacrificed, and a scapegoat was chosen to carry away the sins of Israel.

In the Piscean Age, the Fish became the symbol of divinity. The Sun God is said to have fed the masses with two fish. In the frontispiece of Ancient Faiths by Inman, the goddess Isis is shown with a fish on her head. The Indian god Krishna, in one of his incarnations, was thrown from the mouth of a fish. Jesus is also called the Fisher of Men. John P. Lundy explains: 'The word Fish is an abbreviation for the full title, Jesus Christ, Son of God, Savior, and Cross. As St. Augustine said, "If you join together the first letters of the five Greek words,   (Jesus Christ, Son of God, Savior), they spell   , which means Fish. In this word, Christ is symbolized because He was able to live in the depths of this world without sin."' (Monumental Christianity). Many Christians honor Friday, a day sacred to the Virgin (Venus), by eating fish instead of meat. The fish was one of the earliest symbols of Christianity, and when drawn in the sand, it served as a secret sign that identified one Christian to another.

Aquarius is known as the Sign of the Water Bearer, symbolized by the man carrying a jug of water mentioned in the New Testament. This figure is sometimes shown as an angelic being, thought to be androgynous, either pouring water from a vessel or carrying it on the shoulder. In some Eastern traditions, the water vessel alone is used as the symbol. Edward Upham, in History and Doctrine of Buddhism, describes Aquarius as a pot with a color between blue and yellow, calling it 'the single house of Saturn.'

When the planet Uranus was discovered by Herschel, the second half of Aquarius was assigned to it. The water flowing from Aquarius's urn is often called 'the waters of eternal life.' Like all zodiac signs, Aquarius represents one of the ways the sun shapes human worship of the divine."

There are two main systems of astrological philosophy. One is the Ptolemaic system, which is geocentric. In this view, the earth is considered the center of the solar system, with the sun, moon, and planets revolving around it. Though astronomically incorrect, the geocentric model has proven reliable when applied to the material nature of earthly things over thousands of years. A close study of the works of great occultists and their diagrams shows that many of them were familiar with another way of organizing the heavenly bodies.

The second system is called the heliocentric model, which places the sun at the center of the solar system, with the planets and their moons orbiting around it. However, since this system is relatively new, there hasn't yet been enough time to fully study or catalog how its aspects affect people and events. Geocentric astrology focuses on earthly concerns, while heliocentric astrology aims to understand higher intellectual and spiritual aspects of life.

An important detail to remember is that when ancient astrologers said the sun was in a particular zodiac sign, they meant that the sun was casting its light into that sign from the opposite one. For example, when the sun is said to be in Taurus, it is actually in the opposite sign, Scorpio, sending its rays toward Taurus. This difference led to two branches of philosophy: the geocentric, which is outward and material, and the heliocentric, which is inward and spiritual. While ordinary people worshipped the outward reflection of the sun in Taurus (symbolized by the Bull), the wise revered the sun's true position in Scorpio, represented by the Scorpion or the Serpent, symbols of hidden spiritual knowledge.

Scorpio has three symbols. The most common is the Scorpion, which the ancients called the "backbiter," symbolizing deceit and perversion. Another symbol is the Serpent, which represents wisdom. The rarest symbol is the Eagle, which reflects Scorpio's highest spiritual nature. While the stars in the Scorpio constellation resemble both a bird and a scorpion, the Eagle—known as the king of birds—symbolizes the highest potential of Scorpio, rising above the earthly nature of the scorpion. Since Taurus and Scorpio are opposite signs, their symbols are often connected. As E. M. Plunket explains in Ancient Calendars and Constellations: "The Scorpion (Scorpio) joins Mithras in his battle with the Bull, and the spirits of the spring and autumn equinoxes are always present in both joyful and sorrowful forms."

The Egyptians, Assyrians, and Babylonians, who viewed the sun as a Bull, saw the zodiac as a series of furrows plowed by a celestial Ox dragging the sun behind it. This connection explains why people offered sacrifices of bulls and paraded decorated oxen through the streets, accompanied by temple priests, musicians, and dancers. However, the wisest among them, who wore the Serpent symbol of Scorpio (the Uræus) on their foreheads, did not participate in these rituals, seeing them as more appropriate for the general population.

The sun is often shown with its rays forming a shaggy mane, connecting it to the lion. Robert Hewitt Brown, a 32nd-degree Mason, explains the link between the constellation Leo and the summer solstice: "On June 21, when the sun reaches the summer solstice, the constellation Leo, only 30 degrees ahead, seems to lead the way, helping lift the sun to the top of the zodiac's arc. This connection between Leo and the sun's return to power explains why the ancients revered this constellation. Astrologers called Leo the 'sole house of the sun,' and taught that the world was created when the sun was in this sign. Both the Egyptians and Mexicans worshipped the lion. The chief Druid of Britain even held the title of Lion." (Stellar Theology and Masonic Astronomy.)

When the Aquarian Age fully begins, the sun will be in Leo, according to the distinction between geocentric and heliocentric astrology. At that time, secret spiritual traditions will once again include initiation rites known as the "Grip of the Lion's Paw," which symbolizes raising the soul to a higher state. (This will be like the story of Lazarus rising from the dead.)

The age of the zodiac is highly debated. It is a major mistake to say that it originated only a few thousand years before the Christian Era. The zodiac must be old enough to date back to a time when the signs and symbols perfectly matched the positions of the constellations, which reflected the sun's activity throughout each of the twelve months. One author, after years of study, believed the idea of the zodiac to be at least five million years old. It is likely that the knowledge of the zodiac came from ancient civilizations like Atlantis or Lemuria. About ten thousand years before the Christian Era, a destructive period began when knowledge was suppressed, and many records, monuments, and artifacts were destroyed. Only a few relics, such as copper knives, arrowheads, and cave carvings, remain as silent proof of those lost civilizations. Some massive structures, like the mysterious monoliths on Easter Island, also serve as evidence of lost knowledge, arts, and people. Humanity is incredibly old. Modern science measures human history in tens of thousands of years, but occult teachings believe it spans millions. There is an old saying that "Mother Earth has shaken many civilizations from her back," and it is reasonable to believe that astrology and astronomy may have existed millions of years before the first white man appeared.

The ancient occultists had a profound understanding of evolution. They saw all life as existing in different stages of growth. They believed that grains of sand were evolving into human consciousness (though not in physical form), that humans were becoming planets, that planets were becoming solar systems, and that solar systems were becoming cosmic chains. Each step in this process continued endlessly. At one stage between the formation of a solar system and a cosmic chain, the solar system transforms into a zodiac. The zodiac's houses, in turn, became the thrones of twelve celestial rulers, or in some cases, ten divine orders. Pythagoras taught that the number ten, which forms the basis of the decimal system, was the most perfect number. He symbolized it with the lesser tetractys—an arrangement of ten dots forming an upright triangle.

The early astronomers divided the zodiac into twelve houses and chose the three brightest stars in each constellation to serve as rulers of each house. They further divided each house into three sections, each containing ten degrees, which were called decans. Each decan was split in half, creating seventy-two smaller sections, each covering five degrees. The Hebrews assigned a celestial spirit or angel to each of these sections, and this system led to the Qabbalistic tradition of seventy-two sacred names. These names correspond to the seventy-two decorations—such as flowers, knobs, and almonds—on the seven-branched candlestick of the Tabernacle, and to the seventy-two representatives chosen from the Twelve Tribes of Israel.

The only two zodiac signs not mentioned earlier are Gemini and Sagittarius. Gemini is usually represented by two children, who, according to ancient myths, hatched from eggs—perhaps the same eggs that the Bull broke with its horns. The myths of Castor and Pollux, along with

Romulus and Remus, may have evolved from the stories of these celestial twins. The symbol of Gemini has changed over time. The Arabians once used a peacock as its symbol. Two bright stars in the constellation of Gemini still bear the names Castor and Pollux. Gemini was also associated with phallic worship, and the two pillars or obelisks found in front of temples and churches carry the same symbolism as the twins.

Sagittarius is symbolized by a centaur—a creature with the body of a horse and the upper body of a human. The centaur is typically shown holding a bow and arrow, aiming into the stars. Sagittarius represents two ideas. First, it symbolizes the spiritual development of humanity, as the human form rises from the animal body. Second, it represents ambition and aspiration, since the centaur aims its arrow high into the sky, just as humans aim for higher goals beyond their current reach.

Albert Churchward, in The Signs and Symbols of Primordial Man, explains the importance of the zodiac in religious symbolism: "The division here [is] into twelve parts—the twelve signs of the zodiac, the twelve tribes of Israel, the twelve gates of heaven mentioned in Revelation, and the twelve portals in the Great Pyramid that must be passed through to reach the highest degree. Likewise, there are twelve Apostles in Christianity and twelve original and perfect points in Masonry."

The ancients believed that the idea of man being made in God's image should be taken literally. They thought of the universe as a vast organism similar to the human body, with every part of the cosmic structure reflected in humanity. One of the most valuable lessons given to new initiates was the "law of analogy," which taught that everything in the universe mirrors aspects of human nature. Because of this belief, studying the stars was considered sacred, as the movements of the celestial bodies were seen as the active presence of the Infinite Father.

The Pythagoreans were often unfairly criticized for spreading the idea of metempsychosis, the transmigration of souls. However, the version shared with the general public was meant to hide a deeper truth. Greek mystics believed that the spiritual part of a person came into material life from the Milky Way, which they called the "seed ground of souls." This descent happened through one of the twelve gates of the zodiac. Each soul was thought to take on the qualities of the zodiac sign it entered through. For example, a soul that entered through Aries was described as being born into the nature of a ram, while one that came through Taurus would carry the qualities of the celestial bull. In this way, all human souls were symbolized by the twelve creatures of the zodiac, each representing the traits needed to incarnate in the physical world.

This belief in transmigration didn't apply to the physical body but to the immaterial spirit that journeys among the stars, evolving by taking on the forms of the sacred zodiac animals over time.

In the Third Book of the Mathesis by Julius Firmicus Maternus, we find an account of how the heavenly bodies were aligned at the beginning of the material universe: "According to Æsculapius and Anubius—who received the secrets of astrology from the god Mercury—the cosmic arrangement at the moment of creation was as follows: The Sun was placed in the 15th degree of Leo, the Moon in the 15th degree of Cancer, Saturn in the 15th degree of Capricorn, Jupiter in the 15th degree of Sagittarius, Mars in the 15th degree of Scorpio, Venus in the 15th degree of Libra, Mercury in the 15th degree of Virgo, and the Horoscope was positioned in the 15th degree of Cancer. Based on this arrangement, they believed that human destinies were aligned with these original positions, as detailed in the book by Æsculapius called (which means 'Ten Thousand Births' or 'Countless Births'). According to this book, nothing in the destinies of individuals can conflict with the original structure of the universe."

The seven stages of human life are each guided by one of the planets. Infancy is ruled by the moon, childhood by Mercury, adolescence by Venus, maturity by the sun, middle age by Mars, old age by Jupiter, and the final stage of life—decrepitude and death—is governed by Saturn.

The Bembine Table of Isis

A manuscript by Thomas Taylor includes this interesting statement: "Plato was initiated into the 'Greater Mysteries' when he was 49 years old. His initiation happened in one of the underground chambers of the Great Pyramid in Egypt. The ISIAC TABLE served as the altar where the wise Plato stood, receiving knowledge that was always within him, but the Mysteries awakened and brought it to life. After three days in the Great Hall, Plato met the Pyramid's Hierophant, a figure only seen by those who completed the three days, three levels, and three dimensions. The Hierophant gave Plato the highest spiritual teachings, each with its own special symbol. After staying three more months in the halls of the Pyramid, Plato was sent into the world to serve the Great Order, following in the footsteps of Pythagoras and Orpheus."

Before Rome was looted in 1527, no records mentioned the Mensa Isiaca (or Tablet of Isis). At that time, a locksmith or metalworker came into possession of the Tablet and sold it at a high price to Cardinal Bembo, a famous historian and antiquarian of the Republic of Venice, who later became the librarian of St. Mark's. After Bembo's death in 1547, the Tablet ended up with the House of Mantua, where it stayed in their museum until 1630, when soldiers under Ferdinand II captured the city. Many believed the soldiers destroyed the Tablet to collect the silver it contained, but this assumption was wrong. The Tablet was taken by Cardinal Pava, who gave it to the Duke of Savoy, who later presented it to the King of Sardinia. When France conquered Italy in 1797, the Tablet was moved to Paris. In 1809, Alexandre Lenoir mentioned it in his writings, saying it was on display at the Bibliothèque Nationale. After peace was restored, the Tablet was returned to Italy. Karl Baedeker, in his Guide to Northern Italy, noted that the Tablet was placed in the middle of Gallery 2 in the Museum of Antiquities in Turin.

In 1559, Æneas Vicus of Parma made a precise replica of the original Tablet, and the Chancellor of the Duke of Bavaria gifted one of these copies to the Museum of Hieroglyphics. Athanasius Kircher described the Tablet as "five palms long and four wide." W. Wynn Westcott stated its dimensions as 50 by 30 inches. The Tablet was made of bronze, decorated with enamel and silver inlays. Fosbroke adds: "The figures are engraved shallowly, and silver threads outline most of them. The bases where the figures sit or recline, which are left blank in prints, were originally made of silver and later torn away" (see Encyclopædia of Antiquities).

Those who know the basics of Hermetic philosophy will recognize the Mensa Isiaca as a key to Chaldean, Egyptian, and Greek theology. Father Montfaucon, a knowledgeable Benedictine, admitted that he could not fully understand the Tablet's symbols. He even doubted the symbols had any real meaning and criticized Kircher for making things more confusing than the Tablet itself. Laurentius Pignorius published an essay in 1605 with a reproduction of the Tablet, but his cautious explanations showed he didn't truly grasp the meaning behind the symbols.

In 1654, Kircher tackled the mystery in his Œdipus Ægyptiacus. After years of research into ancient secret teachings, and with help from other scholars, he made significant progress in understanding the Tablet. However, the ultimate secret still eluded him, as noted by Eliphas Levi in his History of Magic. Levi wrote: "The learned Jesuit guessed that the Tablet contained the key to sacred alphabets, but he couldn't fully explain it. The Tablet is divided into three parts: at the top are the twelve houses of heaven, at the bottom are the different types of work done throughout the year, and in the middle are twenty-one sacred signs representing letters of the alphabet. At the center is a seated figure of the pantomorphic IYNX, a symbol of universal existence, similar to the Hebrew letter Yod, which all other letters evolved from. Surrounding the IYNX is the Ophite triad, matching the Three Mother Letters in Egyptian and Hebrew alphabets. To the right are the Ibimorphic and Serapian triads; to the left are the Nepthys and Hecate triads, which represent opposites such as action and rest, solid and changeable, fire that gives life, and water that creates growth. When these triads join with the center, they form groups of seven. A group of seven also lies at the center. These three groups of seven represent the complete structure of the three worlds and the original alphabet's letters, with one extra sign added, like a zero following the digits one through nine."

Levi's suggestion seems to imply that the twenty-one figures in the center of the Tablet represent the twenty-one major cards, or trumps, of the Tarot deck. If that's true, then perhaps the controversial zero card symbolizes the crown of the Supreme Mind. This crown might be shown by the hidden triad at the top of the throne in the middle of the Tablet. The first creation from this Supreme Mind could be represented by a magician or juggler, with symbols of the four lower worlds arranged on a table before him: a rod, a sword, a cup, and a coin. In this interpretation, the zero card stands apart from the others—it serves as the fourth-dimensional source from which all the other cards emerge and into which they ultimately combine. The circle or cipher on the card would support this idea since it symbolizes the higher realm that gives rise to the lower worlds, powers, and letters.

In 1887, Westcott gathered the few theories available from various scholars and published a rare book that gives the only detailed English description of the Isiac Tablet. This was the first proper English description since Humphreys translated Montfaucon's poor interpretation in 1721. While explaining why he avoided sharing what Levi seemed to believe should remain hidden, Westcott summarized his understanding of the Tablet: "Levi's diagram, which explains the Tablet's mystery, divides the Upper Region into the four seasons, each connected to three Zodiac signs. He also included the four-letter sacred name, the Tetragrammaton, linking Jod with Aquarius (also known as Canopus), He with Taurus (or Apis), Vau with Leo (or Momphta), and the final He with Typhon. This matches the Cherubic symbols: Man, Bull, Lion, and Eagle. The fourth symbol is either a Scorpion or an Eagle, depending on whether it represents good or bad intentions. In the Demotic Zodiac, a Snake takes the place of the Scorpion.

"In the Lower Region, he links the twelve simple Hebrew letters with the four parts of the horizon. See Sepher Yetzirah, chapter 5, section 1.

"The Central Region belongs to the powers of the Sun and the planets. In the middle, we see the Sun labeled as Ops, and below it lies a Solomon's Seal, positioned above a cross. This Seal is made of two overlapping triangles—one light and one dark—forming a complex symbol for Venus. Around the upright dark triangle, representing Fire, he placed the three dark planets: Venus, Mercury, and Mars. Around the inverted light triangle, representing Water, he placed the three light planets: Saturn, Luna, and Jupiter. Water, in turn, symbolizes female power, the passive principle, and figures like Binah and the Sephirotic Mother and Bride in the Kabbalah (see Mathers' The Kabbalah). Ancient planetary symbols contain a cross, a solar disc, and a crescent: Venus's symbol is a cross beneath a Sun disc; Mercury's is a disc with a crescent above and a cross below; Saturn's is a cross with its base touching the crescent's peak; and Jupiter's is a crescent connected to the left side of a cross. Each of these symbols holds deep meaning. Levi's original plate switched Serapis and Hecate but left Apis noir and Apis blanc unchanged—possibly because he associated Bes's head with Hecate.

"Having placed the twelve simple letters in the lower section, the seven double letters must align with the planetary region in the center. The great triad—A.M.S.—the three mother letters representing Air, Water, and Fire, surround the central Iynx or Yod. These are also connected to the Ophionian Triad: two Serpents and the Lion-like Sphinx. Levi's use of 'Ops' at the center refers to both the Roman goddess Ops, the spirit of the Earth, and the Greek figure Rhea or Cybele, often depicted as a goddess riding in a lion-drawn chariot. Cybele is crowned with towers and holds a key." (See The Isiac Tablet.)

In 1809, Alexandre Lenoir published an essay in French about the Tablet. While the essay is creative and original, it adds little useful information. Lenoir argued that the Tablet was either an Egyptian calendar or an astrological chart. Most writers since 1651, including Montfaucon and Lenoir, either relied heavily on Kircher's work or were strongly influenced by him. A full translation of Kircher's original article—eighty pages of 17th-century Latin—has been made for this book. The double-page illustration at the beginning of this chapter is an exact reproduction of Kircher's engraving from the Museum of Hieroglyphics. The small letters and numbers on the figures were added by Kircher to help explain his commentary and will also be used here for clarity.

Like many ancient religious and philosophical artifacts, the Bembine Table of Isis has sparked much debate. In a footnote, A. E. Waite, unable to distinguish between the true nature and the supposed origin of the Tablet, echoed J.G. Wilkinson's views. Wilkinson, another respected scholar, claimed: "The original [Table] is extremely late and can roughly be called a forgery." On the other hand, Eduard Winkelmann, a scholar of great depth, defended the Tablet's authenticity and age. A careful study of the Mensa Isiaca reveals one key fact: even if the person who made the Tablet wasn't Egyptian, they were a highly advanced initiate with deep knowledge of Hermetic philosophy."

Symbolism of The Bembine Table

This short explanation of the Bembine Table comes from Kircher's writings, with some added information from the Chaldean, Hebrew, Egyptian, and Greek mystical texts. The design of Egyptian temples was highly symbolic, with each room's layout, decorations, and tools holding deeper meanings, as seen in the hieroglyphics covering them. Next to the altar, which was usually in the center of each room, there was a pool filled with Nile water, which flowed in and out through hidden pipes. The temples also contained images of gods arranged in connected groups, along with magical inscriptions. These temples used symbols and hieroglyphics to teach new students the sacred knowledge of the priestly class.

The Tablet of Isis began as a table or altar, with symbols that priests used to teach secret knowledge. Different gods and goddesses had their own dedicated tables. The materials used for these tables varied depending on the importance of the deity. Tables for Jupiter and Apollo were made of gold, while those for Diana, Venus, and Juno were of silver. Other superior gods had marble tables, while lesser deities had tables made of wood. Tables were also crafted from metals linked to the planets associated with these gods. Just as a banquet table holds food for the body, these sacred altars held symbols that nourish a person's spiritual nature.

Kircher introduces the Tablet by saying: "It reveals the structure of the threefold world—archetypal, intellectual, and physical. The Supreme God is shown expanding from the center to the edge of a universe made of both living and non-living things, all energized by a single divine force called the Father Mind, represented by a three-part symbol. The Tablet also presents three groups of three from the Supreme One, each showing an aspect of the original three-part divinity. These groups are called the foundation of everything. The Tablet explains how divine beings assist the Father Mind in governing the universe. In the upper panel, we see the rulers of the worlds, with their fiery, airy, and physical symbols. In the lower panel, we find the Fathers of Fountains, who maintain the natural principles and laws. There are also gods of the celestial spheres and wandering spirits, shown as male and female figures facing their superior god."

The Mensa Isiaca is divided into three horizontal sections or panels, which may represent the layout of rooms where the Isiac Mysteries were taught. The middle panel is split into seven smaller sections, and the bottom panel has two gates, one on each side. The entire Tablet has forty-five important figures and many smaller symbols. These forty-five figures are arranged into fifteen groups of three, with four groups in the upper panel, seven in the middle, and four in the lower section.

Kircher describes these groups: "The figures differ in eight important ways: by their shape, position, gestures, actions, clothing, headwear, staffs, and the symbols around them—whether flowers, plants, letters, or animals." These eight ways of representing the figures' hidden powers are reminders of the eight spiritual senses that can help people understand their higher selves. Buddhists express this idea with a wheel that has eight spokes and follow the noble eightfold path to raise their consciousness. The decorative border around the three main panels is filled with symbols, including birds, animals, reptiles, humans, and mixed creatures. Some interpretations suggest this border represents the four elements, with the creatures symbolizing elemental beings. Others see the border as representing the archetypal realms, showing patterns of forms that later appear in the material world. The four flowers in the corners of the Tablet are sacred symbols because they always turn toward the sun, representing the part of human nature that seeks its Creator.

According to the Chaldeans' secret teachings, the universe is divided into four levels: archetypal, intellectual, sidereal, and elemental. Each level influences and reflects the others, with higher levels guiding lower ones, and lower levels responding to the higher. The archetypal level corresponds to the intellect of the Divine Trinity. In this eternal and spiritual realm, all lower forms of life—everything that exists, has existed, or will exist—are contained as original patterns or divine ideas. These archetypes are shown in the Tablet as a series of hidden symbols.

In the center section of the Table is the Spiritual Essence—a being that contains all forms and serves as the source of everything. From this essence come nine groups of energies, each forming a triad: the Ophionic, Ibimorphous, and Nephtæan Triads. This idea is like the Qabbalistic concept of the Sephiroth, where nine spheres emerge from Kether, the Crown. The twelve cosmic rulers—the Mendesian, Ammonian, Momphtæan, and Omphtæan Triads—are responsible for spreading creative forces and are shown in the upper section of the Table. These rulers act according to divine patterns formed in the highest sphere, where the archetypes reside. Archetypes are abstract forms in the Divine Mind that guide the actions of all lower beings.

In the lower part of the Table are the Father Fountains—four triads called the Horæan, Pandochæan, Thaustic, and Æluristic. These beings guard the great gates of the universe, ensuring that the influences from the higher rulers flow properly into the lower worlds. Egyptian teachings emphasize that goodness is the foundation of everything, present to some degree in all things. Everything strives for goodness because it is the source of all causes. Goodness spreads itself naturally, existing in all things, since nothing can give what it does not have. The Table shows that God exists within everything and that everything exists within God; it suggests that all parts are connected, and each reflects the whole. In the intellectual world, there are spiritual versions of everything found in the physical world, so the lowest things reflect the highest, and physical forms reveal spiritual truths. For this reason, Egyptians made images of material things to symbolize higher, invisible powers. They assigned the qualities of eternal gods to these material images to show that the physical world is just a reflection of divine reality. Everything in the hidden, spiritual realm becomes visible through nature.

The Archetypal and Creative Mind first expresses itself through the Paternal Foundation, and then through secondary gods called Intelligences. It spreads its power from the highest realms to the lowest in a continuous flow. Egyptians used the symbol of sperm to represent the spiritual spheres because each contains all the life that comes from it. Both the Chaldeans and Egyptians believed that every effect remains connected to its cause and constantly seeks to return to it, just as a lotus flower turns toward the sun. Through the Paternal Foundation, the Supreme Intellect created light first—the angelic world. From that light came the stars, and from the stars came the four elements and the physical world. In this way, everything exists within everything else, according to its nature. Physical elements are connected to the stars, just as the stars are connected to angels, and angels to God. Therefore, everything exists within the divine world, the angelic world, and the physical world all at once. Just as a seed contains a tree waiting to grow, the universe is God unfolding into physical form.

Proclus explains: "Every divine quality flows into all of creation and shares itself with all lower beings." One way the Supreme Mind expresses itself is through the power of reproduction, which it grants to all living things. Each being—whether a soul, a heavenly body, a plant, or a stone—reproduces according to its type, but all depend on the one creative power in the Supreme Mind. This life-giving force takes different forms depending on what it flows through. In minerals, it becomes physical existence; in plants, it creates life; and in animals, it produces awareness. It gives motion to the stars, thought to humans, intelligence to angels, and essence to God. All forms share the same substance, and all life draws from the same energy, existing together within the Supreme One.

Plato first introduced these ideas, and his student Aristotle explained them this way: "We believe this physical world is a reflection of another, greater world. If this world is alive, then the higher one must be even more alive. Beyond the stars, there are other heavens, more brilliant and immense than these, and they are not separated by space like the heavens we know. These higher realms are spiritual, not physical. There is also a kind of earth there, not made of lifeless matter, but filled with living creatures and natural things, just like here, but of a better kind. There are plants, rivers, and animals, but all of them are nobler than the ones we know. There is air full of eternal life. Although the life there is similar to ours, it is greater because it is unchanging, intellectual, and eternal. If someone asks how such things can exist without physical bodies, the answer is that they exist in a pure state, created directly by the First Cause without taking on material form. They are like mind and soul—they do not experience decay or destruction. Everything there is full of energy, strength, and joy, living a perfect life, all coming from one source and sharing the same nature. These beings are like perfect scents, sounds, colors, and tastes, each keeping its true form without mixing or corrupting each other. Unlike physical beings, they are simple and do not multiply but remain exactly as they are."

At the center of the Table is a large, covered throne with a seated female figure representing Isis, referred to here as the Pantomorphic IYNX. G.R.S. Mead defines the IYNX as "a transmitting intelligence," while others see it as a symbol of Universal Being. Above the goddess's head, the throne is topped with a triple crown, symbolizing the Triune Divinity—the three-part God known by the Egyptians as the Supreme Mind. This divine triad is described in the Sepher ha Zohar as "hidden and unknowable." In Qabbalism, the Tree of the Sephiroth is divided into two parts: the invisible upper part with three aspects and the visible lower part with seven. The three invisible Sephiroth are Kether (the Crown), Chochmah (Wisdom), and Binah (Understanding). These higher aspects are too abstract for humans to understand, but the seven lower spheres can be grasped by human thought. The seven triads in the central panel of the Table represent these lower Sephiroth, all coming from the hidden triple crown above the throne.

Kircher explains: "The throne shows how the three-part Supreme Mind spreads through the three worlds. From these three unseen realms comes the physical universe, which Plutarch called the 'House of Horns' and the Egyptians called the 'Great Gate of the Gods.' The top of the throne is surrounded by serpent-shaped flames, symbolizing that the Supreme Mind is full of eternal life and light, untouched by the physical world. The Table illustrates how the Divine Fire of the Supreme Mind reaches all creatures through the force of Nature, symbolized by the World Virgin, Isis, called here the IYNX, or the Universal Idea containing all forms." Plato used the word Idea to describe eternal forms that exist without matter. These immaterial forms serve as the patterns that the divine power used to shape the physical world.

Kircher describes the 21 figures in the central panel as seven key triads, each linked to a higher world. These triads originate from the invisible flame of the triple crown. The first is the Ophionic or IYNX Triad, which belongs to the fiery, intellectual realm called Aetherium. Zoroaster described this realm as ruled by strict forces. The second, called the Ibimorphous Triad, relates to the ethereal world of moisture. The third, the Nephtæan Triad, governs fertility. These three triads represent the intellectual and ethereal worlds connected to the Father Foundation.

The remaining four triads belong to the material worlds. Two of these triads relate to the heavens: the Osiris-Isis Triad, symbolized by two bulls (representing the Sun and Moon), and another pair of heavenly rulers. The other two triads are connected to the sublunary and underground realms: the Hecatine Triad and the Serapæan Triad. These complete the seven worlds governed by the Genii—the spiritual powers that rule the natural universe. Psellus quotes Zoroaster, saying: "The Egyptians and Chaldeans taught that there are seven physical worlds, governed by spiritual powers. The first is pure fire; the next three are ethereal; the final three are material. The last, called the terrestrial world, lies beneath the Moon and is full of darkness." Together with the invisible crown, these make up the eight worlds.

Plato believed that philosophers needed to understand how the seven circles under the first circle were arranged, according to the Egyptians. The first triad, connected to fire, represents life. The second triad, related to water, is ruled by the Ibimorphous gods. The third, linked to air, is governed by Nephta. From fire, the heavens were formed; from water, the earth; and air served as the mediator between them. The Sepher Yetzirah teaches that these three elements give rise to the seven directions: height, depth, east, west, north, south, and the Holy Temple at the center. The Holy Temple, shown as the great throne of Nature's spirit at the center of the Tablet, is the home of the seven powers that rule the world.

Psellus writes: "The Egyptians worshipped a triad of faith, truth, and love, along with seven fountains. The Sun, as the fountain of matter, rules over all; other fountains include those of the archangels, the senses, judgment, lightning, reflection, and mysterious characters." The Egyptians connected these fountains with specific planets. The Sun represents the solar world, the Moon governs the archangelic world, and Saturn rules the world of the senses. Jupiter is linked to judgment, Mars to lightning, Venus to reflection, and Mercury to the world of symbols. All of these meanings are reflected in the figures of the central panel of the Tablet.

The upper panel of the Table features the twelve signs of the zodiac, arranged into four groups of three. In each group, the central figure represents one of the four fixed zodiac signs: Aquarius (S), Taurus (Z), Leo (C), and Scorpio (G). These signs are known as the Fathers. In the secret teachings of the Far East, these four figures—the man, the bull, the lion, and the eagle—are called the winged globes or the four Maharajahs, who stand at the four corners of creation. The four cardinal signs—Capricorn (P), Aries (X), Cancer (B), and Libra (F)—are referred to as the Powers. The four mutable signs—Pisces (V), Gemini (A), Virgo (E), and Sagittarius (H)—are called the Minds of the Four Lords. This arrangement explains the meaning behind the winged globes in Egyptian symbolism. The four central figures (Aquarius, Taurus, Leo, and Scorpio, known as the Cherubim by Ezekiel) represent the globes, while the cardinal and mutable signs on either side form the wings. Thus, the twelve zodiac signs can be symbolized as four globes, each with two wings.

The Egyptians also depicted the celestial triads as a globe (the Father) with a serpent (the Mind) and wings (the Power) extending from it. These twelve forces shape the world and give rise to the microcosm, which represents both the twelve sacred animals in the universe and the twelve parts of the human body. In an anatomical sense, the twelve figures in the upper panel can represent the twelve convolutions of the brain, while the twelve figures in the lower panel correspond to the zodiacal organs and members of the body. Each part of the human body is controlled by one of the twelve zodiac signs, demonstrating that humans are formed from these twelve sacred animals.

There is also a deeper meaning behind the relationship between the twelve figures in the upper and lower panels. This connection reveals one of the most hidden ancient secrets: the relationship between two zodiacs—the fixed zodiac and the movable zodiac. The fixed zodiac is described as a massive dodecahedron, with its twelve surfaces representing the outer boundaries of abstract space. From each surface, a great spiritual power flows inward, becoming one of the celestial hierarchies of the movable zodiac, which consists of stars that appear to move in the sky. Inside the movable zodiac, planetary and elemental bodies are located. The connection between these two zodiacs is reflected in the human respiratory system: the fixed zodiac represents the atmosphere, the movable zodiac represents the lungs, and the subzodiacal spheres correspond to the body. The energies of the twelve divine powers of the fixed zodiac are "inhaled" by the cosmic lungs (the movable zodiac) and distributed throughout the material universe. The cycle is completed when the lower world's negative energies are "exhaled" into the fixed zodiac, where they are purified by the divine nature of the twelve celestial hierarchies.

The Table can be interpreted in many ways. If the border of the Table is seen as the source of spiritual energy, then the throne in the center represents the physical body, with human nature seated on it. In this view, the entire Table symbolizes the aura around a person, with the border representing the outer shell of the auric field. If the throne symbolizes the spiritual realm, the border represents the elements, and the surrounding panels depict the different worlds or planes that come from the divine source. If the Table is viewed in physical terms, the throne represents the reproductive system, and the Table reveals the process of creation in the material world. From a physiological perspective, the central throne corresponds to the heart, the Ibimorphous Triad symbolizes the mind, the Nephtæan Triad represents the reproductive system, and the surrounding symbols represent the organs and body parts.

From an evolutionary perspective, the central gate represents both the entrance and exit point of existence. It also illustrates the process of initiation, where a person, after passing through various trials, reaches the presence of their own soul, which only they can fully understand. If we interpret the Table in terms of cosmogony, the central panel represents the spiritual realms, the upper panel symbolizes the intellectual worlds, and the lower panel corresponds to the physical worlds. The central panel can also represent the nine invisible worlds, with the figure labeled "T" representing physical nature—the footstool of Isis, the Spirit of Universal Life.

In alchemical terms, the central panel holds the metals, while the border represents the alchemical processes. The figure seated on the throne is the Universal Mercury, also called the "stone of the wise." The flaming canopy above the throne symbolizes Divine Sulfur, and the cube beneath it represents elemental salt.

The three triads in the central panel, also known as the Paternal Foundation, represent the Silent Watchers—the three hidden aspects of human nature. The two panels on either side symbolize the four lower aspects of human nature. There are 21 figures in the central panel, a number sacred to the sun, which consists of three primary powers, each with seven attributes. By Qabbalistic reduction, 21 becomes 3, symbolizing the Great Triad.

It is likely that the Table of Isis is connected to Egyptian Gnosticism. A Gnostic papyrus in the Bodleian Library refers to twelve Fathers, beneath whom are twelve Fountains (see Egyptian Magic by S.S.D.D.). The lower panel of the Table represents the underworld, emphasized by two gates: the great gate of the East and the great gate of the West. According to Chaldean theology, the sun rises and sets through these gates in the underworld, where it travels during the night. Plato, who studied for thirteen years under the Magi Patheneith, Ochoaps, Sechtnouphis, and Etymon of Sebbennithis, infused his philosophy with Egyptian and Chaldean teachings about triads. The Bembine Table visually represents Platonic philosophy, summarizing ancient teachings about the creation and structure of the universe. The best guide to understanding the Table is Commentaries on the Theology of Plato by Proclus. Additionally, many references to these principles can be found in the Chaldean Oracles of Zoroaster.

Hesiod's Theogony offers the most detailed account of the Greek creation myth. The Orphic version of the creation story has influenced many philosophies and religions, including Greek, Egyptian, and Syrian traditions. A key symbol in Orphic mythology is the cosmic egg, from which Phanes emerged into the light. Thomas Taylor explains that the Orphic egg corresponds to the mixture of limit and the limitless, as described by Plato in Philebus. Additionally, the egg is the third Intelligible Triad and represents the auric body of the Demiurge, or the creator god, who shapes the lower universe.

Eusebius, citing Porphyry, states that the Egyptians believed in a single intellectual creator of the world, whom they called Cneph. They depicted him as a figure with dark blue skin, holding a girdle and a scepter, wearing a crown with a feather, and shown with an egg emerging from his mouth. (See An Analysis of the Egyptian Mythology.) Although the Bembine Table is rectangular, it symbolizes the Orphic egg of the universe and everything within it. In esoteric teachings, the highest spiritual goal is to break the Orphic egg, which represents the spirit's return to Nirvana—the absolute state described by Eastern mystics.

In The New Pantheon, Samuel Boyse includes three illustrations of different parts of the Bembine Table. However, his work does not provide any significant new insights. In The Mythology and Fables of the Ancients Explained from History, the Abbé Banier discusses the Mensa Isiaca in detail. After examining the interpretations of Montfaucon, Kircher, and Pignorius, Banier concludes: "I believe it was a votive table, dedicated to Isis by a prince or private individual in gratitude for a favor they thought she granted them."

Wonders of Antiquity

It was common for the ancient Egyptians, Greeks, and Romans to place lit lamps inside the tombs of their dead as offerings to the God of Death. Some believed that these lamps would help the deceased find their way through the afterlife. Over time, this tradition grew, and instead of only using real lamps, people began placing small terracotta models of lamps in the tombs. Some of these lamps were protected inside circular containers, and there are reports of finding the original oil perfectly preserved after more than 2,000 years. Evidence shows that many of these lamps were still burning when the tombs were sealed, and some claimed they were still burning when the tombs were opened centuries later.

The idea that ancient priests could create lamps with fuel that renewed itself as it burned caused much debate among medieval scholars. Some believed these lamps could burn for centuries, though only a few suggested they could burn forever. W. Wynn Westcott noted that more than 150 writers had discussed this topic, while H.P. Blavatsky counted 173. Some argued that the so-called everlasting lamps were tricks used by clever pagan priests, but many others believed the lamps were real. Some even thought the Devil himself created these lamps to deceive people and lead them astray from true faith.

Athanasius Kircher, a respected Jesuit scholar, offered different opinions on these lamps. In his book Œdipus Ægyptiacus, he suggested: "Not a few of these ever-burning lamps were the work of devils... All the lamps found in the tombs of pagans were placed there as part of false worship, not because they could burn forever, but likely because the Devil set them there to encourage belief in a false religion." Though Kircher acknowledged that some trusted scholars accepted the existence of these lamps, he later dismissed the whole idea as impossible, comparing it to myths about perpetual motion and the Philosopher's Stone. However, he also presented another theory: "In Egypt, there are large deposits of asphalt and petroleum. What if these priests connected underground oil reserves to lamps with asbestos wicks through hidden pipes? How could such lamps not seem to burn forever?" Kircher believed this explained the mystery behind the so-called eternal lamps.

Montfaucon, in his Antiquities, agreed with Kircher's later conclusion. He thought that the stories of perpetual lamps in temples were based on clever mechanical tricks. He also noted that when some tombs were opened, smoke-like fumes sometimes escaped, making it seem as though something had been burning inside. When explorers later found lamps scattered on the ground, they assumed these were the source of the fumes.

There are many interesting stories about the discovery of ever-burning lamps in different parts of the world. One such tale comes from a tomb along the Appian Way, opened during the papacy of Paul III. Inside the sealed vault, explorers found a lamp still burning after nearly 1,600 years. According to a report by someone present at the time, the body of a young girl with long golden hair was found floating in a mysterious clear liquid, perfectly preserved, as if she had just died. The vault contained many objects, including several lamps, and one of these lamps was still lit. However, when the door was opened, the draft blew out the flame, and the lamp could not be relit.

Kircher included an inscription in his work, supposedly found in the tomb: "TULLIOLAE FILIAE MEAE" ("To my daughter Tulliola"). However, Montfaucon argued that this inscription never existed and added that, although there was no solid evidence, many believed the body found in the tomb belonged to Tulliola, the daughter of Cicero.

Ever-burning lamps have been discovered in many places across the world. Records from regions like the Mediterranean, India, Tibet, China, and South America tell of lamps that kept burning without needing any fuel. The following examples are selected from various discoveries made over the years.

Plutarch described a lamp that burned over the door of a temple to Jupiter Ammon, and the priests claimed it had remained alight for centuries without fuel. St. Augustine also mentioned a perpetual lamp in an Egyptian temple dedicated to Venus. He said that neither wind nor water could extinguish it, though he believed it was the work of the Devil. During the reign of Emperor Justinian, a lamp was discovered in Edessa or Antioch. It was placed in a niche above the city gate and protected from the weather. The date on the lamp showed that it had been burning for over 500 years before soldiers destroyed it.

In the early Middle Ages, a lamp was found in England that had been burning since the third century AD. The tomb it was found in was thought to belong to the father of Constantine the Great. Another example, the Lantern of Pallas, was discovered near Rome in 1401. It was found in the tomb of Pallas, the son of Evander, who was mentioned in Virgil's Æneid. The lamp, placed near the head of the body, had burned steadily for more than 2,000 years. In 1550, a marble vault was opened on the island of Nesis in the Bay of Naples. Inside, a lamp was still burning, though it had been placed there before the start of the Christian era.

Pausanias wrote about a beautiful golden lamp in the temple of Minerva that burned for an entire year without needing more fuel or even having the wick trimmed. Every year, they held a ceremony to refill the lamp, which also served as a way to mark the passage of time. According to the Fama Fraternitatis, when the tomb of Christian Rosencreutz was opened 120 years after his death, it was brightly lit by a perpetual lamp hanging from the ceiling.

Numa Pompilius, an ancient King of Rome and a powerful magician, was said to have caused an eternal light to burn in the dome of a temple he built in honor of a nature spirit. Another story tells of a mysterious tomb found in England with an automaton that moved when certain floor stones were stepped on. Since the Rosicrucian debate was popular at the time, many believed this tomb belonged to a Rosicrucian initiate. A farmer stumbled upon the tomb, which was brightly lit by a lamp hanging from the ceiling. As the farmer moved, his weight pressed the floor stones, triggering a mechanical figure in heavy armor. The figure stood, struck the lamp with an iron baton, and destroyed it, ensuring that the secret of the lamp's flame would never be discovered. How long the lamp had burned is unknown, but it was believed to have been many years.

There are also accounts of lights found in sealed tombs near Memphis and in Brahmin temples in India. However, these lights extinguished as soon as they were exposed to air, and their fuel evaporated. It is now believed that the wicks of these lamps were made from woven asbestos, which alchemists called "salamander's wool." The fuel was likely a product of alchemical experiments. Kircher once tried to extract oil from asbestos, believing that since asbestos was fireproof, the oil would provide an indestructible fuel. After two years of failed experiments, he concluded that the task was impossible.

Several ancient formulas for making the fuel of these lamps still exist. H.P. Blavatsky reprinted two of these recipes in Isis Unveiled from older works by Tritenheim and Bartolomeo Korndorf. One of these formulas will help give a basic understanding of the process:

"Sulphur. Burnt alum, 4 ounces; turn them into flowers until reduced to 2 ounces. To this, add 1 ounce of powdered Venetian borax. Pour highly purified spirit of wine over the mixture and let it soak. Then remove the liquid and pour in fresh spirit. Repeat this process until the sulphur melts like wax on a hot brass plate, without producing any smoke. This will serve as the fuel.

Now, prepare the wick in the following way: Gather fibers or threads of asbestos until you have a bundle as thick as your middle finger and as long as your little finger. Place these fibers in a Venetian glass, covering them with the purified sulphur mixture you prepared earlier. Set the glass in hot sand for twenty-four hours, keeping the heat high enough for the sulphur to bubble the entire time.

Once the wick is fully coated with the sulphur mixture, place it in a glass shaped like a scallop shell, making sure part of the wick stays above the surface of the prepared sulphur. Set the glass back on the hot sand and melt the sulphur until it grips the wick firmly. When you light this lamp, it will burn with a steady, never-ending flame. You can place this lamp anywhere you like, and it will continue to burn without going out."

The Greek Oracles

The worship of Apollo included the creation and upkeep of places where the gods could communicate with people and reveal the future to those worthy of such knowledge. Many ancient Greek stories tell of talking trees, rivers, statues, and caves inhabited by spirits like nymphs, dryads, or demons, who gave prophetic messages from these places. Some Christian writers claimed that these prophecies were tricks from the Devil to mislead people. However, they could not deny the reality of oracles since their own sacred texts referenced similar events. If the glowing onyx stones on the high priest's robe in Israel could show the will of Jehovah, then it was possible that a black dove, temporarily given the ability to speak, could deliver oracles in the temple of Jupiter Ammon. Similarly, if the witch of Endor could summon the spirit of Samuel to give Saul a prophecy, then a priestess of Apollo could call upon her god to predict Greece's future.

Among the most well-known ancient oracles were those of Delphi, Dodona, Trophonius, and Latona. The oracle of Dodona, with its talking oak trees, was the oldest. While the origins of oracular prophecy remain unclear, it is known that many caves and openings used as oracles were considered sacred even before Greek civilization developed.

The oracle of Apollo at Delphi is one of the ancient world's enduring mysteries. Alexander Wilder believed that the name Delphi came from delphos, meaning "womb," chosen because the cave and its vent resembled a womb. The original name of the oracle was Pytho, which came from the legend of the serpent Python. According to the story, the serpent emerged from the slime left behind by a great flood that wiped out humanity, except for Deucalion and Pyrrha. Apollo climbed Mount Parnassus, fought the serpent, and threw its body into the cave. From that point on, the Sun God, also known as the Pythian Apollo, gave prophecies from the cave. Apollo shared the honor of being Delphi's patron god with Dionysus.

Though defeated, the spirit of Python remained at Delphi to serve

Apollo. The fumes rising from the cave were believed to come from Python's decaying body, and the priestess, known as the Pythoness or Pythia, inhaled these fumes to connect with Apollo. The Greeks believed Delphi was the navel of the world, symbolizing that the Earth was like a living being, and the connection between oracles and the navel held deep meaning in the ancient Mysteries.

The origin of the oracle is likely much older than the story of Apollo and Python suggests. The priests may have created this tale to explain the oracle's power to people they did not think deserved the real, hidden truth. Some say a priest from Hyperborea discovered the Delphic cave, but records show that the cave had been considered sacred for as long as history remembers. People traveled from all over Greece and nearby regions to ask the spirit inside the cave for guidance. The priests and priestesses guarded the cave closely, serving the spirit that gave prophecies to humanity.

The story of the oracle's discovery goes like this: Shepherds tending their flocks on Mount Parnassus noticed that their goats acted strangely when they wandered near a large crack on the mountain's side. The goats jumped and made odd noises unlike anything heard before. Curious, one shepherd approached the vent, which released strange fumes. As soon as he inhaled the vapors, he was overcome with a wild, prophetic excitement. He danced, sang, mumbled strange words, and began predicting future events. Others who approached the vent had the same experience. The fame of the place spread, and people came from far and wide to breathe the fumes and glimpse the future.

Some visitors could not control themselves, and, with the strength of madmen, broke free from those trying to hold them back. Many jumped into the vent and died. To prevent further accidents, a wall was built around the opening, and a prophetess was appointed to communicate with the oracle on behalf of those seeking answers. According to later stories, a golden tripod carved with images of Apollo as the serpent Python was placed over the vent. A specially designed seat was set on the tripod to help keep the priestess steady while she inhaled the vapors, preventing her from falling during her trance. Around this time, the story began to spread that the fumes came from the decaying body of Python, possibly revealed by the oracle itself.

In the beginning, young virgin maidens were chosen to serve the oracle. They were called Phœbades or Pythiæ and became part of the famous Pythian priesthood. It is likely that women were selected because their emotional and sensitive nature made them more responsive to the "fumes of enthusiasm." Three days before giving a prophecy, the priestess underwent a purification ritual. She bathed in the Castalian well, fasted, and drank only from the sacred Cassotis fountain, whose water was brought into the temple through hidden pipes. Before sitting on the tripod, she also chewed leaves from a sacred bay tree.

Some claim the water she drank was drugged to induce visions, or that the priests knew how to produce a gas that caused an intoxicating effect, which they channeled into the cave through underground pipes. However, neither theory has been proven, nor do they explain the remarkable accuracy of the oracle's predictions.

When the young prophetess completed her purification, she was dressed in sacred clothing and led to the tripod, where she sat surrounded by the fumes rising from the open fissure. As she inhaled the vapors, her behavior changed dramatically, as if another spirit had taken over her body. She began to struggle, tear at her clothes, and cry out in strange sounds. After a time, she grew calm, and an air of majesty seemed to come over her. Sitting stiffly with her eyes focused on a distant point, she began to deliver her prophecy. These prophecies were often spoken in hexameter verse, though the words were sometimes confusing or difficult to understand. Every movement she made and every sound she uttered was carefully recorded by five holy men, called the Hosii, who were lifelong scribes selected from the descendants of Deucalion.

Once the prophecy was given, the spirit left her, and the priestess began to struggle again. She was then carried to a room where she could rest until the intense state passed.

In his essay The Mysteries, Iamblichus explained how the spirit of the oracle—thought to be a fiery demon or Apollo himself—took control of the priestess: "Whether the prophetess receives the god's message through fiery vapors rising from the cave, or whether she becomes sacred to the god by sitting on the tripod, she fully surrenders to the divine spirit and is filled with the god's presence. When fire rises from the cave and surrounds her, she becomes illuminated by its brilliance. Sitting on the seat of the god, she aligns with his stable prophetic power. Through these two steps, she becomes entirely possessed by the god, who then speaks through her."

One of the most famous visitors to the Delphic oracle was Apollonius of Tyana, accompanied by his student Damis. After making offerings, Apollonius was crowned with a laurel wreath and given a branch of laurel to carry. He passed behind the statue of Apollo at the entrance of the cave and entered the sacred space. The priestess, also wearing a laurel crown with her head wrapped in white wool, gave him a prophecy. Apollonius asked if his name would be remembered by future generations. The priestess said it would, but it would be spoken of with slander. Angered by her words, Apollonius left the cave. However, time proved the prophecy true, as early Christian writers labeled him the Antichrist. (For more on this story, see Histoire de la Magie.)

The priestess's messages were passed on to philosophers of the oracle, whose job was to interpret their meaning. These interpretations were then given to poets, who translated the messages into beautiful odes and songs, making them accessible to the public.

Snakes were an important part of the Delphic oracle. The base of the priestess's tripod was formed from the twisted bodies of three large serpents. Some sources say the young priestesses were made to stare into the eyes of a snake to enter a trance-like state, allowing them to speak with the god's voice.

In the early days, the Pythian priestesses were always young maidens, often in their teens. However, after a series of assaults on these young women, a new rule was made that only women over fifty could serve as the mouthpieces of the oracle. These older women dressed as young girls and followed the same rituals as the first priestesses.

Originally, the oracle gave prophecies only every seventh year on Apollo's birthday. But as more people came seeking answers, the priestess began delivering prophecies once a month. The exact times and questions for these consultations were decided by lottery or by a vote among the people of Delphi.

The influence of the Delphic oracle on Greek culture was immense. As James Gardner explained: "The oracle's words exposed many tyrants and predicted their downfall. It saved many lives and guided countless people along the right path. The oracle promoted useful institutions and encouraged progress. It supported moral virtue and helped advance civil liberty." (See The Faiths of the World.)

The oracle of Dodona was overseen by Jupiter, who gave prophecies through oak trees, birds, and brass vases. Many writers have noted the similarities between the rituals at Dodona and those of the Druid priests in Britain and Gaul. The famous oracular dove of Dodona would perch on the branches of the sacred oaks. There, it not only spoke in Greek about philosophy and religion but also answered questions from people who had traveled long distances to consult the oracle.

The "talking" trees stood together in a sacred grove. When the priests needed answers to important questions, they would undergo solemn purification rituals before entering the grove. There, they called upon the god believed to dwell within the trees. After the priests asked their questions, the trees responded with human voices, giving the answers they sought. Some say that only one tree, an oak or beech at the center of the grove, spoke. Since Jupiter was believed to reside within this tree, he was sometimes called Phegonæus, meaning "the one who lives in a beech tree."

One of the most fascinating parts of the Dodona oracle was the use of "talking" vases or kettles made of brass. These were so well-designed that, once struck, they would continue to ring for hours. Some accounts describe a row of these vases, which would vibrate in unison if one were struck, creating a loud, overwhelming noise. Other sources mention a large vase placed on a pillar, with a second column nearby holding a statue of a child with a whip. The whip had several cords tipped with small metal balls. As the wind blew through the open building, the balls would strike the vase, creating sound. The priests carefully listened to the number and strength of the impacts and interpreted the vibrations to deliver prophecies.

When the original priests of Dodona, called the Selloi, mysteriously disappeared, three priestesses took over the oracle's duties. These women interpreted the sounds from the vases and consulted the sacred trees at midnight. Visitors seeking the oracle's wisdom were required to bring offerings and make donations.

Another well-known oracle was the Cave of Trophonius, located on the side of a hill with an entrance so small that it seemed impossible for anyone to fit through it. After making an offering at the statue of Trophonius and putting on sacred clothing, the visitor climbed the hill to the cave, carrying a cake of honey. Sitting at the edge of the opening, the visitor lowered their feet into the cave. Suddenly, they were pulled entirely into the cavern, which those who entered described as being about the size of a large oven. After the oracle's message was delivered, the visitor was ejected from the cave, usually in a delirious state, with their feet coming out first.

Near the cave were two fountains that bubbled from the earth just a few feet apart. Those about to enter the cave drank from these fountains, each of which had unique properties. The first fountain contained the Water of Forgetfulness, which caused anyone who drank it to forget their earthly troubles. The second fountain held the sacred Water of Remembrance, known as the water of Mnemosyne. This water helped those who drank it remember the visions and experiences they had while inside the cave.

Though the entrance to the cave was marked by two brass obelisks, the cave itself, hidden behind a wall of white stones and surrounded by a grove of sacred trees, did not look particularly impressive. However, there is no doubt that those who entered the cave had strange and intense experiences. After leaving the cave, visitors were required to write down everything they saw and heard during their time in the oracle. The prophecies came in the form of dreams and visions, often accompanied by severe headaches. Some people never fully recovered from the effects of the delirium they experienced.

The priests interpreted the visitors' disjointed descriptions of their visions according to the specific question that had been asked. It is likely that the priests used some type of unknown herb to trigger the dreams or visions, but their ability to interpret these experiences was so precise it seemed almost supernatural. Before anyone could consult the oracle, they had to offer a ram as a sacrifice to the spirit of the cave. Using a form of divination called hieromancy, the priests determined whether the sacrifice was acceptable and if the time chosen for the consultation was favorable.

The Seven Wonders of The World

Many sculptors and architects of the ancient world were initiates of the Mysteries, especially the Eleusinian rites. From the beginning of time, those who worked with stone and wood have belonged to a sacred order guided by divine inspiration. As civilization spread, cities were built and abandoned, monuments were raised to heroes now forgotten, and temples were constructed for gods whose broken statues lie buried in the ruins of the nations they once inspired. Research shows that the builders and sculptors of these ancient structures were not just skilled craftsmen but masters of their art, unmatched by anyone today. The advanced knowledge of mathematics and astronomy found in ancient architecture, along with the detailed understanding of anatomy displayed in Greek statues, proves that these artisans were brilliant minds, deeply educated in the secret wisdom of the Mysteries. This tradition led to the formation of the Guild of Builders, ancestors of the modern Freemasons. When building palaces, temples, or tombs, or crafting statues for the wealthy, these initiated artists embedded the secret teachings within their work. Even now, long after their bones have turned to dust, it is clear that these early craftsmen were worthy of the honors given to Master Masons.

The Seven Wonders of the World, though seemingly built for different purposes, were actually monuments designed to preserve the secrets of the Mysteries. Each was a symbolic structure placed in a specific location, and only those initiated into the Mysteries could fully understand their meaning. Eliphas Levi pointed out a connection between the Seven Wonders and the seven planets. These wonders were built by those known as Widow's sons in honor of the seven planetary spirits. Their symbolism is connected to the seven seals in the Book of Revelation and the seven churches of Asia.

1. The Colossus of Rhodes was a massive bronze statue, about 109 feet tall, and it took more than twelve years to complete. It was created by an initiated artist named Chares of Lindus. For centuries, people believed that the statue stood with one foot on each side of the harbor entrance, allowing ships to pass between its legs, though this theory has never been proven. Unfortunately, the statue stood for only 56 years

before an earthquake destroyed it in 224 B.C. Its broken pieces lay scattered on the ground for over 900 years until they were sold to a Jewish merchant, who transported the metal on 700 camels. Some say the bronze was turned into weapons, while others believe it was used for drainage pipes. The statue, with its crown of sun rays and raised torch, symbolized the Sun Man of the Mysteries—the Universal Savior.

2. The architect Ctesiphon proposed a plan to the Ionian cities in the fifth century B.C. to build a monument in honor of the goddess Diana. Ephesus, a city south of Smyrna, was chosen as the site. The temple was made of marble, and its roof rested on 127 columns, each 60 feet tall and weighing more than 150 tons. The temple was destroyed in 356 B.C. by an act of black magic, though the blame was placed on a man named Herostratus, who was believed to be mentally disturbed. Although the temple was rebuilt, its original meaning was lost. The first temple was designed as a miniature version of the universe and dedicated to the moon, which represents the cycle of creation.

3. After being exiled from Athens, Phidias, the greatest Greek sculptor, went to Olympia in the province of Elis, where he created a colossal statue of Zeus, the king of the Greek gods. No detailed description of this masterpiece remains, though a few old coins provide some idea of how it looked. The statue's body was covered in ivory, and its robes were made of beaten gold. Zeus was said to hold a globe with a figure of the Goddess of Victory in one hand and a scepter with an eagle perched on top in the other. His head, crowned with an olive wreath, was bearded and archaic. The statue sat on a beautifully decorated throne. This monument was dedicated to the planet Jupiter, one of the seven great spirits who serve the Sun.

4. Eliphas Levi lists the Temple of Solomon as one of the Seven Wonders of the World, taking the place of the Pharos, or Lighthouse, of Alexandria. The Pharos was named after the island it stood on and was designed by Sostratus of Cnidus during the reign of Ptolemy (283-247 B.C.). It was made of white marble and stood over 600 feet tall. Even in ancient times, its construction cost nearly a million dollars. Fires were lit at its top to guide ships at sea, and the light could be seen from miles away. An earthquake destroyed the lighthouse in the thirteenth century, though remnants of it were still visible until 1350 A.D. As the tallest

of the Seven Wonders, it was associated with Saturn, the Father of the gods, symbolizing enlightenment for all humanity.

5. The Mausoleum at Halicarnassus was a grand structure built by Queen Artemisia in honor of her deceased husband, King Mausolus, whose name inspired the modern word "mausoleum." The building's design came from Satyrus and Pythis, and four renowned sculptors decorated the monument. It measured 114 feet in length and 92 feet in width and was divided into five main sections, representing the five human senses. At the top was a pyramid, symbolizing the spiritual side of humanity. The pyramid rose in 24 steps—a sacred number—and a statue of King Mausolus riding a chariot stood at its peak, with the figure measuring 9 feet 9½ inches in height. Although many attempts have been made to rebuild the mausoleum after it was destroyed by an earthquake, none have been fully successful. The monument was dedicated to the planet Mars and built by an initiate to spread wisdom to the world.

6. The Hanging Gardens of Babylon, also known as the Gardens of Semiramis, were located within the palace grounds of King Nebuchadnezzar, near the Euphrates River. These gardens were constructed in a series of terraces that formed a pyramid, with a water reservoir at the top to irrigate the plants. Built around 600 B.C., the name of the designer has been lost to history. The gardens symbolized the different planes of the unseen world and were dedicated to Venus, the goddess of love and beauty.

7. The Great Pyramid was the most important of all the temples connected to the Mysteries. Its astronomical symbolism suggests it may have been built as far back as 70,000 years ago. It served as the tomb of Osiris and was believed to have been constructed by the gods themselves. The architect is thought to have been the immortal Hermes. The Great Pyramid symbolizes Mercury, the messenger of the gods, and it stands as a universal symbol of wisdom and knowledge.

The Life and Philosophy of Pythagoras

While Mnesarchus, the father of Pythagoras, was visiting the city of Delphi on business, he and his wife, Parthenis, decided to ask the oracle whether it was safe for them to sail back to Syria. However, when the prophetess of Apollo sat on the golden tripod above the vent of the oracle, she didn't answer their question. Instead, she told Mnesarchus that his wife was expecting a son who would surpass all others in beauty and wisdom and greatly benefit humanity throughout his life. Mnesarchus was so moved by this prophecy that he changed his wife's name to Pythasis to honor the Pythian priestess. When the baby was born in Sidon, just as the oracle had predicted, they named him Pythagoras, believing he was destined for greatness.

Many strange stories surround Pythagoras's birth. Some say he wasn't just an ordinary human but a god in human form, sent to guide and teach humanity. Like other sages and saviors, his birth was said to be miraculous. Godfrey Higgins, in his Anacalypsis, draws parallels between Pythagoras and Jesus, noting that both were born in Syria—Pythagoras in Sidon and Jesus in Bethlehem. Both fathers were given prophecies about their sons being future benefactors to humanity. Both mothers were away from home when they gave birth: Mary had traveled to Bethlehem, and Pythagoras's parents had journeyed to Sidon for business. Higgins also notes that Pythasis, like Mary, had a spiritual encounter—hers was with a spirit of Apollo, who told her husband not to touch her during her pregnancy. Because of these similarities, Pythagoras was called a "son of God" and believed to be divinely inspired.

Pythagoras, one of the most influential philosophers, was born sometime between 600 and 590 B.C. He lived nearly 100 years, dedicating his life to the pursuit of wisdom. His teachings show that he was well-versed in both Eastern and Western esoteric traditions. Pythagoras traveled widely, learning from Jewish teachers about the secret traditions of Moses. The Essenes later focused on interpreting Pythagorean symbols. He was initiated into the Mysteries of Egypt, Babylon, and Chaldea. Although some say he studied under Zoroaster, it's uncertain whether his teacher was the same figure revered by the Parsees. Historians agree, however, that Pythagoras traveled extensively and studied with many masters.

After mastering the teachings of Greek philosophers and likely being initiated into the Eleusinian Mysteries, Pythagoras traveled to Egypt, where he faced many challenges before finally being initiated into the Mysteries of Isis by the priests of Thebes. From there, he journeyed to Phoenicia and Syria, where he was initiated into the Mysteries of Adonis. He then traveled to the Euphrates Valley to learn the secret knowledge of the Chaldeans near Babylon. His most important journey was to India, where he studied with the Brahmins of Elephanta and Ellora. According to Ancient Freemasonry by Frank C. Higgins, Pythagoras is still remembered in Brahmin records as Yavancharya, the Ionian Teacher.

Pythagoras is credited with being the first person to call himself a philosopher. Before him, wise men referred to themselves as sages, meaning "those who know." However, Pythagoras preferred the more humble term "philosopher," meaning "one who seeks wisdom."

When he returned from his travels, Pythagoras established a school in Crotona, a Dorian colony in southern Italy. Although people were initially suspicious of him, he soon earned the respect of leaders from neighboring colonies, who sought his advice on important matters. He gathered a small group of devoted students and taught them the secret knowledge he had gained, as well as the basics of occult mathematics, music, and astronomy—disciplines he believed formed the foundation of all arts and sciences.

At around sixty years old, Pythagoras married one of his disciples, a brilliant woman who gave him seven children. She not only inspired him during his life but also continued spreading his teachings after his death.

Like many great thinkers, Pythagoras's outspokenness earned him both political and personal enemies. One man, angry after being denied initiation into Pythagoras's school, sought revenge. He spread false information about Pythagoras, turning public opinion against him. Without warning, a group of attackers stormed the community where Pythagoras and his students lived, burning the buildings and killing the philosopher.

The stories about the death of Pythagoras differ. Some say he was killed along with his followers, while others claim that after escaping from Crotona with a small group, he and his disciples were trapped in a house that was later set on fire by his enemies. In one version, when the disciples realized they were trapped inside the burning building, they threw themselves into the flames, forming a bridge with their bodies so Pythagoras could escape. However, he is said to have died soon after, heartbroken over the failure of his efforts to enlighten humanity.

After his death, his disciples tried to keep his teachings alive, but they faced constant persecution. Today, only a little remains to honor the greatness of this philosopher. It is said that Pythagoras's followers never referred to him by name, instead calling him "The Master" or "That Man." This could be because the name Pythagoras was believed to contain a special arrangement of letters with sacred meaning. In The Word magazine, T. R. Prater wrote that Pythagoras initiated his students using a formula hidden within the letters of his name, which might explain why it was held in such high regard.

After Pythagoras's death, his school gradually fell apart, but those who had benefited from his teachings continued to honor his memory just as they had respected him during his life. Over time, Pythagoras was seen not just as a man but as a divine figure, and his scattered followers were united by their admiration for his extraordinary wisdom. In Pythagoras and the Delphic Mysteries, Edouard Schure tells a story that shows the strong bond among Pythagoras's disciples:

"One of the disciples fell ill and became poor. A kind innkeeper took care of him, and before the disciple died, he drew a mysterious symbol—most likely a pentagram—on the door of the inn. He told the innkeeper, 'Do not worry, one of my brothers will come to pay my debt.' A year later, a stranger passing by noticed the sign on the door. He told the innkeeper, 'I am a Pythagorean. One of my brothers died here. Tell me what I owe you for his debt.'"

Frank C. Higgins, in Ancient Freemasonry, gives a helpful summary of the teachings of Pythagoras:

"Pythagoras's teachings are of the greatest importance to Freemasons. His ideas reflect the combined wisdom of the leading philosophers of the ancient world and represent knowledge that everyone could agree on, free from controversy. His firm belief in the unity of God supports the idea that the supreme secret of ancient initiations was the oneness of God. The Pythagorean school functioned like a series of initiations. Students had to pass through several stages, and they were not allowed to meet Pythagoras in person until they reached the higher levels. According to his biographers, there were three degrees of initiation. The first was 'Mathematicus,' where students learned mathematics and geometry—subjects that formed the foundation of all knowledge. The second degree was 'Theoreticus,' which focused on practical applications of science. The third and final degree was 'Electus,' where students were fully illuminated and ready to absorb the deepest wisdom.

Students at the Pythagorean school were divided into two groups: the 'exoterici,' or those in the outer grades, and the 'esoterici,' who had passed the third degree and were entrusted with the secret teachings. Silence, secrecy, and absolute obedience were the core principles of this great order."

The Hermetic and Alchemical Writings of Paracelsus

Paracelsus

Foreword

This is a collection of five alchemical writings by one of the most renowned alchemists, believed to have discovered the Philosopher's Stone. In these texts, Paracelsus tries to explain the nature of the Philosopher's Stone and the scientific principles that confirm its existence and reveal how it works. Like many alchemical writings, the language used is intentionally cryptic and symbolic, making it difficult for those considered unworthy to understand.

About the Author

Paracelsus (1493 – 1541)

Paracelsus was an alchemist, physician, astrologer, and occultist, born in Einsiedeln, Switzerland. His birth name was Phillip von Hohenheim, but he later adopted the name Philippus Theophrastus Aureolus Bombastus von Hohenheim. Eventually, he began using the title Paracelsus, meaning "equal to or greater than Celsus," a Roman writer from the first century known for his work on medicine.

Paracelsus authored many writings on alchemy, focusing primarily on the nature of the Philosopher's Stone. Unfortunately, he met an early and violent end, killed by those who were envious of his superior knowledge and irritated by his arrogant demeanor.

Prologue to The English Translation

You, who are skilled in Alchemy, along with others who hope to gain great wealth or dream of making gold and silver through its promises, take note. Many of you willingly endure hard work and frustrations, refusing to give up until you reach the rewards you believe this art will bring. Yet, experience shows that out of thousands, hardly one person achieves their goal. Is this failure caused by Nature or by Art? I say, no. It is instead due to fate or the lack of skill on the part of the alchemist.

Since those familiar with this art already understand the symbols, star signs, and planetary influences, as well as the ingredients, tools, and instructions, there is no need to repeat them here. These elements still serve a purpose when used at the right time, but this book offers a new way of approaching Alchemy. It will be explained through Seven Canons, following the order of the seven metals. Although this approach avoids unnecessary words, these Canons cover everything that should be separated from Alchemy. They also reveal many hidden secrets and insights into other areas of knowledge. In fact, this method may challenge the ideas of older alchemists and philosophers, but it is backed by careful testing and experimentation.

The most important truth in this art, though little known and rarely trusted, is that failure in Alchemy comes entirely from a lack of skill or using the wrong amounts or types of materials. Many people are driven to poverty, while others waste their efforts simply because of these mistakes. Success comes only when the process is done correctly, and if followed precisely, the substance being transformed steadily moves closer to perfection each day. The right path is simple, but only a few ever find it.

Sometimes, an alchemist may try to invent a new method out of curiosity, whether it works or not. But he need not try to create something out of nothing— or turn something into nothing—just for the sake of it. Even so, there is truth in the saying: "Destruction reveals what is good." This is because the good remains hidden beneath what covers it. Until this covering is removed, the good cannot shine in its full brightness. For example, a metal hidden within a mountain, sand, earth, or stone cannot reveal itself until its covering is removed. In the same way, each visible metal conceals the presence of the other six metals.

Through the element of fire, everything that is flawed or imperfect is destroyed and removed—such as the five metals associated with Mercury, Jupiter, Mars, Venus, and Saturn. However, the perfect metals, Sol (gold) and Luna (silver), do not burn up in this same fire. Instead, they remain in the fire, and from the destruction of the other imperfect metals, these perfect ones take shape and become visible. The way this transformation happens is explained in the Seven Canons. From these Canons, you can learn the nature and properties of each metal, how they interact with one another, and what powers they have when combined.

It's important to understand right from the beginning that these Seven Canons cannot be fully grasped on a quick read or after just one attempt. Complex and hidden ideas are not easy for everyone to comprehend. Each Canon requires thoughtful study and discussion. Many people, filled with pride, assume they can easily understand everything in this book. They dismiss its contents as worthless, believing they have better ideas of their. .

Coelum Philosophorum

Paracelsus

Part I.

Concerning The Nature and Proper- Ties of Mercury

All things are hidden within everything. One thing among them acts as the container for the rest—their physical, visible, and moveable vessel. This vessel reveals all processes of melting or liquefying. It is a living, physical spirit, and when it holds something solid or frozen inside it, those things become restless, wanting to escape. There is no proper name for this process of liquefaction, nor for where it originates. Since no natural heat can match it, it is compared to the fire of Gehenna. This kind of liquefaction is entirely different from those caused by ordinary heat or solidified by cold. Such weak transformations have no effect on Mercury, who rejects them altogether.

From this, we understand that earthly elements, in their destructive processes, cannot add to or take away from celestial powers, which are known as Quintessence or its elements. These higher forces are beyond the influence of earthly elements and cannot be controlled by them. Celestial and infernal forces do not obey the four basic elements—dry, moist, hot, or cold. None of these elements can act against a Quintessence. Each higher power holds its own abilities and operates independently, without needing to rely on the elements.

Concerning The Nature and Proper- Ties of Jupiter

Within what is visible—specifically, the body of Jupiter—the other six physical metals are spiritually hidden, though each one is concealed with varying degrees of depth and strength. Jupiter does not contain any Quintessence in its makeup but consists of the four basic elements. Because of this, it melts under moderate heat and solidifies under moderate cold. Jupiter has a natural connection with the melting processes of all other metals. The more it resembles another metal, the easier it is for them to join together. Similar things interact more smoothly and naturally than those that are very different. Something distant will not affect or influence something else strongly. Similarly, distant things are neither feared nor desired, no matter how powerful they might be.

This explains why people do not strive to reach higher realms of creation—they seem too far away, and their greatness is beyond human understanding. Likewise, lower realms are not feared, since people are distant from them and unaware of the suffering they contain. Because of this, spirits from the underworld are considered insignificant. The farther away something is, the less valuable it appears, while things close to us are given more importance. Each thing changes based on its place, becoming better or transforming according to where it belongs, as shown by many examples.

Jupiter is farther away from Mars and Venus but closer to the Sun (Sol) and Moon (Luna). Because of this, Jupiter contains more qualities similar to gold and silver. The closer it is to Sol and Luna, the more beautiful, powerful, visible, and valuable it becomes—far more so than a distant object. On the other hand, the farther something is, the less value it seems to hold, and things nearby are always favored over distant ones. As something nearby becomes clearer, what is farther away becomes hidden. As an alchemist, you must seriously consider how you can move Jupiter to a distant place occupied by Sol and Luna and bring Sol and Luna closer to where Jupiter is now. The goal is to have Sol and Luna present before your eyes in their full physical forms, just as Jupiter is.

There are practical methods for changing metals from imperfection to perfection. First, mix the metals together. Then, separate the pure parts from the impure. This process is simply one of transformation, carefully guided by proper alchemical work. Take note that Jupiter contains a significant amount of gold and some silver. If you combine it with Saturn and Luna, Luna will increase in its presence and strength.

Concerning Mars and His Properties

The six hidden metals have cast out the seventh, making it solid and giving it little power while making it heavy and hard. In doing so, they have transferred their own hardness and ability to solidify into this new body. However, they have kept their color, ability to melt, and noble qualities for themselves.

It is difficult and takes great effort to turn an ordinary man into a prince or king. But Mars, with a strong and aggressive nature, takes control and seizes the throne. Even so, he must stay alert, guarding against unexpected traps that could capture him off-guard. It is also important to consider how Mars can rise to power and take the place of the king, while Sol, Luna, and Saturn take over the role that Mars once held.

Concerning Venus and Its Properties

The other six metals have transformed Venus into an external body by giving it their color and melting properties. To fully understand this, we should use some examples to show how something obvious can become hidden, and how something hidden can be made physically visible through the use of fire. Anything that can burn can naturally change its form through fire, turning into lime, soot, ash, glass, colors, stone, or earth. This earth can, in turn, be reshaped into new metallic bodies.

If a metal is burned or weakened by rust, it can regain its flexibility and strength through the careful application of fire.

Concerning The Nature and Proper- Ties op Saturn

Saturn speaks of himself in this way: "The other six metals have cast me out as their examiner. They have pushed me away from their spiritual state and given me a physical, perishable body as my dwelling, making me into something they are not and have no desire to become. My six brothers are spiritual in nature, and whenever I am placed in the fire, they enter my body and are destroyed along with me—except for Sol and Luna. These two are purified and made more noble by my waters. My spirit is like water, softening the rigid and frozen bodies of my brothers. However, my body is drawn toward the earth, and anything that enters into me takes on the same nature, becoming part of a single unified body through us.

It would do the world little good to know, or even believe, what lies hidden within me and what I am capable of achieving. It would be more valuable for the world to discover what I can do with myself. By abandoning the complex methods of the alchemists and focusing only on what I possess within me, people could find what I am truly able to accomplish. Within me lies the cold stone, a type of water that causes the spirits of the six metals to freeze together, creating the essence of the seventh metal. This process supports the transformation of Sol and Luna."

There are two types of antimony. One is the common black variety, which purifies Sol when it is melted within it. This black antimony has the closest connection to Saturn. The second type is white and is also known as magnesia or bismuth. It shares a strong connection with Jupiter, and when mixed with the black antimony, it increases the power of Luna.

Concerning Luna and The Properties Thereof

The attempt to transform Luna into Saturn or Mars is no easier than turning Mercury, Jupiter, Mars, Venus, or Saturn into Luna with great success. It is not useful to change something perfect into something imperfect; instead, the goal is to transform the imperfect into the perfect. Still, it is important to understand what Luna is made of and where it originates. Anyone who cannot figure this out will not be able to create Luna.

So, what exactly is Luna? It is one of the seven metals, standing as the seventh. It exists externally as a physical, material substance, but within it, the other six metals are spiritually hidden. These six spiritual metals cannot exist on their own without a physical metal to contain them. Similarly, a physical metal cannot exist without these six spiritual elements. All seven metals can mix easily when melted together, but this kind of mixture is not enough to create Sol or Luna. Even when combined, each metal retains its own nature—either remaining stable in the fire or being burned away by it.

For example, if you mix Mercury, Jupiter, Saturn, Mars, Venus, Sol, and Luna into a single mass, the result will not be a transformation of the other metals into Sol or Luna. Even though they all melt together, each keeps its own essence. This is how physical mixtures work. However, when it comes to the spiritual mixture and unity of metals, it is important to understand that no separation or destruction of the spirit is truly possible. Spiritual elements cannot exist without physical bodies. Even if a body is destroyed and transformed a hundred times, the spirit within will always gain a new, more noble form. This process is the transformation of metals from one level to another—moving from a lesser form to a higher one, such as Luna. From there, the metal can be perfected into Sol, the brightest and most royal of all metals.

It is true, as mentioned before, that the six metals will always generate a seventh from within themselves, revealing it clearly in its true form.

One might ask: If Luna, like all metals, comes from the other six, what are its properties and nature? The answer is that no other metal besides Luna can be formed from the combination of Saturn, Mercury, Jupiter, Mars, Venus, and Sol. Each of these metals contributes two key qualities to Luna, making a total of twelve virtues. These twelve virtues represent the spirit of Luna, and each metal offers something unique to its composition.

Luna gains liquidity and its bright white color from Mercury, along with influences from the zodiac signs Aquarius and Pisces. It receives its whiteness and resistance to fire from Jupiter, along with traits from Sagittarius and Taurus. From Mars, along with Cancer and Aries, Luna gets its hardness and clear, ringing sound. From Venus, along with Gemini and Libra, Luna gains the ability to solidify. From Saturn, along with Virgo and Scorpio, Luna inherits a consistent body and weight. Finally, from Sol, with influences from Leo and Virgo, Luna receives its pure, spotless nature and strong resistance to fire.

This is the essence of Luna's spiritual and physical qualities. It is a combination of the six metals and their virtues, reflecting both wisdom and the natural order of exaltation, briefly summarized for understanding.

It is also important to explain what kind of body metallic spirits take on during their initial creation through the influence of the heavens. When a miner crushes a seemingly worthless stone, he melts it down, corrupts it, and completely breaks it apart with fire. During this process of destruction, the metallic spirit takes on a new body—one that is stronger and more refined. Instead of being brittle, it becomes soft and flexible.

Then the alchemist steps in, further corrupting, breaking down, and carefully refining this metallic body. Through this process, the spirit within the metal takes on an even more perfect form, revealing itself more clearly—unless it is Sol or Luna, which are already perfected. At last, the spirit and the body of the metal become fully united. They are now protected from the effects of ordinary fire and have reached a state where they cannot be corrupted.

Concerning The Nature of Sol and Its Properties

The seventh metal, after the six spiritual ones, is Sol, which is purely fire in its nature. Outwardly, it is the most beautiful, brilliant, clear, and noticeable of all metals. It also has the heaviest and most uniform body. This is because it holds within itself the frozen essence of the other six metals, combining them into one solid form. Sol's ability to melt comes from either the heat of fire or the hidden influence of Mercury, along with the zodiac signs Pisces and Aquarius, that exist spiritually within it. We can see proof of this because Mercury blends effortlessly with Sol, almost as if in an embrace.

However, after Sol melts and the fire's heat is removed, cold takes over, causing it to harden. To make Sol solid and stable, it requires the essence of the other five metals—Jupiter, Saturn, Mars, Venus, and Luna—each of which contributes its cold nature. Because of this, Sol is difficult to keep in liquid form without the constant heat of fire. Mercury cannot provide enough heat on its own to keep Sol melted, nor can it resist the coldness of the other five metals. Mercury's natural role is simply to stay in liquid form and flow, not to harden or make anything solid.

Heat and life belong to the same nature, bringing movement and fluidity, while cold brings hardness, stillness, and the absence of life, which can be compared to death. For instance, the six cold metals—Jupiter, Saturn, Mars, Venus, Luna, and even Venus again—can only be melted by the heat of fire. Snow and ice, being cold, will only cause things to harden further. Once a metal melted by fire cools, the cold seizes it, making it solid and frozen in place.

As for Mercury, in order to remain fluid and full of life, it depends on heat, not cold. Anyone who claims Mercury lives through cold and moisture misunderstands nature and follows common but mistaken beliefs. The truth is that life comes from warmth and fire, while cold brings death. Sol's fire is pure—it is not a living fire, but it is solid and contains the colors of sulfur, a perfect blend of yellow and red.

The five cold metals—Jupiter, Mars, Saturn, Venus, and Luna—each give Sol part of their nature. They contribute solidity through coldness, color through fire, hardness through dryness, weight through moisture, and sound through brightness. Gold, which is Sol's material form, cannot be burned or destroyed by ordinary earthly fire. This is because one fire cannot burn another fire; instead, adding fire to fire only makes it stronger.

The celestial fire we receive from the Sun on Earth is not the same as the fire in heaven or the fire we know on Earth. The fire from the Sun, when it reaches us, becomes cold and frozen—it forms the body of the Sun as we experience it. Therefore, earthly fire cannot overcome the fire of the Sun. Instead, the Sun's celestial fire melts objects, like snow or ice, but is never burned itself. Fire does not have the power to burn fire, because Sol is fire—its essence dissolved in the heavens but solidified here on Earth.

Gold is in its
1 Celestial
Dissolved Essence three
2 Elementary} and Fluid fold
3 Metallic is Corporeal.

Part II

God and Nature Do Nothing in Vain

The eternal nature of all things, existing beyond time, with no beginning or end, is always at work. It operates even in places where no hope can be found. It accomplishes what seems impossible. What once appeared beyond belief or hope reveals itself as truth in a marvelous and unexpected way.

Note on Mercurius Vivus

Whatever gives a white color carries the essence of life and the qualities of light, which naturally bring life into being. In contrast, anything that produces blackness shares the nature of death, carrying the qualities of darkness and the forces that lead to death. The earth, with its cold nature, symbolizes this hardness, as it solidifies and fixes things. A house, for example, is always lifeless, but the person who lives inside it is alive. If you can understand the power of this idea, you have gained mastery.

Tested liquefactive powder: Burn the fat of verbena.

Recipe: Four ounces of saltpeter, half as much sulfur, and one ounce of tartar. Mix them and melt.

What Is to Be Thought Concerning The Congelation of Mercury

Trying to solidify Mercury and turn it into Luna, while also refining it through great effort, is a waste of time. This process only leads to the loss of the Sol and Luna already present within Mercury. There is a much simpler and quicker way to transform Mercury into Luna, without the need for freezing or excessive labor. This method minimizes waste and saves effort, making it possible to create silver and gold with ease.

Anyone can learn this alchemical process since it is straightforward and simple. By using it, one can produce large amounts of silver and gold in a short time. Long, complicated explanations are unnecessary—most people prefer clear instructions. So, follow these steps, and you will create Sol and Luna, which will bring you wealth. Pay close attention as I explain this process briefly. Keep these instructions well in mind so that, by working with Saturn, Mercury, and Jupiter, you can produce Sol and Luna.

There is no easier or more effective method in alchemy, and it requires very little effort to master. The process for making Sol and Luna is so fast that no further books or detailed lessons are needed—writing more about it would be as pointless as documenting last year's snow.

Concerning The Receipts of Alchemy

What, then, should we say about the recipes used in alchemy, along with the many different tools and vessels? These include furnaces, glassware, jars, waters, oils, lime, sulfur, salts, saltpeter, alum, vitriol, chrysocolla, copper greens, black inks, orpiment, green vitriol, white lead, red earth, thucia, wax, lutum sapientiae (the clay of wisdom), ground glass, verdigris, soot, eggshells, crocus of Mars, soap, crystal, chalk, arsenic, antimony, red lead, elixirs, lazurite, gold leaf, sal ammoniac, calamine stone, magnesia, Armenian bole, and many other substances.

Moreover, the steps involved—such as fermentation, digestion, testing, dissolving, cementing, filtering, refining, burning, distilling, purifying, and more—fill alchemical books to the brim. Then there are the materials drawn from herbs, roots, seeds, woods, stones, animals, worms, bone dust, snail shells, other shells, and pitch. Many of these things, however, only make the work more complicated. Even if Sol and Luna could be made with them, they would slow down the process rather than help it. The truth is that the art of creating Sol and Luna is not learned from these things. Therefore, they can be ignored, as they do not help when working with the five metals to make Sol and Luna.

Someone might ask, "What is the quick and easy way to create Sol and Luna, without unnecessary effort?" The answer is that this process has already been explained clearly and thoroughly in the Seven Canons. There is no point in trying to teach it to someone who does not grasp these Canons, as it would be difficult to convince them that this knowledge can be understood, though it must be approached in a hidden way rather than openly.

The art is this: Once you have created heaven, or the sphere of Saturn, and allowed its life to flow across the earth, place upon it the planets—whichever ones you choose—ensuring that Luna plays the smallest role. Let them run their course until Saturn, or heaven, has vanished entirely. At that point, the planets will remain lifeless, with their old, corruptible forms discarded. However, they will have gained new, perfect, and incorruptible bodies.

These new bodies are the spirit of heaven. From this spirit, the planets receive new forms and life, and they continue as they did before. Take this body, born from both life and earth, and keep it. It is Sol and Luna. Here, then, is the entire art, explained plainly and completely. If you still do not understand it, or have not practiced it, that is fine. It is better that this knowledge remains hidden and not revealed to everyone.

How To Conjure the Crystal So That All Things May Be Seen In It

To conjure means nothing more than to observe something correctly, to know what it is, and to fully understand it. A crystal is a representation of the air. Whatever appears in the air—whether it moves or stays still—also appears as a reflection or wave within the crystal or mirror. This is because air, water, and crystal are the same in terms of how we see through them. They function like a mirror, showing a reversed image of whatever is reflected within them.

Concerning The Heat of Mercury

Those who believe that Mercury is naturally cold and moist are mistaken. In truth, Mercury is warm and moist by nature, which is why it remains in a constant state of fluidity. If it were cold and moist, it would behave like frozen water, always solid and hard, requiring fire to melt it, as is the case with other metals. But Mercury doesn't need fire to become liquid. Its own natural heat keeps it fluid, giving it the ability to move freely, or "quick," meaning it cannot be killed, solidified, or frozen.

It is important to note that when the spirits of the seven metals, or however many are combined, meet fire, they compete with one another—especially Mercury. Each metal tries to display its powers and virtues, working to dominate the others through liquefaction and transformation. One metal will take on the life and properties of another, giving a new form and nature to the one it overtakes. The heat stirs the spirits or vapors of the metals to interact with each other, constantly changing one into another until they reach perfection and purity.

What, then, must be done to Mercury to remove its natural warmth and moisture, and replace them with extreme cold that will solidify, bind, and fully harden it? Follow this method: Take pure Mercury and seal it tightly in a silver container. Place this container in the middle of a jar filled with pieces of lead. Allow it to melt for twenty-four hours, or one full day. This process removes Mercury's hidden heat, adds external warmth, and introduces the coldness of Saturn and Luna, two planets with cold properties. This forces Mercury to freeze, solidify, and become firm.

It is important to understand that the cold needed to solidify Mercury is not the same as the cold we feel from snow or ice. Instead, this cold has a different quality—on the surface, there may even seem to be some warmth. Likewise, the heat that keeps Mercury fluid is not the same kind of heat we normally experience. Instead, Mercury can feel cool to the touch, which has led some scholars, who speak more than they understand, to wrongly conclude that Mercury is cold and moist. They mistakenly suggest that heat will solidify Mercury, but instead, heat makes it even more fluid, as they continue to discover at their own expense.

True alchemy, which teaches the only way to make Sol and Luna from the five imperfect metals, offers this principle: "Only from metals, within metals, by metals, and through metals can perfect metals be made." In some metals lies the essence of Luna, and in others, the essence of Sol.

What Materials and Instruments Are Required in Alchemy

All you need are a foundry, bellows, tongs, hammers, cauldrons, jars, and small refining dishes made from beech ashes. After gathering these tools, introduce the metals—Saturn, Jupiter, Mars, Sol, Venus, Mercury, and Luna. Let the process run its course, finishing with Saturn.

The Method of Seeking Minerals

The hope of finding metals within the earth and stones is very uncertain, and the effort required is immense. However, since this is the most direct way to obtain them, it should not be dismissed but highly praised. This desire to seek metals should be encouraged, just as the natural desire for marriage in youth and adulthood is accepted. Just as bees are drawn to roses and other flowers to create honey and wax, so too should people—apart from greed or selfish ambition—seek metals within the earth. Whoever does not search for them is unlikely to find them. God grants not only gold and silver to some but also poverty, hardship, and suffering.

Some people, however, are given special knowledge of metals and minerals, enabling them to discover easier ways to create gold and silver. These methods are faster than digging and smelting, allowing them to extract precious metals from their original forms. This applies not only to things found underground but also to metals refined from imperfect minerals. Gold and silver (Sol and Luna) can be made from any of the five metals—Mercury, Jupiter, Saturn, Mars, and Venus—although some are easier to work with than others. Sol and Luna can be made more easily from Mercury, Saturn, and Jupiter, while it is more difficult to create them from Mars and Venus, though it is still possible with the addition of existing Sol and Luna. For example, Luna can be produced from Magnesium and Saturn, while pure Sol can be made from Jupiter and Cinnabar.

A skilled alchemist, through careful thought and study, can perfect the transformation of metals better than by relying on the movements of the twelve zodiac signs or the seven planets. It is unnecessary to follow these celestial movements, whether they indicate favorable or unfavorable days, good or bad planetary influences. These things neither help nor hinder the process of natural alchemy. If you have a working process, you can perform the operation whenever you choose. However, if something is missing from your method or understanding, no alignment of stars or planets will make up for it.

Metals that remain buried in the earth for too long not only rust but can also transform into natural stones over time, though this is known to very few. In fact, old coins from ancient times, bearing various images, are sometimes found in the earth. These coins were originally made of metal but, through the slow transformation of nature, have turned into stone.

What Alchemy Is

Alchemy is the deliberate effort to change one type of metal into another. Each person, using their own understanding, can find the best path and discover the truth, as truth is revealed to those who pursue it with dedication. It is essential to understand both stars and stones because the spirit of all stones is linked to the stars. Sol (the Sun) and Luna (the Moon), representing celestial bodies, are also connected to a single stone. The stones of the earth originate from these celestial stones. Through fire, purification, and separation, these earthly stones are made bright and pure, much like their celestial counterparts. The entire earth is made from a mixture of materials that have solidified into a stony mass resting within the larger sphere of the universe.

Precious stones found on earth are the closest in perfection to the heavenly stones. These earthly stones possess purity, beauty, brilliance, strength, and resistance to fire, just like celestial stones. However, they are often found in rough environments, and most people mistakenly believe these stones were created exactly where they were found. They assume that these stones were simply polished and traded for their beauty, color, and value. A brief description of these stones follows:

The Emerald is a transparent green stone. It is said to improve eyesight and memory and protect purity. If the person carrying it loses their purity, the stone will lose its perfection.

The Adamant is a black crystal, also called Evax, known for bringing joy to those who carry it. It is dark, with a metallic color, and is the hardest of all stones. However, it can dissolve in goat's blood. It rarely grows larger than a hazelnut.

The Magnet is a stone made of iron that attracts iron to itself.

The Pearl is not truly a stone since it forms inside seashells. It is white and grows within living creatures, like fish or mollusks, which makes it different from typical stones.

The Jacinth is a yellow, transparent stone. Its name also refers to a flower, which legend says was once a man.

The Sapphire is a stone with a heavenly color and is considered connected to celestial qualities.

The Ruby glows with an intense red color.

The Carbuncle is a solar stone that shines as brightly as the sun itself.

The Coral is a stone that can be white or red. It forms in the sea, growing like a plant or shrub. When exposed to air, it hardens and becomes fireproof.

The Chalcedony is a stone with mixed colors, sitting between transparency and opacity, often with cloudy or liver-colored patterns. It is considered the least valuable of the precious stones.

The Topaz is known to shine at night and is found among rocks.

The Amethyst is a stone with a purple or blood-red hue.

The Chrysoprasus shines like fire at night and resembles gold during the day.

The Crystal is a transparent white stone that looks like ice. It forms from the essence of other stones through extraction and purification.

The key to understanding these stones lies in knowing their origins and connection to metals. The truth is that metals are the most refined part of common stones. They contain elements like oil, fat, and grease, but they remain impure and imperfect as long as they are mixed within the stones. To create perfect metals, these elements must be identified, separated, and extracted from the stones through a process of melting and refining. Once purified, the substance becomes a metal comparable to the stars, which are themselves like separated stones from the heavens.

Those who study metals and minerals must be guided by reason and intelligence. They should not limit themselves to exploring only the known metals buried deep within mountains. Often, valuable metals are found closer to the earth's surface, while deeper layers may not yield the same quality. Every stone—whether a large boulder or a simple rock—must be examined carefully, for even a stone that seems worthless might contain hidden value, sometimes more valuable than livestock. The place where a stone is found does not always determine its true worth, as the influence of the sky plays a role in its formation. Even common earth, dust, or sand can contain traces of gold or silver, and those who look carefully will notice this.

The Book Concerning the Tincture of The Philosophers

Paracelsus

Preface

Since you, O Sophist, insult me with false and foolish words, saying that, being from rough Helvetia, I am incapable of understanding or learning anything—and also criticize me for being a physician who travels from place to place—I have decided to write this treatise to show the ignorant and inexperienced what true arts existed in the past. I will demonstrate the value of my knowledge against yours, and yours against mine, so that future generations will know how to follow my path in this enlightened age. Look back at Hermes, Archelaus, and others from the early times—see what great philosophers and alchemists lived then. Their work proves that your so-called mentors, O Sophist, are nothing more than empty images and idols. Even if those you call fathers and saints refuse to acknowledge this, the ancient Emerald Tablet reveals more wisdom and skill in philosophy, alchemy, and magic than anything you or your followers could ever teach.

If you still cannot understand how great these treasures are, then tell me: Why did no prince or king ever succeed in conquering the Egyptians? And why did Emperor Diocletian order all the Spagyric books to be burned wherever they could be found? If the contents of those books had remained unknown, the people would have continued to suffer under his oppressive rule. Know this, O Sophist: One day, a yoke just as heavy will be placed upon you and your companions.

In the middle of this age, the authority over all arts has been given to me—Theophrastus Paracelsus, Prince of Philosophy and Medicine. I have been chosen by God to eliminate the empty, false works and misleading words of Aristotle, Galen, Avicenna, Mesva, and their followers. My teachings, which are based on the light of Nature, are solid and unchanging. Though they may seem unappreciated now, in the 1,558th year they will begin to flourish. At that time, people of all kinds—craftsmen and ordinary folk—will see proof through extraordinary signs and fully understand how unshakable the Paracelsian Art is, no matter how hard the sophists try to maintain their flawed knowledge with the support of papal and imperial privileges.

You call me a beggar and wandering sophist, but the Danube and the Rhine rivers will speak in my defense, even if I remain silent. Your lies about me have angered many courts and princes, as well as noble orders and cities. I have a hidden treasure in a city called Weinden, part of Forum Julii, stored at an inn—a treasure so valuable that neither Leo of Rome nor Charles of Germany could buy it, no matter their wealth. Even though the symbol of the star has been applied to your names, only those who follow the divine Spagyric Art know its true meaning.

So, you worm-ridden Sophist, since you think me—a master of hidden knowledge—a foolish and wasteful quack, I now choose to explain, through this treatise, the proper way to prepare and use the famous Tincture of the Philosophers. This explanation is given to honor all who seek the truth and to ensure that those who dismiss the true arts will suffer poverty. This great secret will illuminate the final age, making up for all past losses through divine grace and the reward of true wisdom. From the beginning of the world until now, no growth of knowledge or wisdom will ever have equaled what is to come. In the end, vice will not be able to defeat virtue, and no matter how many resources evil people gather, they will not harm those who remain righteous.

The Book Concerning The Tincture of The Philosophers

I, Philippus Theophrastus Paracelsus Bombast, declare that, through Divine grace, many different paths have been taken toward discovering the Tincture of the Philosophers. In the end, however, they all reach the same goal. Hermes Trismegistus, the Egyptian, followed his own method. Orus, the Greek, used a similar approach. Hali, the Arabian, stayed committed to his process. Albertus Magnus, the German, also followed a long and complex path. While each of these philosophers advanced according to their chosen methods, they all reached the same outcome—achieving long life, which philosophers have always desired, along with the means to sustain it honorably within this troubled world.

Now, in my time, I, Theophrastus Paracelsus Bombast, Monarch of the Arcana, have been given special gifts by God so that all seekers of this ultimate philosophical knowledge must follow my example. No matter whether they are Italian, Polish, French, or German—or from anywhere else—they must imitate my path. All philosophers, astronomers, and spagyrists, no matter how renowned, must come after me. I will reveal and teach them—both alchemists and doctors—the secrets of bodily regeneration. I will show them the tincture, the hidden knowledge (arcanum), and the quintessence, which contain the foundations of all mysteries and works.

Everyone must only believe in what they have tested through fire, for it is by fire that the truth is separated from falsehood. If someone presents a theory that goes against this method of practical experimentation in alchemy or medicine, there is no reason to trust them. Only those who work in the light of Nature will see this truth, as the light of Nature is given to help us test everything. With this light, we will demonstrate, using the best methods, that those before me—who relied too much on their ideas and speculations—only harmed themselves with their foolishness. For this reason, I have seen many simple people rise to greatness through hard work, while many nobles, trusting only in their imaginations, have fallen into foolishness, thinking of "golden mountains" in their minds before they even touched the fire.

The first things you must learn are digestion, distillation, sublimation, reverberation, extraction, solution, coagulation, fermentation, and fixation. You must also gain experience using all the necessary tools, such as glass vessels, cucurbites, circulators, earthen vessels, baths, blast furnaces, and reverberatory ovens, along with materials like marble, coals, and tongs. Only through mastering these tools and processes will you succeed in alchemy and medicine.

However, as long as you cling to fantasy and opinion, relying on false books, you will never be able to achieve anything in these fields.

Concerning The Definition of The Subject and Matter of The Tincture of The Philosophers

Before I explain the process of creating the Tincture, it is important to introduce the subject properly. Up until now, this knowledge has been kept hidden by those devoted to truth. The Tincture, when understood in a Spagyric sense, is something that passes from three essences into one through the art of Vulcan—or it can remain in that state. To give it its proper name, as used by the ancients, it is often called the Red Lion, though few truly understand what it is. With the help of Nature and the skill of the alchemist, it can be transformed into a White Eagle, producing two from one. For the alchemist, these two together shine more brightly than gold itself.

If you do not understand the teachings of the Cabalists and the ancient astronomers, then you were neither destined by God for the Spagyric art, nor chosen by Nature for the work of Vulcan, nor created to speak on the subject of alchemy. The essence of the Tincture is a great treasure—like a pearl of immense value—and it is one of the most noble things on earth, second only to the revelation of the Divine and the pursuit of wisdom among men. This Tincture is the true "Lili" of both alchemy and medicine, a treasure that philosophers have sought tirelessly. Yet, because of their incomplete knowledge and lack of proper preparation, they have never achieved the full result. Through their experiments, they managed to discover only the first stage of the Tincture. But the real foundation—the one my fellow alchemists must follow—was left for me to uncover, ensuring that no false ideas would interfere with our true purpose.

With the right to do so, and based on my extensive experience, I correct the errors of other Spagyrists and separate truth from falsehood. Through my long research, I found just reasons to criticize and change many aspects of the old teachings. If I had discovered that the experiments of the ancients were better than my own, I would not have devoted myself to such difficult labor. But I willingly endured these efforts for the benefit and progress of all true alchemists.

Now that I have explained the Tincture and revealed its essence faithfully, in a way that one brother would share with another, I will move on to its preparation. After presenting the discoveries of the earliest ages, I will add my own inventions. In time, the Age of Grace will embrace my contributions, no matter which of the ancient teachers, O Sophist, you choose to follow in the meantime.

Thank You for Reading

You've Just Read a Piece of the Greatest Library Ever Rebuilt

Thank you for reading.

This book is one of thousands we're restoring, reimagining, and translating as part of the **Modern Library of Alexandria** — a global movement to preserve and share humanity's most important ideas.

What was once lost to fire and time is now rising again — not just as memory, but as living, breathing knowledge, freely accessible to all.

What You Can Do Next:

- **Keep Reading** - Explore more legendary works in print, audiobook, or digital at LibraryofAlexandria.com.

- **Build Your Own Library** - Every title is available at true printing cost — paperback, hardcover, or collector's boxset.

- **Spread the Light** - Share this book. Support the mission to translate every timeless work into every language.

By finishing this book, you've already taken part in something extraordinary.

Join us at LibraryofAlexandria.com

Together, we're rebuilding the greatest library the world has ever known.

With gratitude,

The Modern Library of Alexandria Team

Visit:

www.libraryofalexandria.com

Or scan the code below: